WASP CANYON

WASP CANYON

DANIELLE MCCRORY

ISBN-13: 978-1-7377043-1-7 (Paperback)
ISBN-13: 978-1-7377043-0-0 (Ebook)
ISBN-13: 978-1-7377043-2-4 (Hardcover)

Cover design by: Ryan McCrory

In Loving Memory of
Larry Dufour

Prologue

Push it. A little harder. A little further. A little faster. Be stronger. Be better. Be more. Past the boulder with the crust of lichen on its southern face. Past the century plant whose stalk is beginning to list to the side. Past the two saguaros shaped like a man caressing a woman. And past the towering, golden cliff faces that stand at the edge of the desert, marking the entrance to a canyon cut deep into the sun-baked mountains. The unforgiving desert heat is left behind as she enters the canyon, replaced by a cool breeze that caresses her sweat-streaked face and gently tugs at her long hair.

Miles: 4.3
Speed: 4.8 mph
Time: 1 hour, 7 minutes
Heart rate: 134 bpm

This is where she goes to feel the fresh air and to escape from everything, both past and present. This is where she goes to listen to her breath as she pushes herself up and down the rises and falls of the trail. This is where she goes to be alone and to prove to herself that she can get better—that she can make progress. As she runs along the trail she forgets about the pain, and she forgets about what she is fighting to overcome. On the trail it is just to run a little harder, a little further, a little faster. She can be stronger on the trail. She can be better. And she can be more.

Miles: 6.4
Speed: 4.7 mph
Time: 1 hour, 49 minutes
Heart rate: 137 bpm

Something up ahead is blocking the trail. Something that doesn't belong. She has come to know this trail like a person comes to know the body of their long-time lover—every curve, every mole, every scar. She knows when she must swerve to the left to avoid the sweeping branches of an aging mesquite tree. She knows when she must slow her pace to conserve her energy for the steep incline that lies ahead. And she knows when she must watch her footing to avoid tripping on the jagged stones jutting out of the hard, desert soil.

But now there is something stretched across the trail— something unfamiliar and *wrong*. Like finding a fresh wound on the landscape of that lover's flesh that you thought you knew better than your own. Something is lying across the trail, blocking her passage to the desert beyond, and to her car, her home, and to the life she is struggling to enjoy living again.

Something up ahead doesn't seem right—doesn't seem safe—and an overwhelming sense of danger sweeps over her. It pulls her from her reverie of happy moments long since passed. She slows too late, her eyes fixated on what's ahead and not what is directly in front of her. Her foot strikes a rock with violent force—another surprise on the trail she thought she knew so well. She is sent careening to the canyon floor with little ability to slow her descent. She lay in the dirt, looking at what was now sprawled across the trail. *Her trail,* one she has run every day for months. But now, not too far from where she lay injured, something foreign was blocking her path. Something that wasn't there before. She sits up, her ankle already beginning to swell, and stares at what lies ahead. That same sense of danger sweeps over her again, stronger this time. She knows she is no longer safe here. She knows this isn't *her* trail anymore. She needs to get out of here. She needs to escape. But the only way out is to go forward. Whatever she does, she needs to hurry. Time is running out.

Miles: 6.5
Speed: 0.0 mph
Time: 1 hour, 51 minutes
Heart rate: 179 bpm

PART I

GRIEF

CHAPTER 1

"I just don't understand," Jessica Cleary muttered. She sat in an overstuffed armchair in the center of the office, curled into a defensive position with her legs pulled up to her chest. She was a petite woman, her small frame even further dwarfed by the large, beige chair. Lines of stress had already begun to etch into her young face. At the tender age of twenty-four, she had already been dealt a great deal more pain and heartache than those many years her senior. The pain in her eyes was unwavering and complete, the defeated stare of someone that has already given up.

"No matter how much time passes I just can't seem to understand," Jessica continued. "It's like he was here every day—*all day, every day*—for my entire life. And now he's not." She sighed and continued to fiddle with a strand of blonde hair, a sign of nervousness Dr. Cynthia Wyatt picked up on many sessions ago.

"Everyone was saying how sad it is and how sorry they are," Jessica said with mock sympathy, "but really they just want to move on." Her voice hardened, taking on a bitter tone.

"No one wants to talk about it. Nobody wants to talk about something that is depressing. It will just bring them down and ruin their day. So they rather pretend it never happened at all. If it didn't happen to them, then they don't give a shit. They don't *really* care about how you feel, they care about you keeping your mouth shut and not bumming them out. So when they ask how you are doing, they expect you to say you're doing just fine. They don't want to hear you say the truth—that you're dying inside—because that's depressing. And they may feign sympathy if you do say you're sad, but really they are just thinking 'Why the hell have you not gotten over it already?' Deep down they just want you to move on and shut up about it." Jessica fell silent. It was the most she had spoken since her therapy sessions began two months ago.

Wyatt sat quietly with her hands clasped in her lap. The executive office chair she sat in was currently situated in front of her large, mahogany desk. Wyatt had brought it out from behind the desk prior to the start of Jessica's appointment— something she did for every treatment session. She didn't like having anything between her and her patients when she was trying to connect with them. It was too formal to sit behind a desk—too *impersonal*. She wanted to be available to her patients with no barriers in the way, both figuratively and literally.

Wyatt waited another moment, wanting to give her patient the opportunity to continue speaking if she chose to do so. Jessica hugged her knees, one hand continuing to tug at a strand of hair. She stared blankly out the picture window to her right, her face turned away.

Wyatt watched her, looking for any indication that Jessica may further voice her thoughts pertaining to her father's death. It had taken many sessions for Jessica to speak so freely, and Wyatt wanted to allow her a few more seconds to speak her mind if she wished to continue. Her troubled young patient appeared to be through, though. Jessica sat in silence in the beige chair that Wyatt had painstakingly picked out—a chair that was already beginning to show signs of wear.

The treatment office was a spacious one, each item inside carefully selected by Wyatt herself. The plush chair sat in the center of the room, facing Wyatt's large, uncluttered desk. Multiple plaques hung above the desk, awards from Wyatt's many years of being voted "Best in the Southwest" for her achievements in psychology. Bookshelves lined the opposite wall, filled with textbooks on psychology and pathological disorders. A picture window took up the bulk of the northeast-facing wall, offering a generous view of the mountain range.

The chair Jessica sat in was the first item Wyatt had selected when she decided to start her own practice. After spending many years working in a group practice setting, Wyatt decided that self-employment was a much more desirable option. She bid farewell to the agency, stepped into the land of private practice, and never looked back.

Wyatt selected a perfectly suitable office building on the northwest side of town with a treatment office that overlooked the Santa Catalina mountain range. She took great care in selecting the correct furnishings for her waiting room and treatment office, believing everything mattered right down to the light fixtures and coffee table. She wanted a soothing environment where her patients would feel comfortable opening up and confiding in her.

Wyatt believed the chair she selected for her patients was of utmost importance. This would be where her patients would sit, would think, and would grow. Lying on an uncomfortable leather couch staring at the ceiling seemed absurd, so she made sure to steer clear of such clichés. She wanted a chair that would be comforting and safe—something large and cushioned to make her patients feel protected. The oversized arm chair had the desired effect, the chair seeming to have a womb-like comfort that allowed her patients to feel safe talking about their innermost thoughts and feelings. Once one of these chairs began to wear out she would promptly order another of the exact same make and color. She had now been through eleven chairs since beginning her private practice.

Jessica was sitting in chair number twelve, staring out the window and absentmindedly yanking on the same strand of hair. After a long silence she said, "I can't move on. I can't just wake up one day and say 'Okay, I'm better now.' My dad is dead. I don't understand how I am supposed to just live my life like normal knowing that my dad is dead. It all feels like a lie. Being normal feels like a lie. Smiling feels like a lie. I go to work and smile like an idiot all day, and then cry all the way home. It's all just *one big lie*." Jessica shifted her weight in the chair, turning her body away from Wyatt and toward the picture window. Wyatt could almost hear the girl shut down.

"Jessica, what you need is a way to channel it," Wyatt said, hoping to pull her patient's attention away from the window and back to the subject at hand.

"Channel it?" Jessica asked, turning her vacant stare away from the mountains. Her eyes cleared and she focused on Wyatt. "Channel what exactly?"

"Your anger," Wyatt said. "The anger you feel towards your friends because they want you to get over it. The anger you feel towards your mother for making you come here. And the anger you feel towards your father, for dying."

"I am not mad at my father!" Jessica exclaimed.

Wyatt lifted her hands a few inches from her lap, quieting her patient before she could make further protest. "Maybe not directly," Wyatt said. "Maybe not in the same way you are mad at your friends and your family. But you are mad that your father has died. You are mad that he has left you, even if that was never his intention."

Jessica let out an exasperated sigh and returned her gaze to the picture window. "You can't be mad at someone who is dead," she whispered.

"Sure you can," Wyatt said. "We can get mad at anyone we want to, living or dead. And we do, believe me."

Wyatt saw a trace of a smile touch Jessica's lips. "So what did you mean about channeling it?" she asked.

"I mean channeling everything you are feeling into a productive activity. The anger, the sadness, the hopelessness. Channel those things into something you can actively do to get your mind off of it. Or hell, use that activity to get your mind *on* those feelings. Everything you are feeling is as normal as it is debilitating. If you dedicated a part of each day into allowing yourself to feel those emotions, and channeled them into something productive, maybe they will become less overwhelming to you. And maybe, with time, they will also become less negative."

Jessica turned away from the window. Her hand dropped from her hair and she clasped it loosely in her lap. "Losing a parent is always negative."

"Of course it is. But your life doesn't have to be negative forever." Wyatt glanced down at her lap, and to the elegant, golden watch she had strapped to her wrist. The Rolex's minute hand was nearing the top of the hour, indicating that Jessica Cleary's session was about to come to an end. "Just give it a try, Jessica. Try channeling those feelings into a productive activity and see how you feel."

"What activity?" Jessica asked. She uncurled from the fetal position and placed her feet on the floor. She looked at Wyatt with genuine interest.

Wyatt considered the question. Finally she said, "Something that gets you out of the house. Something that gets you away from the friends, family, or coworkers that are making you feel negative right now. And," Wyatt smiled, "something that provides you with some much needed endorphins."

Jessica leaned forward in the carefully selected beige chair, eyebrows raised.

"Exercise!" Wyatt declared.

Jessica made a face like she just smelled sour milk. She looked at Wyatt incredulously. "Exercise? Like Pilates?"

Wyatt put up her hands. "Here me out," she said. "I don't mean watching *Buns of Steel* videos in your living room or running on a treadmill in a smelly gym. I mean exercise outdoors, in the fresh air, out in nature. Arizona is known for its hiking trails and breathtaking scenery. Take advantage of it. It could be hiking, running, cycling…"

"I fell off a bike when I was a kid and broke my arm," Jessica said. "I haven't been on a bike since. And hiking sounds boring."

"Running then. Go out, in nature, and start running."

"Running…" Jessica said, her brow furrowed. Then: "But I don't know how to run."

Wyatt smiled. "Luckily, it's something all us humans can pick up pretty quickly. If you have any trouble, just pretend something is chasing you."

Chapter 2

Jessica stood in the electronics section of Target, looking over the selection of fitness watches. Per Dr. Wyatt's suggestion, she had stopped after her therapy session to pick out a fitness tracker for her new running project. *Running. God, this is going to be stupid. Or painful. Or both.*

Jessica had never been one for physical fitness. She detested team sports, and never felt much drive to incorporate exercise into her daily routine. She had always been slim, her eating habits never catching up with her waistline. Her best friend, Claire Barnett, would often comment on the unfairness of life: Jessica getting to eat whatever her heart desired while Claire always saw the proof of that slice of pizza on her hips the following morning. Not that Jessica was much of a junk food eater. Before her father's passing she had kept to a fairly healthy diet. Now she ate little, and not often. Her weight loss in the past nine months had not gone unnoticed by her mother, and, more recently, Dr. Wyatt.

Jessica stood at five foot six inches tall. Before this whole mess started, she weighed in at one hundred and thirty pounds. Now she guessed she was around one hundred and ten, although she hadn't bothered to weigh herself in quite some time. Taking care of herself had slowly become less and less of a priority as she spent more and more time caring for her father during his final months. Once he finally passed, caring for herself ceased all together, which was part of the reason her mother insisted on Jessica beginning her sessions with Dr. Wyatt.

Her mother had discovered Dr. Cynthia Wyatt on a Google search. Jessica found the whole idea of seeing a shrink as silly and unnecessary, but her mother insisted. And after all her mother had been through, Jessica thought she might as well humor her with these stupid therapy sessions. So for the past two months she had faithfully gone to Dr. Wyatt's office once a week.

The sessions started generically enough. Where are you from? *Tucson.* Where do you work? *Minstrel's Steakhouse.* Do you have a boyfriend? *Screw you.* Slowly the sessions became more focused, Dr. Wyatt edging closer and closer to Jessica's actual purpose for being there: her father's recent death and her apparent inability to move on. Like this is something you can move on from. Like this is something seeing a stupid shrink was going to fix. *Poof! Your dad isn't dead. Poof! Life is normal again. Poof! Your will to live has been restored.*

That's not how grief works. Grief can change you. It can alter your perception—your reality. A future that once appeared promising and hopeful can transform into a nightmare of menacing shadows and foreboding turns in the road ahead. Silver tarnishes, a sunset fades to a murky gray, flowers wilt, fruit darkens and decays, and the brightness in one's soul can dwindle away until it is nothing but ashes with a few embers struggling to stay lit.

Jessica shifted from side to side in the electronics aisle, impatient to finish this stupid shopping expedition. Now humoring her mother with these therapy sessions was going to cost her $129.99 plus tax. Sitting on the center shelf, surrounded by a colorful advertisement of fit, smiling people, was the QuikFit 2.0. The ad said it came equipped with the latest fitness tracking app, heart rate monitor, step counter, and Bluetooth capability so she could link all her fitness stats to her phone for easy review and comparison. It could also link to a Spotify account, and even had a speaker to play music if she didn't want to be burdened with headphones. *Heaven forbid.* All someone could ever ask for when it comes to analyzing how long it takes to huff and puff up and down a mountain. Apparently, for the low, low price of $129.99, you are one step closer to becoming an Olympian. Plus tax.

Jessica grabbed the QuikFit 2.0 box off the shelf without giving much thought to the other models and brands that were available, absentmindedly grabbing the one that came with a plum purple wristband. She had always liked purple, although she rarely paid attention to what color she wore anymore. Her clothes now sagged on her unflatteringly, and her hair often hung limp and lifeless on her narrow shoulders. She once had been considered a beautiful woman—a real stunner her dad would say—but her care in her appearance had diminished and eventually disappeared altogether. Before her dad got sick, which felt like many years ago and not just two, she had long, wavy blonde hair, startling green eyes, and an infectious smile. Jessica found that it was never hard for her to get a date; however, the desire to date, along with the care in her personal appearance, had died along with her father.

Jessica's phone buzzed in her pocket. She fished out the Samsung (also purple) and tapped the **Home** button. Claire's smiling face illuminated the screen next to an icon for **New Text Message**. Jessica clicked on it and a message from Claire appeared.

From: Claire Bear :-)
Date: May 31, 2018
Time: 4:52 PM
Message: Hey gurl. How wuz the quack 2day? Im thinkin beers @ Lindy's 2nite. U in?

Jessica hit **Reply** and began typing, tucking the QuikFit 2.0 box under her arm.

Compose Message: Hey U. The quack was f'ing fabulous as always. I got dinner with my mom 2nite. Beers 2morrow?

Jessica hit **Send** and shoved the phone back into the pocket of her sagging jeans. She started working her way down the aisle toward the registers and the front door. She loved the self-checkout registers that had started taking over in the past few years, eliminating the need to make small talk with one of the fake-smiling cashiers. It was one less person she has to talk to. Thank God.

CHAPTER 3

Jessica was born in Tucson, Arizona, in the winter of 1994. Her mother and father had her later in life, both nearly forty by the time Jessica was born. Her childhood was a pleasant one, full of school projects, festive holidays, and laughter around the dinner table. Looking back, those early memories always felt warm, joyful, and full of love.

One of Jessica's fondest memories from childhood was the monsoon season that arrived every summer without fail. She could remember running out each afternoon when she heard the deep rumbles of thunder traveling across the desert, her bare feet burning on the hot patio as she left the shelter of the porch and looked up eagerly at the mountains. The white, cotton candy tops of the cumulus clouds would appear first, peaking over the mountains in bright, pillowy bunches. As the clouds grew in size and poured over the mountain tops, their dark bellies would become visible, distant lightning illuminating their curves and crevices in brief bursts of light. Jessica would count the seconds after each bolt, continuing the count until she heard the deep rumbles of thunder that followed each flash. *One one thousand, two one thousand, three one thousand.* She could almost taste the electricity in the air as the clouds swept closer, the thunder louder, the lightning brighter. The landscape would turn an eerie yellow just before the clouds blotted out the sun. And then the desert would be drenched by an onslaught of rain, a torrential downpour that pounded the hard soil and drowned out all other sound. Jessica would dance in the wetness and take in the wonderful smell of desert rain, a glorious earthly smell that could not be matched by any perfume.

It was always around this point when her father would insist that her rain dancing was done for the day. That she needed to get under the porch's roof and away from the lightning and the trembling trees, their branches rattling overhead as gusts of wind tore through their leaves. Jessica would begrudgingly return to the shelter of the patio, shivering in her wet clothes when only moments ago she was sweating in the desert's heat. Her dad would attempt to pat her dry with a towel, tickling her in the process. She would giggle, throw her arms around his neck, and say, "I love you, Daddy" in his ear. She had to speak loudly to be heard over the rain. And he would always reply, equally as loud, "I love you too, Jess, even though you just made me a mess." She would then look wide-eyed at his wet shirt and fall into another fit of giggles, ones he would eventually join with hearty laughter.

Roger Cleary fell in love with the desert when he moved to Tucson with his blushing bride, Andrea. The terrain, the animals, and the native plants all fascinated him. Back east saguaros were just things you saw in cartoons and inside *National Geographic* magazines. Their tall, thick trunks and swooping arms seemed like things of fantasy, but here in Arizona they were everywhere. In Tucson, saguaros covered the countryside and succulents bloomed on your front porch.

Roger made a hobby out of identifying different desert plants, cataloguing them in notebooks, and attaching snapshots he took with those disposable point-and-shoot cameras from the convenience store. He found the resilience of these plants awe-inspiring. Cacti could sprout from the toughest of soils, could survive for months or even years without water, and their spiny defense mechanisms were as impressive as they were beautiful. The spines came in all kinds of colors, shapes, and patterns, jutting out of the cactus's smooth, green surface in a haphazard yet organized fashion. No two cacti were alike, and Roger enjoyed spending his free time scouring the desert trails in search of new species to add to his ever-growing notebook collection.

When he wasn't on the hunt for a new cactus to catalogue, Roger was a teacher at North Tucson High School. His biology classes were always well-received by his students, but his best student of all had always been his daughter. Roger taught Jessica all about the desert in which they lived, his lessons including the types of rock the mountains were made from, the variety of animals they shared the land with, and—his personal favorite—the various plant-life that covered the terrain. As Jessica grew into a curious, young girl, Roger would take his little botanist into their backyard to point out the different types of cacti and succulents. Jessica would look at their spiny surfaces in awe, sometimes reaching out to touch one of the cactus's needle-like spines. Roger would snatch her up before she could prick her finger, give her a kiss, and say, "Jess, if you touch that plant, you're going to be a mess." She would giggle and then demand to be set down to see more "pokey plants".

As Jessica got older her interest in "pokey plants" lessened, but she was always willing to go out back with Roger to observe some of his latest findings. She would lean forward and marvel at the red, curled barbs of a barrel cactus or gaze up at the copious arms of a well-aged organ pipe. And while Jessica may have only feigned interest in her father's newest succulent discovery, her love for spending time with him never wavered.

In the final months of Roger's life, Jessica would sometimes urge him to go out and look at some cacti with her. She would insist she had found a new jumping cholla or prickly pear that he hadn't seen before, although she was pretty sure there wasn't one cactus Roger had missed during his cacti quests and meticulous cataloguing. Roger at first would humor her, grab his cane, and carefully try to navigate the rocky backyard to the supposed new cactus. He would then exclaim, "Wow Jess! I can't believe I missed this one!" and they would smile at each other, neither acknowledging that this particular cactus was already photographed and sitting in one of Roger's notebooks.

As the cancer began to eat away at Roger's body, he found he no longer had the strength to go out and see Jessica's "newest finding" in their great expanse of a backyard. Jessica at first would try to urge her father to accompany her, however, her gentle urging began to lessen as she saw the life slowly draining from her father's eyes. In the last few weeks, when Jessica mentioned a new cactus, Roger would pat her hand and simply say, "I'm sorry, Jess. I'm just too much of a mess." And he was right—in the end, it was all just so much of a mess.

CHAPTER 4

Jessica arrived at her parents' house—correction: mother's house—shortly after six. She pulled her aging Camry into the driveway, turned off the ignition, and stared at the garage door. The door, along with the rest of the house, was light beige. Several years back her mother had the house repainted, and despite Jessica's gentle teasing, her mom had decided to paint the house the exact same color it was originally. The paint from the more recent paint job was starting to peel around the edges of the garage door, the harsh desert sun taking no pity on Andrea Cleary's beige paint. *At least the paint underneath is the same damn color*, Jessica thought. *No one will even notice.*

Jessica dragged herself out of the car, leaving the Target bag containing the QuikFit 2.0 on the passenger seat. She brushed some of her lifeless hair out of her face and tried to smooth her wrinkled T-shirt over her slightly stained jeans. *Should have done the laundry,* she thought. *Now Mom is really gonna think I'm not making progress with Dr. Wyatt.*

She took a deep breath and made her way up the driveway toward the front door. She made sure to keep her eyes pointed straight ahead, not allowing herself to look at any of the saguaros, chollas, or ocotillos that covered her parents'—correction: mother's—front yard.

"Hey, Mom," her daughter said with a wan smile as Andrea opened the door.

Andrea had a marked resemblance to her only child, both women having blonde hair and striking green eyes. She had a small, sturdy frame and toned features shaped by years of Pilates and yoga. Unlike Jessica, Andrea kept her hair at shoulder length, something she considered any woman over sixty should do. Her makeup was lightly applied, and she found she never required much even in her older years. However, since her husband's passing, she did notice her under-eye concealer was disappearing at a faster rate. While Andrea was great at concealing her pain and loneliness to others, those dark circles under her eyes were becoming harder and harder to hide.

Andrea was deeply affected by the loss of her husband, although she did her best to not burden those around her with her grief. She never expected to become a widow at the age of sixty-two, but here she was trying to create some semblance of a life in the wake of her husband's untimely death. Roger and her had married in their early twenties and had made it thirty-eight years before cancer came between them. Andrea had supported Roger every step of the way, sometimes having to carry him along both emotionally as well as physically, but in the end the cancer had won.

Life went on, as it always seems to do, and Andrea tried to go on with it. She did her grocery shopping, completed the household chores, attended her Pilates classes and book club meetings, and kept up with her hair appointments. And late at night, as she lay alone in a bed that was meant for two, she would quietly cry in the dark and miss her husband so much she thought her heart would literally stop beating altogether. Somehow, her heart continued to beat, the sun eventually rose over the eastern mountains as it always did, and another day would begin. Andrea would dab a little extra concealer under her eyes as she readied herself in the morning, and then go about the day's tasks, never mentioning the sobs that racked her in the night and left her eyes swollen in the morning.

Jessica stood in the doorway, yanking on a strand of hair with one hand and trying to smooth her wrinkled shirt with the other. Her jeans hung loosely on her hips, something Andrea suspected Jessica was hoping to hide with her ill-fitting shirt. Her hair and makeup were not done, but at least it appeared that she had showered.

"Come on in, dear," Andrea said. She ushered Jessica inside and locked the front door behind her. Being a single woman living alone came with its own risks, and Andrea tried to take the necessary precautions to keep herself safe. "It looks like your washing machine might be on the fritz, huh?"

"Oh, well, yeah I guess. I guess I forgot to buy detergent."

"I have plenty here if you would like to bring some home with you. It looks like your clothes would greatly appreciate it."

"Yeah, sure. Thanks," Jessica replied.

"Where's your purse, dear?"

"I didn't bring one."

"But where do you keep your things?"

"I just have my keys and my phone. I didn't really think I needed a purse."

Andrea looked Jessica up and down. Her daughter looked thin, frail even. Her shoulders were slumped, her hair tangled. Where was her vibrant, care-free daughter who laughed often and batted the boys away with a stick? Her daughter who took care of her appearance and wouldn't be caught dead in stained, dirty clothes? Andrea had not seen that daughter in many months. *That Dr. Wyatt sure doesn't seem as competent as promised,* she thought. *Although she certainly does charge enough.*

"But what about your driver's license? Your money?" Andrea asked.

"I have my license and credit card in my back pocket, Mom. That's what pockets are for. God."

"Okay, okay. I'll let it go. I just want to make sure you have everything you need." Andrea paused, wanting to express her concern but not wanting to push too hard. "I worry about you sometimes."

Jessica turned away from her mother, eyes downcast. "Well I am just fine. I'm seeing Dr. Wyatt just like you wanted, and she hasn't committed me yet. So I can't be that bad, right?"

"Oh, that's right, you saw Dr. Wyatt today." Andrea already knew about the scheduled appointment, but wanted Jessica to be the one to bring it up. Now that she had, Andrea figured discussing her daughter's therapy session was fair game. "How did it go today? Does she think you are making progress?"

Jessica walked into the kitchen, shrugging her shoulders as she went. "It went fine, I guess," she said. And after a pause: "She wants me to start running."

"Running? For exercise?" Andrea's eyes widened and her face lit up. "Oh honey, I think that is a wonderful idea."

☼   ☼   ☼

After dinner was finished and Jessica had helped clear the dishes, Andrea decided to push a little harder with Dr. Wyatt's suggestion for her daughter to begin exercising. She thought this was an excellent idea. *Finally* that expensive psychologist was starting to pay off. Exercise will get Jessica out of her apartment, will give her a much-needed boost in her mood, and will hopefully get her to start taking better care of herself. It sounded like a perfect start on the path to recovery.

"You know honey, I really enjoy my exercise classes. I think they make me feel better, both physically and mentally. If you want, I could give you some class schedules for my gym. They have classes for young people as well, not just old fogies like me."

Jessica was facing the sink, scrubbing some remnants of food off the dinner plates. "Mom, I said I don't want to do any classes. I don't want to be around a bunch of people. I agreed to try running. *Alone.*"

"You are already alone so much, hon. That's why I thought a class would bring you some camaraderie. You could even go out with some of the girls you meet after class and maybe make some new friends."

"You know I have friends. I have Claire." Jessica continued to face the sink, even though the dish she was holding was thoroughly rinsed. She held onto it tightly, like a life-preserver.

"I know. And Claire is a lovely girl. I just thought if you made some new friends at exercise class you'd know some people with different interests. Interests in exercise and healthy eating habits maybe. Claire seems to be mostly interested in boys. And drinking."

Jessica turned from the sink, her voice hardening. "Claire is my best friend. She has been my best friend for years and was there for me during all the stuff with Dad. And she isn't a freaking drunk," she snapped. She held onto the dish with such force that Andrea thought it might break. Jessica put the plate down in the sink, harder than necessary, and it made a loud, angry clang as it hit the stainless steel.

Well this escalated quickly, Andrea thought with some dismay. She began back-peddling, trying to find some neutral ground. If only they could openly talk about how they felt.

Unfortunately, that had never been their family's strong suit. "I just want what is best for you, Jess."

"Don't call me that."

"What?" Andrea asked, confused. "Call you what?"

"That's what Dad used to call me. I don't want anyone calling me that ever again." Jessica pushed herself away from the sink and hurried toward the front door.

Andrea dropped the towel she was holding and rushed after her, catching Jessica by the shoulder and turning her around. "Jessica, I love you more than anything. And I hate to see you hurting like this. I just want to help. That's all I want. *Please.*"

The anger drained from Jessica's face. Tears welled up in her eyes, turning their green hue to a shimmering aquamarine. "I just... I don't want to hurt anymore."

"Me neither, honey," Andrea said as she tried to hold back her own tears. "I think this running is a wonderful idea. And if you want to exercise alone then I think that is what you should do. I just worry about you all alone out there in the desert."

"Mom, you always worry too much. There's nothing out there to worry about. And I promise to stick to well-known hiking trails. The worst thing I could come across is a snake, and Dad taught me what to do if I ever saw one of those. There's nothing out there to be scared of."

Andrea smiled, dabbing quickly at her eyes. It was true— she had never come across anything dangerous during her countless hours spent on hiking trails with her husband during the course of their marriage. And Roger trained Jessica well; she knew how to handle herself in the desert. "Okay hon, you're right. There's nothing out there to be scared of. But please, promise me anyway, that you will be careful."

"I promise, Mom. I will be perfectly safe out there."

CHAPTER 5

Wasp Canyon Trail was set back near the base of the Santa Catalina mountain range. Tucson was surrounded by mountains on all four sides, with the Santa Catalinas located on the northeast side of town. The trailhead was located at the end of Wasp Canyon Road—a road known more for its wealthy residents than for its hiking trails. As Jessica drove down the residential street the houses steadily grew in size, each set further back from the road than the one before. The houses eventually disappeared altogether, the only indication of their existence being tall, adobe walls with iron-clad gates stretched across well-kept driveways. By the time Jessica reached the parking lot for Wasp Canyon Trail, she could no longer see any of the houses at all.

Wasp Canyon Road came to a dead end at the entrance to a small parking lot that overlooked the city of Tucson. *All those mansions I passed must overlook the city lights at night,* she thought as she pulled into one of the parking spaces. The lot was surrounded by prickly pear cacti and palo verde trees, some of their green branches reaching over the pavement and close enough to brush against the windows of cars that parked on the perimeter. The parking lot had room for two dozen cars, however no other cars were currently parked there.

"Huh," Jessica muttered as she climbed out of the Camry and stretched her legs, "I thought there would be more people."

She surveyed the parking lot and found the trailhead at the east end. The trail was ten feet across, a slightly crooked wooden post sticking out of the hard earth on the left-hand side. A well-worn path stretched out beyond the post, narrowing as it headed in the direction of the mountains. The path's edges were lined with various cacti. Jessica walked over to the trail and stepped off the asphalt to the soil below. She eyed the faded metal map attached to the wooden post.

Wasp Canyon Trail wound along the desert floor as it headed east. There was a rise midway along the trail that was labeled as Wasp Hill. Eventually the trail straightened out as it entered Wasp Canyon. Jessica traced her finger along the red line that indicated the path. Once in the canyon the trail continued for what appeared to be a great distance before abruptly ending at some unknown point. Perhaps a canyon wall? Or a vista? Or maybe *The Lost World,* equipped with dinosaurs and an aging Jeff Goldblum?

Jessica scanned the rest of the map but there wasn't much else to see. Most of the map was the topography of the Santa Catalinas, with Wasp Canyon Trail snuggly tucked between two of the mountain peaks. There didn't appear to be any other trails that met up with Wasp Canyon, and the path itself was an in-and-out trail. She would have to turn around and head back the same trail when she was ready to leave. Jessica thought that loop trails were more interesting, at least she wouldn't have to backtrack if the trail was a loop. *But oh well*, she thought, *I'm already here.*

Jessica squatted down to make sure her sneakers were securely fastened. As she fiddled with the laces she noticed the quiet for the first time. Away from the roads and shopping centers and bustling city life, the quiet of the desert was startling. She could hear a gentle whisper of wind coming from the direction of the mountains, probably originating from inside the canyon. She could hear birds chirping as they bounced from one cactus arm to another. And she could hear the buzzing of some sort of insect—hopefully not a wasp welcoming her to Wasp Canyon.

Her shoelaces secure, Jessica stood and took a final survey of the empty parking lot. She expected to see at least a few other cars parked there, owned by hikers she would come across along the trail. Well, at least no one would hear her struggling to breathe as she tried to run for the first time since high school PE class. If someone heard that, they might feel compelled to call for emergency medical care on her behalf.

Jessica took a couple steps forward, her feet crunching on the thin layer of soil that covered the hard caliche below. Her father had taught her about desert soils when she was younger, and about how the cement-like substance called caliche was so tough that Tucson homes did not have basements because the caliche was too difficult to dig through. Under her feet, it felt like concrete.

Almost forgot, she thought, bringing her left arm up so she could see her wrist. The QuikFit was there, its purple band tightened to its tightest rung to keep it in place on her frail wrist.

Jessica had tinkered with the fitness tracker back at home to make sure it worked. Once she removed it from the box, she charged the gadget as indicated per the instructions. Then there was the painful process of linking it through Bluetooth to her phone. She could now access all her health stats via an app on her phone, such as her heart rate, speed, distance covered, and elevation. Or she could use the watch's little speaker and play music from her phone. Super cool stuff if you cared about any of it, which she didn't.

The QuikFit had been Dr. Wyatt's idea anyway. She said that if Jessica had a way to track her progress she would feel like she was accomplishing something, no matter how small. If over the course of a month she was able to complete her run faster, or improve her heart rate, she would feel like she moved forward. And making progress—even if it meant taking thirty seconds less to run a mile—was at least something. Something positive in her life, or so Dr. Wyatt proclaimed.

Jessica poked at the watch's touch screen until she was able to bring up **Activity**. From there she followed the menu to **Cardio** and eventually to **Running**. She hovered her finger over **Begin**. *Here we go*, she thought. She pressed down and the menu disappeared. The watch began counting off seconds like a stopwatch. Jessica stood motionless, hearing the wind as it swept through the canyon, and watched the screen of the

QuikFit. She saw that she could customize the front screen and choose what she would like visible during her run. The time was at the top, followed by her distance, speed, and elevation. *Eh, I don't care about elevation*, she thought. She poked at the screen a few more times. *There we go*. Now she had her time, distance, speed, and heart rate illuminated on the device.

It had apparently taken her one minute and forty-two seconds to program the QuikFit to her liking. Distance: 0.0. Speed: 0.0. Heart rate: 72 bpm. *Well, better restart this little sucker*, she thought as she pushed the **Finish** button. The watch showed her a final tally and then went dark. She hit the **Home** button and went through the menu again to start a new run. *Well, no matter what happens right now, I will be able to say I made progress from my first run of 0.0 miles to my next run. And any progress is moving forward, right?* Jessica smiled at the thought, and began to run.

Eight minutes later Jessica was hunched over on the trail with her hands on her knees, gasping in great mouthfuls of air. *Holy mother of God*, she thought, *a fucking infant is more physically fit than I am*. She could hear her heart pounding monstrously inside her head, the sound of the canyon wind drowned out by the blood pulsing in her temples. She thought the blood might just start squirting out of her ears in great red bursts, in sync with her rapid heart rate.

She tried to look at the specs on her watch; however, her arm was shaking too badly for her to read any of the numbers on the small screen. She looked up at the cloudless sky, took in another deep breath, and let it out in a slow, shaky whoosh. Her heart rate seemed to be slowing to some realm of normalcy, and the dizziness started to subside. Again, she tried to look at her QuikFit.

Miles: 0.4
Speed: 0.0 mph
Time: 8 minutes
Heart rate: 168 bpm

Jesus, this is embarrassing. Jessica glanced around to see if anyone was around to witness her pathetic attempt at physical fitness. The trail was deserted. She could hear tiny twigs snapping and leaves ruffling as lizards crawled away from her through the low shrubs. She watched a desert spiny lizard make a hasty retreat, away from the wheezing monster in stretchy purple yoga pants.

Jessica looked up from where the lizard vanished and surveyed her surroundings. A few man-made structures were in the distance—probably the mansions that were set back from the road. She could make out a few adobe walls, a few wrought iron fence posts, the shimmering of some millionaire's oasis pool. Only half a mile down the trail, she was probably still alongside someone's property. Eventually, the trail would descend into the canyon, leaving all human structures behind.

People are strange, she thought. *They keep trying to get closer to nature, but all they really do is push it further away.*

She turned away from the mansions. She wanted to get away from them, from people, and from all things man-made. She looked at the canyon up ahead. That's where she wanted to be.

Wasp Canyon Trail had narrowed a bit, however it was still wide enough to be comfortable and the plant life remained at a respectable distance. Birds continued to chirp and hoo as they pecked at seeds and balanced on narrow tree branches. The landscape was littered with desert shrubs, saguaros, mesquite and palo verde trees, and many forms of cacti that Jessica chose to ignore. All the vegetation was fairly sparse, allowing her to see a great deal into the distance.

She walked along the trail, forgoing running for at least the next few minutes. She had planned to run two miles in, take a break, and then turn and run back. Four miles originally sounded like a good starting off point, however after 0.4 miles of hovering on the edge of consciousness, Jessica thought she might have set the bar a bit high.

Okay, I will walk to the one mile mark, turn around, and then see how far I can run during the return trip. Maybe 0.5 miles instead of 0.4. That would be progress, wouldn't it?

She walked at a leisurely pace, watching the nearby birds and listening to the serene quiet of the desert. The steady sound of wind coming from the canyon was mesmerizing, almost like it was beckoning for her to come inside. *Someday I will make it that far,* she thought. *Someday I will run all the way into that canyon without stopping. But that sure as hell ain't gonna happen today.*

She glanced at her QuikFit. She had been strolling along the trail for nearly fifteen minutes and was now 0.9 miles in.

Wow, time really does fly when you don't feel like you are actively dying, she thought. She realized that she was surprised by just how beautiful the desert was. Somewhere along the way in her young life she must have forgotten. She hated to admit it, but Dr. Wyatt might actually have something with this whole running thing, or at least the getting outside in nature part of it anyway.

At one mile, Jessica stopped walking and took in a final view of the desert. A large crop of jumping cholla stood next to the trail on the right side, its spiny boughs bursting with cream-colored daggers. The jumping cholla was the most feared of all the chollas—their boughs broke off easily, almost like they were jumping at you. Even a strong breeze could knock one off and send it on a collision course with your bare ankle. Once, as a child, Jessica ended up with one embedded in her skin after playing in the backyard. Her mom had to use kitchen tongs to pluck the chunks of cholla out of her leg. Oh, how she had wailed!

Thankfully, these chollas were set back a few feet from the trail. Hopefully far enough to not be a danger on a windy day. *Okay then, the jumping chollas are my one-mile marker,* Jessica thought. She turned, took a deep breath, and began running back the way she had come.

The agony did not take long to arrive, as she knew it wouldn't. The opening in her throat seemed to narrow, the blood once again throbbed in her ears, and her side began to cramp. But she kept pushing, kept running. *I said I could make it half a mile without stopping. And I'm going to fucking make it half a mile without stopping.*

Her quadriceps trembled with overexertion, and dizziness once again crept into the sides of her mind. But she kept running, checking her watch every few seconds until it reached 1.5 miles. As soon as the mile counter hit 1.5, she staggered to a stop in the middle of the trail, bent forward with her hands on her knees. She stared at the blurry desert floor, waiting for the dizziness to subside and for everything to come back into focus. Once it did, she stood up, took a deep breath, and walked the remaining half mile to the parking lot. *I did it. I ran 0.1 mile further during my second try. I made progress. I did better.*

It wasn't until Jessica got into her car that she realized she had not thought about cancer, or her father's death, even once during her first run through the desert.

CHAPTER 6

Lindy's Eatery was a single-story brick building on the northwest side of town. It was set back from the road, its undecorated entrance not even visible to passersby. Only a small wooden sign with chipped paint alerted drivers to its whereabouts. The building itself was surrounded by an expanse of dirt parking lot, one that was mostly vacant during the day and always strewn with cars in the evening. The lack of midday patrons was probably due to the fact that Lindy's Eatery had stopped serving food nearly two decades ago—something none of the bar's regulars seemed to mind. What Lindy's lacked in mediocre bar food, it made up for in liquid refreshment, which was what most of the locals were interested in anyway. As one ambled up to the building, dirt from the unpaved lot crunching underfoot, he or she could hear the sound of country music drifting out into the night. Inside, the dusty concrete floor was rarely swept and the overhead lights didn't quite do their job of adequately lighting the pool tables and dance floor. The bar itself was much better lit, the well-worn wood of the bar top glowing under the warm incandescent bulbs that hung from the ceiling.

It was obvious that Lindy's Eatery was a dive bar that had seen better days, but the college kids and blue collar workers seemed to like it all the same. It had a welcoming atmosphere that the trendy nightclubs down by the college seemed to lack. And the construction crews and other outdoor working-types never had to worry about getting dust from their work boots on the floor. Rarely did visitors or snowbirds (just another version of visitors, except they chose to stay for extended periods of time and only during the agreeable winter months) ever venture into the dusty tavern, and if they did they would politely get one beer at the bar, finish quickly, and then turn tail to find a more respectable establishment.

Jessica and Claire sat at two of the coveted bar top stools, seats that filled early on a Friday evening and didn't turn up empty until closing time. Most of Lindy's patrons ended up standing by the pool tables watching their friends play a game of nine ball, dancing on the just-dim-enough dance floor, or sitting out on the patio smoking cigarettes and playing cornhole. Jessica and Claire almost always found themselves a seat up at the bar—a little gift from Lindy's owner, Howard Dunlap. Howie was an old friend of Claire's family, even attending some of Claire's childhood birthday parties where the drink of choice was lemonade instead of Dragoon IPA. Howie always kept a couple of stools tucked under the bar for his top patrons, pulling them out only when one of these special few arrived so they had a place to sit and shoot the shit with him. Howie considered Claire something like a daughter, which often landed her and Jessica at the end of the bar sitting on Howie's specially reserved stools.

"Hey Howie! Us ladies would love a second round if you feel so inclined!" Claire called across the bar.

Howie looked up from the tap, one large hand holding a half-full glass of golden beer, the other holding the handle for Lagunitas IPA. He was a burly man of sixty, always with a five o'clock shadow on his face and receding white hair that was in need of combing. He wore a plaid button-up shirt, the buttons taught over his considerable midsection. "Be right with ya, darlin'," he called back.

Claire smiled and lowered herself back onto her barstool. She was a petite brunette, her almond-shaped eyes always lined with black eyeliner which caused them to stand out dramatically against her fair complexion. Her dark hair was often streaked with one color or another from her latest salon trip. Tonight, red highlights weaved in and out of her shoulder-length waves. Claire crossed her arms and rested them on the bar, her low-cut tank top showing off her ample cleavage. This warranted many glances toward the end of the bar as young men—and some not so young—worked their way to and from the patio.

Jessica took no notice of the lingering stares cast in their direction. Instead, she stared at her phone with growing frustration. "Stupid freaking thing. Why won't you work?" she muttered as she jabbed at the screen, hitting various buttons. The phone went dark. "Fuck." She dropped the phone onto the bar and looked up at a couple of thirty-something guys that were ogling Claire from across the way.

"What's going on, girl? You've been staring at that thing all night." Claire looked away from the thirty-something guys and down at Jessica's phone.

"Yeah, I know. Sorry. I'm just trying to open this stupid app for my QuikFit and I can't get it to load. Stupid thing."

Claire reached across the bar and grabbed Jessica's phone. "You really are getting into this running thing, huh?"

"Into it? No, uh, not really. I only did it the once so far. I'm just supposed to be able to see my stats or something and I can't get it to work. That's all." Jessica took the last sip of her beer and met Claire's eyes.

Claire took Jessica's arm and looked at her with an expression much too serious for a Friday night at Lindy's. "Hon, it's ok if you are excited to do this running thing. I haven't seen you show much interest in anything since, well, you know. This could be a good thing." Claire turned on Jessica's phone and started tapping at the screen with one of her hot pink nails.

"Yeah, well, we'll see. I really suck at it so far."

Howie arrived at the end of the bar and placed his large, worn hands on the bar top. "Well, ladies, what'll it be?"

"Two more of the same, Howie my dear," Claire said, batting her eyes with exaggerated enthusiasm.

"Now don't choo' be callin' me that, young lady. I am Mr. Howie to you."

Claire laughed. "My apologies, *Mr. Howie*."

Howie disappeared and returned a moment later with two pints, filled to the brim. A small stream of foam oozed down the side of the glass he placed in front of Jessica. "How are ya doin', darlin'? I haven't seen you 'round these parts as much as usual. I know thing's been tough for you and your ma lately."

Jessica looked up from her beer, where she had been watching the foam as it made its slow descent to the smooth wood of the bar below. She forced a small smile, and tugged at a piece of hair. "I'm hanging in there, I guess. Just doing the usual. Plus, I got this one here always looking out for me." She lightly elbowed Claire in the ribs.

Howie leaned forward and dropped his voice. "Kind of annoying, ain't she?" he asked, winking at Jessica.

"God, she really is, isn't she?" Jessica groaned. Howie chuckled and she joined in.

Claire's mouth dropped open. "Hey now you two! Not nice! Not nice at all! I am a delight to be around!"

Jessica and Howie laughed harder. He gave Claire a wink and headed back down the bar toward a group of college-age men impatiently waving a twenty in the air.

Claire turned back to Jessica. "You know, with that kind of attitude I don't know if you deserve my expertise when it comes to phone apps."

"Oh come on, Claire. You know I love you." Jessica took a sip from her beer.

"Well, I suppose I will still help you then," Claire said. She returned her attention to Jessica's phone, and after a moment, started to giggle.

Jessica looked up, confused, and then heard Britney Spears coming from her QuikFit, confessing that her loneliness was killing her. "Claire, what the—"

"Jesus Christ, Claire, turn that pop shit off!" Howie hollered across the bar.

Claire cackled. Jessica fumbled with the QuikFit, trying to figure out how to turn the speaker off. She felt her face grow warm and her cheeks begin to burn. Finally, Claire relented, hit a few buttons on Jessica's phone, and Britney Spears disappeared.

"God, Claire. You couldn't find anything better to play?"

"It was either that or N'Sync."

"How about just making the app work?" Jessica asked. The heat in her cheeks faded. How could such a loud sound come out of such a tiny speaker?

Claire spent another moment pushing buttons on Jessica's phone, then handed it back. "Okay, so you see that icon there? That's your QuikFit app."

Jessica clicked on the icon for the QuikFit application and followed Claire's instructions to open her logged activities. Claire continued, "So then you go to cardio, then running, and then you should have your runs listed in chronological order. See there, that's the one from today."

Jessica clicked on her most recent—and only—listed activity. The screen opened up to a summary of her run on Wasp Canyon Trail. The date and time were at the top, followed by her distance covered, average speed, average heart rate, and elevation change. She scrolled through and saw that she could click on any of the items and they would get further broken down into graphs and charts that showed how much time she spent at different speeds and how much her heart rate fluctuated. Fascinated, Jessica went through the various components of her run, oblivious to Claire who was leaning over her shoulder and also observing her stats.

"Wow," Claire interrupted, "you really suck at this."

Startled, Jessica dropped the phone on the bar and looked up at Claire. A grin crept across her face, and both girls started to laugh.

CHAPTER 7

The Wasp Canyon parking lot was deserted once again when Jessica arrived the following morning. She wondered if maybe the time of day had something to do with the lack of hikers. Or perhaps it was the time of year.

Tucson was a bustling town in the winter months. The ample sunshine and average highs in the seventies made it a prime destination for people from all over the country to escape the snow and icy temperatures back home. And for those with deep enough pockets, it was a great place for a second home so they could avoid the harsh winter months in their hometowns all together.

The summers in Tucson were a different story. As May gave way to June all the winter travelers and snowbirds packed up their houses and condos and headed back east, not returning until the temperatures dropped back out of the triple-digits. From June through September, Tucson was a much quieter, calmer town. And a much hotter town. Temperatures often soared well over one hundred degrees, not cooling to the nineties until late in the evening. Outdoor activities were often forgotten, locals only venturing outside to go to work or run errands. Prime parking spots were selected by shade, not by distance from the storefront. And indoor activities like going to the movies and shopping at the mall were considered favorite pastimes.

The only reprieve from the scorching summer heat was the long-awaited monsoon season. Every July and August the weather patterns across the Pacific shifted, causing moisture to come up from the south and provide southern Arizona with more than half its annual rainfall in the course of two months. Afternoon skies filled with dark cumulus clouds and the stifling heat mixed with the growing humidity made the air feel thick like syrup—like something that would stick to the roof of your mouth if you drank it.

And then the thunder would come, deep rumbles that spread across the desert and sounded like the ominous growls of an angry predator. The sky would begin to flash, bolts of lightning emanating from deep within the clouds and striking the ground somewhere off in the distance. You could feel the electricity building in the air. The wind would sweep in, bringing the smell of moisture and wet desert soil to your nose. And all at once the sky would open up, and a deluge of rain would beat down in torrents so heavy you couldn't see more than ten feet in front of you. Thunder boomed, lightning flashed, and wind shook the trees hard enough for branches to break free. And suddenly the violence would stop as quickly as it had begun. The sky would close back up, taking its lightning and thunder with it. A few final rumbles would travel across the rain-soaked desert, like a beast satisfied with a kill it had made. And then it was over.

Jessica never understood why the snowbirds and winter visitors would leave during the summer and miss the show—a breathtaking show that used to happen almost daily. However, over the years, the storms had become less and less frequent. *Got global warming to thank for that,* she thought. These days you were lucky to get a few good storms a year.

This summer was supposed to be different, though. According to the news, a lingering El Niño was expected this year, bringing tropical storms to the eastern Pacific and more moisture up to Arizona. Increased rainfall was forecasted for all of the southwest this summer, especially in southern Arizona.

Jessica glanced at the sky, an expanse of blue with not one cloud to blemish it. She hoped that wouldn't be the case for long. With it being early June, it would still be a month before monsoon moisture would arrive, and that would only be the case if it arrived on time. Nature could be fickle that way.

June in Tucson was hot, dry, and unforgiving. Plants desperately clung to life, hoping to survive until the rains came. Animals came down from the mountains and could sometimes be seen in backyards drinking from swimming pools. And temperatures over 110 were not uncommon. *And of course this is when Dr. Wyatt suggests I take up outdoor exercise,* Jessica thought. *Nothing like June in Tucson to take in the desert scenery. And forget about your dead dad. I guess if I pass out from heatstroke I will forget, even if it is only for a little while.*

Jessica suspected that's why the Wasp Canyon parking lot was empty again: anyone who lives here isn't dumb enough to go outside in June. And those that are dumb enough already went back east for the summer.

Another possibility was because it was very early in the day. Jessica decided to do her runs right after sunrise, when the day was coolest. That way she could get it over with and not have to worry about it for the rest of the day. Her work schedule also supported this decision. Jessica was a server at a local steakhouse, which meant evening shifts and free mornings. So here she was, in a deserted parking lot at 6:35 in the morning. The breathtaking oranges and pinks of the sunrise had already faded, and she could feel the day's heat starting to fill the air. *Better get this done. Maybe if I finish quick, I will have time for a nap before work.*

CHAPTER 8

Getting her QuikFit going was easier this time, only taking Jessica a brief moment to pull up and begin her running program. The running itself, however, was just as difficult as it was the first time. Jessica's throat narrowed, the muscles in her legs quivered in protest, and the blood pounded in her ears. There was also one new, and rather unpleasant, sensation that she didn't have during her first run: nausea. A sickening weight began sloshing around in her stomach at 0.3 miles and was now threatening to rise up into her throat. *Beers. It was the freaking beers. I knew I shouldn't have let Claire convince me to get a third last night.*

Jessica pushed on despite the growing need to calm her stomach. She could hear her labored breathing, the scraping of her sneakers on the ground, and the grumbling from within. *Point six. Gotta make it to 0.6 miles. Gotta do a little bit better than last time.*

In the end, her stomach was stronger than her perseverance, and at 0.5 miles she bent over at the edge of the trail and vomited her fried egg and strawberries that she had had for breakfast. There was also a sour, hoppy aftertaste that could not be mistaken for anything other than IPA. She stared at the bleached soil between her feet. In the center was a liquidy blob of yellow, red, and brown—not liquid, not solid, but some mashed up combination of the two. Jessica spat out as much of the hoppy bile as she could and swore to herself to never again drink beers the night before she went running.

Jessica grabbed the tube of her CamelBak and took a long swallow of water. The burn of stomach acid in her throat eased off, but not completely. The CamelBak had been her father's. It was worn out from frequent use, but still functional. Andrea had found it in her closet and insisted Jessica use it on her runs, listing off the many dangers of dehydration and heat stroke. Jessica took it begrudgingly, but was now relieved she had it. She took a few more drinks of water and let the tube fall to her side.

Discouraged by her inability to reach her goal, she meandered along the trail and allowed herself to look at some of the cacti and succulents along the way. *Organ pipe cactus, barrel cactus, century plant, saguaro, prickly pear, aloe vera, ocotillo, another saguaro.* Jessica kicked at the dirt when she felt her eyes start to burn with the threat of oncoming tears. *This is stupid. This running thing is stupid. I'm telling Dr. Wyatt I tried it and it isn't going to work. At least I tried, though. She can't get on me as long as I tried.*

Jessica saw the crop of jumping cholla come into view. Her mile marker. In the distance she could see the mountains coming together, leaving a narrow opening that was Wasp

Canyon. And beyond that, who knows? More Tucson? Mexico? The magical land of Narnia?

She wiped at her eyes and stopped just short of the jumping chollas, making sure to stand on the opposite side of the trail. The slow but steady whisper of wind echoed in the canyon beyond. *I wonder if there really are wasps in there,* she thought. *Who would name it Wasp Canyon if there weren't any wasps?* She took a few steps forward, moving past the chollas, transfixed on the canyon in the distance. *I wonder what else might be in there. Gila monsters? Bobcats? God, I'd love to see a bobcat. Or maybe a gray fox.*

Jessica kept walking along the trail, her QuikFit forgotten. Her feet scuffed along the ground, her ankles shifting to accommodate the rocks embedded in the desert floor. She grunted with effort as she began to ascend a rise in the trail, the rocks requiring her to pay close attention to her footing. *This will be a pain in the ass to run up and down if I ever get to that,* she thought.

When she reached the top of the rise she was able to see the trail's progress as it weaved through the rocks and cacti, eventually disappearing inside the canyon. The walls of the canyon were sheer cliffs with little plant life except for a few stubborn shrubs. Quite a few trees were growing around the entrance, their branches obstructing her view of the path beyond.

Jessica's stomach made an unhappy grumble. *Not today I guess,* she thought as she turned around. She glanced down at her QuikFit and realized she had hiked an additional mile past the chollas. Where she was standing at the top of the rise was

2.1 miles from the parking lot. *So this makes mile marker number two. The top of the hill is two miles in.* Jessica smiled, realizing that she was standing on top of the rise she had seen on the trail map. *Wasp Hill. I'm standing on top of Wasp Hill.*

She made her descent down Wasp Hill, being careful to find the right footing on the juts of rock sticking out of the caliche. She doubted these stones had moved in decades, if not centuries.

The heat was becoming much more noticeable as she worked her way back toward the parking lot. Her stomach, although still not pleased with her, had at least calmed itself now that it was empty. The chollas came and went. Her QuikFit diligently counted her progress, reaching 4.2 miles as she arrived at the parking lot. Jessica stepped up onto the asphalt and turned to look at the trail once more. *So no wasps on Wasp Hill, huh? Well, maybe they are inside the canyon instead. Maybe what I can hear out there isn't wind coming from the canyon at all. Maybe it is thousands and thousands of wasps.*

Jessica got into her car and pulled out of the small parking lot. Whatever was in that canyon, she was going to find out.

CHAPTER 9

Early summer can be a miserable time in southern Arizona. It's hot, it's monotonous, it's *boring*. No one wants to go outside to sweat and swelter in the heat. So they stay locked inside, watching Netflix and praying that the air conditioner doesn't break. A few brave souls will venture out in the early morning hours, trying to get some time outdoors before the heat really sets in, but mostly people stay locked up inside and hope the monsoons will arrive early.

Jessica was also hoping for the monsoons to be early and plentiful. She kept hearing promises from the nightly weather reports to expect a real doozy of a monsoon season, but so far the skies remained empty and the blistering temperatures unyielding. Luckily, the heat had not managed to hinder her progress with running, though. She found that as long as she got out there early enough, she was usually getting in her car to return home before the heat got a really strong hold on the day. And as long as she stayed away from the beer, she was able to avoid another projectile breakfast situation.

Over the past few weeks Jessica's endurance had improved. She was now able to make it one mile without stopping, although she still felt like she might explode or collapse once she made it to the jumping chollas. She continued to push herself further and further, with the unwavering goal to get inside Wasp Canyon driving her on. Unfortunately, her endurance still wasn't enough to carry her to the canyon's mouth. Jessica could now run/walk for three miles without darkness entering the corners of her vision and her throat completely closing up, but she still had the return trip to think about. Three miles in meant three miles out. And the entrance to the canyon, which she estimated to be around the four mile mark, meant eight miles round trip. And that didn't even get her *inside* the canyon.

Jessica decided she would try to improve her endurance for the first month, running for longer periods and with shorter rest breaks. Once she was able to run a reasonable distance without stopping—or passing out—she could then hopefully start venturing further. Her current mile marker was a monstrously tall crested saguaro which stood approximately three miles into the trail. The top of the saguaro had a large fanned headdress, which earned it its name and set it apart from the other saguaros. This type of saguaro wasn't rare, but it was not nearly as plentiful as the typical saguaros of the Sonoran Desert.

Jessica's current plan of attack was to run to the jumping cholla, walk to the top of Wasp Hill, and then run to the crested saguaro. Three miles in. At that point her body would begin to protest, first in the lungs, then in her legs, and eventually in her head. She would collapse at the saguaro, hands on knees and head down, waiting for the swimmy feeling inside her skull to pass. After staring longingly at the canyon for a moment—still a mile out of reach—she would turn around and start heading back the way she had come.

Once in the car, Jessica would snatch her phone out of the glove compartment, upload her latest run onto her QuikFit app, and analyze her progress. *Okay, heart rate is doing a little bit better. Speed is about the same, definitely slower on the second leg of the run than the first. And I really need to pick up my pace during the walking portions. I'm practically going on an evening stroll during those parts.*

Jessica placed the phone on the passenger seat and started her car. Still no other cars in the parking lot, and still no clouds in the sky. Tomorrow was July first. *Come on monsoons. Where the hell are you?*

Four days later, as Americans across the country celebrated their independence with burnt hotdogs and patriotic medleys, the monsoons arrived in Tucson, Arizona. Thunder rumbled, lightning competed with fireworks, and rain poured down over the scorched earth. And deep inside the walls of Wasp Canyon, something stirred.

PART II

FLIGHT

Chapter 10

"Happy Fourth of July, Mom," Jessica said when her mother opened the front door. Jessica held a bag of potato chips in one hand and hamburger buns in the other. Claire stood beside her, holding a bottle of red wine.

Andrea gave the girls a warm smile and ushered them inside. "Come in, come in," she said, directing them toward the living room. Andrea shut the door and grabbed the bottle of wine from Claire. "Thank you so much, dear. Please, go have a seat. I'll bring out some glasses and some chips to snack on."

"Thank you, Mrs. C," Claire said. "And might I say you look lovely tonight."

"Oh goodness," Andrea replied. "You are too kind to an old woman like me. And you are looking just fabulous as always, Claire."

"Just trying to show my American spirit." Claire was wearing a white crop top with a sequined American flag across the front. A sparkling red gem glittered from her pierced navel.

"Well, I certainly believe you succeeded," Andrea said. She gave Claire one more smile and then went to the kitchen where Jessica was already setting down the bags of food on the counter. "She's looking well," Andrea said to Jessica.

"Be nice, Mom," Jessica said, giving her mother a sidelong glance. "She's my best friend."

"I know, I know. I really do enjoy her. Now get out of my kitchen and go join Claire in the living room. I'll grab us some glasses for a toast."

Jessica lingered for a moment, watching her mother grab wine glasses out of the top cabinet. Last year, her father had grabbed those same glasses and poured drinks for everyone. That Fourth of July had ended up being the last holiday they had spent together. Jessica felt a pang of heartache so strong she felt she might collapse. No matter how much she ran, she would never outrun her own grief. Grief has teeth, and it never fully releases you from its jaws. At any moment you might feel those teeth clamp down on you, crushing your chest, and suddenly you are unable to breathe. It doesn't matter if you are waiting in line at the supermarket, sitting at a traffic light, or standing in the center of your kitchen—the grief will find you. You can't run from something that is inside of you. Jessica forced herself to turn away from the kitchen, and the memory, and headed into the living room to sit with Claire.

Andrea emerged a moment later carrying three glasses with one hand and the open wine bottle with the other. "I don't know how you do it at the restaurant, Jessica. I couldn't possibly carry all those dishes and glasses without dropping one. And that is why I will be letting you ladies pour our toast." She set down the empty glasses and handed the wine bottle to Claire.

"It really isn't that hard, Mom. You get used to it."

"And how is work going?" Andrea asked. "You getting a lot of tips? I know the summers can be tough with less people being in town."

"It's going alright," Jessica said, accepting a full glass from Claire. "Geez girl, what are you trying to do? Get me drunk?" They giggled as Claire poured wine into the next glass.

"Here ya go, Mrs. C." Claire handed the glass to Andrea and then poured herself a glass.

Andrea turned back to Jessica after accepting the glass of wine. "Well, as long as work is going alright, then I won't bug you about it. But if things get tight moneywise, please let me know."

"Okay, Mom. I will. Thank you."

"A toast!" Claire announced, standing from the couch and holding up her glass. She gestured to Andrea to make the toast.

Jessica stood up, holding her overfilled wine glass carefully to not spill it. "A toast," she repeated.

Andrea joined them. "Happy Fourth of July, ladies," she said. "Here's to a much better year than the last one."

"Oh, please God," Jessica said.

They clinked their glasses together, and just as Jessica brought her glass to her lips thunder boomed overhead.

"It's he-ere," Claire said in a spooky, sing-song voice. She took a large sip of wine and returned to sitting on the couch.

Jessica sat down beside her. "Thank God. We could really use some rain."

"What about your running, honey?" Andrea asked as she peered out the living room window. Dark clouds covered the sky and the wind had picked up. The bows of Andrea's mesquite tree bounced up and down as downdrafts of wind from the approaching storm swept across the yard. "Looks like this might be quite a storm. I bet the washes will be running." Andrea turned from the window. "You better watch out for flooding."

"We'll be fine, Mom. We just got here. I'm sure the storm will be over way before we leave."

"So what about the running then?" Andrea asked again. She sat down in the armchair opposite the couch. "Do you think you'll be able to continue running with the monsoon season going on?"

"Well, I always run early in the morning, so I really don't think it will be an issue. The storms always happen in the afternoon anyway."

"We just want you to be safe, girl," Claire said. She grabbed a few potato chips from the bowl. "You know, I can always go out there with you sometime. Work some of these things off." She gestured to the potato chips and popped one into her mouth.

"Naw, it's okay. I'm tracking my progress with my app and I think it will skew my results if I'm not alone."

"So you're saying I'm gonna slow you down?" Claire raised an eyebrow at Jessica and popped another chip into her mouth, chewing noisily.

Jessica laughed. "No, that's not what I'm saying. I just think we'd get busy talking and I wouldn't push myself as hard." Jessica shook her head when Claire offered her the bowl of chips. She took one small sip of her wine. Tomorrow she was planning to go for a run and she didn't want a wine-stained puddle on the side of the trail.

"Well, I must say I think it is working, whatever *it* is," Andrea said. "You are looking a little bit healthier, I think. You were just wasting away before."

"She is eating more," Claire agreed. "I saw her eat a whole half of a sandwich the other day." She continued to work on the bowl of chips.

Jessica knew her appetite had started to improve. Sometimes when she returned from a run, she would feel almost ravenous. It didn't take more than a few bites of something to make her stomach ache from overfilling, though. Jessica always forced herself to eat a few more bites, despite the aching, knowing that she needed it for energy if she was ever going to get strong enough to get into the canyon.

"The running can make me hungry, I guess," Jessica said. She didn't want to tell her mother or Claire about the canyon just yet. It was her secret goal, and might one day become her own private getaway from the world and reality. A special place just for her.

Harsh white light lit the living room as lightning flashed overhead. A deafening crack of thunder followed. All three women jumped in their seats, wine sloshing dangerously close to the edges of their glasses. Except for Claire's, whose glass was bordering on empty. Rain began to hit the window in sheets, brought in sideways from the wind.

"My goodness!" Andrea exclaimed. "Well, I'm certainly happy we aren't barbecuing tonight!"

"We certainly are getting a great fireworks display, though." Claire laughed and helped herself to some more wine. She turned to pour some more into Jessica's glass but it was still mostly full. "You don't want any more, girl?"

Jessica looked at her glass and shrugged. "I'm going to go running early tomorrow. Just trying to avoid a hangover."

"Good for you, Jess," Andrea said. And then quickly: "Jessica."

Jessica gave no indication of the name slip. Instead, she stared out the window at the raging storm. Night had almost fully taken over, and the splattered window was transitioning into a reflection of the well-lit living room. A year ago her father had been sitting in the living room with them, a thin ghost of his former self. He tried to act like he was having a good time, but Jessica could see the strain on his face as he tried to pretend he wasn't tired or in pain. In the window's reflection she stared at her father's empty chair, the reflected image obscured by the last hints of light outside.

"What do you think, hon?" Andrea asked.

"Huh?" Jessica jerked back into reality. "I'm sorry, I got distracted looking at the storm."

"Do you think the weather guy is right about this being a big monsoon year?" Andrea asked again.

"They said yesterday they thought it would be the most rain we've seen in years, possibly decades," Claire said. It appeared she had found the bottom of the chip bowl.

"It certainly looks like it," Jessica agreed. She turned her gaze back to the rain-streaked window, lightning turning the backyard into a photo negative each time it flashed.

CHAPTER 11

Mud. Mud everywhere. Jessica brushed at her leggings, where a splattering of mud was now drying. The bottoms of her sneakers were also caked in mud. *Jesus, Jess. You are a mess.*

Her run had gone well enough, although there was more slipping and sliding than usual as she made her way along the muddy trail. Yesterday's downpour had turned Wasp Canyon Trail into quite the obstacle course. There was still the scattering of rocks and stones jutting out of the caliche, but now there was also a collection of muddy puddles. Patches of the trail had already dried and returned to the hard, unforgiving surface that was Tucson's soil; however, in other areas where the earth dipped down, water had pooled and softened the tough clay into a soup. Once the gooey mixture coated her shoes and began to dry, it was almost like running on chunks of cement.

Jessica stood at the edge of the asphalt, trying to scrape the hardening mud-clay off her shoes. She balanced on one foot and dragged the bottom of her sneaker across the pavement's edge, then repeated on the other side. When she managed to get off what she thought was a respectable amount, she headed toward her Camry in the parking lot. She had just reached the car door when she heard the unmistakable sound of approaching footsteps on the pavement.

"Hello there!"

Every muscle in Jessica's body tensed at the sound of a man's voice. She whirled around from the car, her hand still on the handle, and stared at the man standing in the middle of the parking lot. He wore khaki shorts and a salmon-colored button-up shirt. He had a khaki hat to match his shorts, sturdy hiking boots, and a set of walking poles.

"Where did you..." Jessica trailed off. Her head darted from side to side as she scanned the parking lot for another vehicle. There weren't any.

"I didn't mean to startle you," he said with a chuckle. "Name's Cameron Jasper."

Cameron took a step forward to offer his hand, but stopped when he saw Jessica take a step backward. "I really am sorry, ma'am. I just wanted to say hello before you headed out. It's rare to see someone else around these parts this time of year."

Jessica's posture relaxed, however she refused to relinquish her grip on the door handle. "Yeah, uh," she stammered, "this is the first time I've seen someone out here." She looked around the parking lot again, as if the vehicle the man arrived in must have materialized since the first time she looked. "Where exactly *did* you come from?"

"East Texas! I doubt that's what you meant though." He smiled broadly. "I actually live in one of these fine estates on

Wasp Canyon Road." He gestured to the desert surrounding the parking lot. "That's why there's no car. I simply walk from my home to the trailhead."

Jessica finally let go of the door handle. She blushed and offered a small smile. "I'm sorry if I acted weird. You just took me by surprise."

"That's quite alright, ma'am. A young woman must be cautious. And prepared. I wholeheartedly believe it is ever so important to always be prepared." Cameron winked.

"Prepared for what?"

"Well, anything, I suppose. I believe it is important to be prepared for anything life might throw at'cha." Cameron stood in the center of the parking lot, making no attempt to step closer to Jessica. His posture was non-threatening and his warm smile had a calming effect. He certainly didn't appear to have any ill intentions.

Jessica took a step forward. "I—I'm Jessica." She offered her hand to Cameron.

Cameron took a few steps forward and grasped her hand in a hearty shake. "Pleased to make your acquaintance, Jessica." He surveyed the parking lot and also seemed to realize that no other cars were parked in the lot. He returned his gaze to Jessica. "Anyhoo! I just wanted to say hello to a fellow traveler. Like I said, I rarely see people out this way this time of year."

"It's nice to meet you," Jessica said, smiling. Cameron seemed to be a nice enough man and she could feel her tension starting to dissolve. She guessed he was probably in his mid-fifties. His hair was graying at the temples and he had laugh lines etched across his tan face. From the looks of his clothing and tanned features, Jessica guessed Cameron was no beginner when it came to hiking Tucson's trails.

"You've been hiking this trail a long time?" she asked.

"Not as much as I like, but I try to make it out here at least a few times a month. I work from home, but those pesky businessmen in Texas sure keep me on the phone quite a bit."

"What kind of business do you do?"

"Investments," Cameron said. "Not the most exciting of enterprises, but it did help me snag a nice little bungalow in Wasp Canyon Estates."

Jessica laughed. "Bungalow? From what I can see these houses are much more than bungalows."

"Potato potato," Cameron said, pronouncing the word identically.

"You mean potato *potato*?" Jessica asked, pronouncing the first word with a hard "A" and the second with a soft "a".

Cameron laughed. "Nope! Potato potato," he said, once again pronouncing them the same way. "It is all the same thing, my dear Jessica, no matter how we pronounce it."

Jessica smiled. "So you say you come here a lot?" She gestured to the empty parking lot. "Is it always so empty?"

"In the summertime, yes. That's why I come in the summer." Cameron winked. "In the winter, good luck finding a parking spot, let alone a quiet moment alone with nature. Those snowbirds come around, taking selfies and yammering on their headsets. It's like Disney World without the rides." Cameron laughed and looked wistfully at the trailhead. "I make sure to stay clear of that chaos. I come up here to clear my mind and listen to the canyon, not listen to tourists discussing where they want to go for happy hour that night."

Jessica grinned. "I can respect that, Mr. Jasper."

"Cameron, Cameron! You make me sound like an old man."

"Cameron then," Jessica said, smiling. She surveyed the parking lot one last time and then turned back to Cameron. "So this place stays pretty quiet during the summer then?"

"Like a ghost trail. Perfect place to come and get away from it all. As long as you aren't afraid of ghosts, that is." He winked again.

Jessica's smile lost altitude. "Believe me when I say ghosts are the least of my problems."

Chapter 12

"How has the running been going?" Wyatt asked. She sat in her executive chair across from Jessica, her hands loosely clasped and a notepad lying in her lap. Today her office had a warm glow, in contrast to the gloomy grayness that hung outside the window. The monsoon rain had been coming often and mercilessly since the first storm arrived on July Fourth. In the past week it had rained five of the seven days—substantial rainfall for any monsoon season. The clouds appeared over the mountains every afternoon like clockwork. Wyatt had a perfect view from her picture window, where she could watch as the clouds expanded both outward and upward, eventually blotting out the blue expanse of sky. The winds would then pick up, bringing the rain with it. As the onslaught of rain began, the mountains would become obscured, eventually disappearing into a gray mass of wind and water.

Jessica sat in a chair that was no longer slightly worn. Wyatt had promptly replaced it when she noticed the first few loose threads.

"Your chair feels funny."

"It's new. I had the one you were sitting in last week replaced."

"Why would you replace it with the exact same chair?"

"Because some of my patients come here because they are feeling out of control. They don't want surprises or changes; it would only make them feel even further out of control. This room is the same each time they come in. It is reliable. And reliability is comforting."

"Makes sense."

Jessica had been talking more during her last few appointments. Although she still skirted questions regarding her father, she was engaging in conversation more often and with more interest. Her pallor had decreased and her features were noticeably less gaunt. Her clothing was still wrinkled, but it did appear to have been washed recently. All good things.

"I would love to know how your running has been going." Wyatt looked down at her notepad. "Still Wasp Canyon Trail?" she asked.

"Yup," Jessica said, nodding.

"You were still struggling to make it a mile and a half without stopping when we spoke last week. Is that still the case?"

Jessica turned her gaze from the window and looked at Wyatt. More progress.

"Yeah, I'm still having trouble with that. I think it is because of this, though," Jessica pointed out the window. "The rain is making the trail all muddy. It sticks to my shoes and I think it is slowing me down. Plus it makes it kinda slippery in some places."

"What does your QuikFit have to say about your progress?"

"It seems like I'm doing okay. My heart rate has gotten a lot better anyway. And before all the rain, I was running a little bit faster."

"That is excellent news, Jessica. You really are applying yourself." Another glance at the notepad. "And how about your eating? All the running must make you hungry."

"Yeah, I'm eating some. When I skip dinner I can't run as fast the next day. So yeah, I'm eating more, I guess."

"Such fantastic news. I am very pleased with how dedicated you have been with this project."

"Thanks." Jessica offered a timid smile.

Wyatt leaned forward in her chair, lowering her voice as if she was about to tell Jessica something in confidence. "Dare I say you enjoy it?"

Jessica blushed and looked down. Her hand went up to a strand of hair, hesitated for a moment, then dropped back to her lap. "Yeah, I actually think I am. Uh, thanks for the suggestion."

Wyatt leaned back in her chair, made a small notation on her notepad, and then returned Jessica's gaze. "I am here to help you in any way that I can."

Rain pattered on the window. The downpour that was raging when Jessica's appointment began had now dwindled to a sprinkle, as if the clouds were spitting out the last bits of moisture they still had in their dark bellies. The mountains remained shrouded in a gray haze.

No one spoke for a moment, both listening to the rain as it softly tapped on the window. Jessica was the one to break the silence. "What's on the other side? Of the mountains?"

"What do you mean?"

"Well, the trail I run on goes into a canyon. I've been wondering how far the canyon goes. Or what's on the other side of the mountains."

"I'm afraid that is a question I am unable to answer. As much as I love this city, I am no geography expert. I imagine that there is more desert on the other side of the mountains, that I can be almost sure of. But as for how deep Wasp Canyon goes, or if it comes out on the other side, that I do not know."

"Can you come out on the other side?"

Wyatt sensed the change in topic, thrilled that Jessica had brought it up on her own. However, she did not want Jessica to pick up on her excitement. Wyatt kept her expression neutral, a skill she perfected after many nights of practicing in the mirror.

"Yes, Jessica, I wholeheartedly believe that you can. That anyone can, as long as they put in the effort."

"I hope you're right," Jessica said, turning her attention back to the window. The rain had finally stopped.

Wyatt opened her mouth to ask a question, then stopped herself. Jessica had opened the door of discussion, and then closed it. It was the first time she had opened it at all, and Wyatt didn't want to lose ground by pressing her further.

"Have you seen any animals along the trail?" she asked instead.

"Birds, some lizards. Not much else. I'm actually kind of surprised. I thought I would have seen at least a little bit more wildlife."

"It is a heavily populated trail from what I researched. I'm sure the animals just like to steer clear of all those humans."

Jessica leaned forward in the new chair, her eyes bright and interest peaked. "That's the weird thing, though. There aren't any people. I'm always the only one out there. So what are they hiding from?"

Wyatt's expression became concerned. "You are the only one out there? You've never met another person?"

"Well, one. He said hello in the parking lot. But that's it, all this time."

"Only one…" Wyatt tapped her pen on the armrest of her chair, a habit she had stubbornly worked off during her college years. She set the pen down and clasped her hands on the top of her notepad. "How was the gentleman you met? You said he greeted you."

"Oh, he was fine. Seemed like a nice enough guy. Cameron Jasper, I think he said."

"Cameron Jasper! Well, I've heard of him!"

Jessica's eyes widened. "You've heard of him? How?"

"He's in the paper sometimes. The Jasper Group. It's an investment management company. He made a name for himself in… where was it?" Wyatt paused, thinking hard. "Texas, I think it was."

"Yeah, that's where he said he was from!" Jessica exclaimed.

"From what I have read of him, he was very successful in Texas. He built his company from the ground up and hired a strong group of businessmen. And then he decided to up and move to Arizona. Manages the company from here. He was in the Fortune 500."

"The what?"

"It's a list of the top five hundred corporations in the US. *Fortune* magazine publishes one each year," Wyatt said absentmindedly. She realized she was losing track of the conversation—something she rarely did. She tried to redirect the course of discussion for the little bit of time they had left in the session.

"Well, Jessica, it sounds like you made quite the acquaintance. I would like you to be careful out there, all the same. Business tycoons or not, being in the wilderness alone is not always a safe situation. I was not aware that you were so isolated during your runs. I would much prefer you stick to a more populated trail."

"Yeah, I understand," Jessica said, "but I am really starting to enjoy this trail. I'm comfortable with it now." And then quietly to herself: "I've got mile markers."

Wyatt looked at the increased color in Jessica's cheeks and the fuller features of her face. The running was obviously doing her a lot of good. She didn't want to derail her progress by insisting on an alternative trail.

"I understand your reasoning," Wyatt said at last, "and I will not try to persuade you otherwise. But I would like to emphasize the importance of being careful while you are out there. Drink plenty of water, be aware of your surroundings, and carry your phone with you at all times. Neither of us want you getting injured out there and being unable to make it back."

Jessica smiled at Wyatt. "Of course, I always do."

Wyatt decided to leave it at that. The session had gone so well, the last thing she wanted to do was to spoil it.

CHAPTER 13

Miles: 3.7
Speed: 2.1 mph
Time: 1 hour, 9 minutes
Heart rate: 146 bpm

Jessica's breathing started to slow, her lungs began to unclench, and the stabbing pain in her left side faded to a dull ache. The morning heat was starting to set in, and she could feel sweat dripping down her spine, working its way between her shoulder blades. It was 7:32 a.m. on the morning of July seventeenth, and the sun was already well past the horizon. In the summer months sunrise came early, dawn's light invading the darkness before 5:00 a.m. By 7:32 the day was bright with sunshine, and with the sunshine came the heat. And with monsoon moisture came humidity. Arizona's notoriously dry climate disappeared during these few months, and the humidity hung in the air like a damp, smothering embrace.

She had run past the chollas without slowing, pushing hard until she reached the top of Wasp Hill. *That hurt.* From there she walked for the better part of a half mile, willing her heart rate to slow and her breathing to get under control. And then she pushed on. The crested saguaro came and went. Her QuikFit silently counted the distance. At 3.7 miles she couldn't find the strength to make it another step, the muscles of her thighs threatening to give way and send her to the dirt.

The sound of the wind was stronger than ever, the mouth of the canyon practically within throwing distance. *Almost,* she thought. Jessica spread her feet, lifted her arms overhead, and stretched from side to side. The cramp in her left side stubbornly held on, but it was losing ground. Soon it would fade away completely.

There it is. God, I'm almost there. If I called out would my voice echo on the canyon walls? She couldn't seem to find her voice, though. There was such a hush on the landscape that it felt wrong to break it by shouting. Only the wind was brave enough to speak—a steady rushing sound that could almost be mistaken for running water. *It must go all the way through. Right? With all that wind, it must go all the way through to the other side.* Jessica felt a pang of disappointment when she realized she would probably never know. She had every intention of exploring the depths of the canyon, but there was no way she would ever make it all the way through. She would have to camp in there. Be gone for days. And that's where she drew the line.

Today's the day, she thought. *Dear Diary, on this day, the seventeenth of July, I, Jessica Anne Cleary, will step inside*

Wasp Canyon. She walked forward, her feet crunching on the soil below. The wind continued to whoosh and sigh. She was only a few hundred feet away from the entrance now.

The mouth of Wasp Canyon was narrower than she thought, the opening only twenty yards across. There were more trees along the trail now, some pressing close to the path. They were different from the traditional desert variety—instead of seeing mesquites and palo verdes she saw aging oaks and cottonwoods. The trail wound left and right through the trees, making it impossible for Jessica to see what was around each bend. She made her way along the path—left then right, left, then right again—until she stood with the canyon's walls on either side. She looked up. The cliff faces towered overhead, reaching into the sky like the desperate hands of a drowning man. The walls had a golden tint, with layers of limestone and granite creating waves of color on the rocky surface.

Jessica lowered her eyes, her neck aching from the effort of looking up for so long. She surveyed her immediate surroundings. The foliage was much fuller here, and not like desert plants at all. The trees were bigger, their branches more lush with leaves. And there was underbrush covering the ground, more bushes now than cacti. Jessica could still see patches of the desert floor underneath, but she guessed the further she went into Wasp Canyon, the less she would be able to see. *Must get a lot more water in here,* she thought. *The rain must flow down the canyon walls and keeps everything saturated. Lets the plants grow more.*

The plants looked much greener, and much healthier, inside the canyon. *The shade must keep them from dying off during the dry season.* She realized that some of the bushes and plants were foreign to her, and that all the beloved cacti and succulents her father had filled his spare time with were disappearing. A few prickly pears still sat among the bushes, fighting for a chance to survive, but they appeared to be losing the battle. *Oh Daddy, I don't think you would have liked it in here. All your cacti have been taken over.*

Jessica thought about the cacti that her dad loved, and how he always told her how resilient they were and how they could survive practically anything. Looking around, it didn't look like they could survive in here. *Like Dad,* she thought. *So tough, so strong, and he couldn't make it either.*

Jessica walked slowly along the trail, deeper into the canyon. The air was noticeably cooler, ten degrees disappearing in a matter of steps. And the soil felt softer beneath her sneakers. Out on the open trail it felt like running on asphalt, however the further she walked into the canyon, the more give the soil had. She could even feel her feet sinking into it at times.

She shivered. *What the hell? I'm shivering… in Tucson… in July.* The drop in temperature and the persistent wind had caused her sweat-slicked skin to break out into gooseflesh.

She had ventured approximately a half mile into the canyon when she glanced at her watch, more interested in the time than the distance. *8:01. What the hell? I've been in here for almost half an hour?* She sighed. *Time to go.*

Jessica turned and started heading out the way she came. She still had the four miles back to the car, and it was bound to be getting pretty hot out on the trail by now. Plus she had agreed to cover an opening shift at the restaurant, and she needed time to shower, eat, and get ready.

As she weaved along the trail in the direction of the entrance her ears picked up on something, barely audible above the constant whistle of the wind. *An exhale? Like a grunt?* She paused, listening. The wind washed along the canyon walls, but other than that: silence. Jessica turned back toward the canyon and tilted her head in the direction of where she thought she had heard the sound. Nothing. *Just the wind. It plays tricks on you in the canyon. Must echo on the walls or something.*

She turned and resumed her walk toward the entrance. A faint odor drifted past, brought to her by the breeze and then quickly swept away. It was not a pleasant one. It smelled like rotting meat in the dumpster behind the restaurant. A sweet, putrid stench, like decay. Or carrion. A memory flashed in her mind, one of her dad holding her hand at the zoo. They were at an enclosure for one of the big cats or something, and it smelled bad. Not overwhelmingly bad, but like the stench a predator can give off. She was yanking on her dad's hand to tell him it was stinky, but his attention was directed toward whatever was in the enclosure. She kept yanking on his hand—and then the memory was gone, also taken away with the breeze. The smell, and memory, were so fleeting that she wasn't even sure why the zoo had popped into her head in the first place.

She lingered on the trail a moment longer, finding herself confused as to why she was standing there at all when she needed to get going. There was no smell—just the deep, earthy aroma of wet soil from yesterday's storm. And there was no sound—only the wind. She turned to the mouth of the canyon and once again started walking along the trail, this time not slowing her pace or looking back.

CHAPTER 14

"Great day for a stroll, isn't it, young Jessica?" a voice called from the top of the hill. Cameron Jasper was cresting Wasp Hill with the aid of his walking poles, heading in the direction of the canyon.

Jessica slowed to a jog, and then stopped altogether when she reached where Cameron was standing. "Good morning, Cameron!" she panted, trying and failing to hide how out of breath she was.

"Looks like you worked up quite a sweat out there. And it feels like it's going to be a warm one today."

"Yeah," Jessica said between ragged breaths, "it sure is."

"Take your time, catch your breath. I assure you that I get out of breath far more frequently than you do."

"Somehow I doubt that." Jessica grinned, her breathing finally under control.

Cameron returned her grin and winked. "I got started a little later than I care for today. Those dimwits in Texas kept me on the phone far too long."

"Yeah I heard that you were, uh, kind of a big deal back in Texas."

"Well, I wouldn't call it a big deal," he said. "I just happened to be skilled at a certain task and it led me to be quite successful in my business endeavors. Nothing more than that."

"I think you're being modest, but okay."

"I guess it depends on what you measure as a *big deal*," he said, making quotation marks with his fingers. "I think someone who has honed their body enough to be able to compete in the Olympics is a *big deal*. Or a couple that has been happily married for fifty years, that's a *big deal*. I, myself, only made it four years before I realized that marriage was not one of my strong suits. I am, however, good at managing investments. Successful yes, but *big deal*? I don't know about that." He smiled and adjusted his walking poles.

"Well okay, if you say so." Jessica looked around. She could see the roof of a large house in the distance. "You were able to get one of the houses out here. That seems like a big deal to me."

"Now that, young Jessica," Cameron paused and held up his index finger, "I cannot argue with. I do love it out here, and my business success did make it possible for me to acquire a home in this desirable location. And with the dimwits running things back in Texas," he shrugged, "I am able to live out here full time and consult with them from the comfort of my own home."

"Sounds pretty nice." She took a gulp of water from her CamelBak.

"I do wonder how you came across my *big deal* status," Cameron inquired.

"Oh, my thera—" Jessica stopped. She had not meant to divulge to Cameron that she had a therapist. "My, uh…" she stammered.

"Jessica, we all have a therapist. In one way or another, we all need help sometimes. Some confide in a friend or a spouse, others need a more professional confidant."

She smiled gratefully. And before she knew it the words slipped out: "My father passed away recently. I… I'm having a hard time dealing with it."

"My dear girl, I am so sorry to hear that. I lost my parents when I was young and it was a very difficult journey to find happiness again. Nature helped some, but a lot of it was time. So don't be too hard on yourself, and absolutely do not feel ashamed for needing help."

"Thank you. I really needed to hear that." Jessica marveled at the thought that an eccentric hiker/business tycoon/millionaire ended up being the first person she told about seeing a therapist—besides Claire of course. She glanced at the cityscape of Tucson, visible from the rise of Wasp Hill. She really needed to get back, but wanted to ask Cameron something before she headed out. "Cameron, have you ever been inside the canyon?"

A large smile spread across his tan face, making him look ten years younger. "Did you finally make it inside?"

"Yes, I did. Not very far, though," Jessica said. "I have to make it back for work later today."

"Well, the canyon certainly is a treat. And yes, I have been inside of it numerous times. You have to set out a stretch of time to allow for it though, that's for sure. It can take the majority of your day to hike in and then make it back out, especially before nightfall."

"Does it have an end point?"

"That I do not know. If it does, I have not discovered it yet. I can say that it does go for quite some distance." He paused, reflecting on some memory that he did not choose to share. "It is lovely in there, though. That much I know. Like another world."

"It really was," she agreed. "And I didn't even make it that far inside."

"It only gets more beautiful the further you venture inside. Sometimes I feel like I'm on the east coast and not in the desert at all. The foliage gets so green, and the temperature so cool!"

"Yeah, I noticed how much cooler it was in there!"

"Very much so. All I can say is that Wasp Canyon is a wonderful escape. I like to go sit in a certain spot—I have my own special rock, you see—and listen to the wind. It's very peaceful."

"Yes, I imagine it would be."

"However, you make sure to be careful in there, young lady," he said. He smiled, but she could see a touch of concern in his eyes. "If you get caught in a downpour in there, the water can come rushing through the center of the canyon. And with the rainfall we have been having, that can be very dangerous. You also must make sure to provide yourself with plenty of time to get back. The canyon can be a very scary place if you find yourself there alone in the dark."

"You've been in there at night?" Jessica gasped.

"Not on purpose, of course! As a younger man I was not nearly as cautious as I am now. I went exploring the canyon and lost track of the hour. I find it's easy to lose track of time in there. Anyway, I ended up having to stumble all the way back through the dark. It resulted in a sprained ankle and a very stern lecture from my then-wife. Like I said, I was a much younger man then. And much more foolish."

"Well, as much as I would like to explore the canyon, I definitely don't want to be stuck in there at night." Jessica thought nights in the desert could be creepy enough as it was, with all the wildlife coming out, either crawling, slithering, or stalking. "That reminds me, do you see any wildlife out here? Or in the canyon? It seems so… quiet, I guess."

"Well, I like the quiet, that's for sure. But to answer your question, no I have not. Not recently anyway. Seems a bit odd now that you mention it, but I suppose I never noticed it before. Perhaps the different climate inside the canyon makes it less desirable for the likes of our typical desert critters."

"Yeah, I guess that's possible. Anyway, it was wonderful to see you again. I really must be going now, though."

"Of course, being accountable at work is very important. And that advice is coming from a *big deal*," he said with a wink.

"Goodbye, Cameron. Enjoy the trail."

"Of course, Jessica. I always do."

CHAPTER 15

The monsoon rain continued through the rest of July with no sign of stopping or slowing down. Jessica worked at the restaurant, hung out with Claire, and ate dinner with her mother at least once a week. She had put on some weight, and a golden tan now spread across her face and shoulders. A few freckles had appeared on her sun-kissed cheeks, and her hair had faded to a lighter shade of blonde from so much time in the sun. Her father was still often on her mind, but the mind-numbing despair she had struggled with each and every day was starting to fade. Like the sharp pain of a cramp that slowly eases off while running, the pain from her father's passing had now faded to a dull ache. It was always there, but it no longer felt like she was being constantly stabbed by the loss with a sharp blade. At first it had felt like she was suffocating, bleeding out from the constant despair, unable to ignore the replay of her father's last few weeks—days—hours—in her mind. It was like a movie reel in her head that she could never turn off, or even pause. Helping him walk when he no longer could on his own, holding his hand while his wasted body lay in a hospital bed and he no longer knew who she was, the midnight phone call from her mother, the frantic drive to the hospital in the middle of the night, kissing his cheek before they wheeled him away and feeling how cold his skin felt against her lips. These thoughts used to run through her head on replay, an endless home movie—nightmare—that she was forced to watch again and again. Now when the projector in her head woke up, lights flickering and the reel beginning to slowly turn on its spool, she was able to gently turn it back off. The projector light would fade, and so would the image of her father's wasted frame in the hospital bed. She was beginning to realize this was what they called acceptance, knowing that the film reel in your head would always be there—that the pain would always be there—and sometimes it would turn on and the film would play, and sometimes it wouldn't. Sometimes it would turn on at very inopportune moments, like when she was serving a table. And sometimes days would go by and the projector would remain dormant, sitting quietly in her mind and starting to collect dust on the reels.

The running helped. As much as she hated to admit it, it really was helping. Dr. Wyatt was right, and in turn her mother was also right. After all, she was the one who suggested—no, insisted—that she start seeing Dr. Wyatt in the first place. When she was running and the film reel turned on, sometimes she would just let it play. Hospital bed, midnight call, hospital room, kissing his cheek. In the last couple weeks, something amazing started to happen, though. Every now and then, when the film reel coughed and sputtered into life and images started projecting on the screen of her mind, she found that sometimes she could change those images. She could switch the memories out for something better. Something brighter. Instead of a hospital bed, it was her dad squatting next to a barrel cactus and pointing out the barbed, pink spines when she was eleven. Instead of a midnight call that awoke her in the dark, it was her dad calling her at the exact minute she was born on her birthday each year. Instead of driving to the hospital in the night, shaking and drenched in cold sweat, it was her family driving to San Diego for summer vacation, her parents arguing over music stations while she sat in the backseat and watched the mountains roll by. Instead of kissing his cheek that last time, it was giving him a big hug and a kiss after she got soaked in the monsoon rain. *Oh Jess, you made me a mess.* Sometimes these new, brighter memories on the projector screen made her smile. Sometimes they made her cry so hard she had to stop on the trail, sit in the dirt, and sob until she had no more breath. Either way, she preferred these memories to the dark ones that had been on replay for eleven months. These memories might make her cry, but they didn't make her suffocate. They didn't make her bleed out. And for that, she was grateful.

CHAPTER 16

Push it. A little harder. A little further. A little faster. Be stronger. Be better. Be more.

Miles: 4.3
Speed: 4.8 mph
Time: 1 hour, 7 minutes
Heart rate: 134 bpm

She was inside the canyon, a stiff breeze rushing all around her. Her breathing was heavy but controlled. Her muscles ached but didn't cramp. Goosebumps covered her bare arms and shoulders, where her skin was damp with sweat. She had been making great progress, getting a little further each run.

She pressed on, her goal being to make it a mile and a half inside the canyon today. The trail was thin, narrower than three feet at times. The trees were plentiful this far in and a heavy layer of bushes covered the ground. Berries grew on some of the bushes, a splatter of red mixed in with the greenish-gray leaves. All the cacti were gone.

She glanced at her QuikFit, saw she had made it to 5.5 miles, and slowed to a stop. *That's it for today, time to turn around.* She stood in the soft earth and leaned from left to right, stretching her hips and torso. She could feel her body getting stronger and her endurance improving. Her legs didn't ache like they once did, and her throat no longer threatened to collapse. She took a deep breath of the cool canyon air, closing her eyes and listening to the breeze wisp through the trees.

Got lunch with Mom today. I really need to get going, she thought. She took a sip from her CamelBak and began walking back along the trail, following the footprints she pressed into the earth only moments ago. The soft soil held her prints well, unlike the hard caliche outside the canyon. A light rain had drizzled on and off for most of the night, leaving the trail smooth and unblemished. Her footprints from yesterday morning had already been washed away.

She walked along the trail for half a mile, planning to then run the rest of the way back to the mouth of the canyon. She could then pace herself for a mile or two and catch her breath. Her goal was to finish strong with a two mile run clear to the parking lot—no stopping allowed. Her endurance really was improving. *Small victories,* she thought. *Or maybe not so small after all.*

She started running again, setting her breathing into a rhythm and letting the wind be her guide. The closer she got to the entrance, the stronger the wind became. Her mind started to drift off, the movie reel in her head slowly turning. She had become so engrossed in a memory of a childhood Christmas that at first she didn't register the foreign object lying across the trail up ahead. Her eyes saw, but her mind did not engage. She was watching her mom open a Christmas gift from her dad, seeing her mom's smile grow and grow as she opened the tiny jewelry box. As a child, she didn't understand why her mom could be so excited about such a small box.

She was watching the memory of her mom opening the tiny box when her eyes finally took over her mind and brought her back to the present. *Something's in the trail.* Before she could register what it was, her left foot collided with something hard. She was mid-stride and hit the object at full force. Jessica felt a sharp pain in her toes, heard more than felt a crack in the front of her foot, and then the pain shot upward into her ankle. Her foot was yanked violently to one side as she continued to move but the object did not. Her arms flew out in front of her as she catapulted forward, and suddenly the soft soil of the canyon floor was against her face. It had all happened so quickly.

Jessica lay on the ground, dumbfounded. Slowly she started to register what was injured and how much. Her palms stung from protecting her face when she hit the ground. Her shoulders ached, probably from absorbing the impact. Her arms weren't what worried her, though. What worried her was much lower than that. Her left foot and ankle, which had been an eye-watering pain only seconds ago, now felt strangely numb. She did not like that. *Where did the pain go?* She vividly remembered the exquisite pain she felt when she hit the object, but now she felt very little from her ankle downward. Just a slight ache, and numbness.

She carefully pushed herself up from the damp soil, dirt clinging to her cheek where she landed face down in the dirt. Her shoulders ached with the effort and she heard a groan escape her lips. *What the hell did I just run into?* She sat up in the dirt, her legs stretched out in front of her, and looked down at what had caused this unpleasant turn of events.

A rock. A big one. It had to be the size of a beach ball. Definitely not the same consistency, though. The rock—make that a small boulder—was lying smack-dab in the middle of the trail. *Now how the fuck did that get there?* Jessica stared at the rock—boulder—for a long time. Her mind ran through countless explanations, but none of them explained how a boulder materialized in the center of the trail. Or how the hell she didn't see it on her way in. *Could I have run right past it? I was so engaged in my daydreams that I just ran right past it?* Doubtful. The boulder was in the center of the trail, and the trail was only four feet across. *No way in hell would I have missed that.*

Her thoughts shifted to her ankle. She had forgotten about it since the pain miraculously subsided. She felt a flutter in her stomach as she looked down, not wanting to see the damage that was done. Finally she allowed her eyes to focus on her left leg.

It took Jessica a moment to figure out what exactly she was looking at. It didn't look like her ankle at all. For one thing it was twice the size of her other ankle, the skin stretched taut and shinier than normal. The skin was also changing colors before her eyes. She was wearing capri leggings that stopped at mid-calf. Her skin was a light tan where her leggings stopped, but the closer it got to her ankle the more the color changed. *Purple,* she thought. *Not pink, or even red. But a deep, almost bluish, purple.* The color was patchy and mottled, and she could tell the purple was spreading.

Jessica took a deep breath and closed her eyes. *Stupid. So. Fucking. Stupid. I was thinking about stupid Christmas for God knows what reason and I tripped over a rock. No.* A *BOULDER. Stupid stupid stupid.* Her mind went blank for a moment. Something was missing in her memory, like a small piece of her movie reel had been snipped out.

The boulder wasn't there when I came into the canyon. No, that wasn't it. That was disturbing all on its own, but that wasn't it. *Why didn't I see the boulder? It's rather obvious, sitting in the trail like this. And what the hell put it there? It must weigh a gazillion pounds.* But no, that wasn't it either. Something else was missing, something on the edge of her mind.

When she remembered, a small gasp escaped her lips. *There's something up ahead in the trail,* she thought. Something she recognized. It didn't belong out here, but she knew what it was all the same. It had distracted her, and that's why she tripped on the boulder—she didn't see the rock because she was looking up ahead.

Jessica's hands clenched into fists, handfuls of soil sifting out between her fingers. She let go of the soil and pressed her scraped palms against the ground, turning her upper body to look behind her. When she sat up from her fall she was facing into the canyon, looking at the where-the-fuck-did-it-come-from boulder. Now, she twisted through her back and craned her neck to look behind her at the way out of the canyon. Her breath was stuck in her throat, refusing to go either in or out. She could see the trail now. It extended fifty feet before veering left and disappearing around a bend, swallowed by the branches and undergrowth. Right at the bend, right before the trail disappeared, she saw what had distracted her. The bushes obscured most of them, but she knew what they were all the same.

Feet. *Somebody's feet.* One foot was bare and the other one was wearing a hiking boot. There were legs, but that was as far as she could see. The feet weren't moving. Whatever they were attached to wasn't moving either. She knew this much, though: there was a body up ahead in the trail. A body that wasn't there when she ran into the canyon. A body that had to have shown up in the last half an hour. The breath that had been caught in her throat came out in a long, shaky exhale. She couldn't remember how long it had been since she last breathed. Her eyes stayed fixated on the feet. The unmoving feet. There was a body in the trail, and her only way out of this place was to go toward it.

CHAPTER 17

Jessica tried to stand. She needed to get out of here. She needed to get out of here *immediately*. Suddenly it seemed absurd that she ever wanted to come out here in the first place. Suddenly it seemed absolutely insane that she ever started running at all. It was all insane. This canyon was insane. Running was insane. Her dad dying was insane. A couple years ago she was a happy twenty-something girl still trying to figure out what she wanted to do "when she grew up". Now she was a young woman, alone in the wilderness, with what was very likely a dead body. A dead body that wasn't there half an hour ago. And an ankle that she very likely couldn't walk on. *What the fuck is happening?*

She pressed herself up from the ground, grabbing a branch from a nearby tree. The bark rubbed against her scraped palm, sending a bolt of pain up her arm. She hadn't even bothered to look at her palms to see how badly they were injured. *Ha, you think some scraped hands are your biggest priority right now,*

Jess? I can think of a lot of other things that matter more than your fucking hands right now.

Jessica stood upright with the help of the tree branch. She balanced on her right leg, her left hovering over the ground, dreading the moment when she would step down on her left foot. *Well, at least it is the left foot. If I ever do make it to the car at least I will be able to drive. Thank God for small favors.* She giggled. It sounded odd and unsettling inside the canyon. The only other sounds were the wind and her heart thudding in her chest. After all that work to lower her heart rate, here it was beating out of control.

Jessica stepped down with her left leg and cried out, part swear and part agony. *Well, that fucker is shot,* she thought. She tried again, gritting her teeth together and exhaling as she did so. The ankle sent lightning bolts of pain up her leg, stretching all the way to her groin and making her stomach churn. *It might hold me up,* she thought. She pressed down with her left foot. The pain brought tears to her eyes and her periphery faded toward black, but the ankle held. By some act of God, the ankle held. Jessica focused on her breathing, concentrating on not holding her breath. *Don't pass out don't pass out don't pass out.*

She began limping in the direction of the feet. *Check it out Dad, I'm Jack Nicholson in* The Shining. She put her left leg in front, then lurched forward with her right leg. *Left, then right. Left, then right.* The unmoving feet were getting closer. In a moment she would make it around the bend in the trail and see what they were attached to. *Maybe they just passed out. Maybe someone was hiking the trail after me and passed out. That's why they are there now and not before. Just passed out. With one shoe on. It fell off when they passed out. That can happen. It definitely can happen.*

"Hello?" Jessica called out. "Are you alright?" No response. "I—I hurt my ankle… Hello? Are you hurt?" Nothing. Just the wind.

The bend in the trail loomed ahead. Just a few more lurches and she would be there. She had the sudden, almost uncontrollable urge to just sit down in the center of the trail and wait. Someone will come and get her. She can just sit down right here by the feet and wait for rescue. They will be looking for the feet, and when they find the feet, they will find her. She doesn't have to go around the bend. She doesn't have to see what they are attached to.

Stop being freaking stupid. She could feel the anger rising in her chest, and giving in to it wasn't something she could afford to do right now. She needed to stay focused. And calm. With some effort, she pushed the anger back down.

Left, then right. Left, then right. The knees appeared, then the hips, then the torso. Jessica stopped just short of the feet, finally able to see who they belonged to. She grabbed her stomach, her other hand going up to her mouth. She leaned over and threw up everything she had eaten that morning. And anything that might have been left over from the night before. In that moment, bent over on the side of the trail with her eyes squeezed shut, she wished she would throw up until she passed out. Just so she wouldn't have to look at it ever again.

CHAPTER 18

The legs were the most intact part of what was left of the body. The calves appeared to be muscular. They were well-tanned and covered with coarse, dark hair. A man's legs. The inner thigh of the left leg was torn open, jagged chunks of bright red muscle clung to something white deep inside. Bone. It had to be bone. There were taut, whitish-gray cords stretched across the opening. Tendons probably. Or ligaments. The right leg was almost completely torn from the body, attached only by some more of those whitish-gray cords. A circular bone was sticking out of the chunk of meat—*I guess it is meat now*—that was left of the man's upper right leg.

The abdomen was open, revealing lumps of different colored organs and tissues inside. A purplish-brown, smooth piece—*probably the liver*. Tendrils of light pink cords—*gotta be intestines*. Jessica could even make out linked white pieces of something cylindrical in the depths of the bloody mess—*and that's the spinal column*.

The right arm had numerous puncture wounds, especially around the hand. And the left arm was tucked underneath the torso in such a way that it was almost certainly dislocated, only muscle and tissue holding it together.

Jessica looked up at the canyon walls. *Did he fall? Could a fall have done this? And that's why the boulder was there, too? Because it came down with him?* She looked back at the body. *No, not a fall. A fall couldn't do that to someone's face. Not even a fall from an airplane.*

The face was gone. Just... gone. Jessica could see the man's teeth; they stood out in stark contrast to the deep red tissue that was left of his face. The lips were no longer there, and the pale, pink gums were clearly visible. The eyes stared straight up, protruding from the skull and no longer concealed by eyelids. The skull was almost completely scalped, only a few chunks of gray hair remaining at the nape of the neck.

Jessica never felt in her entire life like giving up more than she did at that moment. The phone waking her in the night, lying in the dark and knowing before she even answered it that her mother was going to tell her that her father was dead. Driving to the hospital in the dark. That cold kiss. Standing at his grave as the dirt got shoveled in, wondering how it could possibly be sunny on such a horrible day. All of that felt distant, hazy. Standing on the trail with a stretch of bright red gore in front of her—all Jessica wanted to do was sit down, curl into a ball, and wait for it all to be over.

A grotesque smell filled the air, causing her to gag. She remembered learning in school that the olfactory system was closely linked to memory, and that a certain smell could cause someone to recall a specific moment from their past. She never really gave it much thought. None really. But when that rotting, putrid, slightly sweet stench invaded her nostrils she immediately remembered. She remembered that smell, fleeting though it was, drifting out of the canyon on the breeze that one day. She remembered that smell when she was at the zoo with her daddy once, much milder but still lingering near the enclosure. It was the smell of a predator. Of a carnivore. The smell of its breath, rotting meat still clinging to its elongated canines. It was the smell of dead animals. Of decay on the side of the road. Only this time it wasn't a gentle whiff on the breeze. It wasn't fleeting. This time the smell was strong, overpowering even. And it was coming off the breath of something that still had rotting meat in its teeth. Something that was dangerously too close. *An animal did this… and it's still here.*

Every sense of giving up evaporated when that smell took over. The urge to lie down was gone. The stench was almost sticky in the air, the odor a rabbit might smell as the jaws of a coyote wrapped around its throat. The smell of a predator, only this time she was the prey instead of the rabbit. *It's watching me. Right now. It's been watching me this whole time.*

Jessica stumbled over the remains of the body, gritting her teeth against a new wave of pain, and began to run.

CHAPTER 19

She had been running nearly fifteen seconds when she heard a branch break—if the frantic limping she was doing could even be called running. Jessica stepped forward with her mangled left foot, then lurched her entire body forward with her right. *Left, then right. Left, then right.* The pain was intense, but the fear was stronger. She could taste the fear now—a metallic bitterness that seemed to be rising from her throat.

Before stumbling upon the boulder, and the grisly scene that lay beyond, Jessica had made it a mile of her return trip. That meant she still had half a mile to go until she was out of the canyon. And she wasn't going very fast.

To her surprise, the pain began to fade, adrenaline tampering it down to give her a fighting chance. Not fighting. Running. A running chance. There was no way in hell she was going to fight whatever did that to that man.

The rotting stench followed her down the length of the canyon, keeping pace with her. *Maybe it's just getting carried by the wind. Whatever it is, it's far away and I'm just downwind of it. It's actually really far away and sleeping somewhere.*

Her wishful thinking had been shattered when she heard the branch break. And that sharp crack of wood was not far away at all. It was mind-numbingly close. Forty or fifty yards away at the most. Another branch broke seconds later, alarmingly closer than the first. Jessica didn't dare turn around.

A low growl emanated from somewhere inside the canyon. It echoed on the canyon walls and Jessica could feel it inside of her chest. Or maybe what she felt in her chest was her heart threatening to stop. Her breath came in sharp, jagged gasps and she felt like she was running on a piece of gnarled wood dipped in cement. *Left, then right. Left, then right.* Then: *left right left right left right.* The limp lessened as the adrenaline coursed through her. *Fuck the ankle. They can cut off the foot later if I ever get out of here. I do NOT want to end up like that guy. Left right left right left right. Bear? Mountain lion? Bear? Mountain lion? Bear? Mountain lion?*

Jessica ran. This might be the last run of her short life, so she better make it count. *Push it. A little harder. A little further. A little faster. Be stronger. Be better. Don't die. Don't die don't die don't die.* Her face felt wet. She didn't know when exactly, but she had begun to cry.

She could hear it now, somewhere behind her on the trail. Branches snapped, bushes rustled, and even worse, there were feet running on the trail. Not human feet. That's for damn sure. They thudded with the weight of whatever it was, and the scratching noises on the dirt could be mistaken for nothing other than its claws. Jessica envisioned monstrously long claws, kicking up soil as the thing galloped forward.

She could hear its breathing now, could hear snarling and grunting somewhere behind her. The sounds were getting closer. At first it seemed to be toying with her, a snapped branch here, a bush rustle there. Now it was running, and to Jessica's dismay, gaining on her. She wound her way along the trail, forever grateful that she knew each bend and every turn so well. *As long as the fucking thing didn't put another rock in the road,* she thought. Somehow, she knew the boulder she had tripped over was put there for her—that it was done on purpose. It injured her and now it was playing with her. Idly chasing her, knowing it would catch her eventually, just wanting to tire her out first. *Goddamn cat and mouse bullshit.*

And was it whimpering? *No wait, that's me,* she thought. Jessica had started to make an anxious, whining noise each time she exhaled. *Daddy, I don't want to die. Please. God, please. I don't want to die out here. In here.* Exhaustion was starting to set in. She was pushing with everything she had, yet she could tell she was losing speed. She could see the mouth of the canyon now, but there was still so much desert beyond that. She was going to die. Just like that man did. *At least die in the sunshine. Get out of the canyon. At least don't die in the shadows. Not in the dark.*

The thing seemed to be done playing games, and it began running forward with purpose. Everything seemed to be happening as if underwater—a slow-motion scene from hell. She could hear her breath, its breath, claws scraping on the soil, blood thudding in her ears. She could feel sweat dripping down the center of her back, tears on her face, the wind from the canyon pushing her forward.

Daylight loomed ahead. She was less than a hundred yards from the canyon's mouth. *Please Daddy, just help me get out of here.*

She hadn't looked back since the chase began, hadn't dared even a glance in fear she would trip over something and become an all-you-could-eat buffet. Jessica knew if she turned she would be able to see it. It was close enough now, closing the distance between them. The sweet stink of its breath was nauseating, and she thought she could even feel the warmth coming off of it. It was probably only thirty feet away—make that twenty. Jessica cringed, waiting for the impact of claws and teeth on her bare skin. It must be about to spring at her, ready to jump up with its muscular legs and launch itself onto her back, pinning her face down in the dirt. Then it will tear her open, just like that man—

Jessica's skin kissed sunlight. She burst forth from the canyon in one final surge of strength and willpower. She felt the warmth on her skin, the sun caressing the gooseflesh covering her bare shoulders. And then she was flying. The final surge of energy that launched her out of the canyon also caused her to stumble on the uneven terrain. With such momentum going, she ended up flying through the air almost comically. She smashed into the ground on her right side and tumbled once—twice—make that three times—before coming to a stop on the warm, hardened caliche. She whirled onto her back, prepared to fight with the last glimmer of strength she had left.

Only it wasn't there. Not on top of her, or even next to her. Jessica jerked her head toward the canyon. She saw her pursuer, thirty feet back, standing in the shadows just shy of the sunlight. When she launched herself into the sun she had managed to tumble thirty feet from the canyon's mouth. It stood there, snarling, its features obscured by the heavy shadow of the canyon's walls. She only saw it for an instant before it disappeared completely into the shadows.

What she saw was in no animal book she had ever looked through. It never graced the pages of *National Geographic* and it was never featured on the Discovery Channel. It was large, bigger than a mountain lion but smaller than a bear. But not much smaller. She could see elongated canines protruding from its withdrawn lips as it snarled at her, but most of its facial features were lost in the shadows. Long, sickle-shaped claws jutted out from its sizable paws. And it was hairless, or at least almost hairless. Its skin was a dark gray, or was that just because it was in the shadows? And its spine protruded from its muscular back much further than any animal she had seen before. And then it was gone, abandoning the chase right when she was sprawled helplessly on the ground. Had it been toying with her all along? Or had something stopped it?

Jessica let out a gut-wrenching sob, staggered to her feet, and kept going.

CHAPTER 20

Push yourself. A little harder. A little further. A little faster. Past the dry creek bed with river stones that had seen much more sun than they had ever seen water. Passed the saguaro that looked like a man caressing a woman. Past the century plant with its stalk listing to the side.

Jessica saw a walking pole lying in the dirt not far from the entrance to the canyon. She stumbled over to it and picked it up. *Was it here when I ran by this morning?* The pole was partially concealed by a couple of shrubs; she could easily have missed it if she wasn't paying attention. Hell, she didn't even notice the stupid boulder in the middle of the damn trail. She leaned on the walking pole, grateful for its support.

The going was slow, each step agonizingly painful. The adrenaline that had carried her through the canyon, helping her run on her badly damaged ankle, was dwindling. The pain increased with each step, and each time she put weight on her left leg her ankle made a mushy, shifting sensation that she did not care for. She didn't dare look at it.

What she did do was look behind her, obsessively so. Whatever caused it to stop might be gone, or maybe it just decided to resume the chase. It wanted to let her think she had escaped, and then it would slink up behind her, creeping past the prickly pear and aloe verde, to finally sink its teeth into her exposed neck. Killing her is not nearly as fun if she knows it's coming.

The heat of the day was already stifling, and she could make out the tops of white cumulus clouds on the horizon. It was going to storm later today, and bad. She needed to tell the authorities what happened, they needed to find the man before all the evidence got washed away. *What evidence? It's not like he got killed by Jack the Ripper,* she thought. *Although there was a lot of ripping involved.* She shuddered. She just needed to get the hell out of here. To her phone, and to the safety of her car.

Jessica passed the crested saguaro. Three miles to go. She desperately wished she would see Cameron coming over the rise of Wasp Hill. He would run to her, see what state she was in, and link his arm under her shoulder. He would help her walk out of here; drive her to the nearest hospital. He would call the authorities and she could go to sleep. They would fix her ankle. And everything would be alright. She kept pushing away the thought that she might have already seen Cameron this morning. *Was this one of his walking poles?* She couldn't be sure.

The trail tilted upward into an incline. Wasp Hill. Ascending the hill was more grating on her ankle than she expected, if that was possible. It mushed and squished with each step.

Jessica also noticed she was bleeding from various locations. During her sunshine somersaults she had gotten scraped up pretty good by the unforgiving desert floor. She had cuts and abrasions covering her arms, and there was a rather unsightly gash on her right shoulder where she must have landed on a rock. The blood from the cut oozed sluggishly down her dirt-smeared arm. A fine layer of dust covered her entire body, darker streaks standing out where sweat had dripped down. *Oh Daddy, your Jess is such a mess.*

She limped her way over Wasp Hill, looking over her shoulder for any signs of the canyon creature. Nothing. The temperature ticked up steadily as the day worked its way toward noon. For the first time since before the boulder she thought to look at her QuikFit. It was 10:02 a.m. *This will make for an impressive activity log for today,* she thought. Then: *Wait a minute. They could use it. The authorities. They will be able to see where I fell on the trail so they will know where the body is located.*

She started walking forward with a new purpose. The police needed to know, and she could help. She could direct them to the exact location of the nightmarish scene, and they could possibly make it before the rain came. Maybe even capture it—or kill it—before nightfall. She hobbled along and didn't even bother to deter to the other side of the path as she passed the jumping chollas. *I would rather hug a cholla than ever go through anything like this ever again.*

The chollas meant she was only a mile away from the parking lot. Jessica could feel her fear starting to creep in again. She was suddenly convinced it was following her all along, keeping off the trail and waiting until she was almost safe before bursting out in front of her, teeth bared and claws extended. And then where would she run? Back toward the canyon? Her heart rate increased and she began hyperventilating, on the verge of a panic attack. *Come on, Jess. You are literally almost there. See there? That's asphalt. That's the parking lot. Just a little further.*

She pressed on. The lot was coming into view, and for one terrifying moment she thought her car would be gone. All this to be stranded in a parking lot surrounded by desert and mega mansions. But her car was there, sitting alone in the parking lot in her usual parking space.

A short, silent prayer went through her head as her right foot stepped up onto the asphalt. No more trail. No more canyon. No more *monster*. As the word monster went through her head she quickly looked over her shoulder again, almost falling in the process. Still nothing. The empty trail stretched out into the desert. She could hear a very distant rumbling. *These storms are going to start early today. I better get a move on.*

Jessica arrived at her car, feeling a wash of panic followed by immediate relief when she discovered her car key was still in her pocket. She opened the door, thought about tossing the hiking pole to the ground, then decided to put it in her backseat instead. She groaned as she lowered herself into the car, taking care to bring her left leg inside without bumping her foot. She shut the door, locked it, then looked up at the trailhead. It was empty. The slightly tilted post stood alone, its map glimmering in the morning sunshine.

CHAPTER 21

"But you have to go now!" Jessica demanded, her voice shrill and sounding nothing like herself. She sat upright in her hospital bed, her knuckles white from her grip on the bed rails.

"Ma'am, Search and Rescue is already in route. My department is on standby pending what Search and Rescue discovers," Officer Taylor Kilburn said. He was a tall man, with a broad, muscular chest and a crew cut of sandy-blond hair.

The frazzled blonde girl, her ankle wrapped in a giant swath of bandages, was making him nervous. Her story had been unwavering and highly detailed, unbelievable as it was. But it was over now, and he wanted to get the hell out of here. Hospitals made him uncomfortable. They smelled like piss and disinfectant and there were always all these *sick people* all over the place. But instead of getting the hell out of Dodge, he was stuck behind some cheap teal curtain with a dirt-covered crazy chick insisting that they get their asses up to Wasp

Canyon to find a mutilated body and a monster creature. Kilburn's head hurt, and this chick's yelling was not helping.

At 10:54 that morning, the Northwest Police Department received a call from a near-hysterical woman claiming that some sort of creature killed a man in Wasp Canyon and then tried to attack her. Very little was gleaned from that phone call due to the woman's state of distress. Officer Kilburn was assigned to go to the hospital to get a more detailed—and less hysterical—statement from the caller, while Detective Moser gathered a team to head out to the canyon. The old bastard was probably getting his ass in gear quicker than usual since Wasp Canyon was the home of all those rich fuckers, and heaven forbid you upset one of them. And instead of assigning Kilburn to the recon team heading out to the canyon, he got sent to the damn hospital to interview some dipshit blonde who probably had one too many mochas and hallucinated the whole damn thing. It was probably just some homeless man out there, avoiding the heat by staying inside the canyon. And one less bum wasn't going to upset nobody, in Kilburn's humble opinion.

"But it is going to rain!" Jessica hollered.

Kilburn sighed. Why the hell was he here and not with Moser's team? He had spent what he thought were many admirable years on the force, and yet he was still getting cleanup duty. Get the statement, dot the I's, cross the T's, yada yada yada. All the while, Detective Moser and three other officers were gearing up to go to the site, pending what Search and Rescue discovered. If anything this raving chick said was true, then it sure didn't sound like this fellow was going to require any rescuing. Yet here he was, on clerical duty, in a disgusting hospital room trying to get a statement from a crazy chick that wouldn't let him get a word in edgewise.

"They need to go *now*!" Jessica insisted. "Tell them to stop fucking around and get out there!"

"Jessica!" Andrea Cleary exclaimed. She stood to the side of the hospital bed, looking nervous and pale under the hard, fluorescent lighting.

"Ma'am," Kilburn said, "I understand that you are upset. But I'm going to need you to calm down."

"There is a man up there who was literally torn apart," Jessica said. "Whatever did that to him almost did it to me, too. *And it is still out there!*"

"Yes, but, um," Kilburn flipped back a page in his notebook, "you said that it stopped."

Jessica gawked at him, her forehead scrunched into a furious collection of wrinkles. "What does that have to do with anything?" she snapped.

"Well," Kilburn said, trying not to further agitate the crazy, infuriated ditz, "per your report you said this—thing—chased you for a substantial distance. And then right when you fell down and it was about to attack you, it decided to stop? Just like that?"

"I don't know why it stopped! Maybe it didn't want to leave the canyon or something!" Jessica threw her hands in the air, exasperated.

Kilburn flipped his notepad shut and looked at Jessica. He had had just about enough of this shit. Maybe there is a body up there. Maybe something did chase her away from the kill, that's normal predatory behavior. If a bear or a cougar had offed something—human or otherwise—they would guard it to make sure another predator didn't try to steal it. *She probably stumbled on a bear kill, the bear spooked her, and now I have to deal with this instead of going up to the scene. I've never even gotten to see a damn bear victim*, Kilburn thought.

"Ma'am—"

"Stop calling me that!"

"Ma—Jessica, the amount of damage you described regarding the body was most likely the result of a bear or mountain lion attack. Those attacks can be pretty gruesome." *And I'll never get to see one,* Kilburn thought with irritation.

"But I *saw it.* When it stopped chasing me *I saw it.* And it was *not* a bear. Or a mountain lion. I'm sure of it," Jessica said.

"But did you see it?" Kilburn asked. "I know you saw something, you clearly stated that. But you also said it was in the shadows and pretty hard to make out. And with the amount of fear that you were in…" He gestured into the air in an attempt to find the right words. "All I'm saying is that fear can make your memory fuzzy. Or it can make you see things that might not have been there."

Jessica stared at him, mouth hanging open. It didn't appear that she was buying his explanation, but at least she wasn't yelling anymore. "I saw what I saw," she said finally, her voice low and even. She lowered her eyes to the floor.

"Of course, ma'am," Kilburn said, tucking his notepad into his back pocket. *Complete waste of time,* he thought. "If you think of anything else, anything at all, please call our department." He reluctantly extended a business card to her. He did not want this woman calling their department, and he sure as hell didn't want her asking for him when she did. She didn't reach for the card, so he placed it on the bed near her bandaged leg.

"We will keep in touch." Kilburn turned and headed for the teal curtain.

Jessica called after him, the hysteria gone from her voice. "Your men better be careful out there," she said. "It's still out there." And then after a pause: "And it knows how to set a trap."

Kilburn looked back at Jessica for a moment. He kept his face even as he gave her a final nod, but inside he felt a chill go up his spine.

CHAPTER 22

Andrea sat with her daughter and waited for the doctor to arrive. Although she appeared calm, Andrea was overwhelmed with worry regarding Jessica's injuries. Her frail daughter looked like she had fallen down a mountain, and that was just her upper body. Andrea was very anxious to find out what was hiding underneath all those bandages on Jessica's ankle. *She had been doing so much better,* Andrea thought wistfully, *and now this.* She shook her head, but only slightly. She didn't understand how God could help her daughter start to get better, then throw a giant hurdle in her recovery. A hurdle in the shape of a dead body, no less. Jessica had already seen far too much death this early in her young life.

Jessica hadn't said much since the officer left. Andrea noticed her tugging at her hair with one hand, a nervous tick that she had ceased doing in the past few weeks. Andrea sighed. "Oh honey, you were doing so much better." She squeezed Jessica's hand. "I am so sorry this happened to you."

Jessica looked up, opened her mouth to say something, but then the doctor came in. *You certainly have incredible timing, don't you, Doctor?* Andrea thought. She shook off the momentary irritation and prepared herself for what she hoped was good news. Or at least not horrible news.

"Hello, Jessica. My name is Dr. Reisen. I've been going over your imaging and it appears you have taken quite a tumble." Reisen was a portly man with a neatly trimmed mustache and receding hairline. His white lab coat was unbuttoned, and he wore a navy blue dress shirt underneath.

"Yeah, I guess you could call it that," Jessica muttered.

"Dr. Reisen, is my daughter going to be alright?" Andrea asked.

"Yes, she most certainly is. She may look worse for the wear, but I believe she will be able to make a full recovery. The bumps and bruises will heal with time." Reisen paused to look at the cut on Jessica's right arm. "This laceration will require some stitches, I'm afraid. And I will be prescribing some antibiotics to ward off infection." Reisen turned his attention to Jessica's bandaged leg. "My main concern, however, is the ankle."

Jessica looked up when Reisen mentioned her ankle. Her face, still covered in dust and streaked from tears, was etched with worry.

"Your ankle and foot sustained considerable damage during the incident you had up in the canyon," Reisen said.

"No argument here," Jessica said, looking down at her bandaged leg.

"When your foot struck the rock in the trail, three of your toes were fractured. Unfortunately your hallux—that's the big toe—was one of the ones broken. The recovery from a hallux fracture can take much longer than the other toes and *may* require surgery.

"As for the ankle, you have sustained a grade three sprain of your anterior talofibular ligament and the calcaneofibular ligament. These ligaments are located on the lateral aspect of your ankle—that is what we call the outside portion. These types of sprains are caused by forced inversion of the ankle joint, which means you rolled your ankle inward when you collided with the rock."

Reisen paused, waiting to see if anyone had any questions. Jessica was poking at the bunched up sheet that was spread across her lap, where smears of dirt and few splotches of dried blood stood out on the white fabric. "And what is a grade three sprain exactly?" she asked.

"A complete rupture of the ligaments involved, meaning they tore completely. Being able to run with this severity of an injury is almost unheard of."

"Getting chased by some sort of hell beast is pretty motivating," Jessica said as she rubbed at a reddish-brown smudge on the white linen.

Andrea held her daughter's forearm, her eyes also drawn to the smudges on the hospital sheet. She looked up at Reisen. "What does this mean for my daughter, Doctor?"

"I believe we can give conservative measures a try for now," Reisen said, "meaning we can allow your injuries time to heal on their own. However, if we do not see any improvements within a few weeks, surgery may be necessary."

Jessica looked up from the bed. "What are *conservative measures*?" she asked.

"An orthopedic walking boot," Reisen said. "A controlled ankle motion boot, to be precise. That's a CAM boot for short."

"A boot?"

"Yes. The marvels of modern medicine, I know. The boot has a metal or plastic base to keep your ankle fixed at a ninety-degree angle. It is secured with Velcro straps and then inflated with a pump to further stabilize the ankle. The compression from the air pump will also assist with edema reduction, meaning it will help to reduce your swelling. And the boot will take the pressure off of your toes as well, allowing the fractures an opportunity to heal."

"Okay, and then what happens?"

"Hopefully the fractures in your toes will set and your ankle will begin to heal. If so, we will continue to follow these conservative measures. If not, we will have to consider surgical intervention. Either way, I see a lot of physical therapy in your future."

"That's not so bad, honey," Andrea said, rubbing Jessica's forearm. "After physical therapy you'll be as good as new."

Jessica smiled weakly at her mother.

"I'm going to have someone come in to stitch up that wound on your arm, or *maybe* we could get away with some surgical glue. We'll get you cleaned up and your wounds sterilized. And I will send orders for your CAM boot, a course of antibiotics, and some pain medication you can take as needed. Let's schedule a follow-up appointment in three weeks and then we can determine if surgery will be necessary," Reisen said. "Any questions for me before I go write up your orders?"

"Yeah, just one," Jessica said. "Will I ever be able to run again?"

"I certainly hope so," Reisen said, "but I don't see that happening any time soon. For now you can't put *any* weight on that leg without having your boot on. And running is out of the question for the foreseeable future."

"But what if something happens where I have to run?"

"Well, let's hope that it doesn't come to that," Reisen said, and left the room.

CHAPTER 23

A few hours later, Andrea and Jessica sat at Andrea's kitchen table, Subway sandwich wrappers and crumpled paper napkins spread out in front of them. Andrea asked multiple times if Jessica would like a home-cooked meal, but Jessica had declined. Jessica nibbled at the sandwich and had eaten half of it, but her appetite seemed to have already disappeared, along with her ability to run.

Andrea gathered the napkins, wrappers, and plastic bags. Jessica poked at her phone, willing it to ring. *God, I hope they made it up there in time,* she thought. The rain had come shortly before three that afternoon. Finding the thing in the canyon was going to be pretty damn difficult in all that rain. *I wonder if they even made it to the body in time.*

Jessica looked out the window. Outside, the rain had finally stopped. The ground was sodden and the plants were drooping, their leaves beaten down and heavy with water. Dark, low hanging clouds slowly made their way across the bruised sky.

She shoved her phone aside and looked down at her brand new orthopedic walking boot—CAM boot for short. It was a cumbersome thing, black and bulky, and it held her ankle like a vice. Her entire lower left leg and foot were enveloped inside a tomb of plastic, metal, polyester, and—apparently— air.

Her ankle was beginning to throb. At first it just felt heavy, but now a dull ache was beginning to come from deep inside. It crept its way along her ankle and down into her toes. And *everything* was starting to pulsate with waves of a much sharper pain. She couldn't see her ankle inside the CAM boot, but she imagined what it must look like, and was grateful that the boot was in the way.

When her phone buzzed, Jessica jumped in the kitchen chair, startled by the sudden vibration on the table. She grabbed the phone and looked at the caller ID. The screen said **Unlisted**. *It must be them,* she thought. *Just please let it not be Officer Dumbass.*

It wasn't. A deep, burly voice introduced himself as Detective Moser. "Good evening, Jessica," Moser said. "How are you feeling? And how is your ankle doing?"

"Uh, it's fine. Hurts. But I'm sure it'll be fine," Jessica said. "So how did it go? Did you find him? Did you find… *it*?"

Moser paused for what felt like an eternity. "We did find the man that you informed us about," he said finally. "He was in a similar state to what you described. There were extensive injuries to the face, torso, and extremities. I think it is safe to say that he died from his injuries, although we will need the medical examiner to confirm. Another possibility is that he died of natural causes on the trail and predators came along afterward and fed on the body."

Moser paused again. Jessica could hear papers shuffling around and could picture a large man sitting at an even larger desk, surrounded by countless documents. The shuffling stopped and he spoke again. "Although," shuffle shuffle, "this theory that the body was damaged after death seems unlikely given your statement. You said the body was in the trail during your return trip, but not when you entered the canyon. Is that correct?"

"Yes, yes it is," Jessica said. She could feel her stomach fluttering. She hoped this man would believe her, and that she wouldn't get dismissed as crazy or confused again.

"Whether he died from his injuries or they occurred post-mortem, it is odd that he was moved onto the trail during the short period of time you were in the canyon. You said you didn't hear anything that may have been an attack? No cries for help? Or maybe screaming?"

"No, nothing."

"And you didn't pass him on the way in?"

"No, I didn't see anything. There was a walking pole near the entrance when I came out, but I might have missed it on my way in. It was off to the side of the trail, not in it. It helped me get back to my car."

"It is possible he got attacked the day before," Moser said, "or very early in the morning, depending on when he began his hike. The medical examiner will need to determine the time of death." Papers shuffling. "Anyway, in regards to the body's location, I suppose a predator could have heard you go by as you entered the canyon and then decided to move the remains to another, more secure, location. The animal didn't expect you to come back so soon and abandoned the body on the trail when it heard you returning to the area." The speculation in Moser's voice diminished. He continued, "And once you got too close to its food—to the body, I mean—it felt it needed to defend its meal from you, therefore chasing you out of the canyon."

"But…" Jessica trailed off. Moser's theory sounded believable. Hell, it even sounded *probable*. But that's not what it felt like out there. Not at all. It wasn't your basic predator relocating a kill for later consumption. It set a goddamn trap, for Christ's sake. *Fear makes you remember things differently.* That's what Officer Dumbass had said. But she knew what she saw and what she felt. And it all felt… *wrong,* somehow. "But what about the rock? The one I tripped over?"

More paper shuffling. "The rock was unfortunate," Moser said, "but very likely could have been knocked onto the trail by the animal when it was trying to relocate the deceased. It heard you, quickly went from its current location to the body, knocking the rock over in the process. It began moving the body to a location it felt was more secure, heard you coming back, and abandoned the body in the trail. You arrive, it determines you are not a threat to its safety, but it still doesn't want you near its food source. So it chases you off until it thinks you are far enough away to not be a threat to what remains of its meal." Moser sounded like he had just solved the mystery of the killer's identity in a slasher movie only part way through the film—pleased and a little bit proud of himself. Case closed. Over. Done. *Finito.*

Jessica felt mounting fear in her gut, the throbbing in her ankle forgotten. Had she imagined the whole thing? *The trap? The monster?* What the detective just explained sounded so likely that she could feel her mind already starting to accept it, shuffling her memories around so they fit this new explanation. *But they didn't.* Deep down she knew that was not what happened out there. That rock was not just knocked over accidentally as the animal went by. That rock weighed a million pounds. It would have been a chore for your run-of-the-mill mountain lion, or even a bear, to move that thing. It was put there on purpose. *It had to have been.* Which meant the body was put there on purpose as well.

"Jessica? You still there?"

"Uh, yeah, sorry," she mumbled. "But the rock was so heavy. It couldn't have just been knocked over by accident."

"Bears and mountain lions are very strong, formidable predators. Their strength can be easy to underestimate. It is very possible that the rock ended up in the trail by accident, knocked over as the animal went by."

"But it wasn't a bear or mountain lion," Jessica protested. *"I saw it."*

More papers shuffling. She was really starting to hate that sound. "In your statement you said you saw a bear-sized creature, no fur, with a protruding spinal column. Is that correct?"

"Yes…"

"And what you saw was heavily covered in shadows?"

"It was in the shadows, but I could still see it. And I know it wasn't a bear or a mountain lion. It was something else."

"There are certain skin conditions animals can get. Mange is one that comes to mind. We once had to remove a rabid coyote from a resident's back yard. Awful thing, I almost felt sorry for it. It had this skin disease called mange, something having to do with mites or some other parasite on the skin. Anyway, it made all its fur fall off. And the skin was red and blotchy underneath." He paused. "Horrible disease. And then with the rabies, too… We had to put the poor thing down, of course."

Mange? I got chased by a sick animal with mange? If it's sick how could it move that rock? How could it chase me all that way? And how could it do that to that guy? She said nothing.

"And as for the protruding spine," Moser went on, "if this animal is ill with mange, or another condition that caused its hair to fall out, it might also be too sick to hunt and kill its normal prey. If malnourished from disease or starvation, its spine might appear more prominent, and even more so due to the lack of fur. Its poor health was probably why it went after a human being in the first place. Much easier prey." He stopped then, having explained everything that required an explanation.

Detective Carl Moser leaned back in his sizable chair in the precinct office. Now all he needed was an ID on the victim and he could put this unsettling case in the closed pile and be done with it. Kilburn could draw up all the paperwork and notify the next of kin. Grubby little guy, Moser never quite cared for him. Let him deal with the rest of this mess.

Moser enjoyed his job to the fullest, and for the most part considered himself a pretty decent cop. He had a knack for answering the tough questions and getting the job done. This animal mauling, though—now that he did *not* care for. Gory encounters such as this belonged in horror movies and those Stephen King books, not in his jurisdiction. He never cared for bloody carnage in the past, and he didn't care for it now. Seeing that gentleman disemboweled and disgraced in such a way—he wanted nothing to do with it. Which was why it was such a relief that he had solved the case and could now put it behind him.

The girl still hadn't spoken. He was beginning to wonder if the line had been broken when she finally asked, "So that's it?"

"For now, yes. We will need to identify the victim and notify the family."

"I told the other guy it might be Cameron—"

"Jasper. Yes, I saw that. But you're not *sure* it was him."

"He carried walking poles…" Jessica trailed off.

"Well, a lot of hikers around here have walking poles," Moser said.

"He's also the only other person I've ever seen out there."

"We will have to wait for a positive ID on the—"

"Have you been able to get a hold of Mr. Jasper?" she asked.

"As a matter of fact, we have not. But we cannot make any assumptions," Moser said. "Anyway, we will be getting Fish and Game out there ASAP to find and terminate the animal responsible. Shouldn't be too hard to find. It might be getting pretty weak from disease and starvation by this point. Didn't look like it ended up consuming much of the victim."

"And you don't find that odd?" Jessica asked.

"Find what odd?"

"That it killed that guy, mutilated him, chased me away to keep its food source safe, and then didn't even bother to eat it?"

"It's hard to say. Perhaps it was exhausted by the amount of energy it expelled during the attack, and then the subsequent chase when you came along. It might have gone to rest once you left, feeling its food source was finally safe. And then we came along before it got a chance to… uh, a chance to…" he paused, searching for and failing to find a word that was less upsetting. "A chance to feed," he finished.

"So it did all that and then decided to take a nap?"

"I'm afraid we will never have a concrete answer for why it behaved the way that it did. All I can say is that it is sick, and that we will probably be doing it a favor when we find it and euthanize it."

"So that's it then?" she asked again.

Moser said that it was, agreed to keep in touch if they needed anything else from her, and ended the call. This animal attack stuff really irked him, and he was more than eager to get it behind him. By tomorrow, after the victim was ID'd and the sick animal destroyed, it would all be over and done with.

And then he could try like hell to erase the image of the dead man from his memory.

CHAPTER 24

Andrea insisted that Jessica spend the night in her old room. She was very concerned that Jessica was in no state—emotionally or physically—to be alone in her apartment after what happened. She might have nightmares, or she might wake up in the middle of the night in pain and not be able to make it to her pain medicine or to the bathroom. *It would be much better if you stay here with me where I can help take care of you, at least for a little while,* Andrea had urged.

Jessica made a half-hearted attempt to get her mother to take her to her apartment, however she knew it was a losing battle, so she didn't try very hard. Her ankle was starting to hurt like hell and the thought of hobbling out to the car and then up the stairs to her second-floor apartment sounded dreadful. Instead, she let her mother tidy her old room, help her inside, and tuck her under the pink flower-print bedspread that had been there since Jessica's teenage years. Andrea had always refused to redecorate Jessica's old room, insisting that someday she might need it again, and it turned out she was right about that one. So Jessica willingly crawled under the pink covers in her childhood bedroom, a room that still had posters of *The Beatles* and *Lady Gaga* thumb-tacked onto its lilac-colored walls, and tried to get some sleep.

At first she was worried she wouldn't be able to sleep at all that night. She expected to jolt awake every time she heard a board creak or the AC kick on, certain the creature was in her room or just outside her window. In the dark, it seemed perfectly logical that the creature had found out where she lived and was now creeping around outside, ready to finish what it had started. The more she thought she had gotten away, the more satisfying the kill would be. As soon as she drifted off to sleep it would use its claws to pull the window back, silently slink inside, and then inch closer and closer to her as she slept, relishing every moment before the final, horrific encounter. It would pounce on her, just as she stirred, pin her down, and clamp its jaws around her throat as she tried to scream for help. But no sound would come out because it had already severed her vocal chords. And then it could take its time, leaving her mutilated body at daybreak for her mother to discover.

Sleep eventually came, and when the darkness crept into the corners of her mind, this time she welcomed it. Anything to stop her from listening for the sounds of claws scraping along her bedroom window.

The phone rang a quarter after eight the following morning. Jessica wasn't sure if it was the ringing that woke her, or if it was the dream itself. She was in Wasp Canyon, standing in the center of the trail with her walking boot on. She was watching as the sun descended toward the horizon. Soon it would disappear from sight and leave her alone in the dark. Only she wasn't alone, something was there with her, breathing heavily and smelling of rotting meat. *Not alone!* her mind screamed into the darkness, and then she jerked awake.

She was disoriented at first, not sure exactly where she had woken up. This wasn't her apartment; the sunlight was coming from the wrong direction. And the pictures on the wall were all wrong. Her eyes focused on a poster of *No Doubt*, bathed in morning sunshine, without really seeing it. Jessica struggled through the fogginess that hung heavily in her mind, and was finally able to grasp the realization that she was in her childhood bedroom, and more importantly, that she was alone. Despite her return to reality, her dream voice continued to echo in her head: *Not alone! Not alone! Not alone!*

And something was making an awful buzzing noise. *Wasps,* she thought, a fresh wave of panic sweeping over her. She checked frantically around the room, convinced that thousands of wasps had invaded her bedroom while she slept. They would be crawling on the walls, their stingers pulsating as they writhed together like a living wallpaper. And then the wallpaper would explode—thousands of wasps taking flight and ready to land on her bare arms and screaming face. They'd crawl on her eyelids, enter her mouth, and she would choke on them as they crawled down her throat, cutting off her scream…

The corners of the bedroom were empty, and not a wasp was in sight. Jessica continued to search the room—nothing on the walls, nothing on the bed, nothing on her skin. But where was the buzzing coming from? Her mind finally caught up with her consciousness, and the panic receded as she realized the buzzing was coming from her cell phone.

She grabbed the phone off of the nightstand and looked at the caller ID: Claire Bear :-). She had left Claire a message the night before knowing she probably wouldn't answer. Claire had told Jessica a couple days ago that she was going downtown to a dance club with her work friends last night. Jessica didn't expect a call back until today, and not nearly as early as it was now.

"Hello?" Jessica croaked. The throbbing in her ankle was becoming harder to ignore as she lay in bed, her right hand clutching the cell phone. There was also a persistent throb in her bladder. She was going to need to make it to a bathroom and pronto. And double pronto on the pain pills.

"Jessica, what the hell?"

"Hi, Claire," Jessica said.

"Jessica! What the hell happened? I've been calling all night!"

"You have?" Jessica pulled the phone away and looked at the screen. Six missed calls. "God, I'm sorry Claire. I must not have heard it while I was sleeping."

"Your message said you were in the hospital! That you were attacked? What the fuck is going on?" Claire sounded frantic.

"Yeah, during my run yesterday." Jessica told Claire what happened, feeling her ankle and bladder throb in unison as she told her story. When she was done, she waited for Claire to respond.

"It was a *what?*" Claire asked finally.

"I have no freaking idea. The cops think I imagined it."

"Do *you* think you imagined it?"

"I—I don't know. I was pretty sure I saw what I saw, but… the detective's explanation sounded so damn convincing. Maybe he's right," Jessica said, feeling defeated.

"Whether he is or not, are *you* okay? I can call out sick today. I'll come right over—"

"No no no. I'm okay. I'm staying with my mom for now."

"Well, can I come over after work then? I want to see you," Claire insisted.

"Yes, of course. Please come over after work. But right now, "Jessica said, "I really have to go pee."

"And I really have to go throw up the half bottle of tequila I drank last night. I will come over as soon as work is over, okay?" Claire said. "God, your message scared the shit out of me!"

"I'm sorry, Claire," Jessica said. "Go. Vomit. I will see you this afternoon."

"You sure will. And Jessica—" Claire paused.

"Yeah?"

"I love you."

"Love you too, girl," Jessica said. She hung up the phone and stumbled out of bed, heading in the direction of the bathroom and the medicine cabinet.

CHAPTER 25

Tucson Daily Tribune
Investment CEO Found Dead on Hiking Trail

By Audrey Summers
August 3, 2018

Early Wednesday morning a gruesome discovery
was made on a local hiking trail near Wasp
Canyon Estates. Wasp Canyon is a well-known
trail, frequented by visitors and residents
alike, that cuts across northwest Tucson as it
heads in the direction of the Santa Catalina
Mountains. After four miles the trail enters
Wasp Canyon, and it was a short distance
inside where the remains of a man's body were
discovered.

Cameron Jasper, age fifty-six, appears to have been mauled and killed by a wild animal. Police have not identified the type of animal involved, nor have they released any details regarding the extent of Jasper's injuries. Jasper's body was discovered by a local hiker, although the hiker has yet to be identified.

The Northwest Police Department has deployed Arizona's Fish and Game to track down and euthanize the animal involved in the attack. It is suspected that the animal in question was either a black bear or mountain lion, and that illness or disease had rendered it incapable of hunting its traditional food source. When asked how the search for the predator was going, Detective Carl Moser declined to comment.

Cameron Jasper, originally of Houston, Texas, was the founder and CEO of The Jasper Group, an investment management company based in Jasper's hometown. Over the course of twenty-eight years, Jasper grew his company from the ground up. The Jasper Group has been included in the Fortune 500 for the past seven years. Jasper relocated to Tucson in 2006. He has been controlling his company via telecommunication since his move to Arizona.

Jasper owned a home in the highly sought-after Wasp Canyon Estates, located off of Orion Street and set against the Santa Catalina mountain range. These multi-million dollar estates offer grand floor plans, substantial acreage, and privacy for their residents. They also happen to be located within walking distance of the Wasp Canyon trailhead.

Other residents were shocked and horrified when they heard the news of Jasper's attack. Ava Cuthbertson, of Wasp Canyon Estates, said, "I can't believe such a horrible thing could happen to such a good person. Cameron was always kind to me, always willing to lend a helping hand when I needed assistance with something around the house. He was never too good or too busy to help an old woman in need."

Cuthbertson was one of Wasp Canyon Estate's earliest residents. When asked about her safety in Wasp Canyon, Cuthbertson said this: "I have always felt perfectly safe in my home. I think that what happened to Mr. Jasper is horrible news, but I do not feel threatened for my own safety."

A service for Cameron Jasper will be held...

CHAPTER 26

Carl Moser detested animal attacks. He always switched stations when a story about an animal mauling came on the news. He flat-out refused to watch any of the Animal Planet shows that depicted animals attacking people, or even attacking other animals for that matter. And he put as much distance between himself and any case that came along which involved snake bites, dog fighting rings, or family pets that went berserk on one of the neighbors. Moser desperately wanted this case behind him, but things had just gotten a lot more complicated. Why couldn't a construction worker or an out-of-work actor been attacked out there, instead? Why did it have to be a millionaire? Why did it have to be *Cameron fucking Jasper?* One of the most well-known—and richest—guys in town.

Moser tossed the newspaper onto his desk. *How the hell do they already know about the victim's ID? Somebody must have leaked it. This is going to be a PR nightmare,* Moser thought miserably. Those damn reporters weren't going to let this thing go after just one article. He could see the headlines now, appearing day after day and monopolizing the front page: *LOCAL BUSINESS TYCOON TORN IN TWO IN NORTHWEST TUCSON. ANIMAL STILL ON THE LOOSE. POLICE HAVE NO LEADS.* And the headlines would be correct. Fish and Game had not found one trace of the sick bear so far. All the damn rain had washed away any evidence there might have been. They were lucky to have even gotten out there and found Jasper's body before that godforsaken downpour started, let alone collect any evidence. All they had was the body itself, and a few hairs that didn't appear to belong to the victim. The hairs were sent to the lab for analysis, where they were going through whatever steps necessary to identify them.

What type of hair it was wouldn't have mattered nearly as much if it had been some drifter or minimum-wage hiker that went down out there. No one would really have cared, not *really*. There would only be one article, and in the middle of the paper—a blurb really—that mentioned that a local man was attacked while hiking. It would urge readers to be careful, keep an eye on their pets, blah blah blah.

But not anymore. This was way past a blurb now. The richest man in town just got filleted by some canyon beast— God, he could see those newspaper freaks giving it a name like that. *The Beast of Wasp Canyon*. And it was going to be front page and center—above the fold. Day after day after day. *Just had to be animal attacks,* he thought. *I'd take a double homicide over this any day.*

Moser rested his arm on his desk and started massaging his right temple. There was no way he was going to be putting this mess behind him anytime soon. All he had to go on was a mutilated millionaire, a twenty-something girl, and a few animal hairs found on the body. *This is going to be a fucking nightmare,* he thought again.

Moser grabbed a couple of aspirin from his desk drawer. It was going to be a busy day, and he couldn't afford a headache. He washed the aspirin down with the cold coffee that remained in his U of A mug, grimacing as the pills clunked their way down his throat. Moser set the mug down and stared at the college logo embossed on the side, trying to figure out where to begin.

He needed to get a leg up on this thing, and he was pretty sure he knew where to start: the hairs on the body. If he could get the comparison results at least he would be able to tell the press *something* when they asked again about what attacked Tucson's wealthiest bachelor. *That was one small grace, though,* he thought in passing. *At least we don't have a grieving widow on our hands. Thank God for small favors.*

Moser picked up the phone, rubbing his temple and wishing for his budding headache to ease up. *How long does it take aspirin to work anyway?* He planned to call the lab first, in hopes that the hair analysis had already been completed. When the victim's ID came up as Jasper, they had put a rush on the hair microscopy, and Moser hoped he'd have that all sorted out before the press resumed their incessant calling.

After calling the lab, Moser planned to touch base with Fish and Game to see if they had any luck with the damn bear yet. If they did, and if the hair matched the bear they put down, then maybe this thing really could be over by the end of the week. *Please Jesus, please let it be over by the end of the week. Or sooner. Sooner would be even better.*

Before Moser could dial the lab extension, the call-waiting light began to flash, indicating that he had an incoming call. Maybe Fish and Game was calling because they caught the damn thing. Prayer received and answered! God, what a relief that would be! He answered the call and braced himself for the good news, but instead of feeling relief he felt his heart sink. It wasn't Fish and Game or the lab, it was a reporter. And she wanted to know what the police were going to do about the animal that killed Cameron Jasper.

Moser sighed, said he had no comment, and hung up. He rubbed at his temples again, this time with both hands.

CHAPTER 27

Cynthia Wyatt set the newspaper down with trembling hands. She let out a shaky breath and closed her eyes. An uneasy weight had filled her stomach as she read Friday's *Tribune* article: guilt. It was an emotion she did not feel often and did not care to be burdened with. But she could not shake the guiltiness away; it gnawed at her insides and refused to be silenced. After all, it was *her* grand idea to send Jessica out there. It was *her* idea to have her patient go gallivanting into the wilderness. Alone. She sent a fragile, grieving girl into a slaughterhouse. *Well, a slaughter canyon actually.*

Wyatt took another deep breath and straightened her suit jacket. Straightening her clothing was a nervous tick Wyatt had worked hard to overcome in her early thirties. It had been two decades since she compulsively pulled at her suit jacket, or attempted to rub away wrinkles that weren't there. But today, she kept finding herself smoothing the front of her blouse and pulling at the hem of her skirt.

It was 1:59 p.m. on Monday, August sixth, and Jessica Cleary's appointment was about to begin. Wyatt stood from her desk, pulled at her suit jacket once more, straightened her skirt, and headed to the door of her office.

The waiting room was empty except for Jessica, who was staring blankly at the wall. She did not look up when Wyatt opened the office door.

"Jessica? Are you ready to begin?"

Jessica looked away from the wall, her eyes clearing. She tugged at a piece of hair and shifted uncomfortably in her seat. The left leg of her jeans was consumed by a large, black boot that was securely fastened to her ankle.

Jessica stood up without speaking. Wyatt could see her grimace as she pushed herself up from the chair. It wasn't until she was standing that Wyatt saw the full extent of her injuries. There was a large laceration on her right upper arm that appeared to be held together by some sort of surgical glue. A large purplish-yellow bruise surrounded the laceration. Bruises and scrapes covered her arms and face, although none were nearly as bad as the one on her right arm. Her palms were dark pink with red trails going across them. The raw flesh looked angry and exposed with its top layer removed. And then there was the boot—a clunky, awkward thing that dwarfed the girl's small calf.

Jessica limped toward the door. Her feet made an unsynchronized shuffling sound as she went. *Swish, clunk. Swish, clunk.* She shambled into the office and headed toward the oversized chair in the center of the room. *Swish, clunk. Swish, clunk.* She sat down, grimacing again.

Wyatt closed the door and returned to her desk. She smoothed down her jacket as she went. "How are you doing today, Jessica? Are you having a lot of pain?"

"I'm fine."

"Have they given you something for the pain? Is it working?"

"Yeah, they did. It works fine, I guess." Silence filled the room. Then: "It makes me groggy, though."

"Yes, pain medications can do that. I hope the pain subsides for you very soon." Wyatt looked down at the cumbersome walking boot again. "That is quite the boot they gave you to wear. How long does it have to be on?"

"Six to eight weeks. But I might need surgery if it doesn't heal on its own, so maybe longer. I'll find out in a couple weeks when I see the doctor next."

Wyatt pulled at the hem of her skirt. Her hand, apparently with a mind of its own, went up to smooth her suit jacket. With some effort she brought both hands to her desk and laid them flat. She looked up, flustered. Jessica was watching her. She offered a small, knowing smile when they made eye contact. Wyatt couldn't tell if it was sympathetic or a smirk. She was really off her game today.

"Your mom called me and told me what happened. And I saw the article in the paper." Wyatt gestured to the newspaper she had inadvertently left lying on her desk. She wanted to smooth her jacket, but she kept both hands firmly planted on the desk. "I would really like to hear the story from you, though. If you are willing to tell me."

Jessica stared out the picture window, eyes scanning the mountains. She looked anxious, like something might crawl out of the mountains and come after her. She looked away and tugged on a strand of hair.

Jessica went over the encounter quickly, skimming over the details about the condition of Jasper's body. She tugged at her hair as she talked, and the color drained from her face when she described getting chased through the canyon. Wyatt said nothing as she told her story, however she became increasingly uneasy as Jessica described the creature in the shadows.

Once Jessica finished, Wyatt asked, "And what do you think it was?"

"I don't know," Jessica said in a low voice. She glanced nervously at the mountains. "The police said it was a sick bear, or a mountain lion. But I really don't think that's what I saw. They said my memory can play tricks on me. I don't know. I *really* thought I saw something... else. Everything about the attack felt *wrong*. Normal animals don't do that." She gripped the armrests as she talked, so tight that Wyatt feared the stuffing might burst out.

"A sick animal may behave differently than a healthy one," Wyatt suggested.

"Yeah, but it didn't *seem* sick. Not at all. It set a trap. It came after me. I—I really feel like it was something else."

Wyatt smoothed her blouse. "Jessica, let's look at this rationally."

"Rationally?" Jessica asked, looking wounded. "You don't believe me either."

"Jessica, I do believe you. I believe you went through a very traumatic experience. One that has deeply upset you, as it would have done to anyone. It is miraculous that you made it out unscathed." Wyatt looked down at the walking boot. "What I mean to say is that you made it out alive."

"But you don't believe me. You think I saw a normal animal, just like everyone else does." Jessica made no attempt to mask the hurt in her voice.

"The explanations the police gave you in regards to your description were compelling. The lack of fur due to mange, the protruding spine due to starvation, the aggressive nature due to the same." Wyatt paused, searching for the correct way to proceed. She hated how flustered and out of control she felt. She knew her guilt was at least partially to blame, but this was something that simply could not be undone. Her suggestion to begin an exercise routine was a sound one, and it was working just fine until that damn cougar screwed everything up. She smoothed her suit jacket.

"Fear can do things to our minds," Wyatt continued. "It can meddle with our memories—"

"Yeah, I heard that already," Jessica interrupted. She looked out at the mountains, refusing to meet Wyatt's eyes.

"Jessica, I believe you saw what you saw—something horrifying that was chasing you. I could not imagine that degree of terror. However, I cannot deny that I believe there is a logical explanation for all of this." She pulled at her skirt hem. "The police told me they thought—"

"You spoke to the police?" Jessica asked, turning away from the window.

"Yes, I called them just so I knew what to expect during our meeting today."

"So you already heard their explanation before you even talked to me?"

"I just wanted to be prepared," Wyatt said.

"Prepared to tell me that I'm crazy for thinking it was something else?"

"No, of course not."

"Okay, so what about it setting a trap then? What's your logical explanation for that?" Jessica looked at Wyatt. The hurt was still there, but now anger had joined it.

"Didn't the police suggest that the coug—that the animal in question knocked over the rock when trying to relocate the body?"

"That *rock* weighed a thousand pounds. I really don't think it could just get knocked over, especially by something that was sick or starving."

Wyatt smoothed her jacket with both hands. "I do agree that it is peculiar. But I don't think it is unheard of. Not for a predator of that size."

The anger drained from Jessica's face, leaving only a naked hurt that caused Wyatt to tug at the buttons of her blouse.

"It's because you feel guilty, isn't it?" Jessica asked.

Wyatt stared at her, startled. She placed her hands on the desk.

"Pulling on your clothes like that. You're doing it because you feel guilty."

"Jessica, I—"

"I'm not mad at you for suggesting it," Jessica cut her off. "It was a good suggestion. And there's no way you could have known what would happen. Cameron sure didn't." Jessica squeezed the armrests at the mention of Cameron Jasper. Her knuckles began to turn white. Suddenly, she stood from the chair with obvious effort. The plush chair and padded armrests made it difficult to get out of, something Wyatt was unaware of because she never sat down in the chair she so painstakingly picked out for her patients.

"What hurts me is that you refuse to even consider that what I saw was real."

"Jessica, I am sorry for sending you out there."

"Like I said, that wasn't your fault. I don't blame you for what happened. But why couldn't you at least *consider* that maybe I didn't imagine what I saw out there? That maybe it was actually real. I thought you were here to help me, Dr. Wyatt."

Jessica winced as she put weight on her left leg. She headed toward the door, the sound of her boot marking her progress. *Swish, clunk. Swish, clunk.* She turned at the door, her hand resting on the doorknob. "I was really hoping you'd believe me. How are you going to feel when it gets somebody else?"

She left before Wyatt could respond, shutting the door softly behind her. Wyatt smoothed her jacket and looked at the new chair sitting in the center of the room. A thread had come loose from one of the armrests.

CHAPTER 28

Howard Dunlap owned Lindy's Eatery for the past twenty-two years. He inherited it from Charles Lindy—Chuck for short. Chuck and Howie had been good friends since grade school. They were both Tucson born and raised, neither living anywhere else except for Chuck's stint in the army. Neither man had ever married, and they found it was nice to have a friend that knew you so well. Someone who knew when you wanted to shoot the shit, or when you just wanted to drink a few beers while quietly sitting next to one another, not wanting to talk but also not wanting to drink alone.

Chuck got the cancer back in '96. Didn't take long. Pancreatic, the doctor said. At least he didn't suffer, Lindy's regulars said. And that was true. By the time Chuck found out he was on borrowed time there were only a few months left. He met with a lawyer once, unbeknownst to Howie, and put Howie as the sole beneficiary to Lindy's Eatery and Pub.

Howie found out after Chuck's funeral. A pleasant enough affair, if you could ever call a funeral that. It was in March, when the weather in Tucson was nice and standing in a cemetery much more tolerable—if you could ever consider standing in a cemetery tolerable.

A lawyer contacted Howie later that same day. Told him Chuck left him the bar—bar none, pun intended. Howie damn near shit his pants. He didn't know piss about how to run a bar, let alone a restaurant. That's when Lindy's Eatery stopped doing the eating part. Howie quit his job at the garage without much objection; he never cared much for grease and car oil anyway. He kept on Chuck's bar staff and promised the kitchen crew free drinks if they ever cared to stop by and chew the fat with him.

Howie opened Lindy's right back up and was surprised by the loyalty of Chuck's patronage. He never saw an empty bar top, except when he was closing up for the night. Customers came and went, mostly blue collar workmen on their way home after a long day. As the years went by and the town's college grew in popularity, Howie started seeing more and more young faces in the bar. He didn't quite understand what the draw was for them college-aged guys and gals, but he welcomed them all the same. Maybe they thought it was rustic, these kids from out of town. An authentic southwestern dive bar. Something to tell Ma and Pa about back home.

Whatever the reason, Lindy's was booming with business and Howie had to hire on more help to deal with the demand. He threw in pool tables and a dance floor, and even updated the broken down jukebox that Chuck never quite got around to doing himself. Someday, he might even open up the eatery part of Lindy's Eatery again, but he doubted it. Don't mess with a good thing, that's what his ma always told him.

It was still early in the day on August sixth, the heat almost a living thing outside the doors of the bar. Early for Howie was three fifteen in the PM, and that was prime burning time for an August afternoon in Tucson, Arizona. The term, he believed, was swelterin'. The clouds were making their way over the mountains and he suspected another monsoon downpour before the afternoon was up, which he welcomed with open arms. Get that temperature down and take the burden off his aging air conditioner units. Those things were going to need replacin', and sooner rather than later.

Howie came out of Lindy's kitchen area, which was now used primarily for booze storage. He had opened the doors fifteen minutes ago and expected a few regulars to start trickling in as they got off their early shifts.

He came out of the kitchen, wiping his thick, sweaty palms on the front of his jeans. There was only one person in the bar, and it wasn't somebody Howie would ever have expected at this time of day. He slid around the side of the bar, tucked his bar towel into his back pocket, and ambled over to his only customer.

CHAPTER 29

"Well, you might be the prettiest thing I ever saw walk in here this early in the day," Howie said to Jessica Cleary, who was sitting in her regular seat at the side of the bar despite the ample supply of available barstools.

"Hey, Howie," she said, sounding downtrodden.

Howie glanced around the empty bar, checking the dance floor and pool tables. "Claire in the bathroom?" he asked, more to himself than to the sad girl sitting across from him.

"No," Jessica said with the same downcast tone. "Just me today."

Howie turned his attention to Jessica. He had known Claire's parents from his time in the garage; they had even invited him over for holidays on occasion. Not ripping people off when their car was broke can incite that kind of generosity. Jessica he did not know as well. She seemed plenty nice, although lately she had been looking pretty low and worse for the wear. A year ago her daddy had up and died the same way as Chuck, although Howie wasn't sure if it was from the same kind. He hadn't felt it was polite, or even necessary, to ask.

Today she looked kind of scuffed up, like she had been in a bit of a brawl. Jessica and Claire weren't the fightin' type, though, although Howie had seen plenty of women that were. Her face was scratched up a bit, but it was her arm that looked pretty torn into. Especially that big number near her right shoulder. That there looked like it needed some doctor work.

Jessica saw him looking and smiled wanly. "That's nothing compared to my ankle," she said.

Howie couldn't help himself, curiosity and the cat and all, and leaned forward to look over the bar top. Jessica stuck out her leg so he could see better. A giant, robot-looking, black thing was strapped to her left ankle.

"Well, what in God's name is that thing?" he asked.

"Controlled ankle motion boot," Jessica muttered.

"Fancy stuff for a fancy gal," Howie said. "Now how in God's name did you wind up with that thing on your leg?"

She sighed and tugged on a strand of hair, looking nervous. "Long story."

"Beer?"

"Absolutely," she said, and smiled.

Howie made his way over to the tap and poured a Dragoon IPA. He knew Jessica was partial to IPAs, and with her current state he doubted she cared much which kind it was anyway. He set the dripping glass down in front of her. She watched as foam cascaded down the side of the glass, and he watched her. This girl had been through something. He was sure of it. And it was a lot more than her daddy dying, which was already bad enough.

She took an admirable sip from her glass and looked up at Howie. He knew with her size it wouldn't take long for the beer to start talking for her. He wished that the eating part of Lindy's Eatery was working right now, because he desperately wanted to offer this girl some food. Fries, chicken wings... *God, she needs to eat somethin',* he thought, looking at her thin frame.

He was about to start moving away to give her some space when she asked, "You hear about the guy at Wasp Canyon?"

"Yeah, a bit. Millionaire? Lived in them richy rich houses." Howie couldn't imagine needing seven thousand square feet of living space. Damn near ridiculous, if you asked him. Nobody did ask, though, especially the richy riches.

"I found him," she said, and finished her glass in one large gulp.

Howie took it, without question, and refilled it. He set the full pint down in front of her. He had heard a lot of shit in his day, but finding a mangled up millionaire's corpse out in the desert was something he had not heard before.

Howie shifted uncomfortably from side to side as Jessica told him what happened to her up in Wasp Canyon. Imagining some man-eater chasing down this poor girl did not sit right with him. Not one bit.

"Did you know him?" she asked.

"Cameron Jasper?" Howie had been thinking about getting chased through the desert, and how he would not have fared as well as this young lady. He could barely run to the bathroom when nature was calling a little too loudly; he wouldn't even make it a hundred yards in the desert. Hell, not even fifty. "Naw, Lindy's don't attract them fancy fellas too often."

Jessica smiled. Howie couldn't understand how a smile could look so sad. She looked like she had been to hell and back.

"Do you know of anything like this happening before?" she asked.

"People getting attacked on hiking trails? Well, yeah, I s'pose it happens from time to time. We got our fair share of scary critters out there," he said, thinking about mountain lions, bobcats, coyotes, and maybe the occasional black bear. "I hear more about them snakes, though, more than anything else. Rattlesnake bites. Now those can get a fellar into a pinch real fast."

"Yeah, you gotta watch out for those." She took a sip of beer. "You ever hear about someone getting attacked by something... different?"

"Different how?" he asked, his eyes narrowing.

She looked up at him with large, pleading eyes. "Like not from around here. Like not your normal predators. Take away the bears and mountain lions and rattlesnakes. Have you ever heard about somebody getting attacked by something... else?"

Howie felt growing disquiet in his gut. He didn't like where this was going. "Well dear, I don't really know anything about that." He chose his words carefully, although he was never too good at keeping a poker face. It wasn't in his nature to lie. "I just know you were helluva lucky girl to have gotten outta there." His mouth smiled, but his eyes didn't—

and she knew it. *Awe fuck,* he thought, *she knows somethin'. Awe Christ, not this shit again.*

"Something like this *has* happened before, hasn't it?"

Howie glanced around the bar, which was still empty. It wouldn't be for long, though. He didn't want anyone else hearing what he was about to say. He couldn't lie to this girl, though. It looked like she already had an inkling that some funny business was going on, and it's not like he had all that much to tell anyway. It's not like it happened to him, was it? He just happened to be around when it did happen.

"I don't know exactly what happened before. The newspapers only said so much. And it's not like I'm a big news buff anyway. Mostly I heard men talking 'bout it here at the bar. I was sitting on your side of the counter back in those days. My buddy Chuck was runnin' the place back then. This was, oh, thirty, maybe thirty-five years back. Can't remember exactly, all I do remember is it rained like a son of a bitch that summer."

Jessica perked up at that, as he suspected she would. It was raining like a son of a bitch this summer, too. Sure there were plenty of summers where Tucson saw its fair share of rain— even more than a fair share. Them monsoons brought all that moisture in from Mexico, or the Pacific—one of those two. But this summer was getting a metric fuckton of rain, and Howie remembered that summer all those years ago was high on the metric fuckton-o-meter as well.

"It was one of them El Niños, or La Niñas, or whatever. I don't remember which one does what. All I know is it rained like cats and dogs every damn day that summer. Got those palo verde beetles all over the place. Those big black ones that come out when it's humid. God, I hate them things.

"Anyway, part ways through that summer some of the fellas in here—the regulars that worked at the mine or on one of them construction crews—they started telling stories about their buddies getting kilt. And not normal kilt, like from a machine accident or somethin', but kilt by some sorta animal. And it didn't happen while they were at work, always seemed to happen at night. The guys here at the bar said they went to work like normal and then realized that one of their buddies didn't show up that day. So they'd go check on 'em after they clocked out. These fellas..." Howie paused, shaking his head. He did not like thinking about that summer, not one bit. "These fellas," he continued, "they found their buddies all tore up. Musta happened the night before 'cause they were long since dead by the time they got there in the afternoon. And these guys work early shifts—we're talkin' four or five in the AM. So when these guys didn't show for their shifts, we gotta assume they got kilt earlier than that, sometime in the night."

Jessica looked like she was going to be sick, and he didn't think it was from the beer. Howie kept talking; he wanted this particular story over and done with. "These poor fellas, they had been sliced and diced three ways from Sunday. Authorities kept saying it was a rogue cougar that did it. But I never thought so. Cougars can be mean, but I don't think they would tear up a man for no good reason. Most of the dead fellas weren't even eaten, not much anyways. Just kilt.

"I forget how many. I listened to the news every now and then, but mostly what I found out I heard right here. These workin' fellas sure can talk, especially when they are feeling blue and they got a few drinks under their belts. I remember one guy saying his buddy had his head torn clean off."

"What happened?" Jessica asked, her hands grasping the edge of the bar top.

"'Nothin'. Not much anyway. Went on all summer. Maybe once a week, if not more. There was talk about some serial killer, though I do recall the news people saying no to that one. They said serial killers like young women, not hard-workin' construction crew types. That's another thing—these fellas were *strong*. Worked with their hands for a livin'. I don't know any cougar or other animal 'round these parts that could kill that many strong men. It's not like they were old, some were as young as you. Younger, I reckon. They all died just the same, though."

"Why didn't anyone do anything about it? I mean, where were the police during all this?"

"Well, they were there, I'm sure. But you're forgetting somethin'. These were workin' men. I doubt even half of 'em had their green cards. They all lived in the same general area, down south and to the west of town, near them Tucson Mountains. Not the best area of town. And they sure as hell weren't millionaires. People don't care nearly as much when a miner gets kilt, not really. I'm sure the families were torn up about it, but as for the news and the rest of town, they lost interest as soon as they got their hands on the gory details. No longer interestin' after they satisfied their curiosity."

Howie still felt bad about those men all those years ago, getting forgotten after cashing their checks in such an awful way. He didn't care much for the police not trying harder to capture the animal—or person—responsible, neither. Those men deserved just as much help as them millionaires up in Wasp Canyon do.

"So nothing was done then?"

"Not really. Police never found any leads. Never found a rogue cougar or any other animal that coulda done it. And when the rain stopped, so did the killings. By Halloween, it seemed everybody had damn near forgot about it. I'd bet my bottom dollar those families didn't forget, though. Or the fellas that found 'em."

There was a jingle at the door, and both Howie and Jessica jumped at the sound. A man in construction boots and a sweat-stained T-shirt walked in, heading for one of the barstools. Sweat was beaded across his brow, and some was trickling down from his hairline. "Tall one, Howie," he called across the room.

"Hold your horses, Brandon!" Howie called back.

Jessica watched as the sweaty man sat down at the bar. "One last thing, Howie," she said. "You were saying this all happened in the same area—down south somewhere. You said it was near some mountains?"

"Yeah, the Tucson Mountains. Tucson has mountains on all four sides. Pretty unique in that respect. You got the Santa Catalinas and the Tortolitas up north, the Rincons to the east, Santa Ritas way down south, and then the Tucson ones to the west."

"And all these guys that were attacked lived near the Tucson Mountains?"

"Yeah, pretty damn close, I reckon. I think that town was just south of the mountains. Why?"

Jessica looked at Howie, her eyes widening.

"Just like them millionaires in Wasp Canyon live right up close to the Santa Catalinas?" he asked. After making the connection, he thought, *Well shit on stick. This is gonna be a damn shitshow all over again.* He sighed and shook his head, wishing the damn rain would stop already. He rather just buy them new air conditioners and not have it rain one more damn day this summer.

"How much I owe ya, Howie?" Jessica asked, stumbling as she stood up. Howie wasn't sure if it was the beer or that walking boot, or maybe a combination of the two.

"Not a dime, sweetie," Howie said. "How about a bottle of water for the road and I call you a cab?"

"Yes to the water, no to the cab." Jessica held up her phone. "I have Uber. Is it okay if I leave my car here 'til tomorrow?"

"That's what parking lots are for," Howie said as he reached under the bar and brought a bottle of water back up. He set it down on the bar.

"Thank you so much for the beer," she said. And then quieter: "And for the information."

"Promise me one thing, darlin', before you go."

"What's that?" Jessica asked as she grabbed the bottle of water.

"You take care of yourself. And stay the hell away from Wasp Canyon."

"Absolutely, Howie," Jessica said, smiling with her mouth but not her eyes.

CHAPTER 30

Instead of heading home, Jessica directed her Uber driver to the Kokopelli Public Library. She knew she could do all the research she wanted to do on her laptop at home, but since she was still staying with her mom, she thought it best to use one of the library computers. She also wanted to avoid the endless questions regarding her Dr. Wyatt appointment for as long as possible.

Jessica arrived at the library at quarter to five, right along with the rain. She pulled herself out of the Uber driver's Nissan Juke and took care to not step in any puddles on her way up to the library's entrance. She didn't want her boot getting soaked. A heavy, water-logged CAM boot sounded even worse than a dry one. She could hear her steps echo in the alcove as she made her way to the sliding glass door. She had managed to keep the boot fairly dry, but her sneaker was another story—it made a squishy noise each time she stepped down on the cement. *Squish, clunk. Squish, clunk.*

The door slid open automatically as she neared the entrance. Jessica walked into the hushed world that is any library: muffled whispers, stifled giggles, and pages ruffling. She squish-clunked her way to one of the computer workstations and sat down.

Her phone beeped as she pulled the chair up to the desk. She had three messages: two from her mother and one from Claire. Both of her mother's messages asked where she was and when she was getting home. The first also asked how her therapy appointment went. The message from Claire said *Beauty and the Beast* sounded perfect for tomorrow and that she would be there after her shift was done at the salon.

Jessica silenced the phone and set it down on the desk. She logged onto the computer and clicked on the Google Chrome icon. Her fingers hovered over the keyboard as she tried to decide what exactly she was going to research.

Although Detective Moser's explanation had been compelling, Jessica couldn't shake the feeling that something else, something *worse*, had attacked her in Wasp Canyon that day. Despite the gnawing feeling in her gut, Jessica had been ready to give up on the idea and accept the inevitable—it was just a sick bear, her eyes were playing tricks on her, she's just a confused, grieving girl—after being discredited by Kilburn, Moser, and even Dr. Wyatt.

But then she heard Howie's story about the monsoon murders all those years back. She saw the fear in his eyes, and that felt a lot more real than Moser's explanation ever did. Jessica decided it was time to stop listening to everyone else's theories and start listening to her own instincts. She was the one out there and the only one who saw it. Saw it and survived anyway. Deep down she knew it was something more. And that it was still there… waiting.

Jessica stared at the colorful Google letters and the blinking cursor in the search bar. She decided to begin with the murders that happened back in—what did Howie say? Thirty years ago? That would make it the late eighties, or maybe the early nineties. She could hear fingers tapping on neighboring keyboards, feet softly padded across the carpeted floor behind her, and the printer humming as it printed out copies for one of the library's occupants. An occasional rumble of thunder grumbled from outside.

It didn't take long to find articles referencing the bloody summer Howie had mentioned. The deaths began in July of 1987 and continued through the end of August of that same year. The police believed a total of seventeen deaths were linked to the case, with all the victims being killed in a similar fashion: all at night, all in the same area of town, and all in the same gruesome manner. Broken down, it ended up being eleven men, four women, and—worst of all—two children.

The victims were mostly found outdoors, although the later murders happened inside the victims' residences. One man was walking home in the early hours of the morning when he was attacked, his body found along the roadside the following day. He was last seen alive at a tavern a mile down the road. A few men were found in the backyards of their homes. Police theorized that they heard something outside during the night and went out to investigate. The wife of one of the victims told police she was awoken by a banging sound outside and sent her husband out to check for burglars, which were common in that part of town. She heard her husband screaming and called the police. They were too late.

Jessica read the articles with unwavering interest. It made her queasy, but she needed to know what she was dealing with. She thought of Cameron, his stomach wide open and his face gone. The teeth looking too white surrounded by all that red. And his eyes, still intact, staring up at the sky.

The last two slayings occurred indoors. One man appeared to be attacked outside and tried to seek safety inside his home, but whatever it was followed him in and finished the job. The final attack—one that Jessica had trouble reading all the way through—involved the deaths of a family of four. A husband, wife, and their two children were killed in the early hours of the morning on August twenty-ninth of that year. The husband was found in the kitchen, the wife in the bedroom, and the two children appeared to have tried to take shelter in a closet. The closet door was torn open and one child had been removed from the closet and killed. The other was killed inside the closet itself.

The beers from earlier felt like a lump of sludge inside her stomach. The article went on to describe the bloody scene, and said that the police had no leads on the case. *Just like all the others,* she thought.

Mountain lions were hunted down, along with coyotes, and even one stray dog. People were panicked and the police were unable to offer any solutions. And then the murders stopped, just as suddenly as they arrived. People later speculated that the animal involved—probably rabid, although no proof of that ever surfaced—had simply moved on or died.

And that was it. No more murders, so no more problem. Jessica wiped at her eyes, thinking of the children in the closet. *This shit is not going to happen again,* she vowed to herself.

She started looking up geographical maps of Tucson and the surrounding area. She sent page after page to the printer, getting up each time to collect what she had printed. She didn't want anybody going to get their own print job and seeing what she was up to. Each time she stood from her chair, her left ankle screamed at her. She had forgotten to bring any pain medicine with her when she left home that day, although she doubted she should be taking any after those beers anyway.

Jessica lost track of time. She had printed more documents than she had intended to, once having to go to the front counter to inform the librarian that the paper supply for the printer needed to be replenished. She was engrossed in her latest research when her phone buzzed. Jessica finished the paragraph she was reading and searched for the phone. She found it buried under the papers she had printed.

Her mother again. Jessica answered the phone, told her mom she would be home in half an hour—yes, lasagna would be fine—and hung up. Jessica collected the various papers she had printed on the library's industrial sized printer and logged out of the computer. She thought she had enough information to go on, at least for now.

Her boot clunked as she crossed the lobby, and a few fastidious studiers looked up from their books with disapproval. When they saw the noise was coming from a disabled person they quickly returned their gazes to their books. *It's interesting how people avert their eyes when they see someone who is disabled,* she thought. *They want to see all the carnage up front, but they don't want to make eye contact with the aftermath.*

Jessica walked through the sliding glass doors and into the darkening gloom. It would have been sunset if the sun had a chance to peek out from behind the heavy, gray clouds. Instead of brilliant colors across the sky, the gray just became darker as the sun slipped below the horizon. She headed toward the car that was waiting out front, headlights on and windshield wipers whisking from side to side. She lowered herself into the back seat of the Uber, being careful not to bang her boot on the frame as she got in.

Jessica stared out the window, barely hearing the swooshes and splashes as the driver made his way through the various puddles on the road. She thought about all those months of barely speaking, about all those sessions with Dr. Wyatt where she sat in silence and stared out the window at the mountains. She couldn't be silent anymore, not when others could possibly be in danger. And they were in danger, she was sure of it. It was time to speak. It was time to be heard.

Jessica had searched for another explanation, but in the end she kept circling back to the same thing. And it was a thing. Not a sick bear or a rogue mountain lion. It was a *thing*. And she knew what it was now. She knew what killed Cameron

Jasper, and what killed all those people thirty years ago. If Howie was correct about the rain, it wasn't going to stop until the monsoons stopped. That left over a month of this… slaughter.

Jessica leaned back and let out a long, silent whoosh of air. *Daddy, please help me,* she thought. *It's Jess, and if I'm right about this, there is about to be such a mess.* She stared out the window and listened to the car's tires as they glided along the wet pavement. Night had fallen.

CHAPTER 31

Ava Cuthbertson was an elegant woman. She had been an elegant woman many years ago, standing in a sleek, green gown, when a handsome man by the name of Edgar Cuthbertson came over and asked her to dance. She had been Ava Portsmith back then. She was an elegant woman a year later when Edgar had taken a knee and asked for her hand in marriage. And she had been an elegant woman on their wedding day, standing in front of her groom in a gown that was fit for a queen.

Edgar Cuthbertson was a kind man to his wife, and a ruthless man in business. He had climbed the corporate ladder early in life, and by the time he had approached the stunningly beautiful woman in the green evening gown, he was already a wealthy man. He could have had his pick of women in that ballroom on that lovely spring evening, but his eyes were only for Ava. He proposed exactly one year after their first dance, and their wedding had been a blissful one.

Edgar and Ava lived in New York for much of their marriage. They enjoyed the galas and endless parties, him in his best tuxedo and Ava by his side, wearing one luxurious gown after another. They appeared in the papers often: New York City's most desirable couple. Most desirable, and most wealthy.

Edgar was killed in a traffic accident when returning home from a business venture in upstate New York. His driver skidded on the ice, and the town car was sent tumbling down a snowy embankment. Edgar, not one for safety measures such as seatbelts, was thrown from the vehicle. His body was found the following morning, drifts of snow covering the gore beneath.

The loss of Edgar cut Ava deeply, and she found herself incapable of staying in their brownstone in the city. In fact, she could not bear the thought of living in New York at all. She relocated to a place she thought was just about as far away as she could get: Arizona. She thought a change in scenery would even further improve things. She had had just about as much snow as she could stand.

Ava relocated to Tucson in 1989. She lived in a lovely estate in the central portion of town for many years, however, as Tucson expanded, she found herself once again in a city-type setting that she wanted away from. When Wasp Canyon Estates began construction in 1998, she immediately contacted her broker and real estate agent and sent them on a mission to acquire the most desirable of the estates. She wanted the largest one, with the best view, and with the most acreage. Edgar would have insisted on it.

Ava Cuthbertson's estate was the closest to the Santa Catalinas, pressed up against the base of the mountain range. Her multi-million dollar home was 9,000 square feet, with an impressive twenty-four acres of land. The house was set almost half a mile back from Wasp Canyon Road. The entrance had a thick, wrought iron fence with a large "C" in the center. The gate was now motorized, but in the early days her driver had to get out of the vehicle and push the gate open manually. She no longer had a driver, so the automatic gate was now of utmost importance.

The years had softened Ava. She no longer felt a need to have staff members or drivers. While Edgar's investments had kept her a very wealthy woman, she found in her later years that it wasn't money that she craved—it was companionship. She never remarried. Suitors had tried, but Ava had the heart-sinking suspicion that many were just after her bank account. After so many years she had stopped trying, and now at seventy-two, she doubted there would ever be another opportunity.

She lived in her 9,000 square foot estate alone, sharing the space only with her purebred Persian she named Tofu. Even though she would never have the companionship of a lover again, she found that having a cat seemed to fill at least some of the void. Ava and Tofu spent most of their time in a very small portion of the house. What once seemed like a glamorous idea to have such a grandiose home now seemed silly to her—an elderly woman with arthritis having to walk for an eternity to get from one end of the house to the other.

She spent much of her time in a single wing of the house, the rest sitting quietly and collecting dust.

When things broke around the estate, as they often do in any home, Ava sometimes called on her neighbor, Mr. Jasper. He was a kind man and would often come over to help her with her leaky faucets or broken window shades. Now that he was gone, she supposed she would have to call a maintenance repair company for such things, and she doubted they would want to humor an old woman and stay for tea and cookies afterward. She had begun to look forward to something trivial breaking around the house, sometimes even setting off to find something that needed fixing in the other wings, just so she could call upon Mr. Jasper and eventually sit on the patio with him and make small talk. She had no romantic feelings toward the man; she just enjoyed the pleasure of his company. Tofu was a lovely cat, but purebred or not he was still unable to engage in conversation with her. Except for the insistent meowing at meal time.

On the night of August sixth, Ava walked aimlessly around the inhabited wing of her house, Tofu padding along beside her. Tofu was as pure white as he was purebred, with bright green eyes and a pink nose. He reminded her of the Fancy Feast cat, which was probably part of the reason she was so taken with him.

"You hungry, my love?" she asked, and bent over to pat Tofu on the head. He looked up at her with wide, eager eyes. Ava's hips hollered in protest as she stood back up. She was counting the days until this rainy season was over; the humidity made her arthritis hurt something awful.

She ambled over to the elaborate kitchen and began preparing dinner for one, as always. Such a big kitchen for so little cooking going on, it really was a shame. She gave Tofu a Salmon Primavera Pâté Feast, from Fancy Feast of course. "There's your sister," Ava joked, showing the front of the can to Tofu. He appeared to be much more interested in what was inside of the can than what was glued onto the front of it. She placed the bowl of salmon on the floor, her hips grumbling angrily as she did so, and then started collecting ingredients for her own supper.

After inhaling his food Tofu disappeared, presumably to take a nap. Eating was hard work, after all. Ava brought her dinner—a bowl of soup and half a sandwich—to the dining room table to eat. The newspaper was still lying on the table, the article about Mr. Jasper on the cover. A picture of his handsome, smiling face stared up from the front page. Ava sighed. She missed her friend, which deep down, she had always considered him to be.

After dinner was done, Ava brought her dirty dishes to the sink. Her hands ached with the effort. She washed out the bowl and placed it on her generously sized granite countertop. She was just thinking about making some tea and retiring to the bedroom to read when she heard a thumping noise come from outside. She looked up from the sink and peered into the darkness on the other side of the window. Outside, the storm had passed and the wind had come to almost a complete stop. The mesquite tree opposite the kitchen window was still, the branches barely rustling in the calm that followed the storm. *Maybe a small gust knocked something over,* she thought. It seemed unlikely, though—the branches of the mesquite would still be bobbing up and down if there had been any wind.

Another thump, coming from the backyard. Ava was looking at the tree when she heard it, and she was certain that there was no wind this time. Something had been knocked over.

Her large backyard was tastefully decorated, much like the rest of the estate. A flagstone patio stretched out from the base of the house, surrounded by a low adobe wall topped with a wrought iron fence. Small "C"s for Cuthbertson adorned the iron bars, painstakingly etched into the metal. The wall was not a tall one—more decorative than purposeful. It could not keep out the desert wildlife anymore than it could keep Tofu in. Which was why Tofu was not allowed outside. There were far too many predators out there that would be more than happy to make a Fancy Feast out of her poor Tofu.

At the thought of Tofu, Ava began looking around the kitchen floor. Where was he? Earlier she had stepped outside to water the plants under the awning... could Tofu have snuck out when she opened the door? She doubted it; he was never very good at slinking around. A hunter he was not. But he certainly could have gotten out, couldn't he? She was an old woman with failing eyesight; it certainly was possible he could have snuck past her.

Ava rushed around the countertop, ignoring her aching hips, looking for Tofu as she went. No sign of him on the other side of the counter either. A fresh wave of worry went through her. She tried to remember the last time she saw Tofu, and could only think of when she fed him before making her own supper. Ava got to the sliding glass door and looked out into the night, fear mounting in her chest.

The entire northeast-facing wall of the dining room was floor-to-ceiling windows. The mountains towered over the property, and the dining area offered the best view of Wasp Canyon and the cliff faces on either side. Ava flicked on the patio light and surveyed the yard. The patio was empty, cast in a warm glow from the porch light. No Tofu, just the regular patio furniture and potted plants. Beyond the back wall, the desert was bathed in darkness. Sometimes, on a clear night, she could see all the way to the mountains, covered in cold moonlight with the darkness of the canyon at the center. No moonlight tonight, though—there was still a heavy covering of clouds sluggishly working their way across the night sky.

Ava thought of the predators that came down from the mountain: the coyotes howling in the night, the bobcats creeping about in the underbrush, the mountain lions lying in wait. And a sick bear as well? She couldn't stand the thought of her Tofu being out there, unaware that he was getting stalked by some carnivore. Ava undid the latch, yanked open the sliding glass door, and ran out into the night. She shut the door behind her by habit, accustomed to always closing the doors to keep Tofu from getting out.

Outside it was suffocatingly muggy, the humidity hanging thick in the air like soup. She could not see beyond the wall of her backyard. Ava looked around, growing more and more frantic by the second. She didn't think Tofu would have jumped over the wall and ran into the desert, but she couldn't be sure. She should have brought a flashlight with her.

The sound she heard had come from the left side of the patio, closer to the mountains, so she headed in that direction. The right side of the patio overlooked the city lights of Tucson. It was a breathtaking view, but one she rarely sat out and enjoyed because sitting out alone at night had started to make her feel less and less comfortable as she aged.

Ava headed toward the shadows on the left side of the house. She kept her eyes low to the ground, searching for white fur. "Tofu," she whispered. She wondered why she was whispering; it's not like anyone was around to hear her. Her closest neighbor was almost a mile away. "Tofu!" she said louder, although still not at full volume.

She ventured further into the shadows, fear creeping up in her throat and making it hard to swallow. Tofu wasn't over here, she was certain of it. She turned to head back to the patio and saw one of her flowering pots lying on its side. It was cracked down the middle and soil had spilled out of the top. It was a fairly heavy planter—one she would have had to call on the helping hands of Mr. Jasper to move, if she ever had the desire to do so.

She walked through the spilled soil, missing the smeared paw print that was pressed into the scattered dirt. The print was much larger than a house cat's and didn't catch her attention.

Ava got to the center of the patio and looked around, still calling for Tofu in a harsh whisper. She noticed another toppled planter. It had been obscured by the patio table and chairs when she first came out, but now that she was next to the table she could see it clearly. This pot was by far larger than the first. It was made of poured cement and stood at just over three feet tall. Two men were needed to move it into position on the patio, and that was before it was full of gardening soil. Now it was lying on its side, the soil spread out on top of the flagstones.

Ava's fear was replaced by confusion. What in the name of God could have knocked something like that over? And why? Nothing large enough to knock that pot over would care about the contents inside, which was just dirt and a gardenia bush. The bush was torn out and shredded, white flowers littering the patio.

Ava took a step closer to the planter and the pile of dirt that had been dug out. The flowers obscured what was pressed into the extracted soil. She peered closer, and this time was able to make out the paw print. It was enormous—larger than any she had seen before. She could also see scratches in the dirt, which she realized were claw marks. A fresh wave of fear washed over her. *Tofu didn't do this.* If Tofu was out here at one point, he wasn't anymore.

Ava wasn't sure which she noticed first: the smell or the sound. Maybe they happened at the exact same time, but she supposed it didn't really matter anyway. A rancid smell filled her nostrils, permeating her sinuses and making her head swell. At the same time—or slightly before or after—she heard a growl. It rumbled like oncoming thunder, although she thought the storms were done for the night. *Not thunder,* she thought. She could feel the growl resonating in her chest.

Ava was facing the back wall, and the sound came from directly behind her—on the patio, between her and the house.

The light on the patio dimmed as whatever it was moved in front of the porch light. Its shadow stretched across the flagstones, the top swallowed by the darkness of the desert.

She turned slowly. She could feel her chest tightening up and her breathing cease. She suspected she was having a heart attack. When she turned around, all she could see was a very large silhouette. The animal was blocking the porch light, and there was no light coming from behind Ava to reveal the creature's facial features. All she could tell was that it was large—much larger than the animals she usually saw coming from the canyon. And something about its posture and the shape of its head led her to believe that it wasn't a bear, after all. There was no fur illuminated by the patio light—just rough, gray skin.

Ava opened her mouth to scream but never had the opportunity. It launched at her, its full weight colliding with her fragile, arthritic frame. She heard crunches in her hips and spine as she hit the flagstone—her bones breaking, no doubt. Her face was pointed toward the brightly lit kitchen. In the window, on the inside of the glass, was Tofu. His back was arched, his fur on end, and he was hissing at whatever was on top of her. *He was inside all along,* she thought.

Teeth sunk into Ava's throat and the taste of copper filled her mouth. Blood ran down her throat and filled her lungs, and she could feel herself drowning in it. Ribs snapped and warm liquid poured down the front of her robe. The weight of the thing on top of her was immense. The entire time she stared at Tofu, and thought, *I wish Edgar was here.* Before long, there was blackness. Ava hoped that Edgar would be waiting for her once the blackness cleared.

CHAPTER 32

Claire arrived at the Cleary house shortly after five the following afternoon. She held a grocery bag in one hand and her Coach purse in the other. The grocery bag had Junior Mints and popcorn on top and a bottle of wine hidden underneath. No need to upset Mrs. Cleary anymore than she already was. Claire knocked on the door and waited. She used to be able to walk right in, but ever since Mr. C passed away Mrs. Cleary started locking the doors.

"Good afternoon, Claire," Andrea said as she opened the door. She stepped to the side, allowing Claire space to come in with her bags. "How are you today?"

"Doing just fine, Mrs. C. How are you doing?" Claire smiled at Andrea. She knew she would never be loved by Mrs. Cleary, but she could tell Andrea was making an effort and that she should do the same.

"Just fine, just fine," Andrea replied. She looked distracted. "Please," she gestured to the kitchen, "come on in."

Claire felt nervous. She didn't want to unpack her grocery bag in front of Mrs. Cleary. Pulling out a bottle of wine was just going to upset her, which was why Claire hid the bottle underneath her snack purchases. She knew Mrs. Cleary was planning to go to her book club tonight, and Claire could just see her fretting the entire time she was there, imagining her injured daughter getting drunk with that crazy friend of hers. She might even come home early because of it. The fact that Jessica was a 24-year-old woman didn't seem to calm Mrs. Cleary's worries one bit.

Claire gently set the grocery bag down on the counter. She made no move to unpack it. Andrea looked frazzled, often glancing down the hallway in the direction of Jessica's room. "Is everything okay, Mrs. C? Where's Jessica?"

"Oh, she's in her room," Andrea said, distracted. She looked down the hallway again. "She brought all this stuff home from the library last night and has spent most of the day in her room with the door shut. Whenever I come in to check on her, she turns the pages over so I can't see what she is looking at." Andrea sighed.

Claire glanced down the hallway. She could tell from the way the hall was lit that Jessica's door was shut. Jessica probably didn't even know she was here yet. "I'm sure everything is just fine, Mrs. C."

"Oh, I hope so, it's just…" Andrea trailed off. She finally turned and looked at Claire. "I'm worried about her, Claire."

"Well…" Claire paused. She knew Jessica had fallen off course when she was attacked in the canyon. She had been doing better—a lot better—before that. She was looking healthier, and she was eating. She was even smiling and laughing sometimes. Following Mr. C's death, Claire wondered if she would ever hear her friend laugh again. "Well, I guess you could say she's been acting a little odd since the attack. But that's to be expected, right? It must have been terrifying."

"Oh yes, I know, I know," Andrea said dismissively. "I know it must have been awful. I expected her to be sad. And scared. Perhaps even mad that her ankle was injured and she couldn't run anymore. But she's behaving... differently."

"Differently how?"

"Oh, I don't know," Andrea muttered. "When I ask her what's wrong, she just stares out the window at the rain. I guess I'm worried this... *encounter*... in the desert has affected her more than she is letting on."

"What does Dr. Wyatt think?" Claire asked. "I mean, she saw her the other day, right? Did she mention how it went?"

"Very little," Andrea lamented. "She hardly told me a thing about it. I'm worried it went poorly, but I can't get any answers out of her." Andrea glanced down the hallway again. "Listen," she said to Claire, her voice low, "I need you to help me. Well, to help Jessica."

Claire looked at Andrea with confusion. She glanced down at her grocery bag on the counter.

"Here," Andrea said, "let me open that for you." She reached into Claire's grocery bag and pulled out the bottle of wine. "You don't mind, do you?"

"I—uh..." Claire stammered.

Andrea looked at the bottle. "Yellow tail? Not the best, but I guess it will have to do. At least you got the big bottle." She popped the cork, grabbed two glasses, and poured each of them a glass. "I need something to help me get through book club tonight. It's *Fifty Shades of Grey*." She rolled her eyes and took a large gulp.

Claire stared at her, dumbfounded. She took her glass from the counter and looked at Andrea with awe. "Thanks, Mrs. C."

"Relax, dear," Andrea said, taking another long pull from her glass. "I know you two were going to have a few drinks with your movie tonight. Just please make sure that she eats something, too."

"Of course, Mrs—"

"Andrea," she said. "It's about time you start calling me that."

"Okay... *Andrea*," Claire said.

Andrea finished off her glass and took Claire's hand. "Listen Claire, Jessica is never going to confide in me the way she would with you. I need you to keep an eye on her. If she is thinking about doing something... dangerous, or self-damaging... please, *please*, help her to get back on track."

Claire nodded, confused. "Uh, yeah, I guess so. I—I guess I can do that."

Relief washed over Andrea's face. "Thank you, Claire." She squeezed Claire's hand and let go. "I appreciate this more than you know."

A sound came from down the hall. Claire looked in the direction of the sound and saw Jessica heading down the hallway. *Swish, clunk. Swish, clunk.* She looked excited.

"Hey girl," Jessica said as she entered the kitchen. "Whatcha two doing in here?" She looked at the two wine glasses, one empty, and raised her eyebrows.

"Oh, I'm just catching up with Claire," Andrea said.

Claire looked at Andrea awkwardly, then turned her attention to Jessica. "Hey you! Ready for some Disney action? I got *Beauty and the Beas*t all ready to go."

"Sounds great!" Jessica said with too much enthusiasm.

Mrs. C—Andrea—was right, Claire thought. *She is acting a little different.*

"Okay then, ladies," Andrea said, "I'm off to book club. There is money on the counter for pizza. You two enjoy the movie." And almost as an afterthought: "And keep the doors locked."

"You got it, Mom. Have fun!"

Andrea grabbed her purse. She gave Jessica one last smile, then turned to Claire. She was still smiling, but she also looked concerned. She headed out through the garage door. The girls watched as the deadbolt locked into place, just in case they forgot to lock it themselves.

CHAPTER 33

They stood in the kitchen, listening to the garage door rumble back down and finally come to a stop.

"Girl, you'll never guess what your mom just did—"

"C'mon," Jessica said, grabbing Claire's hand and pulling her toward the hallway. Claire looked longingly at her wine glass as she let Jessica drag her toward her bedroom.

"What's going on? You seem antsy about something?"

"Uh, yeah," Jessica said, distracted. She went straight to her desk once they entered her room, grabbed a large stack of papers, and began shuffling through them.

"Whatcha got there?" Claire asked, feigning enthusiasm.

Jessica glanced up. "Research," she said. She went back to shuffling through the documents that were strewn across her desk.

Claire started to feel uneasy. Her friend looked like she might be going off the deep end. *What's that word when they are way too hyper? Manic. That's the one.* Maybe she could redirect Jessica's attention to something other than all those papers. "So how did it go with Wyatt yesterday?" she asked.

"Shitty," Jessica said, not looking up. "I don't think I'm going back."

"What?" Claire asked, alarmed. "But she was actually helping you, Jess. You can't just... stop."

"Don't call me that," Jessica said, still looking down. She was putting all the papers into some kind of order.

Claire sighed. *When was this whole 'Don't call me Jess' thing going to stop? Just because her dad called her that doesn't mean nobody else could ever call her that.* "Sorry," she said, "it slipped."

"It's okay. You know, there's more room in the kitchen. Let's go." Jessica swish-clunked past Claire and headed back down the hall. Claire sighed and followed her, turning off the bedroom light as she went. At least the wine was in that direction.

Jessica sat down at the kitchen table and spread out the papers. Claire walked past her, nervous to look at what the papers had on them, and grabbed her wine glass off the counter. Claire took a large sip from her glass and poured one for Jessica. She headed over to the table and sat down. *Here we go,* she thought. "So what are we looking at here?" she asked.

"I know what killed Cameron Jasper," Jessica said.

"Did the police figure it out?" Claire asked, perking up. If they found the animal, maybe all this was just her friend feeling relieved and not knowing how to express it. Nothing more than that.

Jessica looked up from her papers. "The police don't know jack shit."

"Oh," Claire said, defeated. She drank from her glass.

"I talked with Howie," Jessica said. "He—"

"You went to Lindy's?" Claire interrupted. *"Without moi?"* She clutched dramatically at her chest.

"Not for fun," Jessica said with a smile. "I went after my therapy appointment. It didn't go well, so I went to Lindy's afterward to postpone having to go home and tell my mom about it."

"How did your mom take it?"

Jessica sighed. "Not well. You know how she worries."

"Yeah, I sure do." Claire took another hearty sip of wine.

Jessica put the papers down and looked at her. "Okay, listen. I have to tell you something. And it's important."

"Okay…" Claire said, nodding. "Roger that."

"After I was attacked everyone said I imagined what I saw. The detective, that shitty cop at the hospital, my mom, even Dr. Wyatt. And I was ready to just accept that, I guess. I mean, I've had to accept a lot of things I don't like this year. But then I talked to Howie. And I realized I shouldn't be listening to all these other people tell me what I saw. Because I know what I saw, whether anyone believes me or not."

"Whoa, whoa, whoa… I wouldn't go that far," Claire said. "I just might believe you. But first you have to tell me what's going on."

"Okay… the thing that attacked me was not a bear. Or a mountain lion. Or a coyote. Or anything else that we know about. It killed Cameron, it wanted to kill me, and it is going to kill somebody else. A lot of somebody elses."

Kill more people? God, is she going to say it's Hannibal Lecter or something? Claire thought. "Well, how about we have a snack, maybe a drink, and then you can tell me the whole story, from start to finish. I'm guessing you haven't eaten anything today."

"I'm not hungry," Jessica said, and resumed organizing her paperwork.

"But I brought popcorn. It's the good stuff, too." Claire gestured toward the kitchen counter. "Look, it even says 'Movie Theater Butter' on it."

Jessica looked up from what she was doing, stared at the popcorn box for a few seconds, then returned to her papers. After a moment, she set the papers down in a stack. She grabbed the glass of wine and took a long swallow. "Okay," she said, "so I told you about the attack. About the rock, and finding Cameron, and getting chased."

"Yes," Claire said, thinking about her description of Cameron's body. A shiver crept its way up her spine, one vertebra at a time. Jessica could have used a little less detail during that part. What happened to him sounded horrible.

"And I told you how the police didn't believe me when I said it wasn't a normal animal. The police said they thought it was a bear with mange or something, and that's why it didn't have any fur. And it couldn't hunt normal because it was sick. And its spine stuck out because it was hungry." She rattled off the details like they were on a check list.

"Yes, you told me all of that."

"Well, I went and saw Howie at Lindy's yesterday and he told me about these murders that happened around thirty years ago. All the people that were killed died the same way as Cameron. All torn up, none of them really eaten. Not a lot anyway."

Claire felt queasy. Maybe from the cheap wine, but most likely from Jessica's story.

Jessica fanned out a bunch of papers in front of her. She looked down at the headlines. "Another Person Slain in South Tucson Community." "The Body Count Continues to Rise in South Tucson." "Family of Four Found Slain in South Tucson Home." Claire glanced through the articles but had no desire to read them.

Jessica continued. "Seventeen people in all, all in the course of two months. And you know what Howie told me that they didn't mention in the papers?"

"What's that?"

"This all happened during a big El Niño year. *Just like this one.*" Jessica took a sip of wine. "Back in '87, when this all happened, there was a shit-ton of rain, *just like this year.* And that community where they all died was right up against the mountains, *just like where Cameron was found.*"

"But they were different mountains," Claire protested.

"Doesn't matter. The circumstances are the same. Whatever it is, it sets up camp in the mountains. Lives there for however long, probably surviving by eating other animals. And then whenever there is a big monsoon season, it comes out of the mountains and starts attacking people."

"Like it gets washed out of the canyon or something?" Claire asked. This was all starting to sound pretty weird to her. No wonder Andrea was concerned.

"Yeah, maybe, I guess so. Whatever the reason, it is linked to the rain. The rain started, the killings started. The rain stopped, the killings stopped. That's why they never found it back then," Jessica pointed to the articles in front of Claire. "It went away when the rain stopped."

"Okay, let's say that's true…"

"But it *is* true."

"Okay, yes, it's true." Claire stood up from the table; she needed more wine for this. She glanced to see if Jessica needed more as well. Claire filled her own glass and topped off Jessica's. She set the bottle down next to the unopened box of popcorn. *Guess we won't be watching any* Beauty and the Beast *tonight,* she thought. She sat back down at the table. "Even with the link to the weather, couldn't it still be a sick bear or something?"

"No, it couldn't."

Claire took another pull from her glass. "And why not?"

"First of all, because these killings were thirty years apart and bears don't live that long. Especially sick ones."

"It could have been two different sick—"

"Second of all," Jessica said, cutting her off, "it set a trap. *It set a fucking trap.*" She said the words slowly, emphasizing each one.

Claire shifted uncomfortably in her seat. Either Jessica was losing her grip on reality or there was some trap-setting monster beast out there. She didn't care for either possibility.

"When I entered the canyon that morning, there was no body and there was no rock," Jessica continued. "It knew when I went into the canyon. It then moved the rock onto the trail for me to trip over. And it put the body just past the rock so I would be distracted and not notice it. The rock I mean. And it *knew* I was going to have to go back that way. It must have been watching me for a while. That's why I smelled it that one time. It was watching me."

"Smelled it?" Claire cut in. "When did you smell it?"

"It smelled awful. Like a carnivore smells. Rotting meat and just... gross." Jessica shook her head.

"Yeah, you told me about the smell before. What I mean is what time are you talking about? When you smelled it the first time? And it was watching you?"

"I smelled something awful one day when I was leaving the canyon. It was just one quick whiff, but when it chased me I remembered the smell. That happened weeks before the attack, so it must have been watching me the whole time. Waiting."

Claire felt the pestering tug of anxiety. This all sounded profoundly creepy. Some beast lying in wait, biding its time, and then setting a trap when the time was right. *Freaking creepy.* "Why you?" she asked. "Why would it spend all this time setting up a trap for little ol' you? You aren't exactly a feast." Claire looked Jessica up and down. Any weight she had gained had already been lost again.

"Probably because I went into its territory," Jessica suggested. She paused, and then nodded as if in agreement with herself. "Yeah, that has to be it. It wasn't quite ready to come out and start attacking people at that point. But Cameron and I went into its territory. So it thought we were a threat or something."

"Okay…" Claire said. "And the fact that it set a trap links this thing to the murders from a long time ago how?"

"Because that thing set a trap, too! Just look at the news reports! It knocked stuff over outside people's homes, luring them outside to attack them."

"Some of these killings happened inside," Claire said, holding up the article about the family of four.

"It got bolder as time went on. The first man was just walking home along the street. Then it was people in their backyards. Eventually it started going *inside* their homes, too."

Claire set the article down, wanting to be rid of it. "Okay, I agree that some fucked up shit happened to these people back then. That much is obvious." She gestured to the papers with her wine glass, almost spilling it. "But there is one big discrepancy."

"What?" Jessica asked, alarmed.

"The time of day, Jessica. All these attacks happened at night. Every single one of them. But you were attacked during the daytime. It doesn't add up."

"If it set a trap and injured Cameron first, like it did to me, he could have been stuck out there until dark. He could easily have been attacked at night."

"But that doesn't explain *you* getting attacked in the daylight."

"Oh… my God…" Jessica said, trailing off. "That's why I didn't die." She looked like she had just had an epiphany.

"Huh?" Claire asked, confused. "What do you mean that's why you didn't die?"

"*The daylight!* God, I can't believe I didn't figure that out sooner!" Jessica looked at Claire, her eyes wide and mouth hanging open. "Listen," she said, "I always wondered why I got away. I mean—it had me. I was on the ground and unable to run another step. It could have killed me no problem. But it stopped. And you know why it stopped?"

"Hanging on the edge of my seat, babe."

"It's because of the sunlight. Don't you see? That canyon was super dark and shadowy. I doubt it ever got much sunlight in there, if any. It chased me through the canyon, almost caught me, but when I got into the sunlight it had to stop. That's why it was standing in the shadows snarling at me. It couldn't get any closer to me. *It couldn't go into the sunlight.* And that's why all the attacks were at night—because it can't go out in the sun."

"Jesus Christ, Jess, if you tell me you got attacked by a goddamn vampire I am literally going to flip my shit."

Jessica laughed. "No, I'm not going to tell you that."

"Thank God for small favors," Claire said, finishing off her second glass. They were going to need to order the pizza soon, before she got too sloshed. She doubted this was the time to bring up pepperoni or sausage, though. "Okay then, are you finally going to tell me what this thing is?"

Jessica picked up one of the papers she had left face down on the other side of the table. She set it down in front of Claire. "It's a chupacabra."

Claire looked at the image on the page for a long period of time. She placed both of her hands on the table and took a slow, deep breath. Claire looked up at Jessica, her eyebrows raised. "It's a chuppa-whatta?"

CHAPTER 34

"A chupacabra," Jessica repeated. Claire opened her mouth to speak, but Jessica pushed on before she could get a word in. "Here me out!" she exclaimed. She grabbed a different stack of papers, suggesting she had printed out a substantial amount of research on the chubby-wubby—or whatever it was. "There have been multiple reports of a creature that comes at night and kills peoples' livestock."

Claire looked down at the paper in front of her. It had a drawing of some sort of nasty dog-bear looking thing in the center, and the title read: "Chupacabra: Real or Myth?" Claire groaned and pinched the bridge of her nose with one hand. She felt woozy. *This is so much worse than I thought it would be,* she thought. *It says* urban legend *on here. My friend thinks she got chased by some sort of chuppa-cuppa and she wants me to help her—what? Catch it?*

Claire looked up from the table. Jessica eyed her closely, her eyebrows furrowed. "Can you at least listen to what I have to say before you ship me off to the loony bin?" she snapped.

"I'm sorry. Yes, I will listen. Please, tell me what you found out."

"Okay, so these reports go back around forty years. But it's very likely it was around before then, it was just never reported. The first recorded sighting was in 1975 in Puerto Rico. A man said he saw a creature in his farm one night. It killed his goat and drained its blood, but it didn't eat it. Three more of his goats were killed on subsequent nights, all in the same way.

"More sightings were eventually reported, mostly in Puerto Rico, but there have been reports from Central America all the way through Mexico. It's MO—its method of attack, I mean—was to kill farm animals, drain their blood, and then leave the bodies for the farmer to discover the following day. In all the reports it was a creature that nobody recognized. Someone said it looked kind of like an alien, but that report was discredited."

That's the only thing that was discredited in all this? Claire thought.

"Most people described it as around three feet tall at the shoulders, much taller if standing on its hind legs. Of course no one has an extremely accurate description of it since all the sightings occurred at night. From what I found, a lot of the people described a hairless creature with a long snout, big teeth and claws, and a spiny back."

Claire stared at her, mouth open. Jessica set all the papers down on the table so she could gesture with her hands. Claire glanced down at the pile of papers, then back up at Jessica.

"Now, what I saw fits a lot of those descriptions. It was about this tall," she brought her hand to the level of her hip, "when it was on all fours. I didn't see it standing on its hind legs, so I don't know how tall it would be then. Probably scary big."

"Does it stand on its hind legs?" Claire asked softly.

"From what I have researched, it is a quadruped. Kind of dog-like, but bigger. And uglier. Some reports said it had wings, but I know that's not true because I saw it."

Claire started to rifle through the papers. There were a lot of vaguely similar drawings of some sort of dog-like creature. In the pictures the thing was always snarling, showing off its large canine teeth. None of the pictures depicted it having hair. And in quite a few it had a large ridge along its back, sometimes with spines or spikes. It reminded Claire of that *Spinosaurus* dinosaur, with the fin thing on its back. *Except the* Spinosaurus *actually did exist at one point,* she thought miserably.

Jessica continued to describe her canyon assailant, speaking at a rapid pace and leaving little room for interjection. "It didn't have any fur, just like the eyewitness descriptions. Well, it might have had a few hairs here and there, but it wasn't furry like most animals. And that ridge they keep mentioning—that's the protruding spine I saw. It's not there because it is emaciated and starving, that's just part of its anatomy. A spine sticking out like that could be confused for spikes, right? Or, like, a ridge on the back?" Jessica gestured toward her own back, trying to mime a spiky ridge along her spine.

Claire stared at her, dumbfounded, then looked back down at the papers she was holding. There was page after page of different eyewitness accounts. Some villages even had a special name for it, like in Puerto Rico where a small community started calling it *El Vampiro de Moca.* The Vampire of Moca? Claire had been much more interested in The Beast of Walt Disney, courting Belle with his books and sad eyes. This thing in the pictures did not have sad eyes at all.

Jessica looked at Claire, her teeth gnawing at her lower lip. "Please say something, Claire."

Claire held up one of the printouts, her expression a mixture of concern and disbelief. "The goat-sucker?" she asked. "You're telling me you got chased and nearly killed by a mythical beast called a *goat-sucker*?"

"Well, that's just what it means in Spanish," Jessica explained. "Because some of the witnesses saw it when it killed their livestock. It drank their goats' blood, so that's how it got that name. Chupacabra… goat-sucker." She shrugged. "They started calling it that in 1995."

"But a lot of these people said it just drank the animal's blood. I don't see anything about shredding them into bits."

"Well maybe it's *changed*, Claire! Maybe it has evolved. Maybe just drinking some blood isn't good enough anymore. Have you ever heard of Darwin and his theory of evolution?"

"Yes, of course I have heard of Darwin," Claire said, rolling her eyes. "What about it attacking people instead of animals? All these reports are about livestock."

"I'm sorry that the eyewitness accounts I uncovered aren't as thorough as you want them to be. It's not like I could go to the zoo and study the damn thing." Jessica sat back down. "And there's still something you haven't considered yet."

"What's that?"

"These are only the accounts of people who saw it and survived. From the looks of how vicious this thing is, I doubt many people who saw it lived to tell the tale. Maybe these farmers and villagers were the lucky ones. They had animals and livestock outside for the chupacabra to go after instead of the villagers themselves. Do you think a lot of the people living out in Wasp Canyon have livestock?"

"No," Claire snorted. She couldn't help but laugh thinking about all those rich bitches going out at five in the morning to milk the cows and feed the chickens. In their Prada shoes and their Versace bathrobes, no less.

"What's so funny?"

"Oh, just thinking of Mr. and Mrs. Millionaire tending to their livestock in their Gucci loafers."

Jessica giggled and took a long pull from her wine glass.

Claire was relieved to hear her laugh. "Okay, well riddle me this," she said. "All these accounts are from Mexico and Central America. Hell, Puerto Rico is a freaking island. How the hell did this chupa-gupa get into southern Arizona?"

"Chupacabra," Jessica corrected. "And there have been sightings in Arizona, although not many."

"But how did *this one* suddenly appear? How did it get here?"

"I have the answer to that as well." Jessica started looking through more of her papers.

"Man, if you had this many answers during your SATs, you could have gone to Harvard." Claire poured some more wine into her glass, tipped it toward Jessica as if to cheers her, and then took a sip. "Full scholarship," she added.

"Oh, shut it," Jessica said, looking up from her papers. A small smile appeared at the corner of her mouth. "Here it is," she said, setting down a printout of a topographic map. "This is Tucson. You can see us here." She pointed to a spot on the northwest corner of the map. "And here are all the mountain ranges surrounding the city." She made a wide circle around the city of Tucson with her finger. She then moved her finger to the mountains on the western side of the page. "These are the Tucson Mountains. And," she moved her finger an inch to the south, "this is where all the attacks occurred in 1987." Jessica glanced at Claire to make sure she was paying attention, then returned to the map. "Now these," her finger slid across the page to the mountains on the northeastern side of the map, "are the Santa Catalinas. And that dark line right there, that's Wasp Canyon."

Claire studied the map. Maybe it was the wine or lack of food—or a combination of the two—but she was actually starting to get intrigued to find out where Jessica was going with all this. She could see the mountains outlined on the map, lighter in color in areas of higher altitude and darker at lower elevations. There was a dark crevice cut into the Santa Catalina range that came out right where Jessica's finger was.

Jessica followed the dark crevice of Wasp Canyon with her finger. It went on until she came to the edge of the page where the map stopped. Claire looked up at Jessica. "Well, where does it go?"

"From what I can tell it goes all the way through the mountain range. I looked at a broader map, and it winds through the mountains instead of just cutting straight through. And as you can see, it appears to go through various mountain ranges. Where one range stops, the canyon picks up at the start of the next one. It must have formed way back when the mountains formed, I guess. And it looks like it goes clear into Mexico. At least I'm pretty sure it does."

Claire felt a few hairs on the back of her neck prickle. Her mind went to the crude drawings of the chupacabra from the eyewitness accounts—its heavy build and lips pulled back into a menacing snarl. The weird protruding spines on its back, or maybe just an elongated spinal column if Jess is right...

Stop it, Claire. You can't let yourself get sucked into this. Even so, she felt knots tightening in her stomach. She decided to blame it on too much wine. She didn't like the prospect that there could be something else making her stomach churn and the hairs on the back of her neck stand on end.

Claire studied the map, focusing on the mountains on the western side of town. She looked at the neighborhood Jessica had pointed out earlier, and then went up an inch to the mountain range. There was another dark crevice etching its way through the white splotches that represented the mountain peaks. Another canyon, no doubt. The unease in her stomach grew, this time laced with a feeling Claire could no longer deny: fear.

"I'm guessing this is a canyon that goes somewhere into Mexico, too?" Claire asked.

"You got it sister."

Claire let out a long, wine-scented breath. "So what's the prognosis on our little mythical hellhound?"

"It's not a dog, Claire."

"Yeah, I know. Well, whatever the hell it is. Based on your ample research," Claire waved a hand at the papers littered across the table, "what happens next?"

"Well, if it is anything like the first time…" Jessica pulled one final paper from the stack and set it down in front of Claire. "This is a map of Wasp Canyon Estates."

The page was a screenshot from Google Maps. It showed a satellite view of Wasp Canyon Estates starting from the border of the Santa Catalinas and going south to Orion Street, which ran parallel to the mountain range. Wasp Canyon Road was off of Orion Street, heading north and then veering east toward the mountains. A lot of the image was brown with specks of green—an unmistakable desert landscape. White, man-made structures littered the brown and green—the tops of large houses set far apart and away from the road. These were the residences of Wasp Canyon Estates. Sixteen in all, eight on each side of Wasp Canyon Road. The road dead-ended near the base of the Santa Catalinas into what appeared to be a small parking lot.

"So what does this mean for Tucson's elite?" Claire asked.

"Probably the same thing it meant for Tucson's undocumented workers down south," Jessica said. "Right here," she pointed at a dark green area at the base of the mountains, "that's the entrance to Wasp Canyon. The trail works its way through the desert and comes out here," she snaked her finger across an expanse of brown on the map and stopped at the little parking lot.

Claire looked at the green, tree-covered entrance to Wasp Canyon. She couldn't help imagining how pretty it must be in there, with all that green. Tucsonans didn't see a lot of green when it came to the landscape. Mostly it was a lot of brown, beige, and taupe.

Claire followed a beeline from Wasp Canyon to the first white square on the map, the most-northern house in Wasp Canyon Estates. And by the looks of it, it was definitely the biggest one, too. From there, the white squares became closer and closer together, although there was still a substantial distance between each one. She followed along, heading south house by house, until she reached Orion Street. She quickly glanced at the Tucson map, wondering how far it was from the intersection on Orion Street to where she lived, some four miles away. She hoped Jessica didn't see her check.

"You think it's gonna work its way down, house by house?" Claire asked.

"I don't really know," Jessica said. "I think it will head further and further away from the canyon, growing bolder and more aggressive as it does."

"And it's going to keep going until the rain stops?"

"If it is anything like the attacks in 1987, then yeah. Maybe the canyons become uninhabitable when it rains this much. Or the normal things it feeds on don't go into the canyons during a big rainy season. So then it has to venture out for food. Humans are pretty easy prey, after all."

Claire and Jessica sat in the kitchen, drinking their wine in silence. Claire had one more question to ask, and it was the one she was dreading most of all. She set down her glass. She still wasn't sure if she believed any of this. She liked to think that she didn't, and that she was just placating a friend in need. Her gut told her differently, though. Then again, she never was one for listening to her gut. God, just look at her love life.

"Alright then, final jeopardy question," Claire said. "How do we stop it?"

Jessica laughed, although there was little humor in it. "So far, I've got chase it with a UV light."

"Like the things they use to grow pot?"

"Yeah. You think your ex will let us borrow his?" Jessica grinned.

"Shut it," Claire said. "I didn't know about that until at least a month into the relationship."

"Didn't stop you from dating him for another two months."

Claire laughed. She looked at Jessica across the table, her best friend forever since middle school. Recently, she had been to hell and back, and apparently she had brought a hellbeast back with her. Claire doubted it was true—hoped it wasn't true—but she knew Jessica was going to see this thing through whether she helped her or not. Claire supposed it would be better if she was there, if only to comfort Jessica when it turns out to be nothing but a pissed off cougar after all. Andrea had asked Claire to look out for Jessica, and going along with all this seemed like the best way to do that for now. She doubted Andrea would agree, but oh well.

"Okay, I'm in," Claire said, then added: "And I'm also drunk."

CHAPTER 35

Carl Moser leaned against the hood of his car, wishing badly for a smoke even though he had quit fourteen years ago. His police cruiser was one of many parked in the large, circular driveway of 1639 North Wasp Canyon Road. There was also a fire truck, an ambulance, a coroner's van, and one goddamn news helicopter that had just materialized overhead. He expected quite a few news vehicles were already at the gated entrance to the Cuthbertson residence back on Wasp Canyon Road, but thankfully the long driveway that led from the road to the house kept them a blissful half-mile away. *Can't do anything about the damn chopper, though,* he thought. *I sure as hell hope they got the body covered up by now.*

Moser patted the perspiration from his brow with a handkerchief he drudged up from his pocket. *Hotter than Satan's asshole out here,* he thought. The summer sun beat down on his shoulders, and the humidity felt like a suffocating hug. *Fucking monsoons. I moved here to get away from the damn humidity. It feels like Florida out here.*

The officer that answered the call to check on the Cuthbertson woman was a rookie. Good lad, happy to be on board and eager to please. *Jimmy Contrell, that's his name.* Ol' Jimmy had answered the call that morning to check on an elderly woman that hadn't shown for some doctor appointment. Easy gig really. Drive up to the mega mansions, ring the doorbell, make sure the old woman hadn't broken a hip. Call the paramedics if she *had* broken a hip. The end. Bada bing bada boom.

Instead, poor ol' Jimmy stumbled into a goddamn slasher movie. One of the ones that care more about gore than plot line or acting skills. When he got no answer at the front door, Jimmy went around to the back of the house to try the patio door. That's where he found the old broad, spread out in the sun and torn up like a dog's chew toy. Poor woman was in her bathrobe, her blood-splattered slippers found in a bush on the other side of the patio.

Jimmy hadn't taken it all too well. He was practically blubbering when he called in for backup. And now he was just sitting in one of the cruisers and staring straight ahead, sweat standing out on his forehead and dripping down his cheeks. At least as far as Moser was concerned it was sweat that was running down his cheeks—not tears—and no one would ever convince him to say otherwise.

Moser surveyed the driveway, filled with cars and people in uniform. It seemed like the whole damn department had come out. Men walked to and from their vehicles in hushed silence, no one wanting to talk about what had been discovered by poor Jimmy Contrell. In fact, the only real noise was from the motor of that damn news chopper overhead.

Fucking vultures have no respect for the dead, he thought as he looked up at the helicopter. "Channel 8 News Now" was printed on the side. Moser suspected they were broadcasting live on all the local stations. *Christ almighty.*

The forensics team was still looking for signs of foul play inside, but so far it sounded like it was a bust. The theory still went that the woman went outside for whatever reason and was attacked by an animal on the back patio. Moser planned to go have a look at the scene as soon as the medical examiner finished up, but really he just wanted to put off seeing the body for as long as possible. From the look of Jimmy Contrell—sitting in the cruiser with that blank stare—Moser didn't want to see what was done to the old widow. He'd have to go over the crime scene photos of course, and read the autopsy results, but he saw no reason why he had to see the body roasting in the midday sun. God, the smell alone must be enough to set you off your lunch. However, he was the lead detective, and he was acutely aware of how bad it would be perceived if he didn't go take a look at the scene.

Moser already had enough weighing on him as it was. The results of the hair analysis had come in, and the hairs found on Jasper's body were not what he had been expecting. His sick-bear theory had lost ground with those results. Had been all but obliterated, actually.

Sarah Gregors, lab tech to the Northwest PD, had called Moser with the results. She informed him that she had performed microscopic comparisons of the hairs to all known local predatory species in southern Arizona, and when the hairs did not match any of the samples, she broadened the search to all known predatory species they had on record. The hairs recovered did not match any of the hair samples in their database. Moser rattled off every carnivore he could think of that might be found in the southern United States, but Gregors dismissed them all. The hair did not match a bear (brown or black), a mountain lion, a bobcat, a coyote, or a wolf. He even mentioned jackals and jaguars, but to no avail. Gregors was adamant that the hair did not come from your garden-variety desert dwellers, or any other carnivorous dwellers known on this green earth.

Moser suggested that a domesticated dog, turned feral, could have potentially done the damage. That got another refusal from Gregors. "I'm sorry, Detective, but I'm telling you it did not match *any known animals* currently in our database."

"Well, what *can* you tell me then?" he asked Gregors, exasperated.

"Not a whole lot, Detective Moser," Gregors said. "We found some similarities in the hair's cuticle and cortex consistent with *Ursus americanus*—that's the North American black bear—and *Canis lupus baileyi*, the Mexican gray wolf."

"Then that must be it!" he exclaimed.

"No sir, I did not say they were a match. I said there were a few similarities to the black bear and Mexican gray wolf, but they are not a match. The medulla is completely different. I've never seen anything like it. This hair sample did not come from either of these animals."

"Then what in God's name did it come from?" Moser asked, his voice rising.

"I'm very sorry, Detective Moser, but we cannot confirm the animal involved based on these samples. The results are inconclusive."

"So you're telling me Sasquatch could have done this?"

"We do not have a Sasquatch hair sample to compare it to," she said, unphased. "The only expert opinion we can offer is that these hairs did not come from the typical predators found in the Sonoran Desert. What they did come from is currently unknown, since we do not have any samples in our database that match the cortex, cuticle, and medulla of the hairs in question."

Moser thanked her and hung up. *Some expert,* he thought bitterly. He reached for his breast pocket to grab his pack of smokes, only to find the pocket empty. Fourteen years and he still reached for his smokes whenever he got bad news.

The medical examiner emerged from behind the white stucco wall on the north side of the house. Moser pushed himself off the hood of his cruiser and headed over to meet him.

"Whatcha got?" Moser asked.

"Geriatric female. Based on the state of decomposition I would estimate she died the night before last, somewhere between the hours of 8:00 p.m. and 4:00 a.m."

Moser nodded. "And the cause of death?"

"Take your pick. She sustained extensive internal and external injuries. Multiple lacerations, removal of the scalp and jaw, removal of some of the internal organs, and the separation of the pelvis from the spinal column."

"The what?"

"The lumbar spine was removed from the sacrum. That's the tailbone. In layman's terms, she was basically severed in half at the waist."

"Jesus H. Christ," Moser mumbled. "And what could have done something like that?"

"Hard to say exactly. I would put my money on a large predatory mammal. Perhaps a bear or a puma. The injuries are pretty extensive." He paused. "There is one oddity though."

"And what's that?"

"If it was a predatory mammal, it seems peculiar that so little of the body was consumed. Or that the body wasn't removed from the site altogether, to be consumed elsewhere at another time."

"Yup, pretty peculiar alright." Moser thanked him and made his way around the side of the house. The men working in the backyard were going around the side of the house instead of through it, so as to not disturb any evidence that might be inside. Moser had a sinking suspicion the forensic crew wasn't going to find anything inside the house anyway— might as well just walk right through the damn thing. At least there would be some air conditioning in there. He wiped the back of his neck. The collar of his shirt was damp with sweat.

Moser walked through the gated entryway and into the backyard. The gate was ajar so men could come and go, but

Jimmy had insisted it was closed when he originally went around to the backyard to check the patio door.

Men were coming Moser's way, wheeling a stretcher with a black bag on top.

"Why didn't you wait for me?" Moser grumbled, trying to feign anger. Secretly, he was relieved he wouldn't have to see the poor woman sprawled across the blood-smeared patio.

The men wheeling the stretcher stopped and looked at him with wide eyes. "Well... the news chopper..." one of them stammered, pointing upward. "We thought... we didn't want them taking pictures of the body and broadcasting it on the five o'clock news. Forensics, the crime scene photographer, and the M.E. were all done so we thought... we weren't sure if you were even coming back so we decided to—"

"Okay, okay," Moser said, cutting him off. He wanted the frightened man with the stretcher to stop yammering. *Fucking animal attacks.* He looked up at the news chopper hovering overhead. "Good work. Get going." He gestured to the open gate with his chin.

Moser stepped aside and pressed himself against the wall of the house so the men could pass by. There was a small shadow there, and it felt blissfully cool compared to the sweltering sunlight. The two men trudged past him with the remains of Ava Cuthbertson. Moser diverted his eyes. He felt like such a goon, getting his knickers in a twist over a dead body. *Why did it have to be animal attacks?* he thought. *Anything but animal attacks. Damn nasty, violent deaths. That poor broad didn't deserve to go out this way. A serial killer would be better than this.* After a moment of consideration, he decided it might be a serial killer after all—just not a human one. First Jasper, now Cuthbertson. Who's next?

God, why couldn't I have stumbled across a Bundy or a Dahmer? Still sick bastards to be sure, but at least they were human. Who the hell knows what is causing all this? Not even Gregors could figure that out.

Moser surveyed the backyard. There were still half a dozen men finishing up with the scene. A couple from forensics and four officers from his department. He approached one of the forensic men, almost tripping over a toppled planter in the process. "Son of a whore, who knocked this thing over?" he asked no one in particular.

One of the officers perked up. "It was knocked over when we got here, Detective. Same with the one over by the body." He pointed toward the patio. A tarp had been placed over the majority of the blood-stained flagstones. At least the news chopper couldn't broadcast aerial shots of the bloody aftermath.

Moser took a look around the rest of the backyard. It was well-kept, all the bushes neatly trimmed and the potted plants blooming beautifully. Except for the two pots that had been knocked over. Large pots, too—especially the one next to the tarp. That one looked like it would take two men, possibly three, to topple it over. Yet there it was, lying on its side with a crack going down the middle.

"You sure none of the guys knocked that one over when they were taking out the body?" Moser asked, looking at the large pot near the tarp.

"No sir, it was on its side when we arrived. Whatcha think could have done something like that? That thing looks like it would be hell to push over."

"Can't say," Moser said. He didn't feel like shooting the shit with this young kid anymore. Since when did his whole crew get so young? Or is it that he got so old? "Why don't you guys head out, Officer..." Moser looked down at the kid's badge, his name having slipped his mind.

The kid saw him looking and said, "Wesley. Ken Wesley."

"Thank you, Officer Wesley. That will be all for now."

Wesley started making his way to the gate with the other officers. Moser called after him. "The men inside finish up?"

Wesley turned around and glanced at the wall of windows facing the back patio. "Yeah, they're all done in there. Couldn't find anything that looked out of place." He pointed at the windows. "They're not sure what to do about that, though."

Moser pivoted on his heels and squinted at the sliding glass door. Down near the floor, a white cat was watching him. He could see the cat's mouth opening and closing. He knew it was meowing even though he couldn't hear it from where he was standing. "How about one of you guys call the local animal shelter? See if they can take it in. It'll end up starving in there otherwise."

"I'm on it," Wesley said. He walked around the side of the house and disappeared.

The two men from forensics were also headed toward the gate. "You find anything?" Moser asked them as they passed by.

"Nothing much," one of the men answered. "Just a few hairs on the body. Looks like they belong to some kind of animal. We're sending them to lab."

"Any chance they coulda come from that thing?" Moser gestured toward the white cat in the window.

"Highly unlikely. Cats have fine fur, and that one is completely white. These hairs were coarse and dark gray, almost black." The forensic men began walking again. One of them paused and looked back at Moser, who was standing alone on the patio next to the carefully positioned tarp. "You thinking a black bear?" he asked.

Moser sighed. "I was."

The man waited a moment to see if Moser would say more, and when he didn't, he turned and headed through the gate with his team member.

Moser listened to the sound of their boots on the gravel until it faded away. He glanced at the red smears around the edges of the tarp, and then at the toppled planter with the dirt spilled out. There were boot imprints in the spilled soil, and crushed white flowers pressed into the dirt.

He looked up at the mountains, not wanting to stare at the red any longer. He could see Wasp Canyon from where he was standing—a dark, shaded crevice between two towering peaks. He felt a chill go up his spine despite the heat of the day. He wouldn't go back into that canyon for all the tea in China, not after discovering the remains of Cameron Jasper between its walls.

And now Cuthbertson. Two of Tucson's wealthiest residents, killed brutally in the span of a week. Forget local news, this was going to be the top story on NBC.

Moser strolled up to the patio door. He could see a great expanse of kitchen on the other side of the glass. He looked down at the white cat that was sitting on the floor on the other side of the window. It looked up at him with large, green eyes.

Moser squatted down to see the cat better, grunting with the effort. The cat got on its hind legs and pressed its front paws against the window. He could hear meowing faintly through the glass.

"How about you? Did you see anything?" he asked. The cat meowed in response. Moser pivoted to look at the tarp and the red smears below, his boots grinding on the flagstone. Perfect view of the patio and the crime scene. He looked back at the cat and mumbled to himself, "If only cats could talk."

CHAPTER 36

When Moser arrived back at the station, the officer running the front desk informed him he had a couple of visitors.

"Who?" he asked. "I wasn't expecting anyone."

"Two girls. One of 'em said she's talked with you before. She wouldn't say what it was about; just that she'd wait until you got back. They've been here almost two hours now."

"Okay, thanks Cal." Moser left the front desk and headed out to the lobby.

A lanky, blonde girl was sitting in one of the plastic, maroon-going-on-brown lobby chairs. She had a large, black medical boot on her left leg. Another girl, shorter and with dark hair, sat beside her.

"Hello, I'm Detective Moser."

The blonde looked up. Moser could see cuts and abrasions covering her arms and face. She was holding a stack of papers on her lap. She stood up with some effort. The brunette jumped up and held the blonde's arm to help steady her.

"Detective Moser," the blonde said, "I'm Jessica Cleary. We spoke on the phone."

"Yes, of course." Moser remembered her now. She was the Wasp Canyon victim that escaped. Looks like she got pretty banged up in the process. He turned to the brunette. "And you are?"

"Tonto. Robin. Samwise…"

"The sidekick, I get it," he said. "And your actual name?"

"Claire Barnett."

Moser looked from Claire to Jessica. "Well ladies, what can I do for you? I'm having one hell of a day."

"Yeah," Jessica said, taking a step forward, "it's all over the news. That's why I thought I should come in. I have some information about the attacks. I would really like to go over some of the stuff—"

"Not here," Moser interrupted. "Let's go somewhere private." He glanced around the lobby. With such a high profile case, he wouldn't put it past anyone to leak some intel to the press for a few extra bucks. "Can you walk with that thing?" He pointed to Jessica's boot.

She looked down. "Yeah, I can. Kinda clumsy, but it works."

"Okay then, follow me."

Moser led the two women to one of the interview rooms. Jessica went in, but Claire lingered in the doorway. "An interrogation room?" she asked. "Some people go in these rooms and then never get to walk out again. Not without handcuffs on."

Moser looked at Claire and smiled. "You do anything that would warrant handcuffs?"

"I stole a lipstick when I was thirteen."

"I think we'll let that one slide." Moser gestured to the table in the center of the room. "Let's head on in."

Claire went into the room and sat down. He heard her whisper to Jessica, "It looks just like it does in the movies."

Moser shut the door and sat down across from them. "Okay Jessica, let's talk."

Jessica set the stack of papers down on the desk. She fanned some of them out into various piles. It appeared she had them in some sort of order. One page had a picture of some sort of strange animal on it. Claire looked away from the picture and started squinting at the mirror behind him. *She's trying to look through the mirror,* he thought with some amusement.

"Okay, here's what I found out," Jessica said. She went over the various papers, showing Moser different stacks as she talked. He saw a map of Tucson, a map of Wasp Canyon Estates, a bunch of articles from back in the eighties, and then, to his growing dismay, a collection of pictures and eyewitness accounts of some sort of goat-sucking demon creature. *Christ, did she hit her head out there, too?*

Moser looked at Jessica. She didn't look like she was off her rocker, but all this urban legend shit certainly suggested that she was. He looked at Claire, who was now picking at her fingernails and ignoring the pictures on the table.

"Okay Jessica, this is quite a bit of information," Moser said. "I want to thank you for bringing it to our attention."

Concussion maybe? he thought. *I wonder if they did any head scans while she was at the hospital.*

"Would you like to make copies of some of these pages? I don't mind waiting," Jessica said.

"That won't be necessary," Moser said as he stood up. "We have plenty of information to go on in our computer system. I'm sure there are details about all the 1978 attacks in there."

"1987," she corrected, her eyebrows dropping. She looked hurt as she gathered up her papers and stood from the table.

Moser felt a gnawing guilt in his chest as he watched her. Poor girl went through all that, and now she's concocted some sort of creature feature to help her cope with what happened. He looked at Claire, who was watching him with one eyebrow raised. Moser shrugged helplessly. Claire looked away and grabbed the last few papers on the table. She handed them to Jessica.

"Thank you for your time, ladies," Moser said. He opened the door and held an arm up to show them out.

Jessica gave him one more wounded look and then limped through the doorway with her slightly crumpled stack of papers. Claire followed, not making eye contact with Moser.

Once in the hallway, Moser heard a bizarre yowling sound. *What in God's name is that?* The yowling drifted down the hall, and it was getting louder.

Wesley appeared, holding a pet carrier. The sound was coming from inside the carrier.

"Wesley, what the hell—"

"It's the Cuthbertson cat," he said. "She had a pet carrier in the house. Instead of having the shelter people drive all the way out to Wasp Canyon with all those reporters around, we're having them meet us here."

"Good thinking," Moser said. "You can take it to—"

"What cat?" Jessica asked, standing in the hallway next to Moser.

He looked over at her and Claire, having momentarily forgotten they were there. Moser sighed. "The Wasp Canyon victim had a cat," he said. "She has no next of kin, so we are getting the cat taken to a shelter. It can't survi—"

"I'll take it," Jessica said.

Claire gaped at her. "You're adopting the dead woman's cat?"

"If I can save even one living thing during this mess, I'm doing it," she said. "Besides, I've always wanted a cat."

CHAPTER 37

Andrea Cleary sat with her hands tightly clasped on the kitchen table. Jessica and Claire sat on the opposite side. A bag of Meow Mix cat food was on the table between them.

"Where's... the cat?" Andrea asked.

"He's in my room," Jessica said, "hiding under the bed."

"What kind of a name is Sushi?"

"It's Tofu. It was written on the top of his carrier."

"Oh Jessica, I don't know. You come home with this cat—apparently the pet of a *murder victim*? And then I find out you spent the afternoon at a police station." Andrea shook her head. "I don't understand. You tell this... outrageous story about a... *chupacabra*? I just—I don't know what to say."

Jessica and Claire didn't respond. They stared at the bag of cat food with blank expressions. *Meaty Morsels Your Cat Will Love!* the bag claimed.

"Is it because of your father?" Andrea asked.

Jessica looked up from the Meow Mix. "What is that supposed to mean?"

"This—this insanity. Is it because of your father? Because of what happened to him?" Andrea watched Jessica with concern.

Jessica looked at her mother and was startled to see how much she had aged in the past year. Andrea's wrinkles had deepened, and dark circles had formed under her green eyes. Andrea had always appeared younger than she was, but now she looked her age. Older even. Jessica felt a pang of guilt. Was some of this because of her?

"Why would this have anything to do with Dad?" she asked.

"God, I don't know, Jessica. You were doing so much better. And now—I don't know. You're talking about made-up monsters." Andrea glanced at Claire, who was still staring at the bag of cat food.

"I am not making this up, Mom," Jessica said. "I got attacked and nearly killed a week ago. And I know what I saw. The police are wrong. There is something very dangerous in Wasp Canyon, and more people are going to die if someone doesn't stop it."

"You think some sort of Mexican hell monster is attacking people! Do you have any idea how ridiculous that sounds?" Andrea exclaimed. "All this time—all this effort—trying to move on. And it's all been washed away by this one week of… awfulness." Andrea dabbed at her eyes, smudging her concealer and revealing darkened skin underneath.

Washed away? Jessica thought. She started thinking about flash floods, the walls of water tumbling through the washes and surging across roads. Cars trying to drive through the raging waters often got carried away. "All my progress hasn't been... washed away," she said curtly.

"That's how I feel right now," Andrea said. "All this work trying to heal and move on, and it's all... *ruined*."

"I'm really sorry you feel that way," Jessica said in a low voice. "It's not my fault I got attacked, though. And I'm just trying to stop more people from getting killed. There really is something out there."

"Yes, a sick wolf. Not a blood-drinking hell monster."

"It's a chupacabra!"

Claire laughed. Andrea and Jessica turned to her, startled into silence.

"Claire?" Jessica asked. "You okay?"

Claire tried to stifle her laughter, but instead fell into another fit of giggles. "No," she said, "I am *not* alright." More laughter. "My best friend's dad died. She went through this horrible depression. She *finally* starts moving on, then gets chased around by some sort of mythical beast." Claire paused, trying to catch her breath through bouts of laughter. "And then somehow we're at a police station taking custody of a dead woman's cat. And now—now we're sitting at the kitchen table discussing the existence of chuppy-wuppies." Claire bent over the table, the laughter having stolen all of her breath. Tears ran down her cheeks.

Jessica and Andrea looked at her with concern.

"Sorry, I don't handle conflict all that well," she said, her laughter finally trailing off.

"They do exist," Jessica said.

"Jessica—" Andrea started.

"Don't," Claire said. "Please don't start arguing on my account." She turned to Jessica. "You have to get this figured out with your mom, Van Helsing. After all, we can't fight the vampires until you get your permission slip signed." Claire fell into a new fit of giggles.

Jessica and Andrea reluctantly turned their attention away from Claire. "This is happening because it is almost the anniversary," Andrea said. "In three weeks it will be the anniversary of your father's death. I should have known this would set you back."

"Something didn't try to kill me in the desert because Dad died a year ago," Jessica snapped.

"It was a *sick wolf.* The police even said so."

"Then why can't they find it? If it was so sick it would be dead by now."

"Not if it got antibiotics," Claire chimed in.

Jessica and Andrea looked at her briefly, then back at each other.

"You need to go see Dr. Wyatt. I know your last appointment didn't go well. That's why I asked for Claire's help."

"You did what?" Jessica looked from her mother to Claire.

"It's true," Claire said. "She did ask for my help. But then Mr. Merlot told me that the best way to help you would be to go along with this whole damn thing. I didn't think it would land me in a police station taking custody of Soybean the cat, though."

"Tofu," Jessica corrected her.

"Right," Claire said. *"Tofu."*

Andrea sighed heavily. "I really don't know what to do at this point. You need to go see Dr. Wyatt. Maybe she can talk some sense into you."

"I don't want to see her anymore. She doesn't believe me."

"If the police and your therapist have both come to a rational explanation, why do you refuse to accept that's what happened?"

"Because they didn't see what I saw."

"Okay," Andrea said, defeated. "I guess we will have to agree to disagree for now."

"Yeah, I guess so." Jessica looked down at the Meow Mix. "Do I get to keep the cat?"

"I think Tofu has been through enough trauma for one lifetime. He is welcome to stay. But you are in charge of taking care of him."

The sound of digging drifted out from the bedroom. Jessica, Andrea, and Claire turned and looked down the hallway. Tofu was using the litter box.

CHAPTER 38

Tucson Daily Tribune
Another Slain in Tucson's Wasp Canyon Estates

By Audrey Summers
August 9, 2018

The police are baffled following the death of another one of Tucson's elite in the Wasp Canyon Estates community. Ava Cuthbertson, age seventy-two, was found outside her Wasp Canyon residence yesterday afternoon. The police were led to the home after Cuthbertson failed to arrive for a dental appointment that she had confirmed the day before.

The Northwest Police Department sent an officer to the Cuthbertson residence for a welfare check, which was when Cuthbertson's body was discovered. Detective Carl Moser declined to comment when asked for details regarding Cuthbertson's condition or possible leads in the case. From what the *Tucson Daily Tribune* has gathered, Cuthbertson was brutally attacked in the backyard of her estate. She had already succumbed to her injuries by the time officers arrived at the residence. It is suspected that an animal was involved in the attack.

Just six days ago, Cameron Jasper, also of Wasp Canyon Estates, was attacked and killed by what police believe to be a wild animal. Jasper was found on the Wasp Canyon hiking trail located near his residence. Both Jasper and Cuthbertson were horribly mauled and it is believed that both died during their attacks. It is suspected that the same animal is responsible. The police do not have any leads as to the type of animal involved or its current whereabouts. Based on the locations of the two victims, it is suspected that the animal resides somewhere along the base of the Santa Catalina mountain range.

Other residents of Wasp Canyon Estates are on edge, demanding the police find the perpetrating animal and destroy it before more people are attacked. Jerry McElroy, software engineer and resident of Wasp Canyon Estates, said, "I don't see how the police have zero leads on this thing. Two of our community members are now dead, and the police aren't doing anything about it. I have my kids to worry about, and my wife is terrified to even set foot outside the front door. This situation needs to be taken care of now."

Ava Cuthbertson, originally of New York City, moved to Arizona in 1989...

CHAPTER 39

Jessica set the newspaper down on the bed, making sure the aerial shot of the backyard was face down. She didn't want to look at the tarp stretched over the smears of red anymore. Claire was sitting on the floor, dangling a string at the foot of the bed. Tofu was somewhere underneath, and it appeared the string was not going to be enough to lure him out. Jessica excused herself and headed across the hall to the bathroom for a much-needed shower.

Fifteen minutes later, she sat on the floor of the shower, her legs stretched out in front of her and her left foot carefully positioned on the tub's porcelain. The sound of the running water was soothing—a white noise that seemed to envelope her and make her feel safe. The steady hum drowned out all other sounds in the house. She could no longer hear her mother moving plates around in the kitchen, and could no longer hear Claire cooing to Tofu to come out from under the bed. It was just her now, safe and warm in the confines of the shower. *Like a womb,* she thought. *Or a coffin.*

Jessica sat under the hot cascade of water, steam hovering in the air above her. She stared at the ruins of her left foot, transfixed by the colorful, lumpy mess that used to be smooth, unblemished flesh. The skin around the ankle was discolored and patchy. The bruising was now a swirling maroon, and it appeared to be on its way toward a sickly yellow. The three broken toes still held on to the black and blue color scheme that her ankle had been originally. She thought the smashed toes looked like little charred sausages. The toenails on all three were black. The doctor told her the nails would most likely fall off, and she suspected they were now well on their way. She tried to wiggle the toes, winced, and stopped.

Her ankle throbbed dully. Without the compression from the boot, her ankle and foot were already beginning to swell again. The pain was slowly decreasing overall, although a lot of that seemed to be due to the boot. It offered a great deal of support to her ankle, and it definitely kept the swelling down. She wondered if she would have to wear it forever—unless she agreed to surgery, that is. The prospect of surgery was becoming less and less desirable, not that the idea had ever been appealing. But now she had so much work to do, especially if the police didn't get on board. She couldn't afford to be laid up in some hospital bed attached to a bunch of tubes while the chupacabra wreaked havoc across northwest Tucson. Who knows how far it would make it before the rains stopped?

Her follow-up appointment with Dr. What's-His-Name was next week, and she was already dreading the day. He told her she might be able to avoid surgery as long as she wore the boot religiously, which she had. But as she sat in the shower and stared at the damage below her left calf, she wasn't so sure it would be enough. *It looks like monsoon clouds during a sunset,* she thought. She didn't want to look at it anymore. She wanted to put the boot back on—not just because her ankle ached less with it on, but because she wanted to conceal the mess that was her left foot. A mess that was caused by some unthinkable evil that was stalking the desert landscape only five miles from where she now sat.

At least she was alive. And she could walk. *You know who never gets to walk again? That woman under the tarp.* She couldn't help but feel a connection to the Wasp Canyon victims. After all, she would have been one of them if she hadn't managed to make it out of that canyon.

Jessica turned the water off, grabbed the towel that she had left within reach on top of the toilet, and dried off. She took extra care while reattaching the boot, making sure to correctly fasten and inflate it until her ankle sat snuggly within its depths.

Back in her room, Claire was sitting on the bed with her knees pulled up to her chest. Tofu was nowhere in sight, presumably still under the bed. The *Tucson Daily Tribune* was lying face down on top of the flowery bedspread. A beam of golden sunlight splashed across the newspaper, making it look like it was part of a display in a department store window.

Jessica gestured toward the newspaper with her chin. "Does it say anything we don't already know?"

"Nope," Claire said. "Just that people in Wasp Canyon are scared. Some guy's wife is afraid to go outside."

"Yeah, I heard him talking on the news earlier." Jessica dropped onto her hands and knees. Sunlight had spread across the bedroom floor, and the warmth of the carpet felt good against her healing palms. She lowered herself to her belly and turned her head so she could peer under the bed.

"Come on, Tofu. We're not going to hurt you," she cooed. She made a few kissing noises, but to no avail. Other than litter box trips, Tofu had refused to leave his hiding spot under the bed. Jessica started placing the food and water bowls underneath to make sure he would at least eat something. Which he did. Scared or not, Tofu certainly did have an appetite. Jessica took that as a good sign.

She pushed herself up from the floor, keeping her left foot hovering in midair so she wouldn't put any pressure on her charred-sausage toes. She sat down in the warm, sunny patch on the floor and crossed her right leg. The left leg she kept out in front of her, the CAM boot big and black against the cream-colored carpet. "Any luck with our new guest?"

Claire shrugged. "He made a trip to the litter box while you were in there. Did an admirable job of covering up his business. Then he went back under the bed." Claire smiled a little. "He really is more fur than cat. I've never seen one so fluffy. What do you think he is?"

Jessica leaned forward and peaked under the bed again. Tofu stared at her, his green eyes twinkling. "Persian, I think," she said, sitting back up. "I hope he ends up liking me."

"You did good," Claire said. "Taking him in, I mean. That poor thing would have been just terrified in some noisy shelter, wondering why his mama left him there." Her voice sounded sad. She offered Jessica a weak smile.

"He's going to be alright. We're gonna take good care of him." Jessica said, studying Claire. "Are *you* okay?"

"I'm—" Claire paused. She looked like she was trying to find the right word. When she couldn't, she said, "Fine. I'm fine."

Jessica brushed a few wet strands of hair from her face. "I'm wondering if I put too much pressure on you. Or asked too much of you or something. Telling you all that, and then making you go to the police station." She let out a long sigh. "Maybe I shouldn't have brought you into all of this in the first place."

"I said I was going to help."

"I know, but I kind of feel like I forced you into it."

"What happened to you in that canyon was awful. No one can deny that. But do you really think..." Claire trailed off and looked out the window. The sky was pale blue, not one cloud blemishing its expanse. The clouds would come later, though. This summer they always did.

"Think what, Claire?" Jessica asked, leaning to the side to regain her friend's attention.

Claire turned and faced her, her expression grave. "Can you just hear me out with what I'm about to say? Please just listen, and think about it before you answer?" She looked at Jessica, a deep line of worry stretched across her brow.

"Um, okay. Yeah, I can do that." Jessica said. The surgical glue holding the cut together on her right shoulder shimmered in the morning sunlight.

"When your dad died there was nothing you could do. I mean, you were there for him of course. Took care of him, held his hand. But you couldn't stop what was happening to him, no matter how much you wanted to. You couldn't fight the cancer, or stop it. It was this *enemy* that you had no control over. Now, literally almost a year since he died, you have stumbled across this monster—this killer thing that you *can fight*. Do you think…" Claire let out a shaky breath. "Do you think that you are wanting to vanquish *this* demon so badly because you couldn't vanquish the one that got your dad? That the reason you are so hell bent on stopping this thing is because you weren't able to stop the thing that killed your dad?"

They sat in silence, Claire on the edge of the bed and Jessica on the floor. They looked out the window at the cloudless sky, listening to the hum of the air conditioner.

Jessica's voice finally cut through the silence. "I couldn't save my dad. I couldn't stop what was killing him. And I know that it wasn't my fault. But Claire," Jessica leaned forward and took Claire's hand, "this thing is *real*. I did not make it up, and I did not imagine it. This thing is out there, and it already killed two people. And I know, deep down in my gut, that it is going to kill more. What about that family out there, the one from the news? They have kids. What if it goes after them next?"

Claire looked at Jessica. She was still holding Claire's hand, waiting. Claire looked at the laceration on Jessica's arm, the yellowing bruises, the black, clunky boot. "Alright," she said. "I believe you. And I'm going to help you." Jessica squeezed her hand, and Claire squeezed back. An uneasy silence filled the room, out of place in the brilliant morning light.

Jessica returned to her reclined position on the floor. "Wow, Claire. Turning this monster into a metaphor for trying to save my dad? Who needs Dr. Wyatt when I have you?"

"That's Dr. Claire to you," she said, the creases on her brow finally softening as she smiled. "So how in the name of God are we going to stop this thing? There's only two of us, and one of us is all busted up already." Claire pointed at the boot.

"That part I don't know. But I do know that we need to hurry."

Tofu emerged from under the bed. He took a few hesitant steps forward, then stuck out his nose to smell Jessica's hand. She let him sniff at her fingers, her hand hovering tentatively in the air. When he didn't shy away, she reached out and stroked the top of his head. Tofu made no move to run, just continued to watch her with his brilliant green eyes.

The smile that spread across Jessica's face was the largest Claire had seen on her friend in well over a year.

CHAPTER 40

Dispatch received the call at 8:52 on the evening of August twelfth. The computer traced the origin of the call to 1637 North Wasp Canyon Road. The caller was an adult male, and there was obvious agitation in his voice.

"Sir, what is the nature of your emergency?" the dispatcher asked.

"There's someone—" the man paused, sounding distracted. "There's someone in my backyard. They're—they're knocking things over." The man spoke in a harsh whisper.

"Are you in a safe location?"

"The doors are locked if that's what you mean," the man said.

"Can you see who is outside your residence, sir?" asked the dispatcher.

"No, it's too dark. Shit—" he cut off. Silence at the end of the line. And then: "They just did it again."

"What did they do, sir? Is there more than one person outside?"

"Hell if I know. I can't see jack shit out there. I don't even know if it is a person. You heard about those attacks   " He stopped again. "Sorry, thought I heard something. Anyway, those animal attacks happened in my neighborhood. You need to send someone right now."

"Yes, I will send a patrol car right away." The sound of a keyboard as the dispatcher sent out a request for a patrol unit. "What is your name, sir?"

"Desmond Arlington. I live at 1637 North Wasp Canyon Road. Are you sending someone?"

"Yes, Mr. Arlington, the police will be there shortly. Are you sure all of the doors and windows are locked in your home?" the dispatcher asked.

"Yes," he whispered. "I live alone. I always keep my doors locked."

"Very good, Mr. Arlington. Can you tell where the noises are originating from?"

Silence as Arlington listened. "It was coming from the backyard, near the pool. I don't hear anything now."

More typing. "And what noises did you hear?"

"Some banging around. Then some clunking noises, like furniture falling over. Now there's nothing."

"Has anyone tried to gain access to the residence?"

"No, just banging around. Do you think it is some sort of prank?"

"I cannot determine that, Mr. Arlington. It would be best for you to remain indoors right now." More typing. "Is there a reason you think someone would want to play a prank on you? Has that happened before?"

"Yes, by a few kids in the neighborhood. But I doubt their parents would let them out with what's been going—shit! I heard it again. Just now. I think my whole goddamn patio table just got knocked over."

"Are you still unable to see who's causing it?"

"I suppose kids could be doing it," Arlington said to himself. "They once threw rocks in my pool..." he trailed off.

"Mr. Arlington, I would like to advise you again to stay indoors and wait for our officers to arrive and secure the scene," the dispatcher said.

"Damn kids, always picking on an old man like me. I bet they're throwing more rocks in my pool right this very minute." Arlington now sounded more irritated than afraid. "I told that McElroy to keep his children off my property." There was the sound of footsteps as Arlington walked through the house.

"Mr. Arlington, please remain indoors."

There was a clicking sound, and then the sound of a door sliding on its track. "Hey you! Whatever you kids are doing you better stop it right now!" Arlington shouted. His voice was further away, the phone no longer up to his ear.

"Mr. Arlington, please go back inside your—"

There was a clattering noise as something was knocked over. Arlington began to yell, "Jesu—" but the word was cut off.

"Mr. Arlington? Mr. Arlington, are you there?" Two words flashed across the dispatcher's computer screen: Connection Lost.

CHAPTER 41

Taylor Kilburn heard his radio crackling inside the squad car. He took a bite of his Miguel's burrito and reached through the open window to grab the walkie. Through mouthfuls of carne asada he said, "Kilburn here."

"We have a possible B and E happening in Wasp Canyon Estates. A resident reported a commotion outside his home. Thought it might be some kids playing around. Connection was lost. We have not been able to reconnect."

"Roger that," Kilburn said, trying to keep the excitement out of his voice. All that shit going on up in Wasp Canyon and he's been pulling patrol duty day in and day out. This might be his ticket into the big time. It would at least get him into Wasp Canyon Estates. If he gets a rapport going with this rich bastard and scares away the little prank-causing kiddies, maybe they'll let him in on the Cuthbertson case. Maybe this old geezer even knew Cuthbertson, or heard something funny that night. This could be his ticket right into the big time— damn straight.

Kilburn got into the driver's seat of his cruiser. "Address?" He listened, then punched the address into his console screen. "I'm on it." He tossed the walkie back on the passenger seat and finished off his burrito. A slow night had just gotten a lot more interesting. He tossed the burrito wrapper out the car window. He thought about hitting the lights—he's got urgent business up in Wasp Canyon, after all—but decided against it as he pulled away from Miguel's Taco Shop. The top lights would only attract attention, and he'd be damned to share this with anyone else. This was *his* ticket, and he sure as hell wasn't going to share the glory with any rookies.

The cruiser pulled out onto Orion Street. And what damn good luck that was, too! He was less than ten minutes away from the old geezer's house. The kiddies might even still be there. He could arrest them for trespassing, or at least pretend to. Make those prank-causing little shits cry.

Kilburn imagined the scene as he drove along Orion Street, watching for the turn onto Wasp Canyon Road. The old geezer would thank him over and over, maybe mention that he heard something strange coming from the Cuthbertson house the night she was killed. Kilburn would take his statement and then head straight to Detective Moser's office after the pissed off parents picked up their little brats. Moser would just about *have to* let him on the case then, since he now had valuable information pertaining to the dead widow. *Absolutely perfecto,* he thought, making a left and heading up Wasp Canyon Road.

The cruiser's high beams were the only source of light. There were no street lights on Wasp Canyon Road, and with the houses set so far back, no light from the homes made it to the street. Kilburn dropped his speed to twenty miles per hour. The last thing he wanted to do was smack into a deer or a coyote out here. That would only slow him down, and he had very important places to be. He had connections to make. And he had a ladder to climb. No more fucking traffic tickets, no more sitting around with a damn radar gun while he desperately needed to take a piss.

He saw a light-colored adobe wall coming up; it stood out brilliantly in the light from his high beams. Four elegant, blue tiles were inlaid into the adobe. One-six-three-seven. The Arlington residence. He had arrived. Kilburn turned into the driveway, passing adobe walls on either side. He again debated turning on the top lights, but decided against it. He wanted to take the pranking kiddies by surprise.

The house was set about a half mile from the road. He passed by prickly pear, saguaros, and Texas-ranger bushes as he made his way along the unpaved driveway. The house finally emerged out of the darkness, a two-story adobe monstrosity that had to have cost millions. *A house like that was just begging to get pranked,* he thought. *I wouldn't mind throwing some spray paint on there myself.*

The west-facing side of the house was one solid wall of adobe. There was one door on the far left side, which must be the entrance. Kilburn guessed all the impressive aspects of the house must be facing the other direction, toward the mountains. This guy sure didn't seem like he wanted to cater to any visitors. This side of the house practically screamed *Go away!* To further emphasize this point, Kilburn saw a "No Soliciting" sign on a post near the front door.

There was a separate building just south of the main house. It was also a giant box of adobe, although this one had three garage doors facing the driveway. *Three!* One of the garages was all the way up to the roof of the building, which was two stories tall, just like the main house. *Must be for the world's largest RV,* Kilburn thought. *That or a damn airplane.*

Kilburn felt for his firearm on his right hip and stepped out of the patrol car. He left the headlights shining on the front door. There were no other lights on this side of the house. *Old hermit, might as well just have a sign that says "Fuck Off" instead of "No Soliciting".*

He stopped halfway to the front door and spun around to look at the cruiser. He had forgotten to radio in when he had arrived. *Oh well,* he thought. *I'll save the old man and then call it in.*

Kilburn rapped on the front door and waited. No response. He tried again, and then a third time. "Mr. Arleton, it's the police!" he called through the door. *Wait, that ain't it. Not Arleton—Arlington, that's it.* "Mr. Arlington! We received a call from your residence! This is the Northwest Police Department!"

Still nothing. Kilburn tried the door, and was not surprised to find that it was locked. "Well, shit," he said, stepping back and looking up at the expanse of adobe. He was going to have to go around to the back door. And it was *fucking dark* out here. He reached for the left side of his utility belt and grabbed a long-handled flashlight. He clicked it on and cast the beam of light up the side of the house. Who the hell would make the entire front of their house one big wall? *Crazy, rich bastards— that's who,* he thought.

He started heading for the left side of the house, his hand running along the rough surface of the adobe. His boots scraped noisily on the desert floor. As he disappeared around the side of the house, he was momentarily overwhelmed by just how *dark* it was. Not a damn light to be seen except for his flashlight. When in the hell did he last change out the batteries in this thing? He knew he was supposed to switch them out regularly, but there's a good chance it had slipped his mind. Kilburn continued along the side of the house, cursing when the thorned branch of a mesquite tree hooked into his shirt sleeve and tore at the skin beneath. He smacked it away and continued on, making a mental note of the tree for his return trip. *What return trip?* he thought. *The old man will let me go through the house on my way out.*

Kilburn could now make out a faint glow up ahead. There was light spilling out from the back of the house. Not much, but he was thankful for any at this point. He doubted the light was enough to be coming from a porch light; it was probably coming out from the windows. Just what he had suspected, all the windows and fancy fixing's were on the back of the house and pointed toward the mountains. He traced his hand along the adobe and continued on, wondering why he had decided to do this alone. He had good reasoning at the time, but in the dark, listening to his boots crunch on the ground and feeling his heart rate increase, he couldn't think of what the reason was.

His flashlight picked up a low adobe wall that jutted out at a ninety-degree angle from the side of the house. *It must be the wall of the backyard,* he thought, quickening his pace. He was almost out of the dark. He had forgotten about the kiddies he was going to apprehend, and about how he would make them piss their pants and cry to their mommies about how sorry they were. If he had remembered, he might have found it odd how quiet it was out here. No giggles, no muffled conversations, and no old man yelling at them to knock it off.

Kilburn was getting closer to the low adobe wall. He could easily hop over it and into the backyard. *Why do these rich guys have such low walls if all they want is privacy?* It occurred to him that tall walls would probably block the view of the mountains and the city lights, and wasn't that why these people were out here in the first place? Plus, they probably didn't expect anyone to go shambling around in the desert in the dark to get into their backyards anyway. Probably thought the scorpions and rattlesnakes would keep them away.

Kilburn threw the beam of his flashlight at his feet, looking for snakes or other creepy-crawlies. Nothing there, just dirt and rocks and a few branches. He didn't see kids' footprints either. That didn't surprise him much. The hard caliche didn't hold footprints well, or even allow them to happen in the first place. Although with the amount of rain they'd been having he thought the soil might be at least a little bit softened up by now to allow for some prints. There were none here, though— no child-sized Converse prints from the kids sneaking around to do their pranks. A feeling of unease drifted over him. How else would the kids have gotten back there, other than to go this exact same route he was now taking? He pointed the flashlight back the way he had come. He could vaguely make out his own boot prints, the soil just soft enough from the afternoon's rain to show partial impressions from his journey through the dark. No other prints, though—children or otherwise.

Kilburn contemplated this for a moment, standing in the dark and staring at the traces of his own boot prints. A bit of thunder rumbled off to the east. Something tugged at the edges of his mind—two circuits that needed to be connected to make the thought a conscious one. *Connect circuit A to circuit B to light up connection C. Think think think.*

He had all the parts; he just needed them to connect. Being alone in the dark listening to his shallow breathing wasn't helping. His breathing ceased entirely when *connection C* finally lit up in his mind. *The footprints. The ground is only getting drier following the storm, so whatever came through here would have stepped on damper soil and left footprints much more noticeable than mine.* He cast the beam of the flashlight back and forth on the desert floor. *But there aren't any. No footprints. Not from a kid, not from an adult, and not from an animal. Whatever knocked shit down in the guy's backyard did not come this way. And since this is the only clear way around the house, that meant it did not come from the driveway, the front of the house, or the road. It came from...* his flashlight rose up in the direction of the mountains, which were shrouded in darkness. *It came from out there,* he thought.

Kilburn had a sudden, overwhelming urge to flee. To run blindly along the side of the house, the mesquite tree cutting into his face as he went. He would burst out into the glare of the headlights, dive into the cruiser, and slam the door shut behind him. He could then radio call in, ask for backup. No one would ever know he turned tail and ran like a little bitch.

But the footprints. Oh fuck. He had already left his boot prints along the side of the house. They would be discovered by the other officers when they came out to investigate. And then he would have to tell them he made it halfway along the side of the house and then got scared shitless and ran. No—*no way.* His humiliation was now drying in the hard, desert soil. Those prints would be there until the next rain. He had to at least make it to the backyard, then he could radio in foul play, and return to the cruiser to wait for backup.

You don't even have to go into the backyard, he thought. *Just get up to the wall, make sure you get your prints near the wall, then you can go back. At least then they will know you didn't turn and run when you were only halfway there.*

His decision made, Kilburn pressed on through the darkness. The low wall loomed up ahead. He could make out some of the backyard now. The light definitely wasn't coming from a porch light, it was too widespread. Kilburn thought of a huge picture window, spilling light from the house onto the patio. And then the desert sucked up what light was left, stealing it off into the night.

He was a dozen feet from the low wall when he first heard the sucking noises. Or was it slurping noises? He supposed the difference was minimal. He inched closer, his breath caught in his throat. He thought of himself as a kid, greedily slurping down a slushy on a hot, summer afternoon. *Same noise.*

The wall was now less than a yard away. It came up to his waist. Kilburn switched the flashlight off, making sure to not let it click noisily as he did so. He reached for his right hip and undid the latch on his holster, where his standard-issue Glock was lying in wait. *Whatever the fuck is making that noise, it's going to be splattered on the pavement real quick.*

Kilburn took a deep breath in preparation to look around the wall. It would be a hard angle to let off a round and expect to hit anything. Especially since he didn't know what the yard looked like. The slow, steady, slurping noises continued. He thought of the slushy on that lazy summer day of his youth. Cherry flavored. It had stained his mouth and tongue red.

Kilburn peeked around the side of the house. He was right about the wall of windows; the entire east-facing side of the house was nothing *but* windows. Bedroom, living room, kitchen—all windows. The shitter probably had a window, too. Light bled across the backyard, cast from the various windows. There was a pool in the center of the yard. The water inside was twinkling in the darkness, the light seeming to dance with it. Beyond the pool, a collection of patio furniture was scattered across the lawn. *Must be pretty pricey to keep a lawn looking like that in Tucson,* he thought. All the furniture was knocked over, including a sizable table that looked like it was made out of heavy stone on top.

Kilburn continued to pan toward the house and the wall of windows—and the slurping noises. He could see movement. It was partially obscured by an outdoor grill set up, but enough was visible to send a shard of ice down his spine.

The patio door was wide open, and a man's feet were lying across the threshold. The feet were bare, although Kilburn saw a slipper on its side near the open door. The man was sprawled face up on the patio. Well, if there had been a face, it would have been face up. The amount of blood was immense. It was puddled on the concrete patio, it was splattered on the glass window of the sliding door, and it was covering the man's bare legs, slick like oil.

And something was crouched over the body, slurping. Kilburn again thought of the slushy, and about how it stained his mouth red. There was so much red now, spread out in front of him like a million cherries had burst.

The thing on top of Arlington was the size of a small bear, probably weighing in around three hundred pounds. Maybe more. It was crouched on all fours, each leg thickly muscled and devoid of hair. Its skin was a darkish gray, and appeared to be tough and calloused. A few dark, crinkled hairs stood out from its elbows and haunches. Large, curled claws extended from flat paws that resembled a bear's. The claws themselves looked much more feline in nature, coated with a layer of blood that obscured what color they were originally.

The thing's spine stuck out at least five inches from its body, the vertebrae grotesquely draped in gray skin. There was no tail.

Its head resembled a canine, the muddy red eyes looking out over an elongated snout. The teeth were mammoth in size, and seemed to dwarf the size of its head—which was by no means small. Pointed ears, like a Doberman's, stood straight up from the gray expanse of its skull. One ear cocked suddenly, pointed in Kilburn's direction.

The creature was looking down at what remained of Arlington, slurping at his abdominal cavity and the pool of blood that sat there like some macabre soup. *It's drinking,* Kilburn thought, fascinated. *It's drinking his blood.*

He was so transfixed by the creature's slow slurping that he hadn't noticed when the ear cocked, pivoting in his direction. The creature looked up from the soup of congealing blood and detached organs, its red eyes searching in Kilburn's direction. The eyes fixed on Kilburn, and he felt his bladder let go.

His gun forgotten, Kilburn turned and fled along the side of the house. The terror that gripped him was like the terror of a child, suffocating and complete, and it allowed no reasonable thoughts to enter. All it said was *Run! Flee! Escape!* And Kilburn did run, blindly through the night, his arms stretching out in front of him as if grasping for someone—anyone—to pull him to safety. His feet thudded on the ground, dwarfed by the sound of something much larger—and faster—thudding behind him. If he could only get to the patrol car, shut the door, peel down the driveway in a cloud of burnt rubber and exhaust. If only—

It was the mesquite branch that did him in. The same branch that had snared him as he passed by only moments ago once again groped out of the darkness and grabbed him. The thorns of the branch hooked deeply into the fabric of his uniform, yanking him backward and turning him in the direction of the oncoming beast.

He opened his mouth to scream, but the creature collided with his chest before he had the chance. He was thrown backward, the ensnared portion of the mesquite branch breaking off and coming with him. He was vaguely aware of the smell of the damp soil as he hit the ground. That smell was quickly overpowered by the stench of the creature before him. He was surrounded by darkness, having dropped his flashlight somewhere along the way. Although he couldn't see it, he could sense that the creature was just beyond his feet as he lay on the cool earth. The only way he knew it was there was because of the smell—sweet and rotting—and the sound of its ragged breathing. There was another smell, too—one of copper and rust. *Blood,* Kilburn thought. *That's what blood smells like.* Not his, not yet. It was the blood from the other man—Arlington. He lay there, waiting for the smell of his own blood to join Arlington's. They were now bound together, in death and in darkness.

Kilburn waited for what seemed like an agonizingly long time. In reality it must have only been a matter of seconds. Then the creature was upon him, tearing his flesh and breathing that hot, stinking breath of rot and pennies into his open mouth. Claws tore at his tender midsection. Buttons on his uniform popped off and something burning sunk deep into his stomach. He imagined a firecracker on the Fourth of July, stuck into his stomach and going off with excruciating intensity. Except there were no sparks, and there was no light.

A firecracker went off on his left cheek, and tore across his face in one clean, ripping motion. His face felt on fire, and yet somehow cold at the same time. Something heavy and wet lay against his right ear. Copper was now pouring down his throat, thick and viscous and tasting like old pennies. He tried to close his lips against the dripping, but found there was nothing there to close.

Another firecracker exploded on his throat, and something heavy and final shattered in his neck. Blissfully, all feeling below his neck ceased. He could feel his head getting pulled from side to side, and he could feel coldness on his burning face, almost thankful for it. And then he could feel what was below his neck getting tugged about.

He realized he was suffocating, although he couldn't feel it. His lungs no longer worked, whatever told them to continue their forever inhales and exhales was now severed. That was fine with him, though—he didn't care to be part of this for any longer. The slurping sounds were now coming from somewhere below his neckline. Endless slurping sounds, like someone enjoying a hearty bowl of soup with no one around to be polite for. *Slurp, slurp, slurp.* Like a cherry slushy on a blisteringly hot Fourth of July. Kilburn's last thought was of his childhood self, smiling up from his melting cherry slushy, his teeth and mouth stained red.

PART III

FIGHT

CHAPTER 42

Detective Carl Moser stared out his office window as dawn broke across the desert. The expanse of mountains that stretched along the horizon was a dazzling pink, competing with an orange sky. His eyes went up and down the ridges, valleys, and cliff faces without really seeing them. The sun was about to crest the top of the Santa Catalinas, and rays of sunlight reached out from behind a rose-colored mountain peak. The beauty of that August morning barely registered to him, though. His mind was elsewhere, swirling around in an endless spiral of frustration, outrage, and fear. Yeah, fear was definitely there.

His chair squeaked in protest as he reclined further into his seat, interlocking his fingers behind his head. How could such a glorious morning follow such a dark and horrendous night? It was as if the sun was mocking him somehow as it rose steadily over the mountains—as if the desert itself was laughing at him. Moser didn't like it—not the sunrise, not any of it. The situation up in Wasp Canyon was getting stickier by the minute. It was bad when Jasper went down, it was worse when the Cuthbertson woman followed—but now? Two more victims? This was absolutely ludicrous. A string of animal attacks like this was absolutely unheard of. The only other time something like this ever happened...

He let the thought trail off, hoping it would seep into the dark corners of his mind and stay there. It wouldn't—*couldn't*—stay there, though, because he knew the only other time this had happened, and it was in 1987. The Cleary girl told him so. Curiosity had gotten the better of him after she left the station that day, taking her sarcastic friend and the Cuthbertson cat with her. Moser had spent the remainder of the evening reviewing old case files from '87. And by God, everything the Cleary girl told him checked out. *Every goddamn thing.* Like everything else he had counted on to wrap up this investigation, his idea that Cleary was just damn crazy had gone into the shitter as well. First the hair analysis, then the idea that the animal would be easily apprehended, and now the 1987 murders. At this rate he could see himself running through the streets yelling '*El chupacabra!*' right alongside her within a week's time. *Fucking animal attacks,* he thought. *It just had to be animal attacks.*

Carl Moser was only four-years-old when his neighbor's dog attacked him. His memory of the incident was cloudy, and in parts, completely blank. He was playing with a toy in his front yard when the neighbor's Rottweiler came running over. He was familiar with the dog, so he wasn't immediately concerned when it started to nudge at him. He vaguely recalled trying to push the dog away, and that's when it bit him. The bite was to his left shoulder, the dog shaking him back and forth before letting go. He remembered screaming, his father running out of the house, and then red towels being pressed to his shoulder. He wondered where the red towels came from since his mommy's towels were all white. Stitches were involved, but in the end, he healed up just fine—physically anyway. Emotionally, the wounds had cut much deeper. Although he barely remembered the attack, there was one thing that stuck in his mind: the feeling of getting tossed around like a human rag doll. That feeling of helplessness stayed with him, and even now, so many decades later, he still sometimes woke in the night, sweating profusely and feeling those jaws on his left shoulder.

He could never watch those Animal Planet shows his kids seemed to be so fond of. They always had some disfigured person talking to the screen, thick cords of scar tissue warping their facial features. Or the camera would pan down and you'd find out their arm was gone. Sick shit like that. The show would then entertain the viewer with dramatic reenactments of carnage, all blurry and red. He could still remember when it was all blurry and red for him—a terrified human rag doll. The thought of watching such crap for entertainment seemed ludicrous, much like his current situation seemed to be.

The call came just after midnight on the morning of August thirteenth—a frantic voice telling him he was needed out in Wasp Canyon Estates. As he lay in bed in the darkness of his bedroom he could feel his stomach drop and his testicles pull up toward his body. His wife had reached for him then, awakened by his muffled conversation, and he had jumped clear out of bed when her hand brushed against his left shoulder.

Déjà vu danced in his head as he drove up Wasp Canyon Road, still rubbing sleep seeds out of his eyes and feeling the roughness on his cheeks that he hadn't bothered to shave. He kept looking to the sky, wishing for the light of dawn to start brushing across the horizon and the night to get swept away. It was still far too early for such things, though, even in the summer when dawn came early and dusk didn't arrive until after the supper dishes were washed and put away.

The scene at the Arlington house was chaos—far more crowded and hectic than the Cuthbertson case. Despite the hour, the house was lit up like a football stadium. Spotlights and headlights on the ground, and chopper lights up above, panning across the desert. Apparently, it was the damn Super Bowl at Wasp Canyon Estates in the wee morning hours of August thirteenth.

Moser killed the engine and staggered out of his car—not a police cruiser this time, but his personal vehicle. He had come directly from home after receiving the call, not wanting to waste time stopping by the precinct before heading to the scene. He was messily dressed in his street clothes, his hair still in shambles from the deep sleep he had been pulled away from.

Officer Wesley rushed over when he saw Moser get out of the car. Moser sighed with relief, remembering the young, competent officer from the Cuthbertson house. "Wesley, fill me in."

Wesley briefed him on the night's events, beginning with Arlington's call to the emergency dispatcher, and ending with the state of the two victims, which he described in painfully intricate detail. Kilburn had answered the call to investigate the Arlington house; however, it wasn't clear why he had never called for backup after arriving. When dispatch was unable to reconnect with Kilburn, another unit was sent to the scene. The two officers that responded found Kilburn's cruiser in the driveway with the headlights still on and immediately called for backup.

Once they began a search of the premises, it did not take long for Kilburn's body to be discovered lying face up along the north side of the house. They assumed it was Kilburn based on his service uniform; however, the face had been removed which made identification difficult. Kilburn was disemboweled and a few of his organs were missing. It was also discovered that he had been internally decapitated. Moser stopped Wesley, wanting to know what exactly that meant. Wesley explained that Kilburn's neck had been broken and his head was now attached to his trunk only by muscle tissue and skin. Moser wished he hadn't asked.

Wesley resumed his report. The caller, Desmond Arlington, was found in the backyard. His body was lying across the threshold of the patio door. He had also been disemboweled and his body partially dismembered. Both men were pronounced dead at the scene. A search of the property and surrounding area did not produce any viable leads. The house was cleared and nothing appeared to be out of place inside.

Moser thought about his two kids, leaning in during their Animal Planet shows to make sure they didn't miss any of the gory details. It took him a moment to realize Wesley was staring at him expectantly, waiting for orders. Moser had none to give. He looked back at Wesley with a blank stare. All he could think about was Animal Planet playing in the living room while he tried desperately to ignore the growling sounds and the monotone narrator describing the attacks step-by-step.

He thanked Wesley and sent him back to doing whatever it was he was doing before Moser had arrived. Wesley gave him a respectful nod and jogged over to a group of men standing near the left side of the house. Moser watched him go, thinking of teeth against his left shoulder and his mother's white towels that were no longer white.

The sun rose into the eastern sky, bringing a breathtaking assortment of colors with it. Pinks, oranges, blues, and pastel turquoise covered the atmosphere, looking like brushstrokes made by the hand of God himself. Moser couldn't understand how such beauty could exist in a world that also held such ugliness. The night had been so black, so gray, and so very,

very red. And now the world was filled with a bouquet of beautiful colors—colors that beautiful women often wore on their beautiful dresses.

A forgotten cup of coffee sat on Moser's desk, even the mug picking up some of the orange hues outside the window. Moser felt more like the coffee inside of the mug: cold, dark, and bitter. The bad news kept coming, and the evidence was starting to point a more and more sturdy finger at an explanation that he refused to believe.

There were now four dead, all killed in roughly the same manner. All had been eviscerated, some dismembered, one practically decapitated. All the victims had been found face up—a detail that seemed unimportant, except for the fact that every victim from 1987 had been found face up as well. The significance was lost on him.

Hairs had been recovered on all four bodies, and Moser had a sinking suspicion that the new samples will prove that the same animal was responsible for all the attacks. What species of animal involved was still *inconclusive*. Lab had not had time to run a full microscopic analysis on the hairs recovered from last night's attacks, but after a quick visual inspection they said they were almost certain they would be a match to the previously recovered hairs. And what exactly were they a match to in the broader sense? Other than to each other, the hairs did not match any animal on record.

El chupacabra, his mind whispered. Moser shook the thought away.

Then there were the paw prints to consider. Moser thought that maybe, instead of a sick animal, it would end up being some sick son of a bitch human instead. None of the bodies were eaten, after all, which was peculiar for a predatory animal attack. Sure, a few bits and pieces were missing, but nothing like what you would expect from a hungry carnivore. And none of the bodies had been taken away from the original attack site, save for the first victim that was relocated to the hiking trail. His kids told him once, following one of their damn Animal Planet shows, that it is common for carnivores to relocate their prey for later consumption. Yet not one body had been relocated during the recent attacks. There was also no evidence suggesting that the bodies were dragged from where they originally fell—no blood trails, no drag marks (again, except for Jasper). So why kill them if not to eat them? That's what led Moser to considering a human adversary. First the Co-Ed Killer, then the Night Stalker, and now the Desert Destroyer.

The paw prints ruined all that. Another one of his theories took its final breath, keeled over, and dropped dead in the dust. Desert Destroyer, indeed. Bloody paw prints were found on the patio, going from Arlington's location toward the side of the house. The soil beyond the back wall had still been damp from the afternoon rain, and animal prints were also found all the way to where Kilburn's body lay. No prints were found past the fallen officer's remains. Moser suspected Kilburn went around the side of the house when he got no answer at the front door, discovered the thing in the act of killing Arlington, and then fled the scene and was chased down. Why Kilburn didn't call for backup when Arlington didn't answer the door, Moser didn't know. Nor did he know why Kilburn never unholstered his weapon. Kilburn had always been a funny one—God rest his soul.

The prints were large and appeared to be mammalian in origin. Based on the print size it was theorized the animal was the size of a bear—a black bear, not a grizzly. Although a grizzly sounded more appealing than the mystery beast that was wreaking havoc with Wasp Canyon's elite. One thing was certain, if only one thing, and that was that whatever was causing this was an animal. The Zodiac hadn't arrived in town and Jack the Ripper must still be somewhere in London, because the Desert Destroyer was most definitely an animal. And a mean son of a bitch at that.

El chupacabra, he thought again, and shoved the thought back into the darkness of his mind where it belonged.

The final thing nagging at him—like a mesquite thorn tearing at his side—was the patio furniture. All of Arlington's patio furniture had been knocked over, including a large stone table that must have been a bitch to flip. Arlington had mentioned kids playing a prank during his 911 call, but Moser didn't think there was a chance in hell kids flipped that table. And listening to the recording of the call, it was obvious everything was not knocked over at once. Arlington had heard something, called 911, and then heard at least two more things fall over during the duration of the call. So something knocked a piece of furniture over, waited, knocked another piece over, waited again, and continued until Arlington went outside to investigate.

Moser thought about Ava Cuthbertson's yard and the large planters that had been knocked over. He had found that

suspicious then, and he found it damning now. Something—
the same something that was at Arlington's house—had
knocked over Cuthbertson's planters to lure her outside. She
had been less apprehensive than Arlington and went outside
sooner, so fewer things were toppled over.

Multiple reports from the 1987 slayings indicated that
backyard items—lawn furniture and the like—were knocked
over in an attempt to lure the victim outside. The wife of one
victim recounted that the noise had awoken her and her
husband, and when he went outside to investigate she heard
him start screaming. He was found in roughly the same shape
as all the Wasp Canyon victims: savagely mauled, face up,
barely eaten.

Moser's mind turned to Jessica Cleary. Not about her at the
station explaining her theory about the creature, but about her
on the telephone the first time he talked to her following
Jasper's attack. Four words kept echoing in his head, like a
broken record playing an endless loop of sickening realization:
it set a trap, it set a trap, it set a trap, it set a trap…

Jessica had been referring to the large rock she tripped
over, causing her to almost suffer the same fate as Cameron
Jasper. And Ava Cuthbertson. And Desmond Arlington. And
Taylor Kilburn. Jessica insisted the rock was not in the trail
when she entered the canyon, nor was the body of Jasper.
What Moser had brushed off as a starving animal's desperate
attempt to hide its meal might have been a trap all along. The
rock, the planters, the heavy patio table. *It set a trap, it set a
trap, it set a trap*…

How smart does an animal have to be to set that kind of trap? A large, powerful, intelligent predator that apparently kills for fun? The Desert Destroyer, indeed.

El chupacabra, his mind whispered yet again. And this time, Moser did not shake the thought away.

CHAPTER 43

Valley Palms Apartments was located two miles south of Orion Street, just past the Arizona Multiplex. The apartment complex was a simple one, the builders forgoing a labyrinth of streets for one road which made a large loop around the complex. Apartments were located on the outer side of the loop, facing outward toward the valley of Tucson to the south or the mountains to the north. A small, modest pool sat in the center of the grounds, a few palm trees towering over the shimmering blue water. Valley Palms was not known for having luxurious living spaces or favorable amenities, but the units were affordable, the grounds safe, and the neighborhood relatively quiet.

Jessica chose Valley Palms due to its proximity to the Arizona Multiplex, the largest mall center in the city. It had an impressive shopping mall, movie theater, and restaurants for all tastes dotting the parking lot. Minstrel's Steakhouse was one of these restaurants, and Jessica had been a server there for the past five years. Her employment at Minstrel's began as a part-time job while she attended the university; however, career options were slim when she graduated with her bachelor's degree in advertising in 2016. Jessica stayed on at Minstrel's, not knowing what the next step in her life should be. Calls from the Federal Student Loan Department became more frequent, and like so many other twenty-somethings, she felt like she was drowning in a new adulthood that held so many possibilities, yet so few at the same time.

Within four months of graduating with her advertising degree, her father's cancer was discovered. Jessica's interest in figuring out the next step in her life withered away as she watched with helpless dread as her father withered away as well. When he passed away on that horrible August morning in 2017, Jessica felt what little motivation she had for her future die with him. She resigned herself to serving, to Minstrel's, and to the Valley Palms Apartments with its single road and single pool.

On August thirteenth, just two weeks shy of the anniversary of her father's death, Jessica stood in her one-bedroom apartment and stared out the window at the cityscape. Tucson's city view was not very awe-inspiring; the buildings were low and the landscape a relentless beige. But at night, as the lights began to twinkle and the beige faded away, the view could definitely draw some attention. However, in the light of day, it appeared drab and lifeless.

Jessica turned away from the window and began pacing again, her boot muffled on the beige-going-on-gray carpet in her living room. Valley Palm's policy was to change out the carpets with each new tenant, but Jessica had now been at the apartment for over five years and the carpet was beginning to show signs of wear and age. The plush beige when she moved in was now becoming a crumpled gray. Jessica had felt like her life was becoming a crumpled gray as well, but now splatters of red were splashed across the gray, screaming at her to get up and take action. Before it was too late.

She paced the length of the room, each time glancing at the dull city view as she came to the window. The wall clock ticked, her boot clunked softly on the carpet, and her jeans swished together as she walked rapidly from one side of the room to the other. A knock finally came at the door, interrupting the mundane quiet. Jessica rushed to the door and opened it without checking the peephole.

☼   ☼   ☼

Claire was quickly ushered inside, startled by how frantic Jessica appeared. "What took so long?" Jessica asked, shutting and locking the door behind her.

Claire made her way over to the single sofa in the room—a lumpy, burgundy thing that was more comfortable than it was eye-catching (as long as you knew where to sit). Claire knew exactly where to sit for optimum comfort, and sat down with a grunt.

"Some people still have to work, you know," she said. Claire already knew what this meeting was about; she had heard nothing but talk about the news all day. *(Two more victims, can you believe it? We have a serial killer in our midst!)* And the fact that Jessica had chosen her apartment for their rendezvous instead of her mother's house was even more foreboding. Whatever Jessica wanted to say, she did not want to risk her mother overhearing.

Jessica grabbed a crumpled pile of papers from the kitchen counter and came over to the coffee table. Instead of sitting next to Claire, she sat down on the floor across from her, placing the stack of papers in the center of the table. Claire recognized them; they were the printouts Jessica had used during her chupacabra discussions. A blurry picture was on the top page—a night scene with a fence and an unidentifiable creature moving quickly on the other side. The poor quality of the photograph left very little for the viewer to identify, except for the glint of what appeared to be large teeth. Claire looked away. She did not need to see those teeth after all the stories she'd been subjected to during her shift at Desert Beauties Salon and Spa.

"I'm assuming you already heard?" Jessica asked.

"Yeah, it was hard to miss. Everyone at work was talking about it."

"That makes four. Four people that have died because of this thing." Jessica pointed to the blurry picture. *"It even got a cop, Claire."*

Claire looked at the picture again. It was almost worse being all blurry like that. It left way too much to the imagination. If you saw what it actually was, maybe it wouldn't be as bad as you thought—maybe the beast in your head was by far more vicious-looking than the beast itself.

"It is that bad," Jessica said, reading her mind.

"Huh?" Claire asked.

"The chupacabra. You think maybe it's not as bad as the papers are making it out to be. But Claire, *it is that bad.*"

"Yeah, I guess I know that already." Claire grabbed the top page and turned it over, wishing for nothing more than those blurry teeth to stop staring up at her. The teeth seemed to have a mind of their own—just tear, shred, and destroy.

"I'm assuming you know all the details then?" Jessica produced a copy of the *Tucson Daily Tribune* from the stack of papers. The front page said "Four People Now Slain in Wasp Canyon Attacks."

Claire nodded. "Yeah, they had a copy of the paper at work. We always have one in the lobby." Claire looked at the expanse of articles and printouts scattered across the coffee table. "Jessica, how do you still have all these papers? I thought your mom would have—"

"I hid them under my mattress," she said. "You figured correctly. My mom wants nothing to do with this. And she wants *me* to have nothing to do with this. She just keeps saying to let the police handle it."

"And where does your mom think you are right now?"

"Dr. Wyatt's."

"Did you cancel or just not show up?"

Jessica shifted her weight on the floor, looking nervous. "Just didn't show up," she said. She pointed to the papers on the table. "I'm too busy right now! And it's not like Wyatt believes me anyway."

"Your mom is going to find out, you know that right?"

Jessica sighed. "Yeah I know. But… God! I love her to death, but sometimes she can be so *suffocating.*" Jessica stared at the window for a while, thinking. "It's like one of those big tarp things that covers a swimming pool in the winter," she said. " It's meant to protect the pool, but if you got it wrapped around you it would end up dragging you down while you struggled to break free. The more you struggle the more entangled you would become. Eventually, it would cover you completely and the surface would be somewhere overhead, but unreachable."

Claire stared at Jessica, speechless.

"Anyway, by the time she finds out it won't matter anymore," Jessica said.

Claire decided to let the whole pool tarp metaphor slide by. She didn't need to be thinking about any more tarps—not for a pool and not to cover up an elderly woman's blood. "Why's that?" she asked instead.

"Because this is all going to be over soon."

Claire leaned forward on the couch, hearing the familiar *ping!* of the loose spring buried somewhere under the cushions. "How do you know that?" she asked.

"Because we are going to stop it before it happens again," Jessica said.

"Why now? In a couple weeks," Claire gestured to the window, and to the clouds that were building on the horizon, "this will all be over. You said it. You said when the rain stops *it stops.* Well, monsoon season is almost over. We don't have to do anything." Desperation filled her voice, shoved up by the fear that was clenching at her chest.

Jessica sighed, disappointed. Claire winced at the sound. Despite all the craziness, she didn't want to disappoint her friend. She had gotten on board with this whole thing, wasn't that enough? And it's not like they were going to stop it. They had zero guns, and were just about as far from Rambo as you could get. They couldn't stop a sickly bear, let alone the actual demon at hand. *And that's what it is,* she thought. *A demon. It certainly looks like it could be featured in some* Nat Geo *book from hell. By God, it could even be the cover art.*

"Monsoon season can last well into September, you know that," Jessica said. "But that's not the point." She fished through some of the papers and pulled out the aerial map of Wasp Canyon Estates. She rotated it so it was facing Claire. Jessica pointed at the green crevice running between two of the mountain ridges. "This is Wasp Canyon."

"Yeah, Jessica, I know that already." Claire rolled her eyes. Even so, she leaned forward to take a better look at the page. The couch *pinged!* again.

Jessica traced her finger to the first, and largest, white roof. "This is Ava Cuthbertson's house."

Claire recognized the circular driveway from the aerial shot in the newspaper. It looked a lot better without all the cop cars and ambulances on it. "I recognize the driveway."

Jessica's finger went down the map, further south. It stopped at the next white roof. "This is Desmond Arlington's house."

The fear grabbing at Claire's chest shot up into her throat. She saw where this was going, and she wanted it to stop. *Just say uncle and run out the door,* she thought. Instead she asked, "Where Arlington and the cop were killed?"

"Yes, that's right." Jessica moved her finger back to the canyon and started listing names as she dragged her finger southward. "Cameron Jasper... Ava Cuthbertson... Desmond Arlington..." Her finger stopped at the next white roof.

"Who lives there?" Claire asked.

"That's Cameron's house."

"Huh? But he died first?" Claire felt foolish the second she said it, her mind already making the connection. She let Jessica explain it anyway, hearing the words made it sound more real.

"Cameron died because he was in the canyon. If he was a homebody—like everyone else seems to be in Wasp Canyon—he would be next on the list instead of first."

"How do you know it is going to go from house to house? Couldn't it go a different way?"

Jessica pointed at the canyon again, jabbing her finger at it as if there was a bug there that needed to be squashed. "It lives in there, Claire. We've already established it can't be out in the daylight. It cannot go too far from the shelter of the canyon. It comes out at night and heads in the same direction to where it has found food before: south."

"But during the attacks in the eighties it didn't go from one house to the next. It jumped around. Houses were attacked all over that neighborhood. Why wouldn't it do the same thing here? It could go across the street next, couldn't it? Instead of south."

"In 1987, it was hunting in a neighborhood where the houses were very close together. It could go to any house it wanted, because there were so many to choose from." Jessica fished out an aerial map of the town in south Tucson and laid it next to the Wasp Canyon map. "Look how close together these houses are. It was practically an all-you-can-eat buffet."

Claire looked at the south Tucson neighborhood. It was true—all the houses were clustered together. Backyards were slim, if there were any at all. Each house was just a stone's throw from the next. And just north of the neighborhood was the mountain range, with a dark green crevice of a canyon running through it. The creature could have easily come out of the canyon at sundown and chosen any house in the neighborhood for its next meal—and still have plenty of time to get back to the canyon before sunrise.

"Wasp Canyon Estates is different," Jessica said, bringing the Wasp Canyon map to the center of the table again. "All these houses are very spread out. Each estate has acres and acres of land. Not to mention the mountains themselves are set back a little further from the neighborhood. I've measured the distance during my runs. *Four miles*. From the mouth of the canyon it takes four miles just to get to the start of the houses. The chupacabra can't be so picky in this situation."

Jessica pointed at the canyon entrance again. "When it comes out of the canyon it will go in the direction it found food before." She traced her finger south from one white roof to the next. "It found food here," she pointed at the Cuthbertson house. "Then here," she pointed to Arlington's house. "The next time it looks for food, it will go here," her finger fell on Cameron Jasper's house.

"But there is no food there, right?" Claire asked. "Since Cameron already died."

"Correct," Jessica said. "But what happens when it doesn't find food at this house? It's not going to start wandering around aimlessly. The houses on the other side of Wasp Canyon Road are at least a mile away from the houses on this side. It's going to continue in the direction it has been going." Jessica's finger headed toward the next white square on the path to Orion Street.

Claire's eyes followed her finger until it stopped at the next roof. "Who lives there?" Claire asked.

"That would be the McElroys," Jessica said. "Husband, wife, and two children."

Claire groaned and leaned back on the couch, a *ping!* issuing from somewhere deep inside. She placed her hands in front of her eyes even though they were already closed, as if closing them and covering them at the same time would make it all go away. Her muffled voice came out from behind her hands, "And how old are those kids?"

"One is seven, the other is twelve."

Claire hid behind her outstretched fingers, listening to the sound of her breath inside her hands. "Fuuuck," she said, drawing the word out during one long, exaggerated exhale. She sat up abruptly, the *ping!* inside the couch going unnoticed. "Can't you call them? Tell them they're next and to get the hell out?"

Jessica shook her head. "And you think they would believe me? If the police say they are fine, why would they listen to some stranger?"

"Well, why the hell are the police saying they are fine?" Claire exclaimed. She was beginning to feel the same outrage and helplessness Jessica had been feeling all along. Why in the name of God were the cops not doing *anything*?

"The police refuse to accept any explanation that isn't logical. That was pretty obvious when we talked with that Moser guy at the police station. I told him exactly what was doing this, and he looked the other way." Jessica paused, looking at the white roof of the McElroy house. Finally she said, "That's why we need to give them proof."

"Proof?" Claire asked. "Please God, don't tell me we are supposed to supply the proof."

"In 1987 they never caught it. We don't even know if it is the same one. I'm not sure how long they live. Anyway, the police were never willing to look for anything other than the usual suspects—mountain lion, bear, deranged person. They couldn't find anything going off those assumptions. Which means they never found it. *And seventeen people died.*

"If we were able to get them to believe us—to show them exactly what they are dealing with—then maybe they could stop it. They could stop looking for a sick bear and start looking for the actual assailant. For the chupacabra." Jessica stopped, waiting for Claire to respond. When she didn't, Jessica asked, "We have to try, don't we?"

Claire stared up at the popcorn ceiling. Finally, she brought her gaze down to Jessica. "And *how* are we going to prove it to the police?"

"By going to Cameron's house," Jessica said.

"Jesus fucking Christ!" Claire yelled. "Are you fucking kidding me, Jessica? You want us to break into a dead man's house—*his mansion*—to what?"

"To take pictures of it. Preferably video, if we can."

"Holy mother of God." Claire shook her head. "What if we get arrested? Or even worse, what if your creature decides to attack *us* instead?"

"We are not going to go outside, obviously," Jessica said. "From what the news said about the Wasp Canyon attacks, and from what I read about the 1987 murders, it makes a bunch of noise to get its victims to come outside.

"And we already know it can set a trap. Just look at my ankle." Jessica pointed to the boot. "So when it shows up and starts knocking stuff over, we film it. And we will leave the lights off inside the house, so it doesn't know we're there. When no one goes outside, it'll leave. Then we show the video to the police." She fell silent. After a moment, she added, "We can wait until morning to leave if you want, so we know for sure it's gone when we leave the house."

Claire said nothing. She stared at Jessica with a blank expression, her mouth ajar.

Jessica pressed on, seemingly unphased. "We *know* it is going to Cameron's house next. It will do what it always does—throw stuff around in the backyard and try to lure the person out of the house. We simply won't go out. Like I said, we will keep the house dark and stay behind some furniture while we film it. We can even call the cops once it shows up, if you want."

Claire broke her silence, her voice sounding shaky and far away. "You want to break into a millionaire's mansion, then call the police and tell him you broke in?"

"To catch the chupacabra!" Jessica exclaimed. "I'm not going to just call and say, 'Hey, I broke in just 'cause I wanted to see how the better half lives'."

"And what if it gets into the house?" Claire asked, still feeling like she was off in the distance.

"What do you mean?"

"The... *chupacabra*." It was the first time Claire said the word out loud. She didn't like the way it felt in her mouth—all slithering and full of menace. "What happens if we are in the house filming it and it knows we're there? And then it comes after us?"

"I don't think that will happen."

"And why not? You showed me an article of a family getting attacked *inside* their home. Why wouldn't it do that to us?"

Jessica pondered the question. "I don't know," she said finally. "In 1987, all of the killings were outdoors—or at least started outdoors—except for the last one. Perhaps when it got so close to the end of the monsoon season, it got eager to get one last meal. You know, like a grizzly bear before hibernation. Those houses in that neighborhood in south Tucson were poorly made. I mean, I think they were known for their shaky doors and flimsy windows. The houses in Wasp Canyon are basically fortresses." She paused for a while, returning her gaze to the window. "All I can say is that it did not behave that way in the eighties, not this soon in the cycle and not in a house as well built as Cameron's. I don't know if it would try to break in or not. I don't think it would, not this early on, but honestly I don't know." She looked back at Claire and waited.

Claire stared at her, unable to speak. How was she supposed to respond to that? I don't know if it will break in and kill us? She had an answer to everything else, for Christ's sake. But nothing when it came to their own safety?

Jessica shuffled through her papers and pulled out a printed picture of a family. It was a Christmas card, all red and green. A mother and father stood with their arms around each other, smiling warmly at the camera. Two children sat on a velvety red sofa in front of the parents, holding hands and grinning in that mischievous yet adorable way that only children can do. All were wearing matching flannel shirts. On the bottom, in cursive lettering, it said, *"Merry Christmas from the McElroys"*.

Claire stared at the picture for a long time. She felt her heart ache in her chest, an almost welcome feeling in comparison to the nauseating fear. "Where did you get that?" she whispered.

"The McElroy's Facebook page," Jessica whispered back. She pushed the picture across the table so Claire had a better view.

"You're telling me that the next house after Cameron's belongs to this family?" Claire pointed at the picture.

"Yeah, that's them."

Claire stared at the two children, a beautiful blonde girl with her hair in pigtails and a boy with sandy hair splashed across his forehead. The thought of those two children ending up like the others broke her heart. The fear was forced out by the heartache—there was no room inside of her for both emotions. And in the end, her heart had weeded out the fear. Well, at least shoved it into the shadows.

"So all we have to do is go to Cameron's house, film it while hiding inside, and then go straight to the police and show them the video?"

"And then they will have to evacuate Wasp Canyon Estates and call in the troops. How could they see a video of the chupacabra, in flesh and blood, and do nothing?"

"Don't mention blood right now," Claire said, thinking again about the tarp stretched over Ava Cuthbertson's red smears.

"And if the police still don't do anything," Jessica continued, "we'll go to the reporters. Tell all the news stations what is actually going on out there. Even if the police continue to deny it, the public sure won't. They'll take one look at that thing and run for the hills. Well, away from the hills actually."

"On two conditions," Claire said. "First, we call the McElroys and see if they will leave willingly. If so, we don't go. We figure out another way. Second, you call that detective of yours one more time. Tell him again what is going on, and see if the police will agree to stake out the place instead of us. Or at least evacuate the area for the time being."

"Agreed. And if both of those conditions fall through?"

"Then I guess I'm strapping on my sidekick jumper and accompanying Van Helsing to the castle to vanquish the dreaded vampire." Claire shook her head, reality still feeling beyond her grasp.

"What's your sidekick jumper look like?" Jessica asked, smiling. "I'm guessing pink with sequins."

Claire rolled her eyes. "When?" she asked, staring at the picture on the coffee table. The McElroy family smiled up at her from their matching flannel shirts.

"Friday night. August seventeenth."

"Why then?"

"Because I have never found an instance of this thing attacking without at least a few nights in between. It fed last night, so I think it is safe to say it won't come out for the next few nights. All the attacks, both in '87 and now, seem to be around five to six nights apart. If we go Friday—that's five days—and it doesn't show, we can just go back the next night."

Jessica looked down at the McElroys, a beautiful family with hopes of a beautiful future. "The father would be the one to go out first," she said, "to investigate a strange noise outside in the night. I can't let those kids grow up without a father. They need every second with him that they can get. Every damn second."

Claire stood up from the couch. *Ping!* "Well then," she said, "if I'm possibly dying in a few days, then I'm having a drink tonight. And you're buying." Claire reached a hand down to Jessica.

Jessica reached up and let Claire pull her to a standing position. "Sounds good to mc. Wc'll drink to our future."

The words hung in the air, like the stench of stale milk. They smiled at each other, but the smiles did not reach their eyes.

CHAPTER 44

Moser sat at his desk, listening to his chair creak as he rocked back and forth. He spent the bulk of yesterday and much of the morning sitting in his office, looking at newspaper articles online and unsure of what to do next. The chief of police was in the building today, and word on the street was he wanted to see Moser in the afternoon to discuss recent events. Moser hadn't wanted to leave the safety of his office since hearing the news about the chief, except for the occasional trip to the john. He had a headache throbbing at his temples, and the fatigue from the last thirty-six hours was beginning to wear on him.

Going home was not an option, though. There was a press conference scheduled for five that afternoon. From what he heard, the chief was planning to have Moser lead the conference—a prospect he was dreading more and more with each passing minute. The press wanted answers about these attacks, and apparently saying "No comment" every time they asked him a damn question wasn't going to work anymore.

That was obvious, with the amount of outrageous articles being published each hour regarding the murders in Wasp Canyon.

Moser's computer was on the right-hand side of his desk, the screen's blue light increasing the throbbing in his temples. He had already clicked through many of the articles regarding the attacks. Damn technology. People used to have to wait until the next newspaper came out, which at least gave the police a little bit of time to get a grasp on the situation. Now, with the help of the internet, all the breaking news was only a click away. There had already been eleven articles issued electronically on the various news websites regarding the most recent deaths. *Eleven,* he thought, shaking his head. *And half of them are the goddamn tabloids running amuck of everything. Fucking reporters. Fucking animal attacks.*

Multiple windows were open on Moser's desktop, all with a different article about the Wasp Canyon murders. Moser's chair issued another sad creak as he leaned forward and began clicking through the articles again.

"Two More Slain in Wasp Canyon Estates." *Click.* "Wasp Canyon's Elite are Dropping Like Flies." *Click.* "Police Are Dumbfounded with Two More Dead in Wasp Canyon." *Click.* "Local Psychic Says More Will Die in Wasp Canyon." *Click.* "Serial Killer on the Loose in Tucson, Police Have No Leads." *Click.* "The Beast of Wasp Canyon Strikes Again." *Click.* "The Murderer in Our Midst, the Rise of Tucson's First Serial Killer." *Click.*

Moser pushed himself away from the computer, his vision blurring as his headache intensified. He massaged his temples, reviewing the web articles in his mind. The major news networks at least stuck to the facts, give or take. They demanded action from the police, and multiple networks were beginning to use the term *serial killer*. The tabloid articles, on the other hand, were just plum outrageous. However, Moser feared that with a killer at large people would gravitate to those articles just as much as the top news stations. Mass hysteria would set in before the week was up. One tabloid said there was a desert-dwelling serial killer that lived off the land and only went after millionaires that lived alone. Another said the serial killer running loose in Tucson was most definitely human and only disguised his gruesome murders as the work of an animal. There was talk about satanic cults and ritualistic sacrifices. And Moser's personal favorite: the killer was a disgruntled ex-millionaire that lost all his money in the stock market and then trained his dogs to kill Tucson's wealthiest citizens as pay back. *Oh lordy, the shit is surely hitting the fan now.*

Most of the department was still operating under the assumption that a rogue or diseased desert predator was to blame. There had been countless searches of the surrounding desert and dozens of traps set—all fruitless so far. The paw prints at the Arlington house had silenced most of the officers that were suggesting a human assailant, although Moser suspected some of them had read the tabloid article about trained killer dogs and were now thinking a crazed madman was stalking Wasp Canyon Estates with a couple of blood-thirsty pit bulls. The paw prints had not resembled a domesticated dog in the least—had not resembled any known animal for that matter—but that didn't seem to stop some tongues from wagging in the department.

And now a press conference was scheduled, where Moser was supposed to say they were following all possible leads (which were zero) and doing everything they could to protect the public (which, so far, had been nothing). Moser had suggested evacuating Wasp Canyon Estates after the discovery of Arlington and Kilburn, but that was quickly shot down by his superiors. Apparently, you can't treat millionaires just like everyone else. You can't expect them to just leave their mega-mansions willingly with no logical explanation of why they must leave or when they can return. *It will bring mass hysteria,* they said. *We could get sued,* they said. Like getting sued was the main threat right now.

Moser leaned his girth back in his creaky chair, and returned his attention to the mountains outside the window. *It's out there,* he thought. *Right now. Somewhere out there it was sleeping, waiting, and biding its time until nightfall. Maybe not tonight, or tomorrow night, but some night very soon, when the darkness came, it will come with it.*

Moser was called in to speak with the chief of police early that afternoon. The word *chupacabra* danced on his tongue as he sat on the subordinate side of the desk in the chief's office, listening to the chief chastise him on his department's lack of progress thus far.

Just say the word, and then it won't just be your problem anymore, Moser thought. *If it gets rebuffed, at least you could say you tried. At least it won't weigh so heavily on your heart when the next widow gets murdered. Just say it. Say the word. Say chupa...*

"Moser? Are you listening to me?"

"Yes sir."

"We're losing a handle on this thing. And you can't keep saying 'No comment' every time a reporter asks you a question. I mean, just look at these articles." The chief picked up a stack of newspapers that was lying on his desk. He began setting them down, one by one. "No comment," he said, and set a newspaper down. "No comment," he said, and set the next one down. He continued for the remaining four newspapers. "Look Moser, I know you don't like talking to the press, but with this being such a high-profile case, I need someone who can communicate with the reporters. Otherwise we just look like a bunch of asses."

"Yes, I know. You're right, Chief," Moser said, looking down at the newspaper on top of the stack. He recognized the article on the front page from one he had open on his computer browser.

"So what can you tell me about leads on the case?"

"No leads so far, sir."

"Then what the hell *can* you tell me?" the chief asked.

Now or never, he thought. Moser wanted out of the room, and away from the conversation, but something deep in his gut told him he had to stick this one out. He needed to face his demons—both literally and metaphorically. It was time to get over his phobia of animal attacks, time to face his childhood fears head on. And it was well past time to stop whatever creature was causing all this. Moser feared he wouldn't be able to live with himself if he didn't. He couldn't run away and hide under the covers like a frightening child while people were dying. He swore to protect them, and it was about time he stopped beating around the goddamn bush and actually did it. Animal attacks or not. Serial killer or not. Chupacabra or not.

"Chief, I think we need to explore the possibility that the victims were attacked by an animal that we are not familiar with."

"What? Like a tiger? Christ, Moser, do you think one of those Wasp Canyon bastards has a pet tiger up there?"

"No sir. I meant the animal responsible might be something that has been rumored to exist, but has not been proven to exist yet. This is an animal that preys on human beings. I'm beginning to believe the animal responsible is a chupacabra."

"A chupa—what? Like the urban legend?" The chief looked at Moser incredulously. "Christ, Carl, are you feeling alright? I know you've always had some sort of aversion to animal cases, but this? An *urban legend*?"

"The evidence is right in front of us. No known animal behaves this way. This creature—"

"Creature? Carl, I can't have you going up in front of the press and saying some sort of mythical creature is responsible for all this. It would be chaos."

"I understand that it would be difficult, but—"

"I've heard enough. I'm pulling you from this, Carl. Take a few days—hell, take a week—to get your head on straight and start thinking clearly. Get some sleep. Spend some time with your wife. Whatever you need. I'll get Helms on this instead."

"Helms? He hasn't even—"

"Let me worry about that. You're done with this case." The chief shook his head. "You're one of my best detectives, Carl. What I need is for you to take some time and get your shit together."

"What about the press conference?" Moser asked.

"Oh hell. I guess I'm gonna have to do it. Helms isn't caught up on everything yet. Alright Moser, get out of here. I have a lot of work to do before five. Go get yourself a beer or something. Clear your head. I'll get you on something a little more low-key when you get back next week."

"Yes sir," Moser said, defeated. He left the chief's office with his head low and shoulders slumped. *Taken off the case? That never happened to him before.* He was about to duck into the men's room when an office aide approached him with an urgent look on her face. *What in God's name happened now? Please let there not have been another one already.*

"Detective Moser, sorry to interrupt," she said.

"No need to apologize. What is it?" Moser felt fear rising in his gut, cutting like acid.

"There's someone on the line that's been waiting for you. I told her you were in a meeting and you would call back, but she insisted on waiting until you were done. She's been on the line for twenty minutes now. She said it was an emergency, but refused to call 911. She said it has to be you."

"Did she give her name?" he asked, although he was already picturing Jessica Cleary in his mind. She was so persistent, and so sure of herself and her conclusions. He almost envied her that.

"Yes sir. Jessica Cleary. She's on line one. Should I—"

"I'll take the call," he said. "Thank you, Charlene."

Moser changed course, abandoning the men's room and heading toward his office. Once inside, he shut the door and sat down in his creaking chair. He took a deep breath and grabbed the phone off its cradle. He tucked it against his ear and pressed the blinking light next to line one. "Moser here," he said.

"Detective Moser? This is Jessica Cleary."

"Yes, Jessica. How can I help you today?" Moser could feel a knot in his stomach, growing heavy with anticipation.

"I heard the news about the Arlington house," she said.

"I had no doubt you would. Is that why you are calling?"

"Well, yes and no, I guess." She sounded flustered.

"Is everything alright, Jessica?" he asked.

"Do you still think it is a sick bear?"

"That is up for debate at this point. I can't discuss details of—"

"The news said there were footprints," she said. Silence followed, then: "Paw prints."

What imbecile leaked that intel to the news? Probably the same bastards running around here thinking some serial killer trained his dogs to attack rich people, Moser thought. He said, "Yes, I suppose there is no harm in confirming that detail. We did find paw prints around the victims."

"Have you thought more about what I said? About the chupacabra?"

Moser said nothing. That damn chupacabra talk was what just got him kicked off the case. *His case.* "I've considered it," he said, "but I haven't drawn any conclusions at this point."

"Even after one of your own men—someone young, strong, and trained to protect others—was taken down by the same thing? A sick cougar might be able to kill an old woman who was caught off guard, but a young police officer with a gun?"

Silence on Moser's end.

Jessica continued. "You really think some sickly animal could do that?"

Moser sighed, "I don't know what I believe anymore, Jessica." And that, blunt as it was, was the truth. He just didn't know anymore. Not at all.

"Well," she went on, "I'm not going to berate you with my beliefs again. I made my thoughts perfectly clear when we spoke last week. I thought these most recent deaths might have been enough for you to consider what I found out, but I guess not."

"Jessica, I—"

"That's not why I called anyway," she said, cutting him off.

"It's not?" Moser asked, surprised.

"I'm not calling to try to convince you that a chupacabra is attacking people out in Wasp Canyon. I'm calling because I know where it is going to go next. Maybe you won't believe me about what it is, but I'm hoping you could at least try to consider the fact that it is going to keep attacking people. And that I know who's next."

"How could you possibly know that?" Moser asked. He began massaging his temple as Jessica explained her theory about the chupacabra going from house to house, and that Jasper's house and the McElroys were next. Moser already met the McElroys; he talked to them while investigating the Arlington case and the victim's assumption that the McElroy kids were involved in a prank. The kids were at a sleepover that night as it turned out, although after seeing what was left of Arlington, Moser hadn't even considered those two kids being involved in any way.

"You need to get the McElroys out of there as soon as possible," Jessica said.

"I can't make people leave their homes without proper cause," Moser said. *I can't make them do anything anymore, since I'm no longer on the case,* he thought miserably.

"You don't think this is *proper cause*?" Jessica asked.

"Proper cause has to be something people will believe. If I go over to the McElroys and say a Mexican goat-sucker is on the loose and it is coming for them next, they will laugh in my face."

"Well, you don't have to say it that way," Jessica said.

"Look Jessica, even if I might be considering what you said is true, that doesn't mean the department—or my superiors—will feel the same way. I cannot issue an evacuation based on a hunch that *only I have.* Many others would have to support this theory, and I'm telling you right now, I will not get that amount of support at this juncture. Not

when I bring up the word *chupacabra* in a police station."
Moser squeezed his eyes shut, feeling the heavy weight of
shame pushing down on him. *Maybe I should have at least
looked at the bodies. The chief is right—I don't deserve to be
on this case.*

Silence from Jessica's end of the line. After a considerable
pause she asked, "Well, can't you stick with the rogue
predatory animal thing? Say it's a bear or a cougar that's
working its way down from the mountains, and that the
McElroy's house could be attacked next. It would at least get
them away from the area while your men try to find it and kill
it."

"No one will ever consider a bear or mountain lion capable
of breaking into one of those homes, no matter how sick it was
or how much of a man-killer it might be. I cannot force them
to leave their home based on that theory—at best I could only
get them to promise not to go outside at night. And I wouldn't
even be able to enforce that." *Especially since I am off the
case.*

"So you're basically saying there is nothing you can do?"
she asked.

The disappointment in her voice matched the growing
disappointment Moser felt in his own chest. *I wonder if this is
how she felt when I turned her away that day she came to the
station. What I did to her, the chief just did to me.*

Jessica's voice cut into Moser's thoughts. "What if I could
prove it?"

"Prove it?"

"Prove that it exists. The chupacabra. If I can prove it, your men would have to act then, right? No more twiddling their thumbs and saying 'Gosh, I just don't know.' They would have to evacuate the entire area and call in for more help to find it and kill it."

Moser frowned. "Yes, I suppose if there was proof of its existence then we would have to change course and act accordingly. But Jessica, there is no way to prove that this— *thing*—actually exists. We have dozens of men looking and they have found no trace of it."

"Can you have your men set up stakeout units around Cameron's house and the McElroy house each night and wait to see if it shows up?"

"The Jasper house? No, I highly doubt I will get approval to have multiple units deployed to watch a vacant house based on the premise that a bear or mountain lion *might show up one night*. I could possibly get a unit over to the McElroy house, but even that is unlikely. Especially since everyone is going off the assumption that this is a normal animal that is incapable of getting indoors. As far as my superiors are concerned, as long as the McElroys stay inside, they should be fine."

"I thought your superiors would want to catch this thing as quickly as possible."

"They do, but they also don't want to make fools of themselves, setting up stakeouts based on the hunch of some waitress. It would make for a lot of bad press."

"And that's what they care about most—saving face and avoiding bad press?"

"Jessica, I hate to say it, but that's what a lot of high-up officials care about most."

"And what do you care about most, Detective Moser?"

Moser sighed, considering the question. "I care about stopping this thing, whatever it might be, before it kills one more person."

"And if I supply you with proof that it is a chupacabra, will you make every effort to get your department on board to hunt it down and destroy it? And to get everyone that's still living out there out of harm's way?"

"Yes, I would do that. You have my word." Moser waited for a moment, and when she didn't say anything else, he asked, "Jessica, what are you planning on doing? How could you possibly get proof that this thing exists?"

More silence. Finally she said, "If your men won't go to Cameron's house, I will. I will get you your proof, and then it is up to you to stop it."

Moser shook his head and let out a silent whoosh of air. "Jessica, I cannot permit you to trespass on private prop—"

"You could come, too, if you want," she suggested. She waited for Moser to respond, and when he didn't, she went on. "You told me what you wanted most was to stop it before it kills someone else. And since your superiors aren't willing to do anything, I don't see any other way. I'm not going to sit back and wait for the breaking news story that two children were slaughtered, or that they lost their dad when he tried to protect him. *No freaking way.* I'm going to Cameron's house Friday night, whether you help me or not. I'll get you your damn proof, and then you're going to do everything in your power to find it and destroy it. That's what matters most, Moser. You said so yourself."

Moser opened his mouth to speak, but Jessica had already ended the call. The line was dead.

CHAPTER 45

The phone rang in the Cleary house almost immediately after Jessica set it back in its cradle. She had just ended a rather unsuccessful call with Jerry McElroy. Or rather, he had ended it when he hung up on her. Jessica tried to explain the situation to McElroy as best she could, trying desperately to convey the danger that his family was in. McElroy kept asking why the police weren't telling him all this if it was, in fact, true. When Jessica failed to produce an acceptable answer to that question, McElroy threatened to call the police himself—only this time it would be to report *her* for harassment. He said he'd had enough reporters sniffing around following the deaths of his three neighbors, just trying to catch him out of the house to snap pictures of his family and shove a microphone in his face. He wasn't going to subject his family to such things, and that's why they were staying put. He couldn't even get out of his driveway to go to work without news vans swarming his car. As long as the police said it was safe for his family to remain at home, then that's what they were going to do—with the curtains drawn and the gated entrance to his driveway securely fastened. He hung up on her, threatening once more to call the police if she called again.

Jessica hadn't expected much to come from the conversation. Her dad would have behaved in the exact same fashion. She still felt she had to try, though, and that's what she had done.

And now the phone was ringing, buzzing in its cradle and its red light flashing. *Now what?* She picked up the phone. It was still warm from when she had talked to McElroy. Jessica expected the call to be for her mom, since it was her mother's phone line, after all. To her surprise, the call was for her.

"Jessica," a familiar voice said, "this is Dr. Wyatt calling."

Jessica felt her stomach flutter. Why hadn't she looked at the damn caller ID? Not that it would have done any good, either her mom would have answered the call or Dr. Wyatt would have left a message that Andrea could have overheard.

"Um, hello Dr. Wyatt," Jessica said.

"I tried to get a hold of you on your cell multiple times, but it seems you were always too busy to answer." When Jessica said nothing, Wyatt pressed on. "We had an appointment yesterday afternoon. Had you forgotten?"

"Uh, no, I didn't."

Wyatt sighed. "I was afraid of that. Jessica, you must not discontinue our sessions. We were making such—"

"Progress?" Jessica interrupted. "Yeah, we were. Until you decided I was crazy."

"Jessica, I never once said you were crazy, nor did I ever think it."

"Yes, you did," she said. "I saw it on your face and heard it in your voice, when I told you that the thing that chased me was not a normal animal."

"Jessica, I hate so much that something terrible happened while you were doing an activity that you actually enjoyed. And something that I suggested. I never thought it would be so dangerous."

"That's not why I stopped coming."

"It's not? Then why?"

"I already told you. You think I'm crazy. Have you even been watching the news?"

"Yes, I have seen the news."

"And you still don't believe me?"

"Jessica," Wyatt said, "I cannot give in to fantastical theories, no matter how much I might want to. It is my job to keep you grounded, and to keep you focused on your recovery."

"My recovery?" Jessica asked. "You think that refusing to even consider the possibility that I could be right is going to help with my recovery? *I trusted you.*"

Silence on Wyatt's end. "I'm a woman of science," she finally said. "I am incapable of believing that there is a mythical explanation to what is happening in Wasp Canyon right now."

"And that's why I can't continue to see you."

"Jessica—"

"I came to you to get help with my grief. Well, I think I have decided that I will handle *my* grief *my* way."

"Jessica, please listen to me—"

"Just let me grieve." Jessica said, and hit the **End** button on the portable phone. She set it down on its stand, reached around the base of the phone, and unplugged the power cord. Her mom had her cell phone if she needed to make a call, and within a few days, this would all be over anyway. She would plug the phone back in when she got back on Friday.

Jessica heard the TV's volume increase in the living room. "Jessica," Andrea called, "come in here and watch this. It's the chief of police. They are having a press conference about Wasp Canyon. Maybe they found the wolf!"

"Doubtful," Jessica muttered. She headed toward the living room. Since last week's argument, neither Andrea nor Jessica had brought up Wasp Canyon. Things seemed to be going back to the realm of normalcy, although both women were becoming quite skilled at feigning a normal routine.

Jessica entered the living room, her boot clunking on the floor as she went. The chief of police was on the screen, looking shiny and uncomfortable under the harsh camera lights. Andrea was sitting on the couch, watching the chief fumble through his speech to the press. Andrea looked up from the screen as Jessica came in, hitting the mute button when she saw her daughter wincing. Jessica sat down next to her, groaning as the weight came off of her ankle.

"How's your ankle doing, dear?"

"Hurts, but it's getting better I think."

"We have your follow-up appointment with the doctor early next week. I hope you didn't forget."

"I didn't. I'm just worried about what he is going to say."

"Well, we will cross that bridge when we come to it." Andrea put her arm around Jessica, and Jessica leaned in and rested her head on her shoulder. "You okay, honey?" Andrea asked.

"Yeah, just tired I guess."

"You're not just saying that to get out of cleaning Tofu's litter box, are you?" Andrea asked.

Jessica laughed. "No, of course not. I would *never* do such a thing."

"Uh huh. *Sure* you wouldn't," Andrea said, and unmuted the television. They sat side by side, watching the increasingly uncomfortable-looking chief drag his way through a storm of frenzied questions coming from a horde of reporters.

Jessica looked over at the recliner that was positioned next to the couch. Tofu was fast asleep with his white belly turned up toward the ceiling. All the yelling reporters had not awoken him. Jessica figured Tofu was unphased by television volume—his previous owner probably liked to have it turned way up on her TV, as well. Anything to make such a big house feel less lonely.

CHAPTER 46

"He really is making himself at home, isn't he?" Jessica asked, watching Tofu prance around the kitchen in preparation for his dinner. The afternoon was drawing to a close, the sun ready to give up its hold on the day and let the night take over. It was Friday, August seventeenth.

"I'll say," Andrea agreed. "You okay, hon? You seem a little more down than usual."

"*More* down?" Jessica snickered.

"No, I don't mean it like that. I just meant—"

"I'm okay, Mom. My ankle just hurts, that's all."

"Do you want me to cancel tonight? It's just dinner and a movie with the book club ladies. We can have our own movie night here instead."

"Naw, you go," Jessica said, watching Tofu quiver his behind as he rubbed up against Andrea's leg. "You were excited about this one, weren't you? You guys were gonna watch the movie based on the book you just finished."

"Yeah, but that always gets me irritated, you know. They always change way too much in the movie. I can stay here if you want company." Andrea set the food bowl down and Tofu began greedily gulping down the contents.

"I got Tofu," Jessica said. "Thank you, though. You go have fun, and I will see you in the morning."

"The morning? I won't be out that late, honey."

"I think I'm going to turn in early tonight. I'm pretty tired, and like I said, my ankle hurts."

Andrea kissed her forehead. "Perhaps that is for the best. You need your rest."

"I sure do." Jessica looked down at Tofu, who had already consumed half of his dinner. "I've been having a little trouble sleeping lately, so when you get home could you leave my door shut? I don't want to risk getting woken up after I manage to fall asleep."

"Well, I suppose so. Are you sure you don't want me to check in on you?"

"I'll be just fine, Mom. You worry too much."

"I know, I know. You sure everything is okay?"

"Yeah, everything is fine. I'm just worried about the doctor's appointment on Monday."

Andrea brushed some of Jessica's hair off her forehead and tucked it behind her ear. "Oh honey, you have nothing to worry about. I'm sure it will go just fine."

"I hope you're right," Jessica said. And after a pause: "I love you, Mom."

"I love you too, honey." Andrea put an arm around Jessica and stroked her hair—something that always calmed her down when she was little. They watched Tofu gobble up the remains of his dinner, Jessica's head resting on her mother's shoulder and Andrea stroking her hair. Outside, the clouds were beginning to break following the afternoon storm. The sun was visible, heading on its western path toward the horizon. In less than two hours time, it was going to make for another stunning southwestern sunset.

CHAPTER 47

Jessica tucked Tofu into her room with a fresh can of Fancy Feast. She arranged her pillows under the covers to make it look like she was asleep—a childhood classic—and shoved her keys and phone into her pockets. She looked out her bedroom window and was relieved to see that Claire's Malibu was already parked out front. *She must have been waiting down the street for Mom to leave.*

Jessica pulled her bottom drawer out and reached under a pile of teenage-era clothing for the last thing she needed. She tucked it into the back pocket of her jeans, shut her bedroom door, swish-clunked her way down the hall, and hurried out the front door.

The sky was beginning to show hints of pink in the dwindling clouds that still hung lazily overhead. Sunset had arrived. Jessica hurried down the driveway to the idling Malibu. She got into the passenger seat and the car shot forward as Claire jammed on the gas. Jessica's body rocked back as the Malibu accelerated.

"Geez, Jess, cutting it a little bit close, huh?" Claire asked.

"I'm sorry," she said. "My mom wouldn't leave. She kept asking me if I wanted her to stay."

"What did you tell her?" Claire looked up at the sky, which was brightening with splashes of orange, yellow, and purple.

"That my ankle hurt and I was tired. I said I was going to bed early." Jessica grabbed at the door frame to steady herself as Claire peeled around a corner and turned onto the main road. "Jesus, Claire, slow down."

"Slow down? It's sunset!" she exclaimed. "It's going to be dark soon. We need to get there and get inside, like now."

"Yeah, I know," Jessica said. She glanced at the brilliantly colored sky. "How long to get there?"

"I dunno," Claire said. She turned on her signal and drifted into the left lane. She passed by a maroon van with windows that were smeared with smudgy child-sized handprints. A tired woman sat behind the wheel, her head jutted forward and a blank expression on her face. "Maybe five to ten more minutes, as long as there's no traffic. You're lucky you live so close."

"I suppose. Only lucky if we can stop it. Not so lucky if it comes hunting in my neighborhood next."

Claire sailed down the road, running a yellow-going-on-red traffic signal as she veered onto Orion Street. "And you're sure you know how to get in? You looked it up?"

"Yeah, there are a lot of YouTube videos on how to pick a lock. You'd be surprised how easy it is." Jessica reached into her back pocket to make sure the lock picking kit was still there. It was. "I practiced at my apartment. I'm getting pretty good at it."

"Is that where you had it delivered?"

"God yes. That's one Amazon package I did not want to explain to my mom."

"Good call," Claire said, keeping her eyes on the road. The speedometer crept past sixty miles an hour as the Malibu careened down Orion Street. Wasp Canyon Road was only a couple of miles away.

The clouds exploded with vibrant hues. Pinks and purples swirled together on the curves of the remaining clouds, and orange streaked across the horizon where the sun was about to disappear.

A sign appeared for Wasp Canyon Estates. Claire slowed the Malibu—although not much—as they entered the intersection. Tires squealed as she turned left onto Wasp Canyon Road.

"Okay, Claire, slow it down now. You're gonna get us killed."

"*I'm* going to get us killed? Do you remember whose idea tonight was? Because it sure as hell wasn't mine."

"Claire, I'm sorry—"

"It's okay," Claire said, taking a deep breath and letting it out slowly. "I just didn't think getting in before dark was going to be the hard part. I don't want to be standing out there when that thing shows up, and you're still trying to fiddle with the damn lock."

"We talked about this. We couldn't get here until sundown because there are still reporters lurking around and they might see us."

"Reporters aren't the thing I'm worried about that might be lurking around." Claire watched the right side of the road, looking for the gate that marked Jasper's driveway. The sky was alight with color and all the cacti had taken on a rosy hue that would normally be beautiful, but instead felt eerie and surreal.

"There it is," Jessica said. The top of Cameron's front gate appeared in the distance.

"You sure that's it?" Claire asked.

"Yeah, I recognize it from Google Maps."

Claire slowed the Malibu to a crawl. "All this rushing to get here and now I just want to turn around and haul ass in the opposite direction," she said. She stopped the car in front of Cameron's gate.

The gate was ten feet tall and made of wrought iron. It spanned the driveway, although there were no walls attached to it. Instead there was a plethora of cacti, spread tightly across the front of the property and making a wall of their own. Chollas, prickly pears, and saguaros lined the road, all bathed in soft pink from the setting sun. A person could possibly make their way through the spiny fortress on foot, but a car didn't stand a chance.

The gate was slightly ajar, a chain carelessly draped over each side but not attached with a padlock. One could easily take the chain off and toss it to the ground. A careless cop, scared to be left alone in the dark to secure the gate, probably tossed the chain on as best he could, then hightailed it back to the safety of his vehicle. Why should he have to get torn apart to secure a gate to a house that wasn't even occupied?

Claire nudged the gate with the Malibu's front bumper. The gate creaked and began to separate, the chain slowly dragging link by link across the iron. Eventually the chain fell off and landed on the hood of the Malibu. It made a loud clang that caused both girls to jump. The chain scraped along the car's hood and slid off, landing in the dirt on the left side of the driveway.

"Eek, you think that's gonna leave a mark?" Jessica asked.

"On this old thing? By now I just consider all the bumps and scrapes as added character."

"Well, I think some character just got added to your hood."

"Something to remind me of all the fun we're gonna have tonight." Claire tapped the gas, and the gate groaned as it opened wide enough for the Malibu to pass by. The gate's clasp dragged along the right side of the car, sounding like one long, sharp claw cutting across the metal. Dirt crunched underneath the Malibu's tires as Claire crept forward along the path.

Jessica turned and looked behind her. The gate was swinging closed again, stopping at the same slightly ajar position it had been in before they went through. Only now the chain that had been draped across the bars was lying in the dirt on the side of the driveway. She turned forward in the seat again, surveying the long expanse of driveway. It was unpaved, with a generous amount of potholes and divots. It would need to be redone once the rainy season had passed—but who would be there to do it?

The brilliance of the sunset was fading from the sky when the house finally came into view. White walls swept upward into a towering arch which covered an elaborate pair of wooden doors. The wood looked thick, solid, and expensive. Metalwork etched through the wood in an intricate pattern. A metal ring hung on each side, made of the same metal that decorated the wood.

Two saguaros stood on either side of the double doors where the archway began. Each one had many arms, reaching out and upward toward the sky. *Must be hundreds of years old,* she thought. Jessica remembered her dad telling her how a saguaro does not grow its first arm until it is at least a century old. These two saguaros must have been brought in from elsewhere, and set up as guards to tower over the front entrance.

Claire pulled up to the archway and killed the engine. Dusk was setting in and the beautiful colors of the sunset had faded to a dull, lifeless gray.

Jessica and Claire got out of the car at the same time, shutting their doors in unison. They looked at each other from across the scraped hood of the Malibu, and then up at Cameron's house. Without saying a word, they walked up to the front door. Jessica dropped to her knees and pulled the lock picking kit from her back pocket. She inserted the pick and followed the steps the same way she had seen the 15-year-old boy on YouTube do it. Claire surveyed the driveway and surrounding desert for any signs of movement. The wind had died down, and not even the mesquite trees rustled in the stillness of the darkening landscape.

There was an audible *click* as Jessica hit the final pin in the mechanism, and the dead bolt rolled away. She stood up, brushing the dust off of her knees, and looked at Claire. Claire turned her eyes away from the deepening gloom of Cameron's front yard, looked at Jessica's hopeful expression, and nodded. A silent communication passed between them—the time to turn back had come and gone as they looked at each other under the grand archway of Cameron's empty estate. An archway he would never get to pass underneath again, and a beautiful home he would never get to return to after his final hike in Wasp Canyon.

Jessica and Claire turned and faced the front door, their backs to the descending twilight. Jessica reached out and turned the etched metal door knob. The front door shuddered, and then creaked open on metal hinges in desperate need of maintenance following the recent spike in humidity. Darkness hovered beyond the door, and twilight was giving way to night behind them. Jessica stepped over the threshold, and Claire followed. Once inside, Jessica turned and shut the heavy wooden door into its frame. She turned the dead bolt, and heard it lock into place. *Here we go,* she thought. She said a small prayer: *Hi Daddy, it's Jess, please let us get through this mess.*

Jessica and Claire took each other's hands and began walking forward, the darkness of the house swallowing them.

CHAPTER 48

Moser sat at his dining room table, picking at his wife's meatloaf with little interest. He wasn't hungry—hadn't been all day. If he really wanted to be honest, he hadn't been hungry for weeks now. Something about seeing people filleted into bloody piles of meat could really damper the 'ol appetite. He poked at the asparagus with his fork, pushing the spears together and then pulling them apart. The congealing butter surrounding the asparagus smeared across the plate like syrup. Moser couldn't bring himself to take another bite. The butter reminded him of the sticky, thickening blood inside the body cavity of Taylor Kilburn—the way it came together into an oily molasses. He pushed the plate away and turned his attention to the kitchen's bay window. Outside, the sun silently slipped below the mountains.

Lynette Moser had noticed the change in her husband's appetite long before the night of August seventeenth. Since the start of the month, Carl's hearty love for food had dwindled, and then disappeared altogether. Carl had tough cases before—plenty in fact. But this complete aversion to food was unheard of in the Moser household, regardless of the rigors of Carl's career.

Lynette always kept out of Carl's affairs when it came to his police work. Although her involvement—or lack thereof—was never discussed, it was a silent agreement that went along with their wedding vows. Carl never brought the stresses of work home with him, and their talk around the dinner table had always consisted of the kids, travel, and projects Lynette wanted to do around the house. Until now. Now there was very little talk around the dinner table, if any. A dark cloud had swept into their lives, and it arrived at the same time as the monsoon clouds.

Lynette knew something was wearing on her husband, the way a wife always knows when something is burdening the man with whom she shares her bed. What may seem like subtle symptoms of stress to others felt like screaming sirens to her. Decades of marriage could do such things. At some point in a marriage your spouse begins to know when you are stressed before you even do yourself. And Carl was more stressed than Lynette had ever seen him before. He puttered about the house, barely ate, and his sleep was fitful and filled with dark dreams. Carl never mentioned these nightmares to her, but after many years of hearing his peaceful slumber and methodical snores, Lynette knew when her husband's sleep was troubled.

The recent animal maulings were the cause of her husband's nightmares. Lynette knew of the dog attack Carl had suffered as a child—it was hard to avoid since the scars still lingered on his left shoulder all these years later. Carl told the story to her once, speaking in a mechanical tone that bothered her more than the story itself. He never spoke of it again, and she didn't press the matter. But, as a wife always knows, she knew the attack bothered him still. Not just by his reluctance to discuss the matter, but by the way he shied away from his children's television programs when they involved animals attacking humans. She could see the unease in his face, the rigidity of his spine, the stiffening of his chin. And then the excuse would come—whether it be showering, yard work, or meeting the guys for a beer at the local watering hole. Lynette would smile and say "Of course, dear"—secretly excited when the chosen excuse was yard work—and then go back to her household duties, acting none the wiser. Inside, she knew better, though. Inside, a wife always knows.

The electric oranges and sultry pinks of the evening's sunset faded away. The last light of the day hovered on the horizon, about to give up to the darkness that had crept across the sky. Stars were visible through the parting clouds, and the moon, nearing the peak of its cycle, cast a silvery glow on the landscape.

The beauty of the desert's twilight was lost on Moser. He barely noticed when his wife removed his plate of uneaten meatloaf. All Moser could think about was the darkness—the overwhelming, suffocating darkness that took over the land. There was no stopping it. The darkness was like a tsunami of black dread that spread across the world and washed away the safety of the light. And with the darkness, dark things came with it. Predators of the night: owls, snakes, wolves, lions... and something else. Something that was the stuff of legends, but had snuck into reality under the cover of that same darkness. Yes, when the darkness came, the teeth and the claws and the snarling came with it.

She must be there by now, he thought. A young girl still scraped and bruised and broken from the first time she encountered the thing of legends. She was there, in that dark house near that dark canyon, trying to make a difference. *Trying to save people.* Trying to save *children.* And here he was, sitting at his dining room table, being silently judged by his wife—who didn't know Moser was very aware of her silent-judgment face. For all that a woman knows, a man knows, too. A slight shift of the eyes, or the vague yet tell-tale signs of disquiet—those things are picked up during all those years of marriage. Entire conversations could be made with a few expressions—for better or for worse. And right now his wife knew damn well what was bothering him, and he knew damn well that not a word would be said on the matter, because they both knew damn well that he could not talk about the teeth and the claws and the darkness. Especially not when that darkness was pressing upon the kitchen window the way that it was.

Moser had made his decision while he was poking at his cold, congealing asparagus. He already knew it in his gut; he was just waiting for his mind to catch up. But instead of acting on it—partially out of stubbornness, but mostly out of fear— he stared out the window at the blackness beyond and thought about Jessica Cleary. About her describing the initial attack, about her waiting for hours at the police station, about her in the interview room insisting that a chupacabra was on the loose, about her hurt expression when he didn't believe her. And most of all he thought about her calm, determined voice on the phone as she told him of her intentions for tonight.

So instead of sending a squad car to the Jasper residence to pick her up for trespassing, Moser had told no one in his department about her intent on breaking and entering. They undoubtedly would have put a stop to it, and then no proof of the chupacabra would ever be obtained. The monsoons would taper off, and the stuff of legends would disappear, becoming a legend once again. But how many more would die before that happened?

He watched the gloom spread across his backyard. Before long, the tree branches would disappear against the inky sky. Moser wondered when exactly he accepted that monsters were real—that something really does go bump in the night, and that the bump might be a trap to lure you out to a gruesome end. He supposed he believed Jessica's story to some degree ever since he spoke to her at the station, after which he spent the night googling articles about chupacabras and stealing glances at his sleeping wife to make sure she couldn't see what he was looking at in the dark. All he knew for sure was he now believed Jessica's theory, and that her plan to obtain proof of the chupacabra might be the only viable course of action. Trying to convince a practical police chief that a fairy tale monster was stalking the countryside had gone badly, just as he suspected it would. But he had to try. And now there was little time to act before more people were dead. If he could provide them with undeniable proof, maybe they could finally come together and put this fucking thing in the ground. And let him back on the damn case. This was *his* case, and he was going to be the one to close it.

Moser's shoulder ached where he had been bitten so many years ago, although teeth had not touched his flesh in over five decades. He expected much more aching before the night was through. He hoped that, come the morning of August eighteenth, he would still be able to say that teeth had not touched his flesh. It was full dark now, and he had waited long enough. Not just for tonight, but for his whole life. Forty-nine years was a long time to hold onto a childhood fear. And it was an even longer time for a grown man—one who had sworn to protect the people, no less—to cower in the corner when what those people needed protecting from had long claws and sharp teeth.

Moser stood abruptly from the table. His chair scraped across the floor and nearly toppled over in the process. The clatter caused Lynette to look up from the sink, a soapy dish in one hand and a sponge in the other. Neither spoke, and the sound of running water filled the silence.

"There's somewhere I have to be tonight," Moser said finally. "Someone from the case I'm working needs my help."

"Oh, yes, of course," Lynette said, her voice sounding soft against the sound of the running faucet. "Will you be gone long?"

"I sure as hell hope not," Moser said as he strapped his holster onto his belt. "But you don't need to wait up for me. I'm not sure how long this is going to take."

"You be careful now, Carl. You know how I worry." Lynette gave him a light kiss on the cheek as he passed by her in the kitchen, on his way to the garage.

"You got it, babe," Moser said, and gave her a wink. A kiss and a wink—that was their goodbye tradition. Only this time when Moser looked at his wife, he didn't see her usual parting smile as she bid him farewell. Moser recognized the look immediately—twenty-eight years of marriage could make you attuned to such things. And even though Lynnette's expression was subtle and lasted only a moment—and she would deny it was ever noticeable in the first place—Moser saw the look of pride that touched his wife's face as he walked out the door.

CHAPTER 49

"It's dark as shit in here right now," Claire said in a harsh whisper. She was breathing heavily, standing in the foyer next to Jessica.

"Claire, we knew it was going to be dark in here," Jessica said, sounding much calmer than her friend. "We just need to let our eyes adjust."

They stood in the foyer, the house silent as a tomb. Even in the darkness, Jessica could sense a large, open space beyond the foyer.

"Claire, you need to stop hyperventilating. We're gonna be fine."

"You sure that detective isn't going to come and help us? Or arrest us?"

"I doubt it. I hoped he would help us, but I guess not. He probably doesn't even think we would actually go through with this."

"Yeah, I'm kinda surprised we got this far myself," Claire said.

Jessica felt along the front door, wanting to double check that it was locked. It was. She turned away from the door and looked at Claire, who was becoming clearer as Jessica's eyes adapted to the dimness of the house. Claire looked worried.

"We're not burglars, Claire," she said. "We're here to help people."

Claire looked at her as she chewed on one of her fingernails. Jessica could see a glimmer of moonlight reflected in her wide eyes. She looked up. A large skylight was cut into the vaulted ceiling above them. Cold, white moonlight splashed across the high walls of the foyer. A long, thin table went along one wall, with a large vase in the center. Wilted, white flowers were in the vase, a few still reaching up toward the skylight. The moon made the flowers appear blue.

Beyond Claire, Jessica could now see that the foyer opened up to a very large room that made up the center of the house. *A great room, that's what they call them,* she thought. The living room was sunken, with three steps leading down from the foyer into the sitting area. Low, modern-looking couches and chairs faced a gigantic square coffee table in the center of the room. A fireplace stood on the left-hand side, and the right side opened up to an equally impressive kitchen. A shimmering counter sat atop a kitchen island that was easily the size of a car. *Shimmering?* Jessica thought, and looked above her. Multiple skylights were cut into the vaulted ceiling of the great room as well, moonlight casting through them and causing the granite countertop to sparkle. Moonlight was also filtering in from the wall of windows that made up the entire northeastern-facing side of the great room. *The sunrise must be spectacular in here,* she thought.

Jessica took a few steps forward, passing Claire to get a better look at the fireplace. Her eyes struggled to make out the dark shape hanging on the bricks high above the hearth. It was narrow and roughly three feet long. "Geez, is that a gun? Hanging over the fireplace?"

Claire was still behind her. Jessica assumed she was also checking to make sure the front door was locked. "Of course he had a gun," she said, preoccupied with the door. "He's from Texas, remember?"

"Yeah, I guess you're right."

"You think it's loaded?" Claire called.

Jessica thought of Cameron, smiling in the sunshine as he told her to always be prepared. For anything life might throw at'cha, he had said. "Yeah," Jessica said, "I'm pretty sure it is."

"You think we might need it?" Claire asked.

"I'm hoping it doesn't come to that," Jessica murmured, staring at the dark shape mounted over the fireplace. She turned her gaze to the wall of windows which stretched two-stories high thanks to the vaulted ceiling. Beyond the wall of glass, Jessica could make out a large patio surrounded by a low, stucco wall. Beyond the wall, the Santa Catalinas were visible in the moonlight. She felt a lump form in her throat at the sight of the mountains. *It must be running through the desert at this very moment,* she thought. *Heading right for us.*

Claire came up beside her, startling Jessica when their shoulders brushed against each other. They stood side by side in the dark and took in the expanse of the great room. "Holy begeezus," Claire whispered. "Your friend Cameron must have been a gazillionaire. Look at this place. Even the ceiling is made out of glass."

Jessica looked to either side of them. A long, wide hallway went in both directions, leading to two different wings of the house. The floors were white marble. *He really was a gazillionaire,* she thought. Jessica pictured Cameron in the great room, enjoying one glorious sunrise after the other. *He'll never get to experience another sunrise,* she thought. *And if we aren't careful, we might not get to see another one either.*

Jessica looked back at the mountains and her stomach fluttered. She wanted to still be around when the sun rose—Claire and her both. "We need to get set up. I don't know when it is going to show up and I want to be ready."

"You sure it's going to come tonight?" Claire asked.

"I hope so. Out of all the attacks I researched, they always seemed to come five or six days apart. So that means tonight or tomorrow."

"I can't believe I'm saying this, but I hope it comes tonight. I don't want to do this again tomorrow," Claire said.

"Amen, sister friend."

Jessica's CAM boot clunked on the marble floor of the foyer. When she reached the steps going down into the great room the marble switched to carpeting and her footsteps softened on the plush carpet. They made their way down the few steps into the living room. As if on cue, the patio lights turned on. Claire jumped and clamped her hand on Jessica's shoulder. The great room was flooded with warm, golden light.

"What the—is it the cops?" Claire asked.

"No, it's just the landscape lights. I'm sure he has them on a timer or something," Jessica whispered.

Ground lights spanned the perimeter of the yard, each one made of beautifully crackled glass. The warm glow lit the low wall and surrounding yard. A large cobblestone patio was on the opposite side of the wall of glass, with a metal fire pit in the center and comfortable-looking patio couches and chairs surrounding it. Jessica could see the valley lights of the city off to the right. *Present situation aside, this must be a wonderful place to sit out and enjoy the fire and a glass of wine,* she thought. She felt a pang of jealousy, quickly followed by guilt when she remembered what happened to Cameron.

"And explain to me again *how* we know your mythical beast won't know we're here," Claire said.

"It's not a mythical beast, Claire. It's a chupacabra."

"Right. So explain to me again how this *chupacabra* will think that nobody is home."

"Because the lights are off."

Claire stiffened under the warm glow. *"Because the lights are off?"* She threw a hand toward the wall of windows. *"Do those look off to you?"*

"I mean the indoor lights. All the other houses had the lights on inside."

"Jessica!" Claire exclaimed. "You are basing our *lives* on the assumption that it will think the house is empty because the *inside* lights are off?"

"Claire, what—"

"Do you know what *assuming* does? With the asses and you and me." Claire gestured rapidly between the two of them.

Jessica sighed. "What are you getting at?"

"That assuming makes you and me an ass! We don't know if it will think we are home or not just based on the inside lights being off. What about the people back in 1987? Some of them were woken up in the middle of the night when they heard it banging around. *They were asleep.* I'm sure all of their house lights were off when they first heard it."

"But they probably turned the lights on when they got up," Jessica argued. "Those houses were also really close together. Some of them even shared backyards. I'm sure *some* of the houses had lights on inside, and when it started banging around, whoever went outside first, that's who it attacked." She shrugged. "From what I read, it bangs around until someone turns on a light and comes outside. If no one turns on a light or goes outside, it moves on to the next house."

"What about the final house? The family of four? No one went outside then."

"That doesn't mean they didn't turn on a light inside when they heard it banging around. They probably turned on the lights to go check on the children."

"You're *assuming* again."

"Yeah, I know. I'm sorry. If you don't want to stay, I underst—"

"Hell no!" Claire exclaimed. "It's completely dark outside now. There's no fucking way I'm going back out there until morning," she said, gesturing toward the front door. "Let's just hope you're right about the damn lights."

"If it attacked every house it came across there wouldn't have been anyone left in that entire neighborhood," Jessica said. "That's why it attacked those certain houses. Someone came outside to check, or they turned lights on inside. And we aren't going to do that."

"What about those lights?" Claire asked, pointing to the crackled glass twinkling outside near the stucco wall.

"A lot of houses have outdoor lighting. That other neighborhood even had *street lights*." Jessica grabbed Claire's shoulders to get her to stop gaping out at the patio. "Claire, we will not turn on any inside lights. And we will *absolutely* not go outside. After banging around with no results it will give up and move on. And this actually works in our favor," Jessica pointed to the lit patio, "because now I will get much better video of the thing."

Claire sighed, defeated. "So now what?"

"We get into position. Let's get behind that couch there." Jessica pointed to the couch that was closest to the glass wall, facing the foyer. They made their way around the other furniture and got down to their knees in front of the couch. Jessica peered around the right side, making sure she had a good view of the patio. Claire did the same on the left side. They returned to the center of the couch and sat down, legs crossed and facing each other.

"Okay, here we go," Jessica said. "I'm going to take the video; you're going to take pictures. Make sure your flash is off."

Claire pulled out her phone, pressed a couple buttons, then nodded. "No flash."

"Okay, good. So you will peek around from that side, and I'll do this side. When it shows up, *do not* get up and *do not* make any noise. We will film and take pictures until it moves on. Then I will call Moser and say we have the proof he needs. And you will call 911 and tell them the McElroys are in danger and they need to get the hell over there."

"Jessica?" Claire asked. Neither had realized it but they were holding hands. "What if it goes straight to the McElroys?"

Jessica didn't respond, although her grip on Claire's hands tightened. Finally she said, "Let's pray that doesn't happen."

They squeezed each other's hands once more and let go. They got onto their hands and knees and crawled to their designated sides of the white sofa. The white carpet felt plush and velvety on Jessica's healing palms as she crawled into place. She lowered herself to her stomach and peered around the side of the sofa at the wall of glass, camera phone at the ready. The patio was empty, the only movement coming from a palo verde tree that occasionally rustled with the breeze.

"Jessica?" Claire whispered from the opposite side of the sofa.

"Yeah?"

"What do you think the monsoons have to do with it? I mean, why does it only come out during monsoon season?

And not just any monsoon season, but only a crazy El Niño one like this one."

Jessica lay in the dark, feeling the luxurious carpet against her stomach. She watched the patio for signs of movement. After a pause, she whispered, "I don't really know. I couldn't find anything about that in my research. Hell, I didn't even make the connection about the monsoons until Howie told me about the attacks in '87." They lay in silence for a while. "I guess it has something to do with the water. I mean, that has to be it, right? All the water in the canyon brings it out of hibernation?"

"I guess so," Claire whispered from her side of the couch. "I just find it hard to believe it can hibernate for years without food."

"There were never any animals around the canyon when I went running. Maybe it ate those first."

"Yeah, maybe. It still doesn't explain why only a heavy monsoon season brings it out of the canyon, though." Silence took over the great room, then Claire added, "You'd think it would want to stay in the dark where it was safe."

"That's why it only attacks neighborhoods near the mountains. It has to get back to the canyon before sunrise."

Claire sighed. "I know. I just wish I knew what it was about the monsoons. If it hadn't rained so much this summer, would we even be here right now?"

Jessica laughed quietly. "We would probably be at Lindy's working on our third beer."

Claire groaned. "Oh, don't *tease* me."

Time crawled by. Jessica started to feel drowsy as the adrenaline gave way to fatigue. She glanced at her QuikFit, the screen saying it was 8:42. Right around the time Cuthbertson and Arlington were attacked, if the newspapers were correct. So where was it?

Jessica was beginning to fear that Claire was right—that the chupacabra wasn't coming at all tonight or it might already be at the McElroy house. Then she heard a thud as something on the left side of the patio fell over.

CHAPTER 50

Moser didn't live nearly as close to Wasp Canyon as the Clearys did. He cursed himself for not leaving sooner, pressing his foot down on the gas pedal as he sped down Carson Avenue. *How long had it been dark now? An hour? Stupid old man with stupid childish fears. I should have been there at sundown. I should have helped her break in, for Christ's sake. If she's even there at all.*

He blasted through an intersection, looking at the signal as he shot underneath. There was no denying that one—he had just run a red light. He scanned his rearview mirror, looking for headlights to peel out behind him and turn on their top lights. And here he was, being scared of the damn cops, when he was a damn cop. He slowed his speed, thought better of it, and then pressed his foot down again. He had to get there, and fast.

Maybe it won't come tonight. Maybe it hasn't been long enough since the last attack. It did get two people last time, it might still be full. Full from what, Moser didn't know. It's not like it ate the bodies. *Chupacabra does mean goat-sucker—* *they named it that because it sucked the blood of those farm* *animals.* Moser's stomach dropped. *That's it. That's what it* *does. It drinks the victim's blood and moves on. We thought* *the victims were low on blood because of their wounds. But it* *drank it all. That's where the blood went—it drank it. All of it.*

Moser moaned, feeling his insides clench down into a cramp of nausea and fear. He thought of the congealing butter on his dinner plate, grateful he hadn't eaten much of anything. He was queasy enough as it was.

Maybe it won't come tonight, he thought again. He'll get to the Jasper house in fifteen minutes—maybe less. He'll stake out the place with Jessica for a little while longer, and then they will throw in the towel and go home. And he can pat himself on the back for trying.

That's right, maybe it won't come tonight. The pit in Moser's stomach did not abate despite his wishful thinking. Instead, it continued to worsen, growing heavier and harder to ignore with each passing moment. Perhaps it was because, deep down, he knew it was already there.

CHAPTER 51

Jessica felt an icy chill slide down her back, vertebra by vertebra. She held her breath, afraid that even breathing would give away her position. She heard a small gasp on the other side of the couch, then nothing but silence. She tightened her grip on her phone, the camera app loaded and ready to record.

The silence stretched out, seeming to go on endlessly on the other side of the glass. She strained to hear movement out there—to hear anything. The plush carpet now felt rough under her stomach and her shoulders ached from her hunched position, but she didn't dare move.

Jessica saw a shadow moving along the dark perimeter of the yard. It was still a distance from the lights that lined the patio wall. From what she could tell, the shadow was curved and had spike-like eminences extending from the bulk of the curve. *Its spine,* she thought. *Those spikes are its vertebrae. God, no wonder the eyewitness accounts said it had spines on its back. The shadow looks like a freaking dinosaur.* And then it was gone, back into the darkness on the left side of the patio.

The shadow was there for such a brief time, she thought maybe her eyes were playing tricks on her. Maybe it was just the palo verde tree after all. She was about to whisper to Claire and ask if she saw anything, when the shadow reemerged, slightly closer to the patio. She no longer needed to ask Claire if she saw it, too—Jessica heard a stifled whimper come from the other side of the couch.

The shadow extended further into the light of the patio. It was still just the long curve of its back, with the protruding vertebrae looking like spines. It went along the perimeter of darkness, but did not enter the light. Jessica realized she wasn't even sure if she remembered what it looked like. She had been so disoriented by fear and exhaustion at the mouth of the canyon, and it had stayed in the shadows and been partially obscured by the branches of a tree. Now it was outside, only feet away from being illuminated by the patio lights.

Jessica could feel her head becoming swimmy from lack of oxygen. She forced herself to take a slow, silent breath through her mouth. She lifted her phone a few inches from the carpet and pointed the lens at the patio, her finger hovering over the red record button.

The shadow hovered on the outskirts of the light. She wondered if it was debating if it should move forward, or if it was figuring out what to knock over next. *Or maybe it is listening for you,* she thought, and fought the urge to shudder. She didn't want to move a millimeter more than necessary. The shadow inched further into the light, the bulge of its shoulders now visible. A large, elongated shape extended from the shoulders: its head. It looked around the patio. *Dear God, was it looking into the house?*

The shadow disappeared back into the darkness, and another thud came from somewhere off to the left. Closer than the first noise, and louder. Jessica wondered what was over there to knock over. *In the morning,* she thought. *We will go take a look at what it was in the morning.* The thought was meant to be comforting, but it came out flat and made her feel worse.

More silence followed the second crash and the shadow did not return. After what felt like eons of time, she heard the muffled, barely-there voice of Claire whisper, "Jessica… I see it." It sounded like Claire was on the verge of tears.

"Claire—" Jessica whispered, then stopped. The shadow was back, heading toward the patio. It stretched across the cobblestones, impossibly long in the warm glow. As the creature got closer to the edge of the patio, the shadow shortened—although not nearly as much as Jessica would have liked. It stopped at the edge of the light. Jessica steadied her phone, not realizing that her hand had been shaking, and pressed the **Record** button.

A timer appeared in the bottom right corner of the phone's screen, counting the seconds of her recording. She remembered hitting **Begin** on her QuikFit the first time she went running, and watching the seconds go by on the small screen. She stared at the recording timer on her phone, transfixed by the changing numbers. Something entered the frame of her video, and Jessica felt her stomach churn. She looked up from the phone and out the window.

The chupacabra stepped into the light. It was over three feet tall at its shoulders. The shoulders were laced with muscles, which bulged and rippled as they extended down its torso. The muscles looked thick and powerful, like those of a pit bull or a lion. The chupacabra's hide was dark gray, the skin thick and hairless. Scraggly, dark hairs stuck up from its elbows and haunches. Elongated claws protruded from the hairless flesh of its paws. The claws stuck out like those of a bear, although they were much more curved.

As the chupacabra entered the center of the patio, fully bathed in the glow from the landscape lighting, Jessica could finally make out its facial features. The face was a hideous thing—something that belonged in the pages of horror novels and in the depths of nightmares. Its snout was extended like a dog's, the muzzle thick and devoid of whiskers, and canine teeth protruded from its jowls. The ears were pointed upward and listening for signs of life in the dark house.

The eyes were the most haunting of all of the chupacabra's features. Jessica would take the teeth and the claws over those eyes any day. She imagined—if she did live through this—she would see those eyes in her dreams every night until she left this world. The eyes were dull, red, and full of hunger and hate. The red irises shimmered lifelessly in the patio light, resembling a doll's eyes more than a living thing. Those eyes were hunting, and they were staring directly at her. She bit the inside of her lips, trying to stifle a scream. She tasted copper on the tip of her tongue.

At the taste of blood, Jessica felt a sudden and overwhelming urge to jump up from behind the couch and run for the front door. This was the creature that chased her through the canyon. This was the monster that murdered Cameron Jasper. The thing that set a trap for her, and so many others. And it was looking at her—looking *through* her. Jessica stared at it, puzzled. It wasn't looking at her; it was looking at its own reflection in the window. The lights outside were reflected in the glass, and the thing was discerning if its own reflection was a threat. A wave of relief washed over her.

The chupacabra turned to a patio chair, grabbed it in its paws, and flung the chair across the yard. The metal chair flew across the patio as if it was made of nothing but plastic and feathers. The crash it made as it hit the stucco wall made her jump. She dropped the phone on the carpet and quickly looked down to retrieve it. She brought the phone up, looking into the screen to center it on the chupacabra, and saw that it wasn't there. She looked up, startled. Where had it gone?

Jessica could hear herself hyperventilating, and willed herself to breathe slower. As she regained control of her breathing, she heard a muffled sound on the other side of the couch. It was Claire. She was crying, and from the sounds of it, trying to get herself under control. The soft sobs broke Jessica's heart, and she wished she had never brought Claire along. She wished she had gone on this dangerous errand alone. Claire didn't deserve to be put into this situation, especially not by her best friend.

"Claire," Jessica whispered, "where did it go?"

Soft sobs from the other side of the couch. "I want to go home," she whispered through her sniffles.

"Claire—"

"It's waiting for us. It threw the chair, then ran into the dark to wait." Claire took a deep breath. Her sobs softened and then came to a stop. "It's waiting for us to go outside."

"Okay, keep taking pictures. And stay *quiet*," Jessica whispered, more to herself than to Claire.

They lay in silence, surrounded by darkness except for the glow of the patio and the moonlight filtering down from the skylights. Within a couple minutes, the chupacabra returned, grabbed the metal fire pit, and dumped it on its side. Coals tumbled out onto the cobblestones. Its red eyes looked up at the dark wall of windows again, scanned it for movement, and then it ran back into the shadows. It moved with a litheness that seemed unnatural for an animal of its size and build. Although, nothing seemed natural at this moment—not anymore.

The seconds ticked by on her phone recorder, turning into minutes. Her QuikFit glowed dimly in the moonlight. Her heart rate was 164. *Just breathe. Just breathe in and out and it will go away soon. You're going to have a freaking heart attack.*

The chupacabra returned, its feet scattering the coals from the fire pit. It tossed the patio couch next, sending it toward the glass wall. Jessica held her breath and waited for the couch to collide with the window, shattering it and removing the barrier between them. The couch stopped just short of the window, lying on its side with its cushions torn. *It's getting angry,* she thought. *It's mad that no one is coming outside.*

It didn't leave the patio this time. Instead of running for the shadows to lie in wait, the chupacabra stood next to the fallen fire pit, its features grotesquely illuminated in the patio lights. The red eyes stared at the window, watching. Jessica was sure it couldn't see them, not with the landscape lights reflected in the glass. Yet there it stood—a muscular pile of gray flesh, curved claws, and horribly long canines. *What is it doing?* she thought, fear rising in her belly. The carpeting felt like sandpaper against her stomach. *What the hell is it doing?*

Claire whispered from the other side of the couch, "Jessica... *why isn't it leaving?*"

Jessica watched, fascinated. She had no idea what it was doing, standing there and staring at the window like that. It made no move to advance, but it also made no move to retreat. "I don't know. Maybe it's deciding if it's time to leave?"

She watched the chupacabra lift its chin into the humid night air. The chin went from side to side, its neck stretched out. The chin seemed to be searching for something. *Not its chin,* she thought. *It's not searching with its chin... it's searching with its nose.* Jessica felt dangerously close to her bladder letting go. She stared at the creature in front of her with dawning horror. *It can smell us.*

She frantically searched the wall of glass for possible openings. Other than an oversized sliding glass door—which was closed—there were no windows that could be opened. *But how the hell is it able to smell us? Those are dual-pane windows, for Christ's sake.* She looked toward the kitchen, and her heart sank. When they came in, she had briefly scanned the dark kitchen. She noticed the sliding glass window over the sink was shut, and didn't give it another thought. It was the light that mattered anyway. What she failed to notice in the dark was the long, narrow jalousie window that was positioned above the sliding window. *Probably to let smoke and steam out when you're cooking,* she thought. *If it's hot outside and you don't want to open the whole big window, you just open the small slat one instead to let the smoke out.* And with the monsoons, Cameron might have opened just that one small window to smell the rain, but not the big one over the sink because then the rain would get inside. She stared at the jalousie window with crushing dismay. There were only three horizontal panes of glass, but they were all open.

She turned her attention back to the patio. The chupacabra lowered its chin and stared straight ahead at the wall of glass. Jessica thought, *It knows. It knows we're here.* She said, "I'm so sorry, Claire. I didn't know."

"Didn't know what?" Claire whispered, sounding panicky.

"It doesn't use the indoor lights to hunt with. It doesn't use the lights at all. I was wrong." Jessica felt tears stinging at her eyes. She watched the chupacabra, motionless on the patio and staring straight ahead. *Staring at us, because it knows we're inside.*

"Jessica, what the fuck are you saying?"

"It hunts by smell, Claire. I should have known. God, I'm so sorry."

"Jess—"

"It lives and hunts in the dark." *Jesus, how could I be so stupid?* "It doesn't rely on its vision to hunt. The lights mean nothing. To find its prey it relies on its hearing… and on its smell." She paused. Claire said nothing, waiting. "There's an open window in the kitchen, Claire. It's a small one. I didn't notice it in the dark."

Claire gasped, louder than Jessica would have liked. She supposed it didn't matter if they made noise, though—not anymore. It knew they were there. The chupacabra hadn't moved from its position on the patio since it smelled the air. It stood there like a statue, staring at the window. *Like one of those Anubis guards in Egypt,* she thought.

"We have to get out of here," Jessica whispered.

"No shit," Claire whispered back.

All Jessica could think of was getting to the front door and to not stop running until she was either tackled or she got inside the car. If she distracted it from Claire at least that would be something—maybe Claire could manage to get away. Right as Jessica pressed herself up from the floor, the chupacabra darted to the left and out of the light. Jessica stopped mid-push and scanned the patio rapidly from side to side. *Where the hell did it go now?*

Claire was already up from her side of the couch. She crouched beside Jessica and began tugging at her arm. "Let's go—"

Jessica continued to scan the empty patio, ignoring Claire's urgent tugging. She pushed herself up to her hands and knees. "Where the hell did it go?"

Claire's head jerked up to look at the patio, unaware that the chupacabra had left its sentinel position by the fire pit. Both girls looked out at the patio, searching.

"Maybe it decided to go after all," Claire said hopefully.

The landscape lighting cut out, and Cameron Jasper's patio was submerged into overwhelming darkness.

CHAPTER 52

Moser hurtled down Orion Street. His speedometer read seventy-eight and he didn't suspect that it was malfunctioning. Wasp Canyon Road was a mile up ahead.

Moser wasn't a spiritual man, nor was he one to believe in palm reading or premonitions. Something, however, had started to claw at him—a deep ache in his belly that stretched into his chest and wrapped its talons around his heart. A horrible sense of dread had come over him that he was almost out of time.

He spent too much time weighing his options, too long debating what was the right thing to do. He knew what was right all along, but he refused to give into it until it was almost too late. He spent so long deciding if he was brave enough to go that now it might be too late for it to even matter. He had finally chosen to face his demons, and that demon might escape him before he even got a chance to vanquish it. And it might do so much more than just escape.

The intersection of Wasp Canyon Road came into view. As he hastily made the turn he saw burnt rubber was already smeared across the intersection. Someone else had come this way, and they were also in a hurry. It had come from *her*. He knew it in his gut. Jessica Cleary was at Jasper's house, and she had gone there in a hurry. He wondered if she had gone alone. He wondered if she was alone with it right now. Or if *it* was alone in the house, having killed her and now waiting for him. The scar tissue across his left shoulder throbbed. Moser flipped on his high beams, and made his way up Wasp Canyon Road.

CHAPTER 53

Jessica's hope of them both making it to the safety of the car died along with the lights. "We have to go." She tried to stand up, but Claire yanked her back down.

"What are you doing? If it comes back, it will see you!"

"It's not over there anymore, Claire," she said, standing up. "It ran off and killed the lights. Besides, it already knows we're here." She reached down, took Claire's hand, and pulled her up. *"We have to get the fuck out of here."*

"Isn't it safer to stay inside?"

"We both know it's capable of getting inside houses," Jessica said. "It's done it before."

"Yeah, okay," Claire said. "Which way? What do we do?"

"God, this is a long shot, but let's try to make it for the car. It's probably still out back somewhere. And if it gets in here, we're dead."

Claire groaned, jumped up and down a couple times to limber herself up, then nodded. "I didn't park that far away from the door," she whispered. "Maybe we can make it."

"Or at least one of us can," Jessica said, grabbing Claire's hand and heading through the dark living room toward the front door.

Claire jerked her hand away, making Jessica stop partway up the living room steps. "No way. *No way.* We're both getting out of here," she insisted. She grasped Jessica's hand again and squeezed it tightly.

"I got you into this, Claire, and I'm getting you out. Now come on." She tugged on Claire's hand, and they ascended the remaining steps into the foyer.

Jessica's boot stepped off of the carpeting and onto the marble floor. It made a loud clunk. *Just great,* she thought. *I'm getting stalked by a monster hell beast that hunts by sound and smell and every time I take a step it makes a loud clunking noise.* If she hadn't known any better, she would have thought the chupacabra planned it this way all along. It makes you feel like you *really* got away, and then it gets you, once and for all. They made their way to the front door, Claire's footsteps silent and Jessica's clunking with each left step.

They stopped at the front door. Jessica pressed her hand against the heavy wood door and said a silent prayer before reaching for the lock to release the deadbolt. *Daddy, it's Jess. Please help me to get Claire out of this mess.*

She reached for the lock, and just as her fingers touched the metal latch, a heavy, splintering crash rippled through the thick wood. Claire screamed. Jessica stumbled back, pulling her hand away from the door as if she had touched fire. Another blow slammed into the front door, and then a third. Jessica could hear wood cracking, but the door held. She remembered the decorative metalwork that adorned the outside of the door. *The metal must be keeping the door from breaking apart.* There was a fourth, final blow, and then silence. Jessica and Claire stood in the dark foyer, clutching each other.

When another blow didn't come, Jessica reached for the door lock. Claire grasped at her with wild hands. *"What are you doing? You're going to open the fucking door?"* she cried.

"The door's bent inward." Jessica pointed at the double doors. "I think it busted the lock. What if the door just swings open when we aren't looking?" Claire loosened her grasp, but not entirely. Jessica reached out and tried the lock. The deadbolt was still in place, but it now seemed to be stuck. The door would not be swinging open anytime soon—whether they wanted it to or not. If they were going to escape to the car, it was going to have to be a different way.

Jessica let go of the lock and looked at Claire. She looked back at her gravely, having come to the same conclusion. "It's jammed," Claire said.

"Yeah."

Jessica turned from the front door and looked desperately around the great room. The room was much darker with the patio lights off, but thankfully the moonlight pouring down from the skylights lit the area enough for them to search for weapons, or a place to hide. Jessica scanned the dark patio, now only lit by moonlight. Nothing was there—no dark shapes, no sentinel guard with gray skin and bared teeth.

Her eyes swept the room and went up to the fireplace. The dark, elongated shape was still stretched across the bricks. In her panic, she had forgotten about the gun. Claire's words echoed in her mind: *Of course he had a gun, he's from Texas.* She should have taken it down then, before the chupacabra arrived. She hadn't thought they were going to need it, though. But an open window and her own ignorance had led them to this moment, and now that mounted gun might be their only chance. *God, please let it be loaded.*

Jessica rushed out of the foyer and catapulted into the great room. She collided with the bricks of the fireplace, her palms making a smacking sound as they hit the hearth. She extended her arm as high as it would go, but she couldn't reach the gun. It loomed above her in the dark. *Fucking vaulted ceilings... everything is too high up,* she thought. *First the window and now this.* Jessica jumped, trying to knock the gun off its mounting, but she was still unable to reach it. Claire ran into the room and grabbed the chair closest to the fireplace. She pushed it a foot toward the fireplace, then stopped. Jessica turned to see why Claire was taking so long. "Claire, I need the cha—"

Claire stood frozen in place next to the chair, staring out at the expanse of windows. Her body trembled in the moonlight. Jessica followed her gaze to the patio. A dark shape had materialized by the fire pit. The chupacabra was back, standing in roughly the same spot as before. Only this time, without the reflection from the landscape lighting in the glass, Jessica was certain it was looking directly at them. It could see them now—see them and smell them. She doubted its vision was impeccable, but it appeared to be decent enough for it to see them standing inside Cameron's great room.

She wondered if it recognized her from the canyon. Maybe it remembered her smell, just like she remembered its stench wafting on the breeze. She could smell the sweat and fear pouring off her body. It smelled like battery acid. Was it smelling her right now as it watched her?

"What's it doing?" Claire whispered.

The chupacabra launched at the window. It collided with the glass and fell backward onto the patio. A spider web of fractures spread across the window, glimmering in the silvery moonlight. *Thank God for dual-pane windows,* Jessica thought. The chupacabra took a step back and shook its head. It arched its back, flexed its legs, and looked up at the web of cracks along the glass surface. It sunk down into a deep crouch.

"Get away from the window," Jessica ordered. She grabbed Claire's hand and pulled her toward the foyer, away from the living room and the fireplace. They were out of time. If they had gone for the gun immediately and not wasted time on the front door, maybe they would have been able to move the chair, climb up, grab the gun. But she had made the wrong choice again—another fatal error. Taking the time to scale the fireplace was no longer an option.

Jessica dragged Claire out of the living room. Claire stumbled backward up the steps, never taking her eyes from the creature outside. "It's gonna come through the glass, isn't it?"

"Yeah, it is. We have to go. *Now.*"

The muscles in the chupacabra's flank rippled. It came up onto its hind legs, making it look fearsomely tall, then fell back to all fours. *It's judging the distance,* she thought. *It's deciding where to hit the glass.*

Jessica and Claire stood in the foyer, staring in horror at the wall of windows. Everything seemed to be happening in slow motion, although only a few seconds had managed to tick by. The chupacabra rose up onto its hind legs, came down to reposition, then rose up again. Jessica noticed two dark shapes lying on the white carpet next to the couch in front of the window. *Phones. We left them there when we tried to run away.*

"Claire," Jessica said through gritted teeth, "we left our phones on the floor."

"Fuck, I'll go grab—"

"No, no time." Jessica looked down at the phones on the ground, then up at the chupacabra that was no longer getting positioned. It was crouched low to the ground, about to spring up at the window. There wasn't time anymore. All that was left was to get it to go after her instead of Claire. It wouldn't be all that bad in the end. At least she would get to see her dad again.

"Claire, go down that hallway," she pointed to the hall behind Claire. "I'll go down this one," she threw a thumb behind her. "I'll make noise and get it to go my way. You find a way out. Run straight for the car, you understand? *Do not wait for me.*"

"But Jess—no. I'm not leaving without you. We can hide in a closet—"

Jessica's mind flashed to 1987, and to the children who were attacked in their closet. "*No!* No closets. No hiding. You have to run. Break out of a window and run. For the car. *Now!*"

"No, Jess—I can't—"

The wall of glass shattered. The sound was all-consuming—a cacophony of crackling that sounded like icebergs breaking and wind chimes during a hurricane. Both girls turned to the window, holding each other, and watched as the entire wall turned into a million sparkling pieces of moonlight. And then the moonlight was melting—the glass plummeting toward the ground. Glass burst as it hit the floor below, new explosions of sound that muted everything else—except the snarling, which somehow pushed its way past the smashing glass and penetrated Jessica's eardrums. The stench of the chupacabra hit her nose just as the sound of its snarls made its way to her ears. The whole world was filled with shattering glass, reeking rotted meat, and snarling rage.

Jessica could see a dark figure emerge from the sparkling moonlight of a thousand broken moons. It was in the living room, the glass continuing to shatter all around it. It seemed to be waiting for the glass to fall before it rushed toward them, although she wasn't sure why. Jessica grabbed Claire, pulling her roughly away from her transfixed gaze at the exploding window. "I love you, Claire," she said, then turned Claire toward the hallway and shoved her in that direction. Claire stumbled, regained her footing, and ran down the hallway until she disappeared around a corner at the far end.

Jessica turned back to the dark form standing in the center of the living room, surprised it wasn't on top of her already. Its heavy, gray body stood out in stark contrast to the lightly colored carpet and furnishings. It seemed to be disoriented, waiting for the deafening sounds of the crashing window to cease.

Jessica pivoted on the marble floor and ran down the hallway opposite of Claire's retreat. She planned to yell as she went, luring the chupacabra down her hallway so Claire had a chance to escape. However, as she ran down the hallway, she realized yelling would not be necessary—her CAM boot emitted a loud *clunk!* with every step she took.

CHAPTER 54

Time slowed down even further—if that was possible—as Jessica ran down the marble hallway, moonlight sweeping across her bare shoulders as she passed underneath the hallway skylight. The hallway was wide with pictures of the desert hanging on either side. She felt like she was in a canyon, in *the* canyon. The movie reel played in her head—the one that always played as she ran through the desert. Only this time instead of full-length memories running their course as she traversed the trail, the projection screen in her mind was only showing flashes of different memories. Every time her boot clunked on the marble a new memory flashed by. There was a flash of her dancing in the rain as her father watched. A flash of her getting her first kiss on a swing set, their swings shifting back and forth in unison as they pressed their lips together. A flash of her having her first beer in college, Claire by her side. A flash of her crying in a bathroom stall of a restaurant right after her dad told her they had found a mass in his lung. A flash of what was left of her dad lying in a hospital bed with tubes coming out of him. A flash of her mom's face on the caller ID at two thirty in the morning. A flash of her keeled over on the hiking trail, trying to run for the first time. A flash of Cameron's feet, lying motionless across the trail. The memories flashed faster and faster, running together into a blur where she couldn't discern one memory from the next.

The hallway came to a T-junction, and Jessica veered to the right and down a new corridor. There were doors on each side of the hallway. It was darker here—the skylights didn't run into this portion of the house. Jessica grabbed a doorknob and yanked it open, revealing a linen closet. *No closets,* she thought. *Anywhere but a fucking closet.* She ran to the next door and yanked it open. A bathroom. Beautifully tiled and the size of her childhood bedroom. She rushed into it, whirled around, and shut the door. She expected an immediate collision into the doorway from the other side, just like the front door, but eerie silence followed instead.

She could smell it, though. The rancid, putrid stench filtered under the door of the bathroom, filling the room and making her head swell. The same smell from the canyon, and the same smell from the carnivore exhibit at the zoo. Jessica gagged. The smell was overpowering in such a small space. She stifled an unexpected urge to laugh. *A small space?* she thought. *This is the biggest bathroom I have ever seen.* In comparison to the great outdoors, she supposed it was a much smaller space, though. She pictured the waves of green stink that cartoons have when something smells bad. She imagined the entire estate, magnificently pristine as it was, covered in a great green cloud with little black flies buzzing around the top.

The smell was getting stronger. It had definitely come down this way. Jessica prayed that Claire was creeping out a window somewhere on the other side of the house. She would get to her car and start driving, throwing dust out behind her as she sped toward safety.

Jessica struggled not to gag again. She didn't want to make a sound. The longer it took for the chupacabra to get to her, the longer Claire had to escape. *It hunts on hearing and smell,* she thought, then added: *I'm so fucking stupid.* She should have known it never had to do with the lights. Why would something that survives only in darkness use lights to hunt by? All those people back in '87—how many of them had their windows open? A lot of those homes in that neighborhood probably didn't even have air conditioning. And after a monsoon storm, with the temperature dropping from one hundred to seventy-four, who the hell wouldn't open their windows to enjoy the cool breeze and the smell of wet desert soil? Jessica suspected every single house that was attacked had at least one window open, if not all of them.

Something fell over in the hallway to the left of the bathroom. There had been a small decorative table at the T-junction—the chupacabra had probably just knocked it over. *Searching?* she thought. *Or doing the same knock-something-over routine that it usually does to lure someone out? Why would it need to do that? Can't it smell me?* Jessica sniffed the air. She couldn't smell anything other than the rotting stench of the chupacabra. The battery-acid smell of her own fear had been overpowered by the rancid odor coming from the hallway. *It can't smell me anymore,* she realized. *This space is too small, and its own smell is too much. It can only smell itself.* Jessica took a long, slow breath through her mouth, trying not to make a sound. Sound was what it was relying on right now. *Only sound.*

Jessica took a step back, away from the closed door. She glanced around the bathroom. Moonlight poured onto the white marble, coming from a large picture window over the garden tub. A double vanity was on the left side, next to the doorway. On the right were a toilet and a bidet. *Fancy stuff for fancy butts,* she thought. A walk-in shower, surrounded by glass, was next to the vanity on the left. She saw that the shower head had a small leak. In the silvery glow of the moon, it looked like a sparkling diamond welling up at the head of the faucet and then plummeting into the darkness of the shower stall. *Even rich people have plumbing issues,* she thought absentmindedly. Everything in the bathroom was white, including the towels. In the moonlight, the room looked like icicles.

Jessica went to take a step toward the tub, then stopped. Her damn walking boot was going to clunk on the tile if she took another step. She held her breath and listened. After all the shattering glass, the silence felt horrifying and complete—like she was already in her grave. The bathroom was a mausoleum made of marble and porcelain, and she had just shut the door to her own tomb. She heard a grunt coming from the hallway, which brought her back to reality. She wasn't in a tomb; she was in a very extravagant guest bathroom. And she was in peril.

Heavy breathing was coming from the hallway. God, she could actually hear the thing breathing now. And something else. A clicking? A tapping? Jessica's stomach churned as she thought, *Claws? Those are its claws on the tile floor.* With every step it took, its claws tapped and scratched across the marble. She strained to discern how close it was to the bathroom. When it grunted again, closer this time, she no longer had to wonder.

Jessica sat down on the cool tile and scooted backward away from the door. She didn't dare try to walk across the bathroom with her boot on. She slid backward on her rear, her left leg hovering in the air. Once her back touched the cold edge of the garden tub, she gently lowered her left leg onto the bath mat that was outside the shower door. From this angle, she could see under the crack of the bathroom door, although all that was beyond the door was darkness.

How much time had passed? A minute? Probably less. She wondered if Claire had time to escape yet. Probably not. The picture window in this bathroom wasn't even capable of opening. She wondered how many windows were on Claire's side of the house, and if there was one she could open and crawl through. Not just crawl through, but be able to do it silently and undetected. She wanted to warn Claire that the chupacabra was hunting by sound alone now, and that she needed to keep absolutely quiet.

Wood suddenly cracked in the hallway, accompanied by snarling and a guttural growl that sent shivers down her spine. *It's tearing down the closet door,* she thought. Banging gave way to splintering, and splintering gave way to breaking. All the while the chupacabra snarled and growled. *I knew the damn closet was a bad place to be.*

Jessica sat with her back against the tub, listening to the destruction of the closet door. *If there is any time to break a window and escape, Claire, now's the time.* Wood burst and exploded in a frenzy beyond the bathroom door. Jessica listened, paralyzed with fear. This room was next, she was sure of it. Sweat trickled down the back of her neck, although her body had broken out into gooseflesh. *Any minute now.* Wood clunked and cracked as it fell to the marble floor in the hallway. *Thorough son of a bitch, isn't it?*

The movie reel played in her head, one memory repeating again and again. She had just danced in the monsoon downpour, ran under the dryness of the porch, and hugged her dad, soaking his clothes in the process. Her dad's words ran on an endless loop in her mind as she watched the moon-splashed bathroom door. *Look Jess, you made me a mess. Look Jess, you made me a mess. Look Jess, you made me a mess.* His voice had sounded so quiet, drowned out by the deafening afternoon downpour. If she hadn't been hugging him at the time, she wouldn't have heard him at all.

Jessica looked at the dripping showerhead in the glass-enshrouded shower stall. She could see the showerhead through the top portion of glass, which was clear and devoid of water splashes. The lower portion of the glass stall was opaque and twinkled in the cool, blue light from the window like freshly fallen snow. Jessica watched the showerhead drip, unable to pull her eyes away. It welled up, dripped, welled up, dripped.

Something tugged at her mind. It felt like a word on the tip of her tongue that she just couldn't manage to remember. Or like the frustrating feeling of walking into a room, only to not remember why you went there in the first place. *Look Jess, you made me a mess. Look Jess, you made me a mess.* Her dad's words barely audible above the noise of the raging storm. Drip, *Jess,* drip, *mess.*

And all at once, like a ray of sunshine shooting through the moonlight in her mind, she knew. All the puzzle pieces had finally fallen into place. Jessica knew why the chupacabra had left the canyon. She knew the connection between the monsoons and the attacks. And—God willing—she might just know how to get out of this alive. *Thank you, Daddy.*

Silence fell in the hallway. The chupacabra had given up on the closet. The tapping of claws on tile resumed, heading in her direction. She heard grunting sounds coming from directly behind the bathroom door. Claws slid through the dark gap under the door and protruded rudely into the pristine bathroom. Jessica held her breath and waited.

CHAPTER 55

The monsoons came every summer in the southwestern United States, bringing much-needed moisture to the plants and animals that relied on its arrival. Flowers bloomed, the beige desert turned green, and animals flourished. Most of the year's rainfall occurred during only those few summer months. And then the storms would fade, the humidity would lessen, and the dry desert heat would return.

This summer had been different, though. The El Niño had increased the amount of tropical storms in the Pacific, leading to unprecedented amounts of rainfall to the area. The Sonoran Desert was being berated by an onslaught of rain on an almost daily basis. The clouds would roll in during the early afternoon, the sky would turn yellow with the approaching storm, thunder would rumble, and by mid-to-late afternoon the rain would begin. Flash floods rushed down washes and water flowed through the streets. Tucsonans chattered endlessly about how they had never seen so much rain in a single monsoon season. Some of the old-timers would chime in then, recalling one other particularly wet season that could rival the likes of this one. And that was the summer of 1987.

The clouds appeared during the hottest time of day, white cotton balls rolling over the mountains and heading toward town. Soon one would be able to see their purple, pregnant bellies, filled with moisture and zapping with electricity. The mountains would get hit first. People in town could see dark sheets of gray pouring down from those clouds and saturating the mountains below. The sheets of gray would creep closer and closer, until the whole sky turned into a windy, swirling gray and the first fat drops of rain hit the earth.

The rain from the mountaintops would flow downhill, pouring into washes and ravines and surging into town as dangerous flash floods capable of washing cars off the road and carrying away the unlucky passengers to their muddy, watery graves. The water would dump into canyons, creating cascading waterfalls as it poured down the cliff faces of the canyon walls. The water would then careen down the canyon, taking rocks and underbrush and desert soil with it. Even hours after the rain had ceased, the canyon was filled with the sounds of water—running, dripping, and babbling along the canyon floor. The sounds would echo on the cliff walls, the entire canyon sounding like a partially submerged cave deep inside the earth.

The movie reel flickered on in Jessica's mind. She was dancing in the rain, and her daddy was standing on the porch. His mouth was moving, but she couldn't hear a word he was saying. He was starting to get his angry face, though, so she decided she should join him.

"Why didn't you come in, Jess? I've been calling to you."

"I couldn't hear you, Daddy. The water was too loud."

Now, sitting in a dark bathroom with the claws of a menacing beast protruding from under the door—a beast Roger Cleary had never believed to exist and had never taught his young daughter about—Jessica knew why the chupacabra was here. She knew that it was driven from the canyon when the rains began, no longer able to hear and hunt its normal prey. The chupacabra relied heavily on its hearing when stalking its victims, and the constant dripping and rushing of water in the canyon interfered with its ability to catch its food. Under normal circumstances, the chupacabra would spend the majority of its life inside the southwestern canyons, traveling from mountain range to mountain range, and only coming out from time to time to snatch the occasional pet or farm animal—maybe an unlucky human if the opportunity arose. But now, with the rain being a constant interference, it was unable to hunt the lengths of the canyon. It was forced to venture out in search of food, whatever that might be. It picked up the available animals in the surrounding desert first, which was why Jessica hadn't seen any animals during her runs. Eventually it moved on for bigger game, an occasional rabbit or coyote not being enough to satisfy its hunger. It was currently confined to the area immediately surrounding the canyon's mouth, needing to make it back to the shelter of the canyon before the sun rose each morning. That's why it attacked that particular town in 1987, and that's why it was attacking Wasp Canyon Estates now. It wasn't going to stop, not until the rains stopped. Or until something else stopped it first.

CHAPTER 56

The first collision with the bathroom door made a sickening *crack!* that filled the confines of the bathroom. Jessica sprang to her feet, letting out a cry that she was unable to contain. The chupacabra growled in response, now certain that what it wanted was hiding on the other side of the door.

Jessica yelled at the top of her lungs, hoping Claire could hear her from the other side of the house. *"Claire! Water confuses it! Turn on all the faucets! Claire—"*

Another heavy thud hit the bathroom door, and a hairline crack appeared down the center. Jessica sent Cameron a silent thank you for having solid wood doors installed in his home. She doubted it would withstand that many more blows, though. Jessica strained to hear a response from Claire, but heard nothing but scratching and snarling on the other side of the door. The angry sounds filled the bathroom, making her ears ache and head throb.

She threw herself over the side of the tub, grabbed the faucet, and yanked the brushed chrome nozzle until the water was on full blast. She then rushed to the toilet, lifting the lid and flushing it at the same time. She grabbed the handle of the bidet and turned it on as high as it would go.

The pounding on the door continued, wood splintered, and the door shook violently in its frame. The chupacabra let out an enraged howl, and slammed its body weight against the door. The door was on the edge of collapse. The pounding and crashing became frenzied, its claws scraping crazily against the wood.

Jessica whirled around and grabbed the nozzles on each side of the sink faucet. She cranked them on, then methodically moved to the other sink and did the same. The room filled with the sounds of running water, although the sound of the door's destruction was still deafening. Jessica had one more faucet to turn on. She ran to the shower door, yanking it so hard that she thought she might tear it from its hinges. The hissing and growling had taken on a different pitch, no longer muffled by the door. The chupacabra had made an opening in the door now, its frenzied growls even louder as it struggled to get inside. *Here's Johnny,* she thought.

Jessica crawled into the shower stall. She unlatched her QuikFit from her wrist, hit the **Spotify** button, and tossed the watch across the room toward the toilets. She shut the shower door, grabbed the faucet of the shower, and turned it on. Cold water poured down on her, drenching her shirt and making her hair stick to her face. She could hear AC/DC begin playing somewhere on the other side of the room. She crouched down in the shower, shaking uncontrollably, and pressed herself against the far end of the marble stall. She couldn't see out through the opaque glass—hopefully that meant it couldn't see in either. The shower was darker than the bathroom, and she tried desperately to blend into the dark shadows furthest from the glass door.

The bathroom door gave a final crack and fell from its hinges, falling to pieces on the bathroom floor. The growling stopped at once, the door no longer an obstacle in the chupacabra's path. Jessica sensed the presence of the creature inside the bathroom, even though she wasn't able to see its bulk through the opaque glass. AC/DC was playing the intro to "Back in Black". The shower's cold water pelted her bare arms and her soaked clothes clung to her thin frame. She felt her skin break out into yet another wave of gooseflesh. She pressed herself against the marble, squeezed her eyes closed, and waited.

CHAPTER 57

Moser shot down Wasp Canyon Road at a speed that it was not intended for. His car bumped and jostled as he scanned the right-hand side of the road with growing panic, looking for Jasper's front gate. At last he saw the familiar wrought iron. There was a chain lying in a pile in the dirt next to the gate, the metal glinting in his headlights. He turned into the driveway, swerving to miss the chain, and hit the gate with some force. The gate shook from the blow, and he suspected that Lynette would later be chastising him for the damage done to the front bumper.

Moser's Cadillac bounced along the dirt driveway leading to Jasper's house. Cacti and desert trees passed by on either side. Finally, he made out the red glint of taillights in the driveway. A beat-up Chevy Malibu was parked there, empty and dark. He didn't know if this relieved him or further increased his sense of dread. She was inside alright, but he wasn't sure what state she was in. He thought of Kilburn's squad car parked outside of Arlington's house, with the headlights still on. That night had not gone so well for Kilburn. Not at all.

Moser parked behind the Malibu, his tires skidding in the dirt as he jammed on the brakes. A small cloud of dust appeared in his headlights. He flipped them off, not wanting to alert any animals in the vicinity to his arrival. For better or worse, he had arrived. For better or worse, he was going to go into that house and face his fears. Moser stumbled out of his car, feeling the comforting weight of his firearm pressed against his hip. He walked toward the house. With the headlights off, it was difficult finding his way to the front door. He squinted against the darkness, using the moonlight to guide him. From somewhere inside the house, he heard screaming. His hand went to his right hip and he pulled out his Glock 19, a gun he hadn't unholstered in the line of duty in nearly eleven years.

Moser reached the front door, which looked beat three ways from Sunday. The door appeared to have given way in the center, but the metal etching that wove its way through the wood had kept it in place. He tried to open the door. *Locked. Fucking locked.* He could hear an immense amount of banging and breaking coming from inside, and something else. *Water? Is the water running in there?*

Whatever the hell was going on, he needed to get his ass in there—not stand around like an imbecile in the driveway, looking around and scratching his balls. Moser scanned the front of the house, hoping for an easily accessible window so he wouldn't have to go around to the back. *Like Kilburn did,* he thought with mounting horror. *Caught on the side of the house and torn apart. Damn thing drank his blood, too.* Moser shook his head. He was not going to let thoughts like that stop him now. He was going to face this thing, once and for all. At least he wouldn't go down with his gun still in its holster.

He stumbled through the darkness toward the left side of the house. He chose the left for no particular reason except that the moonlight was brighter on that side. He could still hear banging sounds coming from the house's interior. It sounded like a whole demo crew was tearing the place apart.

Moser reached the edge of the house and grabbed the wall to steady himself. His heart pounded in his chest as terror became dangerously close to taking over. He took in a deep breath, wondered if it might be his last, and stepped around the corner of the house and into the darkness of the desert. He began to run.

CHAPTER 58

Brian Johnson was singing about nine lives and cat's eyes. Other than "Back in Black" and the sound of running water, Jessica heard nothing. She couldn't even hear the chupacabra's breathing anymore. She knew it was there, though, standing in the center of the bathroom. The putrid stench of it hung in the air, the increasing humidity in the room turning the smell into a horrible soup. Jessica bit into her hand, suppressing the urge to vomit. One wretch and that would be it. Game over.

The chupacabra went for the QuikFit. Jessica heard a horrific crack as the toilet was ripped from the wall, and then gushing water pouring onto the marble floor. Brian Johnson stopped singing. It had found the QuikFit. She wasn't sure if it had swallowed it or simply broken it, but the classic rock disappeared from the bathroom all the same. Now there were just the gurgles and hum of running water.

The seconds ticked by with agonizing slowness. The chupacabra stood in the center of the bathroom, not moving. *It must be working,* she thought, trying not to let herself become too hopeful. *The sound of the water—so much in such a small space—it doesn't know where I am.* She stared at the shower door. She hoped from the outside it just looked like another wall, not a space worth investigating. The chupacabra grunted in rage and confusion, the sound exaggerated in the confines of the bathroom. She could hear the clicking of its claws on the tile as it began to move. *Not towards me, not towards me, not towards me,* she prayed. She pressed herself as far into the shower's shadows as she could, drawing her legs against her body.

It was near the glass door now; she could make out its shadow across the opaque surface. The spines of its vertebrae stood up harshly from the curve of its back. *Oh God... Daddy... please make it not hurt, okay? Please let it be fast.* Tears fell from the corners of her eyes and were washed away by the cold spray of the shower.

The shadow faded away from the shower door. Jessica blinked, dumbfounded. She realized that deep down she had not expected it to work. But it was moving away from her. It was actually *moving away.* It was still in the bathroom; however, its snarls now sounded more confused than enraged.

Jessica heard something big shatter somewhere else in the house. The chupacabra let out a howl of what sounded like triumph, and launched itself out of the bathroom. It hit the wall opposite the bathroom door with a splintering bang.

Jessica heard clicking and growling as it ran down the hallway, the sound fading away. She was left alone in the ruins of the bathroom, water pouring from every faucet. Her mind was running on a loop again, only this time it kept repeating: *Claire, Claire, Claire...*

CHAPTER 59

Jessica threw the shower door open. The bathroom door was in tatters, strewn across the marble floor. She stepped out of the shower, her hands shaking and wet hair plastered to her face. Her boot was logged with water and considerably more heavy. It squished as well as clunked as she took each step. There was a large indentation in the wall opposite the bathroom doorway. She stepped out of the room in one quick motion and faced the T-junction in the hallway. Nothing there except more chunks of ruined doors. The closet door was also in shambles.

She could hear water running down the hallway—Claire's doing. Had she knocked something over while turning on the faucets? *Oh God, was it killing her right now?* Jessica ran down the hallway toward the great room. The weight from the waterlogged boot turned her run into an exaggerated limp, reminding her eerily of her hobbled run out of the canyon. She slipped on the wet marble and almost slammed into the broken table at the T-junction. She caught her balance, straining every muscle in her thighs to do so. She turned the corner and entered the hallway with the skylight overhead. The hallway was still filled with the chupacabra's horrible stench, but any other sign of it was gone. Jessica slowed as she neared the great room.

The large vase in the foyer had fallen over. Shards of broken pottery littered the floor, the wilted flowers lying in clumps across the tile. Jessica stepped over a sizable piece of ceramic and into the foyer. She searched the great room for signs of the chupacabra, but saw none. After the darkness of the shower, the moonlit great room seemed impossibly bright to her. She looked down the long hallway toward the other wing of the house. It either went down there or back into the desert. *And where the hell is Claire?* She didn't hear screaming, so she was fairly certain it hadn't gotten to her yet.

Jessica was about to go down the opposite hallway in search of Claire, when a head popped up from behind the kitchen island. Claire stood in the center of the elaborate kitchen, her hands gripping the thick countertop. The kitchen sink was running on full blast. Jessica made a final look down the long, empty hallway, then carefully stepped over the broken remains of the vase and half-limped/half-dragged herself across the living room to the kitchen.

"Claire, what the hell?" she whispered as she came into the kitchen. "What happened?"

Claire reached out and grabbed Jessica's hands with a fierceness Jessica hadn't felt before. *"Why are you wet?"*

"I hid in the shower." Jessica's eyes darted around the great room for signs of movement. "I told you to get out of here," she whispered, turning her attention back to Claire.

"I tried to go out a window. They all have those freaking sunshield things on them. They're screwed in from the outside. There's no way I could get out without making a bunch of noise. Plus..." she paused, looking down as if ashamed, "I couldn't leave you, Jess. Not in here alone with that thing. I heard you say to turn on the water, so I turned on all the bathroom faucets and came out here. I could hear it breaking things down your hallway so I decided to try the old 'knock shit over and hide' routine. I knocked the vase over, ran over here, and hid. See how it likes being the one that gets tricked."

"Well, where did it go?"

"Down the hall. You were right, the water really seems to be confusing it. It almost stumbled into the front door. Then it turned and ran down the hall." Claire lowered her voice even further, grasping Jessica's hands until they hurt. *"We need to go. Now."*

Jessica looked at the remnants of the glass wall, the great room now open to the night air. If they went running out there, without the cover from the sounds of running water, it would get to them for sure. Once it finished looking down the other hall it would almost certainly come back in here, then run out the broken window to look for them. The sound of them running through the desert in the dark will be hard to miss. It will catch them long before they make it around the house and to the safety of Claire's car.

"Without the help of the water we don't stand a chance. We need to hide."

"*Hide?* But you said not to—"

"That's before I knew about the water. If all the water keeps running, it will get disoriented and go elsewhere. Just like in the canyon."

"Wait—what?"

"Later. Now quick, before it comes back. Grab a phone so we can call 911." She pointed to the phones lying on the carpet. "And help me get that fucking gun off the damn wall."

"How do you even know if it's loaded?"

"Because Cameron once told me to always be prepared. An unloaded gun is not being prepared." Jessica limped across the living room with Claire hurrying after her.

"How long do you think we have?" Claire whispered, scooping a phone off the ground and heading to the chair closest to the fireplace. They shoved the chair up to the bricks and Jessica climbed on top. She reached up with both hands, her fingers sliding across the rough bricks and mortar. Her fingertips touched the stock of the gun. She stepped onto the armrests of the chair, straddling the seat. Water slushed out of her boot, drenching the chair's cushion. She shoved her hand upward again, her fingers wrapping around the double barrel of the shotgun. She lifted and pulled the shotgun from the wall. The weight of it dragged her down and she stepped heavily onto the seat of the chair. Claire grabbed her arm, steadying her. She helped Jessica step down from the chair.

They both looked at the shotgun, frantically trying to figure out how to turn off the safety. Claire found it—a small metal latch on the side of the stock. Jessica clicked it off.

"Wait, shouldn't you check and make sure it's load—"

A low growl drifted out from the foyer. Jessica's back was to the sound, but she felt the hairs on the back of her neck prickle. Her eyes darted up to Claire, who was facing the foyer. Claire's eyes widened in terror as she looked over Jessica's shoulder. *"Jessica, behind you!"* Claire screamed.

Jessica began to whirl around, bringing the barrel of the shotgun up as she did. She only made it halfway through her turn when something immensely heavy collided with her left side. The gun flew from her grasp, something on her left side cracked, and she was thrown to the ground several feet away.

CHAPTER 60

Moser stumbled along the side of the house as quickly as he could go. The moon offered some assistance to light his path, but there were so many damn branches and cacti in the way. More than once, he had to veer away from the house to avoid colliding with a cholla or an ocotillo. He had passed a few windows, the curtains of which were drawn so he was unable to see inside. A utility box came into view. It had been torn from the wall, and the wires shredded. *What in the name of God...*

Moser carefully stepped around the mutilated utility box and kept going. He was coming up on another large window. He could see something shining inside, so he knew this one didn't have the curtains drawn. He stepped around a few saguaro ribs and jogged up to the window. The thing he saw shining was a showerhead, and it was running. He peered through the glass and saw the bathroom in complete disarray. The door was torn to pieces, and every faucet in the room was running. For an agonizing second, he thought he saw a body near the toilets, but after squinting into the dim room, he saw that it was the toilet itself lying on its side.

Moser pressed onward, moving as quickly as the terrain would allow. He had seen pictures of the Jasper house before, following Jasper's death and the subsequent search of his home. He knew the entire back of the house was a giant series of windows. If necessary, he could break a window to gain entry. He just hoped he would make it in time.

He could see the edge of the house coming into view. He had a sickening thought that this is just about the same distance from the yard that Kilburn had been when he was attacked. Instead of the thought crippling him, it faded away as swiftly as it had arrived. He didn't feel the terror anymore; it was giving way to something else. Purpose. He felt a desperate need to get to the girl before it was too late, and that feeling of purpose was pushing the terror to the outskirts of his mind.

He reached the backyard and began shuffling along the stucco wall to the gate. He remembered a gate from the police photos during the search. A younger Carl Moser would have jumped over the wall without a second thought, but that was many years and many pounds ago. He wove his way around one more prickly pear cactus and grabbed the latch of the gate, pulling it open. Just as he stepped into the dark yard, Moser heard a girl yell, *"Jessica, behind you!"* And then the screaming began.

CHAPTER 61

Everything took on a surreal perspective as Jessica crashed onto the floor of Cameron Jasper's living room. She struck the ground on her right side, bolts of pain rocketing up her right arm and into her neck. The crack on her left side had been in her midsection, and she felt the throb of what were probably several broken ribs. Everything felt blurred and far away. She could hear Claire screaming in the distance. And she could hear snarling and growling—a sound she thought would stay with her long after she was dead. She wondered if her dad would be there, waiting for her once the darkness cleared.

But instead of fading away into the dark, she was being tugged at—violently and incessantly tugged at. And not in a metaphorical way. Something—multiple somethings—were literally tugging her up and down, like that Spanish Inquisition torture device. It pulled at her lower body, then yanked at her arm. The haze began to clear, and with the lessening haze the horrible cracking sounds filtered in. Something was breaking below her waist, but for some reason, she wasn't in searing pain. *Paralyzed? Am I paralyzed?*

Reality rushed back, the comfortable haze fading completely. She could hear Claire screaming from somewhere up above her, and she could hear snarling from somewhere down below. Jessica was on her back, staring at the skylights in the vaulted ceiling. The carpet rubbed the flesh away from her spine as she was dragged back and forth.

She looked over her head, beyond her outstretched left arm, and saw Claire. Her best friend's face was strained with effort, her expression contorted into a combination of horror and determination. Claire had both hands wrapped tightly around Jessica's left wrist, and she was pulling with all of her might. Jessica was pulled toward Claire a few inches, and then something dragged her body in the opposite direction. Whatever Claire was playing tug of war with, she was losing.

Jessica was terrified to look down. She didn't want to see what was down there—or how much of her insides were now on the outside. She forced herself to look down at her body. The chupacabra was there, its head looking enormous so close to her small frame. Its eyes were a dead red, the pupils dilated. Its ears were pressed against the gray skin of its skull. And its long, yellow-gray teeth were sunk deep into her CAM boot.

The boot was bent and cracked, but still held together. Shards of plastic stuck up from the black polyester, and water from the shower oozed from the fabric. White stuffing peeked out from the polyester in multiple locations. Despite the horrible appearance of the boot, Jessica imagined the metal frame was the only thing keeping her foot from being torn from her leg.

The chupacabra yanked her body toward the foyer, and in turn Claire yanked her back a few inches toward the broken window. Claire was fatiguing, though—each yank through Jessica's left arm seemed to hold less power than the last. Before long, the chupacabra would overpower her and drag Jessica down one of the long hallways to finish her off.

"Claire... the gun," she stammered, not recognizing her own voice. "Get the gun."

"If I let you go... it will take you... before I get a chance... to shoot," Claire grunted in between tugs. "Jess... I don't think... I can hold on... much... longer."

Jessica looked around for the shotgun. She saw it lying near the chair they had moved against the fireplace. At this rate, she would be tugged right up to it by the chupacabra in just a few moments' time. Being able to grab it, cock it, and shoot it with only the use of one arm was going to be impossible, though. However, if Claire let go, neither of them would have time to grab the gun and fire it before she was dragged away. Jessica felt herself wanting to give up, hopeful her dad would be waiting for her on the other side of this mess.

The chupacabra clamped down hard on her ankle, and the CAM boot finally crumpled under the pressure. It made an audible *pop!* as the air compression burst. Jessica felt the bones in her foot begin to break. A wave of agony radiated up from her foot, and the sense of giving up vanished. She was not going to just lie here and let this thing do that to the rest of her body. And she was not going to let it crush the bones or drink the blood of anyone else either. Through the bolts of pain, she thought, *I'm going to kill this motherfucker.*

CHAPTER 62

Moser stood at the edge of the broken glass wall, staring in awe at the chaos unfolding in front of him. A horrible-looking creature had its jaws clamped down on Jessica Cleary's leg and was pulling her toward a dark hallway. Another girl—this one a brunette—was pulling on Jessica's arm, trying to keep her from getting dragged away. It was a grotesque game of human tug of war, and one the hell beast was apparently going to win.

Moser aimed his Glock at the chupacabra, centering the sight on the creature's wide chest. He didn't want to aim at its head, since Jessica's leg was currently in its jaws. The chances of hitting her were far too great. He was about to fire when the brunette's head was pulled in front of his sights. He pointed the firearm to the ground and took a few generous steps to the left. He aimed again. The chupacabra yanked Jessica several feet toward the hallway, and the brunette stumbled forward and into Moser's line of fire again. He lowered the Glock, frustrated. Shooting from this angle wasn't going to work. He had to get closer. Moser scrambled over the frame of the shattered window, and entered the house.

CHAPTER 63

"Claire…" Jessica stammered. "The gun… get me closer to the gun." Claire said nothing. Jessica could hear her panting from somewhere above her. *She's not gonna make it much longer,* she thought. Her left wrist was starting to feel slick with sweat, and Claire was losing her traction. Jessica lifted her head and looked at the shotgun. It was only a few feet away now, lying near her right foot. The chupacabra clamped down on Jessica's boot again and she let out a wail of pain.

"Claire! Now! Let it pull me toward the gun!" she said through clamped teeth. She could feel her breath hissing through her teeth, her jaw rigid. She sucked in air in long gasps, fighting the urge to hold her breath. Darkness moved into the edges of her consciousness. She was going to pass out soon.

Claire stumbled two feet to the right, pulling Jessica closer to the fireplace. When the chupacabra pulled back, Jessica was dragged a foot closer to the shotgun. She extended her right hand and groped for it, but was still unable to reach it. Claire took another lurch to the right, the chupacabra followed and yanked back. Jessica's body was dragged into reach of the shotgun, her extended fingers brushing against the metal barrels.

"Almost!" she screamed to Claire. She could feel her left wrist slipping out of Claire's grasp, bit by bit. Jessica's right fingertips crawled across the shotgun barrels, searching for purchase. Every inch her left hand slipped from Claire's grasp, she gained another inch of contact with the shotgun. Claire's hands slid to Jessica's fingers. *"Claire... let... go!"*

Jessica's left hand lost contact with Claire, and she was pulled rapidly across the living room floor.

Chapter 64

Moser stood on the edge of the violent scene, facing the fireplace. He had wrapped around the perimeter of the great room, not wanting to lose his element of surprise. Now he was approaching the chupacabra's right side. So far he had gone unnoticed. Blood was beginning to smear across the white carpeting, oozing out of the crushed boot on Jessica's ankle. The red smears matched the creature's dead, hateful eyes. Its teeth were sunk into the boot almost to the gum line.

The scars etched across Moser's shoulder throbbed. He remembered feeling those teeth on him so many years ago. It felt like it was happening right now, all over again. The sharp burning as the skin tore, the pressure of the jaws clamping down, the scrape of teeth on bone. When the beast bit down on her ankle, he felt it in his shoulder. All these years later, he could still feel it with the same intensity he felt as a boy. This was his chance to put that pain behind him—to never again wake in the night feeling those teeth tearing into his flesh.

Moser stepped forward with a grace that was unbeknownst to him, the Glock centered on the chupacabra's chest. He felt the trigger pressing into his index finger as he started to squeeze down. Just then, the brunette lost her grip on Jessica's arm. The creature lurched backward, out of Moser's aim. It dragged Jessica across the living room through the smears of her own blood.

He tracked the chupacabra's retreat, firing into its right side. Light and noise filled the dark room with brilliant clarity. Carl Moser thought of himself as a boy, lying under his mother's red towels. He thought of his nightmares, and waking in the night covered in cold sweat. He thought of the animal shows he couldn't watch. About the teeth he still sometimes felt digging into his shoulder. Moser fired again and again, and continued to pull the trigger long after the clip was empty.

The chupacabra stopped in its tracks and dropped Jessica's leg. It turned its dead eyes on Moser, its muzzle pulling away to reveal long incisors tinged red. Moser dropped his Glock to his side. He watched the chupacabra sink into a deep crouch, like the hammer of a gun being pulled back. A gun that was aimed at him.

CHAPTER 65

The skylight lit up with the first blast. Instead of seeing the star-strewn sky, Jessica saw a momentary reflection of herself, sprawled on the white floor amidst smears of red. Then darkness returned. *Lightning?* Again the skylight lit up and revealed her reflection. This time she could make out the chupacabra near her foot. Darkness returned. Then she could see the chupacabra as it let go of her leg. Darkness. Then she could see her right hand holding the shotgun. Darkness. With every flash of light came a deafening blast that filled the room. *Gunshots?*

The flashes stopped just as quickly as they started, and the moonlight claimed the room once again. Her ears were ringing, and she strained to get her eyes to readjust to the darkness. A photo negative of herself, reflected in the skylight, hid behind her eyelids.

She could hear the labored breathing of the chupacabra. It was still standing by her left foot. It growled with rage, then stumbled. It was wounded, but not enough to incapacitate it.

Someone had shot it a bunch of times, yet it was still standing. Its attention had been diverted from the attack, and as her eyes made out the bulk of its frame in the new darkness, she could see that it was now facing her left side—to where the shots had come from. It lowered itself onto its haunches. Jessica recognized the move from the patio—it was about to launch itself toward whoever had shot at it. *Moser?*

Jessica sat upright, feeling her abdominals contract as she hauled herself into a sitting position. Her legs were splayed out in front of her, the chupacabra just beyond them. It was in a deep crouch now. Her right hand was still wrapped around the shotgun. She pulled it from the floor, feeling her entire upper body strain from the effort. She brought it across her chest and pressed her thumbs hard against the hammers, hearing a very satisfying click as they locked down. She raised the double barrel and pressed the stock firmly against her right shoulder. *Please be loaded please be loaded please be loaded.*

She centered the barrels on the chupacabra—the thing that killed Cameron Jasper, the thing that set a trap to kill her, the thing that tore apart all those people. She felt rage and revulsion surging through her. She shoved the double barrel against the chupacabra's head just as its legs began to flex. *Die you piece of shit,* she thought, and pulled down hard on the trigger.

CHAPTER 66

The blast was much louder than the first shots. The cracking boom filled the great room and echoed across the desert. It reminded Jessica of the crack of thunder she had heard—and felt—as a child when a tree in their yard was struck by lightning. In the flash from the muzzle she saw a red explosion where the chupacabra's head had been. The body of the chupacabra slumped over, landing on the steps leading up to the foyer. It hit with a sickening thud, and lay still. Chunks of meat and bone splattered onto the tile, a few pieces landing on the living room furniture and bouncing off the cushions.

Jessica, Claire, and Moser watched in stunned silence, staring at the motionless heap on the stairs. It was a giant stinking mass of gray flesh and twitching muscle. No one spoke. They held their collective breath, all waiting for signs of life from the beast that lay before them. There were none.

☼   ☼   ☼

Moser stumbled forward, toward the stinking, bleeding lump on the stairs. He was prepared to strangle it with his bare hands if it made any move to attack. As he got closer, he realized there was hardly any neck left to strangle. The entire head had been blown off. A sickening sludge of torn muscle, flecks of bone, and thick blood made up what was left of the head and neck. It was on its right side, its hairless gray legs splayed out like it was about to lunge. *At me,* he thought. *That thing was about to lunge at me. All those gunshots and it was still going to come after me.*

He nudged at one of its legs. Nothing. The chupacabra's claws had lost their menace. And the teeth? Well, who the hell knows where all of those went? Moser kicked at it again, still not eliciting any movement from the body.

"Is it dead?" a small voice croaked from behind him. It was the brunette.

Moser turned from the body, but he still wasn't willing to abandon it completely. Who knows if mythical beasts die the same way as real ones? "Yeah, I'm pretty sure," he said.

"Pretty sure?" Jessica asked. She sat on the white carpet, red smudges all around her. The shotgun was on the floor beside her.

Moser looked at the chupacabra once more. It wasn't breathing. And its head was splattered all over the stairs and tile floor. He could see white flecks and gray chunks mixed into the red—brain matter and skull fragments. *Yeah, this thing is fucking dead.*

"It's dead," he concluded. "You blew its damn head off." He walked toward the two women. He recognized the brunette now; she had been at the station with Jessica. Claire Barnett. He nodded to Claire, who was trembling and hugging herself. "You okay?"

"Yeah, uh… yeah, I think so," Claire stammered. "But Jessica…"

Moser squatted down by Jessica's side. He glanced at her upper body, which appeared relatively unscathed. He then looked down to her left leg. The amount of damage couldn't be seen through the crushed boot, but blood was seeping from the black fabric and she was obviously in need of urgent medical care. "How are you doing?" he asked.

"I'll make it," she said. She looked at him in the darkness. "What made you join the party, Moser? I thought you didn't believe in these things." She gestured toward the bloody carcass on the stairs.

"Well, I decided I just had to see this one for myself," he said. "I didn't think you crazy broads were going to start the party without me, though."

Jessica smiled. "Oh, you know us. Always looking for a good time." She looked up at Claire and smiled.

"Jess—what about your ankle? I could hear it crunching…" Claire trailed off.

"Well, I'm definitely going to need that surgery now," she said. "Luckily, I have that doctor appointment already scheduled for Monday."

"Not Monday," Moser said. "Tonight. I'm calling in for an ambulance right now." He stood up and pulled his phone from his pocket. He spoke briefly on the phone, then hung up. "They're on their way," he said. Jessica nodded.

Moser scanned the room. How were the paramedics going to get in here? He went up the foyer steps, carefully stepping around the stinking pile of dead chupacabra, and went up to the cracked front door. He grabbed the lock and tried to jimmy it from side to side.

"Hey guys?" Claire called from the living room.

"Yeah?" Moser turned away from the door, still holding the lock in his hand, and looked at the girls in the living room. Jessica was looking expectantly up at Claire.

"It was just the one chupacabra, right?" Claire asked.

Moser dropped the lock and took a large step away from the door. "Now, why in the hell would you say something like that?"

In the darkness of Cameron Jasper's living room, they all laughed.

EPILOGUE

Jess stood by the tilted wooden post that marked the beginning of the Wasp Canyon trailhead. The breeze was cold against her cheeks, her breath coming out in white plumes in the morning air. Frost covered the cacti lining the sides of the trail, their spines twinkling in the rays of winter sunlight. The sun had just risen over the mountain crest and the sky was alight with yellows, pinks, and blues. A morning hush covered the landscape, a peaceful silence only the desert knows.

There were no other cars in the parking lot. Jess arrived early to have the trail to herself. She hoped to be done with her run before the lot began to fill with winter tourists, all wanting to take in the desert's beauty when the temperatures were mild and the weather forgiving. Only real Tucsonans braved the hiking trails during the summer months. Real Tucsonans, and an occasional Texan with a kind smile and a loaded gun over the fireplace.

Jess shifted her hips from side to side, twisting her back into a satisfying stretch. Her ribs still ached when she rotated to the left, but her doctors said the pain would lessen over time. The fractured ribs had not punctured her lung, which they said was a miracle in itself.

Her ankle had been a more difficult recovery. Jess had undergone two surgeries to correct the damage that was done to her left foot and ankle. The first one was on the night she arrived at the hospital, smeared with blood but in good spirits. The CAM boot had actually saved her from amputation—its hard, plastic cover and metal frame absorbing the majority of the damage during the attack. That night they set the broken bones and stitched up the bite wounds. A month later, she had to return for reconstructive surgery to further correct the damage and hopefully allow her to be able to walk again. The physical therapy had been grueling, and the healing slow.

Five months had passed since the attack when her surgeon finally gave her the approval to begin running again, and only in small doses. She knew small doses well. She knew when half a mile felt like an accomplishment, her thighs quivering and her heart pounding as she tried to push herself that one more tenth of a mile. She knew it would be months before she could run any real distance. She didn't expect to make it to the top of Wasp Hill this winter, and possibly not even this spring. She probably wouldn't see the crested saguaro until summer crept in and the temperatures soared. But that was alright with her. It wasn't the distance that she craved; it was the chance to be out on the trail at all.

She had almost lost her sanity when her father passed away. She had almost lost her life that fateful morning in Wasp Canyon. And she had nearly lost her foot the night she took on the chupacabra and put a double barrel shotgun to its head. In the end, she had managed to escape with all three— her sanity, her life, and her foot. She doubted she would ever be able to wear a high heel again, but that seemed like a small price to pay.

Jess resumed her appointments with Dr. Wyatt. After a few bumpy visits—visits where Wyatt spent the bulk of the allotted time reiterating just how sorry she was—Jess and Wyatt were able to resume their productive sessions. They made progress. And Wyatt even stopped pulling on her suit jacket. Within a few months, Wyatt suggested they drop their appointments to twice a month, and then to once a month. Before long the sessions would stop completely. Jess no longer needed assistance to cope with her loss. Her grief, although not gone, had become a manageable thing. She still struggled with it from time to time, but it was no longer eating her alive.

Carl Moser returned to his regular duties as a detective for the Northwest Police Department. Any scrutiny he received regarding his actions on the night of August seventeenth dissolved when images of the chupacabra were leaked to the press. Under the new light of this grotesque discovery, he came out a hero for coming to the aid of two young women and for helping vanquish *The Beast of Wasp Canyon*. He received a medal for his heroism, and Jess and Claire were invited to attend the ceremony.

The media had a frenzy regarding the discovery of the chupacabra: the stuff of legends. And nightmares. It made national news, and eventually international news. More eyewitnesses came forward, sharing their stories of when they saw a similar beast in their yards in the night. Some of the stories held credence, many did not. Like all things in the news, the stories faded once the novelty wore off. Talk shifted back to political mishaps, celebrity gossip, and various sporting endeavors. It was surprising how quickly people moved on. But moving on was the human condition, and one must do it to survive.

With time, the truth of the chupacabra began to fade. Eventually it would fade completely, and only be recounted on the animal shows that Carl Moser was no longer afraid to watch. National Geographic, Animal Planet, and The Discovery Channel had a field day with the discovery of this new species—all networks airing special episodes about the mythical beast that turned out to be a creature of flesh and blood. They showed dramatic reenactments of the attacks with actors portraying the Wasp Canyon victims. Much of the episodes were speculation, however, with so little known about the chupacabra itself. Many scientists and zoologists combed through the desert surrounding Wasp Canyon, and eventually ventured down the depths of the canyon itself, however, few found anything worth noting. Any trace of the chupacabra seemed to have been washed away with the monsoon rains.

Jess's sneakers scraped on the thin layer of dirt that covered the hard caliche below. It seldom rained during this time of year, and the soil had regained its unforgiving hardness that came with lack of water. She inhaled deeply, feeling the freezing air as it filled her lungs. When she exhaled, she watched the white plume drift up and disappear into the pink sky. She stretched her left ankle, feeling the deep pull of scar tissue that now lived there. She wanted to get back into shape as quickly as her ankle would allow—she had already talked with Moser and was scheduled to begin basic training at the police academy that fall. That gave her several months to ease her ankle back into shape, as well as the rest of her. She remembered the nausea, pounding heart, and shortness of breath she had felt when she first started running, and she knew all of those would come screaming back to her by the time she made it to 0.3 miles. She welcomed it, though. She made it through that agony once, and she could do it again. Hell, she made it through a lot more than that.

Her phone buzzed against her thigh. She unzipped the pocket of her leggings and withdrew her cell phone. Her mother's face was on the screen. Jess shook her head and smiled. Always up with the sun, her mother was.

"Hi, Mom," Jess said, answering the phone.

"Good morning, honey! You at the trail yet?" Andrea asked.

"Yeah, I am. About to get started. Oye, it's gonna hurt!" Jess adjusted her wool headband. Andrea had knitted it herself and gave it to Jess as a Christmas gift. She insisted that Jess use it on all her winter runs. The mornings were cold and she didn't want Jess's ears freezing off while she was out running in the frigid temperatures.

"Your ankle?" Andrea asked, worry entering her voice.

"No, no," Jess said. "I mean the running in general. I'm really out of shape after not being able to walk on my leg for so long."

"Okay hon, well please be careful and don't push too hard."

"I promise." Jess watched the pink fade to orange in the crystal clear sky.

"Anyway, I called to remind you about your birthday dinner tonight. I already spoke to Claire and she will be arriving at four this afternoon to help set up."

"Mom, you don't have to set anything up," Jess said, smiling. "It's just us, you know."

"Well, it's your birthday and birthday girls get balloons. No argument! Besides, it's not just us. Detective Moser will also be stopping by, remember?"

Jess laughed. "Okay, okay. Balloons it is. I'm sure Carl just loves balloons."

"I'm sure he enjoys them plenty when the occasion calls for it," Andrea said.

Jess could feel the warmth of the sun on her face. It was going to be a beautiful day out on the trail. "Absolutely," she said. She could feel the muscles in her legs twitching. She danced from foot to foot, craving to begin her run. "Anything else, Mom? I'm about to get started."

"I think that's it. Be at my place at five?"

"You got it."

"Oh, and I picked up some of those Fancy Feast Delights that Tofu seems to love. They were on sale. I'll give them to you tonight so you can take them home. You better tell him they are from me, though!"

Jess laughed. "Of course, Mom."

"Okay, hon. Have a good run. I will see you tonight."

"Sounds good. I love you."

"Love you too, birthday girl."

Jess ended the call and zipped her phone back into her pocket. She looked around the parking lot. Still all hers. She might see a few tourists heading down the trail on her way out, but right now, the desert was hers and hers alone. She bent forward, giving her legs one final stretch. She looked at the sunrise, took in a deep breath, and smiled up at the expanse of sky. She liked to think that, somewhere up there, her father was smiling back.

Jess focused on the trail ahead. She could feel her muscles aching to begin. She pulled up her left wrist, selected **New Program** on her QuikFit 3.0, chose **Running**, and hit **Begin**. The seconds began ticking away on her watch. Jess took a step forward, glanced up at the orange sky one last time, and began to run.

Acknowledgement

First and foremost, I would like to thank my incredible husband, Ryan McCrory. His encouragement and endless support were paramount to my success in completing my first novel. He has been with me every step of the way, from the day I announced that I wanted to write a book (out of the blue, might I add) all the way to the day of that book's publication. His unwavering belief in my abilities was what kept me going during times of self-doubt, and I could not have accomplished this goal without him. He even stepped up to be my book editor—and a mighty good one at that. His insightful critiques and well-thought-out suggestions helped to make *Wasp Canyon* what it is today. I also have him to thank for designing the cover art for this book and for taking my author portraits. Ryan's support in my writing, and in all aspects of life, has helped get me to where I am today, and for that I am forever grateful.

I would also like to thank my family, whose support was very much appreciated as I tried to achieve this exciting (and unexpected) goal. They were willing to read my manuscript (typos and all) and provide me with many helpful tips and suggestions. Thank you to my mother, Nancy Dufour, to my father-in-law and mother-in-law, Mike and Betty McCrory, and to my brothers-in-law, Michael McCrory and Randy Ballesteros. I am so thankful to have such an encouraging group of people rooting me on.

Thank you to my father, Larry Dufour, for passing his love of reading on to me. He will forever be missed, and I hope that he had the opportunity to read my first novel, wherever he may be.

And finally, thank you to those who were willing to give my book a try. I hope you enjoyed reading it as much as I enjoyed writing it!

Until next time,
Danielle McCrory

ALSO BY DANIELLE MCCRORY

FOSTER

A Love Story

Skyler Seabrooke lives for helping animals. Those in need of saving, she saves. Those in need of fostering, she fosters. Skyler is a hardworking employee at the local animal shelter, and has dedicated more than half her life to rescuing and caring for animals in need.

When Skyler gets a call about an abandoned animal on the outskirts of town, she doesn't hesitate to go out and rescue it before the animal succumbs to the elements. This infant is different, though, and as it begins to grow under Skyler's foster care, she realizes she is caring for something that doesn't belong in her home. It's something big— something dangerous. Skyler knows allowing it to stay with her isn't safe, but the love she has for her foster pet is overpowering her sense of right and wrong.

As the repercussions for keeping such a dangerous animal become horrifically apparent to Skyler, she is forced to make a difficult decision. Just how far is she willing to go to protect the foster pet she has come to love? She needs to decide quickly, though, because unbeknownst to Skyler, time is running out for the both of them.

ALSO BY DANIELLE MCCRORY

Scarlett Springs

A NOVEL

Katelyn Chambers is overjoyed when her boyfriend invites her to a family getaway in northern Vermont. However, her excitement quickly turns to trepidation when she discovers their cabin is located in what is rumored to be a haunted forest—a forest where a monster walks among the trees, always in search of its next meal.

Despite her concerns, Katelyn does her best to enjoy the mountain retreat, even with the eccentric innkeeper that always seems to be watching her, and the screams she often hears coming from the woods at night. But when someone from their group goes missing, it becomes clear that this rural homestead is far more sinister than it first appeared to be.

Unable to call out for help, the group is forced to choose between staying where they have shelter, or entering the haunted forest to seek rescue on foot. Unfortunately for them, they have no way of knowing whether the monster that's hunting them is in the surrounding woods, or if it's been in the house with them the whole time.

About the Author

Danielle McCrory was born and raised in Tucson, Arizona. She has degrees in Graphic Design and Physical Therapy. Danielle started writing because she believes there are still so many scary stories left untold. Danielle loves horror movies, animals, rainy days, and Halloween. She lives in Tucson with her husband, son, and their two cats.

www.ingramcontent.com/pod-product-compliance
Lightning Source LLC
Chambersburg PA
CBHW051515250626
47156CB00001B/106